ALSO BY MARGARET DRABBLE

A Writer's Britain

The Ice Age

The Genius of Thomas Hardy (editor)

The Realms of Gold

Arnold Bennett

The Needle's Eye

The Waterfall

Jerusalem the Golden

The Millstone

The Garrick Year

A Summer Bird-Cage

THE MIDDLE GROUND

The Middle Ground

MARGARET DRABBLE

ALFRED A. KNOPF   NEW YORK   1980

Library of Congress Cataloging in Publication Data
Drabble, Margaret [date]
   The middle ground.
I. Title.
PZ4.D756Mh 1980 [PR6054.R25] 823'.914 80–7630
ISBN 0–394–51224–3

MANUFACTURED IN THE UNITED STATES OF AMERICA
Published September 15, 1980
Second Printing, October 1980

For darling Becky

THE MIDDLE GROUND

Thoughtfully, Kate cut up Hugo's steak and spread each piece with a dab of mustard, then started to turn over her own spinach with her fork, as though inspecting it. Hugo watched her, and then said (for many things that Kate did were little performances, requiring applause, enquiry or comment), "What are you looking for?"

"Ladybirds," said Kate.

"Why?"

"Once I had lunch here and ate a ladybird without noticing it."

"If you didn't notice it, how did you know what it was?"

"Because there was another one, in the spinach. So I thought back, and realised what the crunchy thing was that I'd just eaten. Anyway, I'd kind of half seen it out of the corner of my eye." Satisfied with her investigation, she looped up a mouthful, and ate it. "It was during that ladybird plague year," she said, "do you remember? They were all over the place, swarming on beaches, biting old ladies on the tops of buses. How's your steak?"

"It's fine. But the courgettes taste of chlorine."

Kate leaned over, helped herself to one, ate it.

"Yes, so they do. Funny, isn't it? I wonder why I go on coming here, it's a terrible restaurant. Loyalty, I suppose."

"Did you send the spinach back?"

"No, of course not. Women never send things back in restaurants, didn't you know?"

And she smiled at him, her wide, infuriating double-edged smile, her smile full of duplicity.

Hugo spiked another piece of steak, and continued to look at her while he ate it. She continued to smile, the smile turning into a sort of bland, mask-like, Medusa defiance, but good-natured still, for Kate was after all relentlessly good-natured, that was one of her problems: and how well she looked, how pink and shining with health, although he knew that she was not particularly well at all, but on the contrary had been rather ill and was now rather miserable, with some cause. Kate had often complained, in the past, as a joke, that the worse she felt, the better she looked, and now she did indeed look healthier than ever, her pale brown hair escaping bouncily from beneath her green headsquare, her white teeth munching the spinach; as though the surface of her resolutely refused to acknowledge any interior difficulties, as though the glow on the surface emanated in direct contradiction from within, in order to confuse, perplex, and throw spectators into disarray. Hugo knew her well enough to stare her out, and would have done so, but she came back to the attack without dropping her eyes.

"Look, Hugo," she said, "it's all very well for you, and I'm as bloody sick of bloody women as you are, I'm sick to death of them, I wish I'd never invented them, but they won't just go away because I've got tired of them. Will they?"

"You could switch to industrial relations. Or Middle Eastern affairs, perhaps," said Hugo, for Kate had just been complaining about her latest visitor, a student from Iraq, who had arrived unannounced and seemed to be intending to stay indefinitely.

"Don't be silly, Hugo. I know my limitations," said Kate.

"That's a very unfeminist remark," said Hugo, provocatively.

"Look," said Kate, ignoring this new angle, and returning to an earlier point in their conversation, "look, do you want to see my morning's post? You don't, do you? But you're going to have to, just the same. Here"—and she started to delve around in the large kitsch carpet-bag she'd been carrying around on her shoulder for years—"here, take a look at this lot"—and she slammed down on the table a great untidy wad of letters and envelopes and brochures, which, when sorted and expounded, proved to contain:

1. A letter from the American Express, addressed to her ex-husband Stuart, asking him why he didn't give his wife the freedom of an Express card. The letter was illustrated by a photograph of an expensive-looking woman in a black evening dress and strings of pearls, standing in an expensive hotel foyer with a lot of shining matching luggage. (Kate had been a card holder for some years: Stuart's credit, as she had no need to explain to Hugo, was not good.)

2. An advertisement for a fire extinguisher, portraying a hysterical woman in a provocative nightdress, shrieking amidst a lot of flames, and asking: "Do You Protect Your Loved Ones?"

3. A life-insurance leaflet with much the same message, but less sensationally portraying a happy family sitting over its cornflakes, the wife in a striped apron, the unsuspecting husband with a heart attack just round the corner, despite the fine executive panache with which he was reading his up-market newspaper.

4. An invitation to attend a fashion show.

5. A letter from the Post Office addressed to Stuart, requesting his signature on her application for a new telephone extension.

6. An invitation from a women's group in Birmingham, asking her to speak to them on the subject of "Women Today."

7. A letter from a BBC producer, asking her if she'd ever thought of writing a play about the liberated woman of today, and if not, why not.

8. A pink letter from a militant American feminist announcing the birth of a daughter, and sending good wishes to dear Kate from Sandy, Steve, Baby, Wiggles, and Mustapha. ("I think calling your cat or dog Mustapha qualifies as racist, don't you?" was Kate's comment on this offering: "and pink notepaper is certainly sexist, wouldn't you agree?")

9. A brochure for expensive Italian shoes, with under-age models posing in Victorian underwear, offering a Try-at-Home Service for Professional Women.

10. A request that she should appear in a fur coat in an advertisement for fake fur, in aid of wildlife conservation.

"Well," said Kate, having thoroughly displayed this interesting selection. "You see what I mean? What else can I do but write *yet another* piece about the image of women in advertising? This was a bit much, all in one post, don't you think?"

"Was that all the post you got?" asked Hugo, chasing an elusive chip around his plate, and finally cornering it against a lump of fat.

"What do you mean, all? How many letters do you get a day? And this was all home stuff, not counting the office."

"I meant, don't you get any nice personal post?"

"Well, no, not today, actually." She leaned forward, widening her pale bright-blue give-away impenetrable eyes at him. They were full of the hard glitter of deep sympathy, deep interest, deep devouring self. "And you, Hugo, how much personal post do you get?"

"Oh, not so much these days," said Hugo. "But then, I realised I'd finally grown up when all I was interested in getting through the letter box was cheques."

Kate laughed.

"Anyway, Kate," said Hugo, "you ought not to complain about a post like that. It's a tribute to your Social Class B Economic Status."

"I'm not really complaining," said Kate. "I'm perfectly complacent, as you know. But it's my social conscience at work. I ought to be worrying about everyone else, oughtn't I?"

"All those women who didn't have your peculiar advantages?" said Hugo: again provocatively, for Kate's past advantages would have taken some subtlety to discern.

"Oh, shut up," said Kate. "You know what I mean."

"No, I don't, as a matter of fact," said Hugo. "But I know we're not likely to agree, on this particular subject."

"Shall we talk about something else? Shall I light you a cigarette?"

"You are so solicitous, dear Kate, you will ruin my health. But yes, please. Have one yourself. Help yourself."

Kate lit a cigarette, and handed it over.

"Did you know the statistics for women smoking have risen by some horrific proportion?" she said. "Smoking women, violent women, what is the world coming to? Freedom is very bad for people." She started to stack up her letters again, casting a look of lingering regret at the fake leopard and mink.

"Anyway, I'm too old and fat to model a fur coat," she said.

"Of course not," said Hugo, gallantly, while thinking that in fact she, marginally, was.

"You know, it's all very well," she said, "but I've been thinking lately, every single bad thing that's happened to me happened to me because I'm a woman. There's no point in pretending it's not so. Even my illnesses. Apart from tonsils when I was ten."

"And colds, and chickenpox, and measles, and mumps, and flu."

"I've never had flu. I don't believe in flu."

"You could argue that all the bad things that have happened to me happened to me because I was a man."

Kate took this suggestion seriously, reflected on it, and nodded, blowing out smoke.

"Well, that all goes to show that I must have been mad to try to pretend that the sexes were much the same; if that's what I used to say. Is that what I used to say?"

"How should I know?"

"I don't suppose I ever had what you might call an ideology. But I certainly used to believe in freedom. And progress."

"Yes, I do seem to remember a few columns of newsprint on those topics. But I hadn't noticed that you'd abandoned them."

"I haven't abandoned them, they've abandoned me. I can't afford to abandon them officially, anyway. I've got to pretend to stick by them." She sighed, heavily. "You know, looking back, I realised I felt as light as air, all these years. I felt as though I was walking on air. I did feel free, I felt so—so undetermined, so unforced, so unpushed in every way. And now I realise it wasn't like that at all. It was all an illusion."

"I don't see why it has to be called an illusion, just because you feel differently now. And you probably only feel different temporarily. It's your age, that's all."

"It's worse than that. Though God knows that's bad enough. Oh dear, what a bore I am these days. How very patient you are, I don't know why you put up with me."

"I don't find you boring."

"Depressing, then?"

"No, I don't find you depressing, either. Perhaps I should, but I don't."

"That's nice of you."

"It's only because I'm an unfeeling cold-hearted creature. I don't really care enough about you to get depressed by you. Anyway, I'm sure you're going to cheer up again one of these days. You're bound to. You can't not."

"That's what I tell myself. But I don't think I believe myself."

"Well, I believe you."

She smiled, dispiritedly, then tried again, and smiled more brightly.

"You know," she said, "I'm beginning to think I feel the same way about women that my father feels about the unions. That it was a good cause in the old days. And that's treachery, isnt it? I've sold out, like my Dad. I thought I was a revolutionary, but I'm not."

"That really *is* age, what you're describing. Don't we all feel the same?"

"Maybe we do, but that doesn't make it any better. Yes, you're right, it *is* age. I used to enjoy the smell of battle, but I've got sick of it, I'm really sick of it. I'm worn out."

"You've done your bit. You can retire."

"What to?"

"I don't think you're tired of fighting, you're bored with finding yourself on the winning side. It's all got too easy for you. That's the real problem."

"Do you think so?" This analysis seemed to cheer her, and she stirred her coffee with a new access of energy. "Do you think I'm just fed up with everyone agreeing with me?"

"You're fed up with them pretending to agree with you. You should find some wonderful new line and annoy them all. Start again, with your back to the wall."

"How can I, when I believe in the old line? Perhaps I should join a group and get my consciousness raised."

"Your consciousness needs lowering, not raising, if you ask me."

"Oh, don't be silly, Hugo. Anyway, I'm too busy to go to a group. I haven't time." She looked at her watch, put on her busy expression, waved for the bill. "Now, look, Hugo, you promise you'll help me out with Mujid? Friday, we agreed. You can talk French to him, and ask him about Iraq. His English is awful, and my French is worse, so you can imagine what a nightmare it is trying to talk politics after a hard day's work."

"I don't know why you take such people on."

"I don't. They just arrive. And I don't know how to say no. Do you know, Mujid believes that not a single nation in the twentieth century won its independence without the support and intervention of the Soviet Union? At least, I think that's what he thinks. It can't be right, can it? I mean, what about Iran? But I just don't know enough to answer back. I'm an ignorant fool."

"I suppose you think men are better than women at saying no."

"I don't think it, I know it. And I also know that when men have other men to stay with them, they don't run around cooking them meals like I do for Mujid, and worrying about whether they like them or not. Do they? So you see, I do need a consciousness-raising group after all." She started to fish in her bag for money. "Is it your turn to pay, or mine? I think it's mine."

"I thought you paid last time."

"No, I'm sure you did, don't you remember, you only had a tenner and he was bloody rude about the change." Kate counted out three notes and some silver, and began to struggle into her coat.

"Actually," she said, "saying yes is my special technique for preserving myself. I know it doesn't sound very logical, but it works. I don't know *why* it works, but it does. It's my way of keeping the upper hand."

"I don't think a group would like the sound of that."

"No, it wouldn't. That's why I don't go." She said this with an air of triumph, as though she had scored a point, though what the point was neither of them could have said.

They walked back to the office in silence, in the October sunshine, for the traffic was too noisy to permit conversation, and Kate reflected, not for the first time, that it was very shocking of her to be pleased that Hugo had lost half his arm in Eritrea buggering around drunkenly with a stray grenade, and indeed pleased wasn't quite the word, for she'd been very upset when the news came through, but nevertheless she was pleased in some wicked corner of herself, for now she could look after him and cut up his meat once or twice a week, and make him duly grateful, without feeling she was imposing on him in any way. A horrible, manipulating, dominating, castrating, busybody woman, that's what I am, she thought, I like everyone to depend on me, why ever is that? And Hugo, for his part, thought of Kate and her history, of their long friendship, of her recent misfortunes, and wondered how she was getting on, really, inside herself, and whether or not she was managing to put herself together again. It wasn't an arm she'd lost, but a baby, and it had shaken her more than he'd believed possible. She had gone to pieces in the strangest way, though not many people knew her well enough to notice. At first he too had been obscurely pleased by her misfortunes, to note that she too was weak, vulnerable, a victim of circumstance, for her high-handedness in her good years had occasionally annoyed even him, as it had certainly annoyed many of their friends and colleagues; it had been interesting to see her waver, make mistakes, make a fool of herself, stop looking so bloody pleased with herself all the time. But this satisfaction had given way to a worthier though equally selfish regret. He wanted her to cheer up, because she was more amusing when she was up than when she was down. She wasn't boring yet, but she would be if she went on like this about women and groups. He knew enough angry, disillusioned, bitter women. Kate had been light relief, of a high quality. Always good for a laugh. He didn't like to see her sink into seriousness. Let her be happy, let her recover, let her be a freak escape from the general doom. Her life had been freakish enough so far, surely she could find a way out of this particular trap?

Hugo thought that he knew exactly how Kate felt about his own accident, and he liked her for it. Secretly, he was quite pleased about the accident himself, in some ways. It had its compensations, and one was that he'd never have to pretend to be a war correspondent again, he'd never again have to pretend that he liked the sound of gunfire, he'd never again have to fly off to some disaster-stricken zone with an air of calm indifference. He could retire from that particular field of masochism, honourably, with decorations. He had done his bit, more than his bit. Nobody expected him to play at being a limbless war hero. He was writing his Middle East book. A much more suitable occupation.

He'd never confessed this feeling of relief to anyone except to the surgeon at the hospital, who had looked at him oddly, and told him an extraordinary story about a patient who had taken it into his head that he was destined by God to model artificial limbs, had studied surgery from a medical textbook, and had amputated his own right leg at the knee one night in his Knightsbridge flat; he didn't make a bad job of it either, said Mr. Pethwick, but he passed out before he quite finished and would have bled to death if his boyfriend hadn't dropped in unexpectedly at the crucial moment. Very strange people are, said Mr. Pethwick, the ways they devise of mutilating themselves.

Hugo had thought this response rather over-sophisticated, but guessed he had asked for it, and took it in good part.

Hugo had no desire to model artificial limbs. So far he had refused even to consider acquiring one for his own use.

Kate can never decide whether she is a special case, and as such of little general relevance, or whether she is on the contrary an almost abnormally normal woman, a typical woman of our time, and as such of little particular interest. Sometimes she thinks one thing, sometimes the other. There is plenty of evidence on both sides. She doesn't even know which she would like to be. At times she feels a sense of womanly solidarity, for the things that have happened to her—marriage, children, love, divorce, illness, ageing parents, lost love, rejection—are the things that happen to many, if not most, people. At other times she feels a giddy solitude, and a sense of strength from this solitude. She used not to worry about this uncertainty, but worry has been forced upon her by what Hugo has not entirely seriously labelled her mid-life crisis. She doesn't even know whether or not to welcome this label, with its suggestion of inevitability. And if it is a mid-life crisis, such as everyone suffers, what on earth is on the other side of it? She has no idea. For the first time, she feels, she has no idea of what will happen next. She has run through what she now recognises were the expected phases of life, though some of them seemed surprising, not to say miraculous, at the time, and she doesn't know what will happen next, nor how to make it happen, and, being an energetic and active person, she strongly dislikes the feeling of helplessness, the lack of direction, that this uncertainty generates. She looks at the component parts of her life—her children, her ex-husband, her ex-lover, her work, her parents—and doesn't know what to do or to think about any of them. Her implacable progress has been halted, a link has been broken, and the past no longer seems to make sense, for if it did, how would it have left her here, in this peculiar draughty open space?

Here is an account of Kate's past history, some if not all of which must have led her to wherever she now is.

Kate Fletcher was born on 7 February 1937, in what is still picturesquely known as the Lying In Hospital for Mothers and Infants, on the Old Pinstead Road in Romley, East London. It was a district where many mothers had their babies at home, both through choice and necessity, but this possibility was not extended to Mrs. Fletcher, who was classified as a health risk. She was extremely overweight, suffered from high blood pressure, and through peculiarities of temperament had none of the little network of friends and neighbours that makes home confinements pleasant. Also, unlike many women of her class, she had no fear of hospitals; rather she enjoyed them, enjoyed being the centre of professional attention, enjoyed the relapse into enforced inertia. She even enjoyed being asked questions about her weight, questions which to most fat people are a torment of shame and a temptation to mendacity. Oddly, despite sporadic attention from the medical profession, Mrs. Fletcher managed to reach the age of fifty-five before anyone thought of asking the question that elicited the information that she was a butcher's daughter, and had been throughout her life in the habit of eating too much meat, meat which she never declared when questioned by doctors and dieticians, not because she wished to deceive, but because she genuinely believed that meat was not fattening. Cholesterol had not then been invented; and she never came to believe in it.

Both Kate and her elder brother Peter were in contrast, at least in infancy, extremely skinny children. They did not seem to thrive as other children did, but suffered from chest complaints, bronchitis, asthma, even eczema. Mrs. Fletcher blamed the bad air of Romley. She was not a woman given to blaming herself, or if she did, it was in the recesses of her spirit, unobserved. Mrs. Fletcher did not like Romley or the neighbourhood of Romley in which, for the early years of her marriage, she was obliged to live. She considered it, with little justification, beneath her; she strove to set herself apart, to cut herself off, and succeeded. She also succeeded in making herself a figure of fun, an achievement for which both her children suffered.

They also suffered on their father's behalf. Walter Fletcher was a man of character, by no means the hen-pecked shadow he inevitably appears in photographs beside his massive wife, but he was an eccentric, and looked it. He was as small as his wife was large, a little, undernourished, grey-faced man, self-educated, self-made, a working-class intellectual with a passionate interest in his work. He and Florrie Fletcher were, physically, a very odd couple, and attracted attention whenever they went out together, which was rarely. But worse than his appearance, from the children's point of view, was his interest in sewage. He worked at the Blackridge Pumping Station, not half a mile from Arblay Street where the family lived when Peter and Kate were little; his father and grandfather had been in the same line of business, over the river at Crossness, and had worked on the ships that used to disappear secretly up the Thames and out to sea to dump their in those days untreated load. Walter's father had been a keen union man, protesting energetically against the supreme and dictatorial authority of the Old World top-hatted manager; he had been one of the select band that had been born, reared, and educated on the works. Walter had inherited his militancy, and had taken it north of the river with him. He had also developed a lively interest in the science of drainage, sewage, and pollution, was forever writing letters to the local paper and the *Sewage Workers' Gazette* about the overloading of drains with new-fangled tampons and contraceptives and indestructible detergents, about fluoridisation and the dangers of water-born viruses.

Kate's feelings about this inheritance are very mixed. On the one hand, she cannot fail to feel respect for her father's achievements; his work, as he was fond of pointing out, was essential, even more so than the work of miners, and he had himself been vocal in campaigns for better pay, better working conditions, better status. His speech at his retirement, during the strike of 1970, was a fine piece of oratory, invoking the great pioneering names of Chadwick and Bazalgette, Simon, Godwin, and Snow, conjuring up the Dickensian horrors of the polluted Thames, nostalgically recalling the heroism of three flashers lost during the great flood of 1953. By 1970, Kate was well placed to appreciate such points, but as a little girl she was much more conscious of the ridiculous aspects of her father's enthusiasms, aspects which caused her and her brother much trouble at school.

Looking back now, she realises that there was no reason why her father's job in itself should have been the cause of so much teasing; many of the children had fathers employed in pursuits that were positively disreputable, whereas her father's position was secure and respectable. And her cousins over the river certainly didn't suffer in the same way. Uncle Bob, who worked at Crossness, was a jolly man, always ready with a joke, full of good stories about rats and diamond rings. He had a ring of his own, of which he was very proud, made from a gold sovereign he'd found in the old King's Pond Sewer; he and his mates were a friendly lot. But Walter was a different matter altogether. There was something purposefully, provocatively irritating and alienating in his manner; he would harangue neighbours about their drains and cisterns and faucets, he was a busybody, aggressive, interfering, self-righteous, and utterly lacking in human tact. Whenever Kate saw him talking to anyone in the street, her heart would sink, for she could catch all too quickly the expressions of bored impatience and sulky resentment with which his temporarily captured audience would listen to his lectures.

He was a useful man, of course. Those whom he had not too deeply offended would call him in when pipes burst or blocked, when ballcocks misbehaved. And Kate is herself a dab hand at washers and plumbing. She cannot bear to waste water, and has been known to leap up from other people's dining tables to turn off a dripping tap, to return smiling defiantly and apologetically with an amusing account of the price of each wasted drop in man hours and money. People always assume that her father instructed her in these skills, but that, she says, isn't so—why should she have needed to learn these things when he was around to do them? No, she learned the hard way, when she got married, from a do-it-yourself book. But the neurosis, if such it be, is inherited. She doesn't think it's neurosis, she thinks it's common sense. She gets very annoyed when people own up to the range of things they flush down the lavatory. Just think, she says, of the people on the receiving end. Luckily, she manages to say these things in a manner that people find endearing, acceptable, even charming. Unlike her father.

Walter Fletcher was useful in other ways. He loved committees, and sat on as many as possible. Local government, the Co-op, the local Sports Association, the local primary school, the local Labour Party—he was involved in them all. He had been shop steward, before his promotion. (They promoted him, Kate later found, to shut him up.) The only thing he kept clear of was religion. His grandfather had been a Plymouth Brother: his own father had defected, in favour of the Municipal Workers' Association, and Walter had inherited his father's deep dislike of anything to do with church, chapel or God. This also used to annoy his neighbours and embarrass his children: not that many of them were in any way devout, but the least devout of them objected to being accosted by virulent rationalism while waiting for a bus or trying to buy a packet of cigarettes. Walter was a proselytizing atheist, and he was stunned by the poor logic of those who claimed to believe in God. He was good at producing definitive arguments against the Deity, and saw religion (with some reason, it must be said, in view of his grandfather's affiliations) as a conspiracy to keep the working man in his place. Kate and Peter must have been amongst the few children who had to plead with their parents to be allowed to attend prayers and assembly and scripture lessons. All they wanted, in these early years, was to be inconspicuous.

So Walter Fletcher, as we see, though in many ways an admirable man, was not an easy father, nor was Mrs. Fletcher an easy mother. The children lived precariously, nervously, subject to teasing, mockery, contempt, outcasts in their own community. It was not, Kate recalls, a very pleasant community anyway, and her mother may have had good reasons for spinning it, but that did not make life any more agreeable. Kate has said several times that she can imagine no way of life more cramping, painful, and pointless than the life of the lower middle-class family aspiring to be better than it is. Their house itself, she says, seemed to suffer from acute indecision and paranoia. Arblay Street was one of those long, low, dull, little streets built round the turn of the century, a street of little artisans' houses, onto which some but not all families had added bathrooms; they had tiny front yards about four feet wide, into which passers-by would chuck newspapers full of fish skin and old chips. At the end of the road ran the sewage bank, which led in one direction towards the Blackridge works, in the other towards the marshy wastes of Pinstead; this grass-covered bank, about twenty feet high, was a secret thoroughfare, a walk through the backways of Romley, the scene of many childhood games and excursions, a green spine through the surrounding brick industrial wilderness, a link with scrubby open space which counted, to the children of the district, as countryside.

The Fletcher house was a corner house, with a slightly wider frontage than the rest of the terrace, and a different motif over its door. It was called, in ancient cracked gold script, Laburnum House, though there was no space for anything as large as a laburnum in its back or front concrete yard. Khartoum Road that led off from the corner, at right angles to Arblay Street, was a better class of road; the houses were larger, they had space for untidy shrubs in their front patches, the paintwork was better, the residents were slightly more house-proud, a nicer class of people. Mrs. Fletcher felt that she belonged to Khartoum Road rather than Arblay Street; when asked for her address, she would always quite unnecessarily point out that she lived on the corner. The sewage bank she deplored as a horrible reminder of the district's grim functional gracelessness, though to Kate it was its most interesting feature.

So there they lived, apart from a brief period of evacuation during the war, until Kate was ten, and Peter thirteen. They were not happy years, as Kate recalls them. She herself could have made friends at school and in the street, for she was tougher and more resilient than Peter, but she condemned herself by taking Peter's side, by refusing to have anything to do with his attackers. Peter became increasingly nervous and withdrawn; he began to grow fat, like his mother, and to stay indoors more and more, as she did, reading, making model aeroplanes, model tanks, and model battleships. His parents thought this model behaviour, and were delighted when he passed his eleven-plus exam and got a place at Romley Grammar School. Kate was not at all interested in such peaceful activities. She wanted to get even with the kids in the street, she wanted to play, she wanted to join in the hopscotch and

cigarette-card swopping and gossip. She concealed these de-
sires very well, learning to return aggression with worse aggression; she was a fierce child, and the other children stopped
teasing her in the end, letting her go her own solitary way,
swinging her satchel proudly and angrily to school, sitting by
herself digging holes in the grassy bank with a ruler and
brooding on revenge.

All seemed set, says Kate, looking back, for a life of truly
gruesome neurosis, such as poor Peter has had to put up with
—how amazing that it didn't quite happen that way! What do
you think saved me? To which her friends shake their heads,
not knowing the answer, if there is an answer, and not as
certain as she that she had after all been saved.

In 1947, Mr. Fletcher was promoted, and the family
moved house, to the other side of the bank, to a thoroughly
suburban district of 1930s semi-detacheds, far from the grim
terraces of South Romley, far from the fish-and-chip shops and
dirty pubs. It was only two miles away, but the social difference was enormous. Mrs. Fletcher was, she claimed, over-
joyed, and settled in to get herself properly straight at last.
She arranged her furniture, she bought new stair carpets and a
new three-piece suite, she made new curtains. Everything was
spotless and shining, and smelled of polish and Window-
clean and Airwick. She ceased to emerge even to shop, and
sent Kate to do all her errands. In 1950, she persuaded Walter
to buy her a television set, and settled herself in front of it.
She became house-bound. Kate, even at ten and eleven, felt
there was something wrong here, that she should not be getting breakfast for her father and mother, then rushing off to
school, then to the shops, or the laundry, or the cobbler's, on
the way home. But she did it, because she was told to do it,
and because Mrs. Fletcher was always telling her how lucky
she was not to have a working mother, like so many of the
other girls. Kate secretly wished she had a working mother,
for the children of these wicked women had the house to
themselves every now and then and could make themselves

little treats of baked beans or tinned spaghetti or dripping on toast, whereas Kate was never alone, and had to live up to high standards.

In fact, Kate realised that she alone in the family was not wholly pleased by its rise in status. She hadn't been happy in Arblay Street, but something in her kept harking back to it fondly, as though it were real life and this were some kind of pretence. She nourished childish fantasies of returning to Arblay Street and making her brother's tormentors eat their words. She would marry a lord and drive back in her Rolls. She would marry a film star and scatter their marbles. She would become a film star, and astonish them all by her radiant beauty. The children in Amalfi Road were weedy creatures, hardly worth astonishing, whose mothers made them stay indoors, do their homework, and go to bed early.

Kate failed her eleven-plus. At the time, nobody was surprised. It had been considered rather a marvel that Peter had passed, and he was, as Kate knew, having a tough time at the Grammar—he was finding it hard to keep up, was sweating away unprofitably at his homework, hated games, had found a new tormentor in the shape of a sadistic vicar who taught mathematics. So Kate wasn't even disappointed to fail. She was, and is to this day, almost totally innumerate—the spectacle of her trying to work out eight per cent of £200 for a VAT invoice is a lamentable one. She reckons she scored something like zero on the maths papers. In those days she took this weakness for granted, but now she is both self-conscious and curious about it—was it a result of sexist conditioning, or is it true that men are better at maths than women, you know the kind of argument. How she managed to do so badly on the rest of the paper is more mystifying—it was, she says, a hot day, she felt sick, it was a strange building, the questions were too silly for words, like which has higher rank, a colonel or a private, and *I didn't know what any one of those three words meant*—"rank," "colonel," "private," I mean—or was there snow at Christmas in Australia, I mean how the hell was I expected to know? And the truth is, I didn't care. I didn't want to go to the Grammar. It sounded horrid, at Grammar School.

So off she went to the Girls' Secondary Modern at Romley Fourways, so named because this rather bleak Late Victorian brick edifice stood at a large road junction on the Old Romley Road, where Roding High Street intersects it. It was in those days a derelict district, for a large area to the south had been devastated by bombs, and not yet rebuilt. The school had been miraculously (or, as some of the staff argued, disastrously) untouched, and it rose from the surrounding sea of rubble and willow herb like a great dark ship.

It was at Romley Fourways that Kate discovered her true talents in life. Or the talents that have got her to this point, anyway, though whether or not they will carry her beyond it is, I imagine, precisely what keeps her awake at nights.

At Romley Fourways, Kate found a whole new set of people, most of whom knew nothing about herself and Peter, about her large mother and her small father, who had never heard the nasty little ditties that had echoed over the peeling front steps of Arblay Street.

> Pete, Pete,
> What does he eat?
> A nice thick sandwich
> Buttered with shit

had been one such jingle. She had a new audience, and audience is the word, for Kate realised, more or less overnight, that one of the ways to avoid being a butt or laughingstock yourself is to make people laugh—not as in the pious old cliché "*with* you rather than *at* you"; no, they had to laugh *at* you, but they had to laugh *because you made them*, because you were funny. Her desire to be inconspicuous, one of the crowd, faded as though it had never been, as she realised that it was fine to be the centre of attention on one's own terms, and that there was nothing, literally nothing, that couldn't be turned into a joke. In fact, the more horrible and discreditable the subject matter, the better the joke. (This, of course, is her technique to this day.) She got in there quick, aged eleven, when everyone else was still nervously looking for new alliances, a new place in the pecking order; and she made them laugh. Astute, she was then.

She blossomed in the unfamiliar sunshine of success, and within two years became a new person, her appearance changing with startling rapidity. The eczema and bronchitis disappeared as though they had never been, her skinny body filled out, her skin began to glow, her hair to shine. The fact that many of her contemporaries made a reverse journey—from clean, odourless girlhood to spotty, greasy, sweating adolescence —gave Kate yet more of an advantage. She was ahead: they looked to her for advice. Womanhood came early to her, and suited her, to her own surprise: was it nature or will power that effected the transformation? She was not sure, and still is not. Either way, it was a new lease of life, and she felt that she could bounce out of the confines of her own past like a rubber ball full of spring. Was she angry, in those days, to be a woman? Not at all, she was delighted—of that at least she is still certain.

It was a sudden leap, from timid, persecuted outcast to queen of the playground, and probably more sudden in her subsequent recitals than in reality. But the metamorphosis was real enough, and she enjoyed every moment of it. She became, she says, merciless in her pursuit of power. She instigated a playground game called Confessions (her profitable flair for journalism was evident this early) which consisted of forcing everyone present to recount the most embarrassing experience of the last twenty-four hours. The girls loved it, and the game became immensely popular, though Kate usually won, simply by being more truthful than everyone else. Also, she had good material to go on—her Mum, her Dad, Peter, Grandpa Fletcher at Abbey Wood, Arblay Street, the secrets of her body, what old Mr. Bly had tried to do to her

when she went to pick up the groceries, Auntie Janey's span-
iel, the sewage works, out they all came, translated into art. It
was like a kind of magic, turning shit into gold, or so she now
tells us. She made them laugh, the hard-baked kids with their
wedge shoes and pierced ears, their waspy waists and painted
toenails, the timid girls with their home-knit cardigans and
schoolgirl sandals. She said things they'd never dare, she made
them turn pale. She did things they'd never dare, just to see
what it was like. All for a laugh. Oh, I had a nerve, in those
days, Kate sighs, looking back. (Kate's jokes about her father
were a fine mixture of defence and aggression; at Junior
School, when others mocked, she had always taken his part,
fiercely partisan, tooth and nail, but as she grew older she
discovered she could avert ridicule by taking the initiative
herself, an exercise which simultaneously disturbed and satisfied her: by betraying she protected.)

The teachers at Romley Fourways did not much appreciate
her line of success. They regarded her as lazy and subversive,
something of a trouble-maker, intelligent enough to do better
if she tried, but she never did try, partly because none of them
found any ways of making her want to try. It was in those
days a dull, restrictive, traditional school which aimed to keep
its girls as quiet as possible, not to let them mix too much with
the boys from Pinstead Green, not to let them write on walls
or in textbooks, not to let them linger too long on the premises
after school. The academic standards were not high; the
brighter girls were steered towards jobs as secretaries and bank
clerks and nursery nurses. The headmistress was an elderly
spinster in the last years of her career, whose outlook on life
was dour, negative, unnerving. The girls were frightened of
her, with her bun of white hair and tailored suits and well-
polished brogues; those were the days when schoolgirls were
still frightened of authority, when threats of bad reports and
detentions and parental summons could alarm all but the most
brazen. Her cultured middle-class tones depressed them and
made them feel inferior. But they did not respect her. There

was something odd about her that prevented respect. Kate never quite worked out what it was—a kind of insecurity, perhaps, that made her adopt a peculiar expression of hard command when addressing the school, and which also lured her into the most astonishing Freudian double entendres. She was fond of speaking to the girls, especially as they grew older, of the perils of sex, and unfortunately this theme seemed to draw her unconsciously into the strangest realm of sexual imagery—she would speak of guns and triggers, of climaxes, of filling the girls in, and of playing ball. The girls, who had never heard of Freud, got them in one. Once she referred to a recently married ex-member of staff as being "firmly bedded down in Billericay," a phrase which even Kate could not resist repeating with delight—for in general Kate disapproved of laughing at those who were unintentionally ridiculous. Laughter should be worked for, in Kate's view.

It was not until years later that Kate, looking back, began to think that Miss Simmons had been physically frightened of her pupils, that the sight of them sitting or standing before her, sullen, bored, ominously fertile, potentially rebellious, must have been as unnerving to her as the sight of an angry mob to a Victorian mill-owner, as the sight of a mutinous hungry crew to a captain far from land. Kate even began, posthumously, to feel sympathy, for on the few occasions in adult life when she found herself before an audience of teen-age girls, she could see that it took a good deal of nerve to face such a mass of young, restless, and hopeful bodies with confident equanimity, and poor Miss Simmons had not had much.

At the time, however, Kate, like the other girls, chafed against restrictions, talked in class, picked up one or two O Levels with not very good grades—she was always good at English, but not at anything else—and found herself, by the age of sixteen, with not much idea of what she wanted to do next. She wanted to leave school, and indeed there was no sixth form to move into; the odd late-developer got shuffled off to the Girls Grammar School in Pinstead. But nobody seemed to care much what she did when she left. In those dark days, there were no Careers Officers, no Sixth-Form Colleges, no Colleges of Further Education. Miss Bates did suggest a nice job with British Home Stores, with opportunities for training, but Kate didn't fancy that. For by this time Kate had realised that she was highly ambitious, that she'd no intention of wasting her life hanging around in Romley running errands for an agoraphobic mother. She didn't yet wish she'd worked harder at school, felt not a flicker of envy for poor Peter, who was swotting away at a failed Physics A Level, but she did realise she was going to have to do something about herself. Little waves of panic swept through her as she sat in the evening during her last term watching *What's My Line* on television while her mother munched her way through boxes of licorice allsorts. What should she do, get a job in the West End, get a job in a coffee bar, get a job in the local chemist's? Become a sheep's-head trimmer, like the lady on the screen, at whom Isobel Barnet was smiling with such chilling charm? She leafed through her mother's copies of *Woman* and *Woman's Own*, wondering what life was really like in offices, in hairdressing salons, in canteens and department stores. She read with attention the narrative advertisements for Horlick's and Lifebuoy soap, she tried to guess which twin had the Toni, she imagined herself as a housewife polishing her furniture to a high gloss with O-Cedar polish or Mim cream. She imagined herself slender and elegant in a Spirella corset, hand-fitted; matte-faced in Charles of the Ritz powder, individually mixed. None of these images seemed very convincing, and she knew from June Barnes, who'd left the year before and got a job in a local estate agent's office, that offices, at least in Romley, were shabby, draughty, full of hardboard partitions and missing stair rungs and boring men who never asked one out to dinner or a drink like they do in the magazines, and who would have been a dead loss if they had. Yet she went on reading the magazines and watching the telly, for something in her was entranced by the gap between fantasy and reality:

the happy endings to the stories of those who found love because they learned about BO in time, who became ballerinas because they discovered hand cream (yes, hand cream), who were promoted to manageress status because they started to drink Horlick's, filled her with a profound and mysterious satisfaction.

And she was not entirely alone in her deliberations. She had friends at school who seemed to have a better grasp of the outside world than she had, whose comments opened windows. There was Denise Scooter, who was determined to be a nurse, and who plodded her way through examinations with awesome purpose, all the more awesome in view of the fact that Denise was so squeamish that she fainted at the very sight of a hypodermic needle or a bleeding knee. There was Lizzy Little, equally determined to be a hairdresser, who would practise on any of the class that would let her; once she cut off so much of Kate's springy brown hair in an effort to straighten it that Kate had to go round with a scarf on her head and everyone thought she'd got lice. And there was Pauline Scott, whose parents ran the Fortunes of War, and who was marked more by panache than determination. Her confessions in the badness stakes had occasionally alarmed even Kate, though she hoped she had never shown as much. Pauline, a handsome redhead, had achieved notoriety in childhood by walking round the parapet of her parents' pub, three storeys up, in her pants, with a plate of sandwiches on her head; her adolescent exploits had been equally dashing though less innocent, and she had placed firmly in Kate's mind the awareness that sex was a possible exit route from Romley. It is perhaps to Kate's credit, in modern ideological terms, that she did not take this traditional exit, much as she appreciated its advantages. A heritage of sewage, agoraphobia, and women's magazine correspondence columns had planted a prudent impulse in her.

Sex, however, was clearly a factor of growing importance, one that could hardly be ignored. During her last year Kate took up with an old flame and tease from Arblay Street, Danny Blick, now in his last year at Pinstead Green. Danny was a sharp lad, a con man and dealer in the making; he and his elder brother had been among the ringleaders of Peter's tormentors, and Kate had once thrown a brick at him, an act for which she had been forgiven, and which indeed had earned her some respect. "You were a right little madam," sixteen-year-old Danny would say admiringly, smart in his winkle-pickers and drainpipes, and Kate would flounce proudly. She liked Danny; he had a bit of spirit, he wasn't one of those who were going to be herded off to the gas works or the jam factory. He had other views of worldly success. His father was a dustman, and Danny had early picked up the art of sorting through rubbish for saleable items. Scavenging was in his nature; during the war, as a small boy, he'd made good pickings from bombed houses, and by the time he was fifteen he had a busy little trade in spare parts, old bottles and buttons, cast-off clothing and old magazines. The pickings of Arblay Street and its immediate vicinity were not very rich, but Danny had followed his Dad into neighbouring districts where the rubbish was of a better quality, and quickly developed an eye for saleable junk; even more usefully, he developed contacts in the markets of the East End. This was before the days when middle-class mothers took to dressing themselves and their offspring from jumble sales and Oxfam shops, but even then there was a certain amount of entrepreneurial middle-class infiltration, and Danny struck up a useful friendship with an ambiguous character called Hunt, a man of indeterminate age and background, with a posh voice and an interesting network of acquaintance. Hunt was not strictly a crook, and certainly did not belong to the organised underworld which Danny might otherwise have entered; the entertainments he offered were of a more rarefied nature, and appealed both to Danny and to Kate, neither of whom would have had the nerve for a life of serious crime.

Hunt knew an amazing variety of people: intellectual im-

migrants from North London, Jewish communists from Brick
Lane, gardeners from country houses, Irish builders, ex-boxers,
and people vaguely associated with the entertainment industry. His centre of operations was an old house in Highbury
New Park, which he claimed had been left to him by an old
woman he met on a bench in Clissold Park. He still lives in
it, along with a shifting population of friends and lodgers. It
took Kate years to realise that the spirit which dissolved and
united the disparate elements of his particular melting pot
was the spirit of homosexuality, for Hunt was not overtly what
we would now call gay; he seemed to be interested in manipulation and domination for their own sake. He was a strange-
looking man—tall, shambling, with dyed yellow hair, given to
wearing shabby green or purple trousers and shapeless cordu-
roy jackets. He collected people as well as articles, and he was
not very nice to the items in his collection. Kate had never met
anybody so rude, and wondered why anyone, including herself, put up with it. His pad, far from being a cosy refuge, was
always seething with ill-will, with sullen or vocal disaffected
acolytes, with emotional dramas, hurt feelings, double cross-
ings, and double meanings. For some reason, she found this
highly stimulating, and was prepared to endure a certain
amount of abuse for the privilege of sitting on a dirty cushion
in a corner listening to what was going on.

Hunt let her sit, keeping half an eye on her. He was of
course more immediately interested in Danny, a round-faced,
rather plump, biddable young man, whom he mocked and
tormented and instructed.

Kate has by now knocked around so much that she says
she finds it hard to remember what a cultural shock the Highbury New Park scene was when she was first introduced to it
at the age of sixteen. For one thing, the dirt, after the shiny
satin surfaces and lustre vases of Amalfi Road, was quite a
revelation. It was unlike the dirt of Arblay Street—it was
antique, accumulated, deliberate. It gave her, she admits, a
thrill. It was an act of rebellion to sit on such a cushion, to

stare at such tattered curtains, to drink tea from so cracked a mug. She risked death at every sip, and the spirit of adventure was in her. She was also aware, she thinks, that she was in the presence of an organising aesthetic intention, despite the shabbiness; that she was being exposed to a fine range of valuable objects, the like of which she had never come across before. "It was almost as though I'd been put down in a shop of life styles, and told, 'There they are, take your pick' "—the greasy shiny red curtains, the plum-coloured, dusty-fringed, velour tablecloth, the threadbare Moroccan rug, the white cracked mugs, the skeleton clock, the grandfather clock, the Windsor chair, the bergère suite, the white deal table, the inlaid cabinet, the extraordinary dresser like a piece of church furniture, the medicine glasses, the stuffed squirrel, the heaps of copies of the *Leathersellers' Gazette*, the games of solitaire, the rows of old riding boots, the ewer full of bottle tops, the jangling cow bells, the bead curtain, the plate inscribed A Gift from Southend, the skeleton fish. And amongst the people, which should she pick? Pale and languid Vic from Chatham, with his violet Vaseline eyelids and his winkle-picker shoes and his guitar? Butch, thick, hairy, squat Clifford, who travelled in Oriental fabrics? Loquacious little Abe Solomon, who worked backstage at the Unity Theatre? Lank, silent, vain Albert from the whelk stall? Runaway Geoffrey, with his white, large, unhealthy, shapeless face and damp black curls? Hunt's court offered a fine variety of the seedy and the exotic, each member of which rated himself for mysterious undeveloped talents, for an unacknowledged secret stardom which Hunt alone had recognised, which Hunt alone could set in its rightful sphere. Sulkily, morosely, they suffered humiliation in exchange for recognition, in exchange for a returned image of hope and possibility: only Abe never sulked, he had the gift of the gab, he answered back, he put Hunt in his place, he was irrepressible.

Of course, Kate did not really have the pick, the sense of choice was retrospective. At the time she was far too humble to ask for anything but tolerance. She was frightened of the others, though she wouldn't admit it; she was even frightened of Danny, thick though he was, and easily fooled. The few times she opened her mouth she bitterly regretted it: once she pointed to a new object standing in the array on the deal table, a green jug with a clear glass handle and a pattern of white spots—"That's nice," she said, not even much meaning it, and Hunt looked up from his tea and drooped his lidded eyes at her and sneered over his big parrot nose and said in his most hoity-toity punishing tone, "Really, child, I see you have an unerring eye for the crap." Kate flinched, perhaps she even blushed: crap was a word not as widely used then as it is now, at least to or by girls, and to hear it in such refined accents was peculiarly painful. On another occasion, she trod accidentally on a wooden Noah's Ark, and broke it (it was hard to avoid treading on things in Highbury New Park): she started nervously to apologise, but was cut short by Hunt's savagely polite "Stow it, Katie: just trample on the cheap stuff, will you?"

He was also unkind about her appearance in a way that she found hard to take. Objects which passed as desirable or stylish at Romley Fourways were scorned: a new plastic pink handbag from Boots was held up for ridicule, and Hunt wheezed with cruel mirth at her black elastic belt and tight black cotton sweater. "We know you've got tits, Katie," he said, "but try to let us forget it, won't you?" In a despair of uncertainty, she took to going round in her old navy school-uniform skirt and blue-striped blouse, which passed without comment for some weeks until Hunt said, this time not unkindly, "Going to wear those for the rest of your adult life, sweetie?"

Why did she put up with it? Because, she says, she deserved it. The pink plastic bag was horrible, and so were the black belt and sweater: as soon as he pointed at them, she wondered how she could ever have thought them smart. Hunt was right. She would have to try again. But where to begin?

There were no women hangers-on to imitate, apart from a strange ugly person who wore sandals, a dirty grey flannel skirt, a flowered blouse, and a cloak, and Kate did not want to look like that. She could see that she could choose to be a freak, but chose not. In the end, she found a new uniform: trousers and one of Peter's school football jerseys. These passed inspection, and she lived in them until she got her nerve back. By then, everybody else seemed to be wearing trousers and football jerseys, and she blended into the background: Hunt never commented on her appearance again, though a year later he gave her a present—a long thin limp old silk scarf, with slanted ends and a black border and a small geometric pattern of green, beige, and white checks and diamonds, a scarf from the thirties, which smelt faintly of age and old-fashioned facepowder and cats and sawdust. She treasured this strange badge of approval, this pledge of womanhood, and still tends to favor small checks: in fact, the only successful evening dress she ever bought was an unconscious imitation of this scarf, a long rayon dress covered in tiny triangles of green and pink and brown. She has got the upper hand with Hunt now, but she recognises her debts.

It was at Hunt's that she met her ex-husband, Stuart Armstrong. She had left school, and was biding her time, working at a photographer's in Leyton during the day, and spending most of her evenings at Hunt's in Highbury. (How Peter envied her freedom. And how impossible it would have been to introduce Peter to her new world.) Stuart was then studying art at the Slade, having left school the year before; he was an old school friend of Abe Solomon's, from a grammar school in North London. Stuart, despite his name, is half Jewish, for his mother Luisa is a Portuguese Jew who left Portugal in the thirties. Michael Armstrong, Stuart's father, is half Scottish, half Irish. The Armstrong household was an artistic household, priding itself rather ostentatiously on its spontaneity, its generosity, its easy-going good humour. Luisa knew a lot of painters, and appears in minor works of the thirties and forties, accompanied in some of them by Armstrong children born and unborn; she herself used to paint, but gave up without apparent regret, under the pressure of five children and a floating houseful of their friends. Michael Armstrong, now largely unemployed, was then a journalist, writing theatre and art reviews for a left-wing daily, since folded. What they live on now is a mystery, for Stuart doesn't support them or indeed anyone, and although two of the other sons have reasonably respectable jobs in journalism, they are always, they claim, broke.

Kate fell in love with Stuart; Stuart fell in love with Kate. There was nothing surprising about this. Kate was an attractive girl, and Stuart in those days was an extremely good-looking young man, slightly effeminate, pale and fine-featured, with dark wiry hair and a seductive gentleness of manner. He was a romantic and read poetry. Kate liked that, and he in turn liked what he saw as her toughness, her familiarity with the back streets of Hunt's kingdom. A perfectly proper alliance, it appeared. Kate fell in love with the whole Armstrong family, which she found warm, uncritical, friendly, a needed antidote to Hunt's biting edge. The Armstrong home, a large, ugly, untidy house between Kilburn and West Hampstead, was full of talk and good meals and dangling strings of onions and vegetables arranged like fruit in wooden bowls. Real paintings hung on the walls. Kate had come across none of these things before. Nor had she ever been in a home with such a high emotional temperature: kisses, embraces, tears, endearments, shrieks of joy and despair were the stuff of daily life. Luisa, with whom Kate is still on good terms, made Kate welcome, encouraged her to stay the night at weekends (nobody ever stayed the night with anybody in Romley, in those days), talked to her, tried to teach her to cook; for the truth is that Luisa loves an audience, she is a frustrated performer, loves to be admired, to demonstrate how warm and wonderful she is. Kate was a willing accomplice in this performance. In those days, Luisa seemed to Kate the ideal mother, strong, resilient, adaptable, excitable, open-minded: a woman of the world, who didn't mind looking at a twenty-year-old portrait of her own large naked pregnant body every day over the kitchen table. A far cry from Romley.

The Armstrongs adopted Kate as protégée, and she responded to their attention by learning fast. She never learned to tell a good painting from a bad one, but at least she learned to look. She still enjoys cooking adafina, one of Luisa's favourite Portuguese recipes (though I fear she gave up on chopped fish long ago). Unlike Hunt, the Armstrongs never made her feel silly and ignorant, though she knew she was; she must have sensed, she now thinks, that the easiest way out of the mistakes and embarrassments of a lower-middle-class life style was not upwards into the middle classes, but out as it were sideways, into a kind of comfortable uncompetitive Bohemia. The Armstrongs were unshockable, and they enjoyed Kate's tales of Romley. When her marriage to Stuart failed, Kate went through a phase of rejecting the whole Armstrong family, trying to read back into their acceptance of her all kinds of sinister motives, recognising that Michael's ideas, which had once seemed so original, were in fact to be found in any old copy of the *New Statesman*, that Luisa's histrionics could be tedious and childish, and that the house, even by Kate's own rather low standards, could do with a touch of *Woman's Own* spit-and-polish (was it really necessary to let the cat sleep on the breadboard next to the communal hairbrush, and the mice it failed to catch scamper along the dresser shelves during supper?)—but her attempts to dismiss them failed; there was a lot wrong with the Armstrongs, but there was also a lot right with them, their warmth was real, not merely a display, and Kate owes to them the ease with which she embraces her own children and colleagues, the liberality of her own endearments: they taught her an emotional style, and she is grateful. They remain genuinely fond of Kate—in fact, too fond by half, she sometimes thinks, as she gets landed with yet another niece or nephew, or forks out yet another small loan to an indigent ex-brother-in-law. But she owes it to them, for they launched her.

It was Stuart's elder brother Alex who decided that Kate ought to chuck her job with the photographer and try for something better. She had confided, one evening, her passion for women's magazines. Alex had a friend who worked for IPC who had a friend who might be looking for a secretary. Kate took a crash course in shorthand and typing, got the job, learned as she went along, and, in brief, prospered. Her career was in fact almost as sensational as those sketched in the Horlick's advertisements, though the reasons for her rise were a little less edifying: her boss, a thirty-year-old graduate alcoholic too fond of large lunches, was incapable of work in the afternoons, and came to rely rather heavily on Kate's helping hand. Kate's copy was brilliant, teetering on the brink between parody and sincerity, and after a while she ditched drunken Robert and got herself promoted, with what splendid results we all know. She worked her way through magazine editorial work, to features, to the secure position she now occupies, with a column of her own in one of the Sundays, and as much free-lance work as she fancies, at prices she or rather her agent can dictate.

Her progress was not, of course, as smooth as this précis might indicate, nor was it unaccompanied by grinding hard work. It was interrupted by marriage, pregnancies, small children, and, to her astonishment, Stuart's opposition. She and Stuart married when she started expecting their first child, Mark; Stuart had just left art school and intended to be a painter, which was all very well while Kate was earning, but not so good when she gave up her job to have Mark. Neither of them objected much to poverty, but Kate found that she objected surprisingly strongly to the suspension of her own income, and at that stage she wasn't nearly well enough established to work free-lance, though she tried. And she found that she equally strongly disliked Stuart's ideas of survival.

Stuart was a borrower. He borrowed money, from anyone who would lend it, and didn't worry about paying it back. Kate tried to see in this an attractive, happy-go-lucky Armstrong trait, but failed. She was surprised by Stuart, and in more ways than one. Their sexual relations, which had seemed so satisfactory during courtship, became less and less so. Stuart was an emotional, impressionable fellow, good at talk and kisses and caresses, but not good at much else. During their early days, he used to amuse and impress Kate by telling her that he could make himself come just by looking at her, a facility which she took as a tribute to the power of love. It gradually dawned on her that this facility had its accompanying disadvantages. Frustrated, dissatisfied, she nursed the baby in the damp basement flat, turning to him more and more for affection, pondering Stuart's defects—was it, after all, significant that she had met Stuart at Hunt's, in a predominantly homosexual milieu? Stuart's looks appealed to men and women alike—was he, after all, basically a homosexual? Kate had nothing against homosexuals, on the contrary she liked them rather suspiciously much (and was heard to say only the other day in mock despair, "Not only are some of my best friends gay, *all* of them are")—but she wasn't sure she wanted to be married to one. Did the fact that she'd married a man like Stuart mean that she was frigid (Lesbian, even?), and if so, why hadn't she thought about it earlier?

These things still worry her, but in those early years, sunk in anxiety about money, she could not contemplate them as calmly as she now does. Her life was at stake. She believed in Stuart, took his word and his friends' that he was talented, but couldn't help noticing his remarkable capacity for ruining his own chances, for doing the right thing at the wrong time. A perverse instinct for self-destruction. He used to be a neo-realist, before neo-realism came in, painting pedantic little interiors, hygienic still lifes, toothpaste tubes and linoleum tiles, then moved on to collages of furry felt and plastic flowers and bits of looking glass. He dabbled in happenings, then moved on to abstract and semi-abstract patterns based on microscopic sections of plant cells and skin tissue. He managed to mis-time each phase with apparently deliberate ingenuity, annoying gallery owners and art critics by his lackadaisical but stubbornly inflexible approach. They got annoyed with themselves for being annoyed, for he was talented, but with so many more manageable people around, why bother to manage him? He was also a lazy bugger, and kept losing teaching jobs at art colleges by not turning up on time. He now lives alone in a small flat in Kentish Town, not far from Kate, knee deep in opened cans and unopened letters and sprouting potatoes. He has taken to painting mould, and Kate says he has plenty to paint. Stuart thinks, and says, that Kate overvalues worldly success. He deplores fashions in the art world, and the commercial exploitation of artists. He says there is no point in this kind of fame. Kate thinks it is not so simple. At times she wonders if it is her own success that has given him this defeatist attitude, and if so, whether she is guilty of the ruin of a fine career. But how can this be so, when she only started to earn money because he didn't? Or is it, again, not so simple?

If Stuart had a flair for bad timing, Kate had exactly the reverse. She had a knack for finding the right thing at the right moment. She started to write new-wave women's pieces sometime before they became fashionable, sharing her pregnancies and exhaustions and indignations with a shocked and enthralled public. Her lower-middle-class origins, onto which she grafted the language and opinions of the artistic and articulate middle class, proved an invaluable asset; she could communicate with a large audience. And she was bold. Squeamish editors tried from time to time to tone her down, but her faith in herself grew with trial, and proved justified; they had to admit that she was onto a winning streak. She was, unashamedly, a women's writer, but men read her eagerly. She created a place for herself, and set a good price on it.

This did not happen overnight, as the envious (and they

are many) now assume. They were hard times, the early sixties. While the press invented swinging London and Carnaby Street, Kate sat in her basement feeding babies, trying to write saleable items, helping out by a cottage-industry job of assembling tin-openers at ten bob a hundred. (The kitchen in those days was full of heaps of strange metal objects, drying nappies, buckets full of soaking nappies, jars of turpentine, sacks of potatoes. They lived on potatoes.) More than once the bailiffs called to remove the furniture, but Kate sat it out, and wrote articles about the bailiffs. Stuart could have let her go back to work, had he agreed to look after the babies, but he wouldn't, although he was very nice to them when he was around. A useful spirit of bitterness and self-reliance grew and hardened in Kate, and an absorbing interest in money. Pride and avarice. By the time the youngest of the three children started primary school, Kate had ceased to care what Stuart thought about her working. He had forfeited the right to care. Back she went, as soon as she could, to a regular job and a salary, to the double life of a working woman, to the over-activity to which she now claimed to be addicted.

Their marriage, eroded at the start by poverty, was finished off by her success. Stuart had an affair with an art student called, of all things (Kate's phrase), Amaryllis, and a prolonged period of acrimony set in, ending in separation and divorce. Kate was so used to running the show single-handed that his departure was a relief. She bought a house just before prices began their astonishing rise, borrowing the deposit from a friend and paying back with conscientious regularity. Stuart continued to visit, but on her terms. At times she would look at Stuart and think, God, what have I done to this man, whatever has happened to us? but most of the time she was too busy for these reflections, and too intent on her own survival, and the survival of the children.

After Stuart's departure, Kate took up with a man called Ted Stennett, who was the husband of a woman she had met through the school's Parent-Teacher Association. Evelyn Stennett and Kate became good friends, chatting in the school playground as they collected their children, calling on one another for tea, going for walks at weekends, for Ted, like Stuart, was something of an absent father, though for opposite reasons. Stuart was lazy, Ted was busy. Ted's career had been even more spectacular than Kate's, though it had not been so exposed to the public eye. Born in Huddersfield, the son of a local government official, he had progressed from Grammar School to Leeds University, where he studied zoology. He went on to do research on the life cycle of *aedes aegypti*, the yellow-fever mosquito, and was given a scholarship by the World Health Organisation (WHO) to continue his work in Gambia, on the role of monkeys as carriers. (It was in Gambia that he met Evelyn, who was then working for the Friends' Service Council.) His work in Africa persuaded him he didn't want to be a microbiologist but a doctor, so he came back to England and read medicine, he and Evelyn produced two children during this period. Having qualified, he decided he didn't want to be a doctor after all and returned to mosquitoes, monkeys, and tropical diseases. His interest in pure research was diverted by an increasing number of invitations to sit on committees advising the government on exotic illnesses, quarantine, and such matters: he is on various WHO advisory lists, and frequently flies off to the Medical Research Council in Gambia, and to conferences and emergency investigations of epidemics. He has a special interest in the history of epidemics, and has written a book on the subject. He is passionately interested in his work, too interested to spend all his time in laboratories. Hugo Mainwaring (again, what a name, as Kate was wont to say in the first days of their friendship, widening her eyes in appreciative mockery), who is Evelyn's first cousin, once spent a flight to Nairobi being lectured by Ted on the collapse of the Panama canal project in 1884 through yellow fever, and on the similar but much-hushed-up collapse of a dam-building project in Africa in 1967, which Ted claimed was the greatest scandal of our time.

But Ted likes disasters. He has a new apocalyptic vision of the end of the world, of a world united not by brotherhood or multi-national combines or oil crises, but by illness. A new pandemic, brought about by increasing air travel, increasingly resistant strains of mosquito and rat, brand-new illnesses from new tissue cultures. Increasing communion and technical sophistication engendering increasing disease. Not exactly the vision of the World Health Organisation, which prides itself on its success in eliminating smallpox. "You don't really think medical science is fighting a losing battle, surely," people say to him, and Ted smiles and says, "No, not really": nevertheless the notion of international disaster excites him, clearly he thinks we deserve it, and that the wrath of God is due to fall once more. Not that he believes in God, of course.

Ted Stennett is not at first sight an attractive man. He is only just of medium height, thick-set, and almost bald; his head is round and shining and ominous, a threatening purposeful head. An aggressive, determined man, slightly manic, a great talker when in action, an enthusiast. He is also, which tends to annoy his friends, a man of considerable culture, who reads heavy Victorian novels for light relief, teaches himself German in order to be able to read papers without translations, attends the theatre and art galleries and parties when he has time. A competitive, ambitious, addictive man, who has harnessed his nature to a useful end, though it breaks out destructively every now and then, particularly with women, for Ted, as well as all the rest of it, is a womaniser, if that old-fashioned term is still current. Like Stuart, he is susceptible, but, unlike Stuart, he clearly offers performance as well as appreciation. Hugo finds Ted's success with women astonishing, for he cannot believe that Ted is considerate in bed, or out of it for that matter, but clearly, he says to himself, he does not understand women, not even Kate, whom he knows quite well. And he concedes that Kate and Ted, in their heyday, were a good couple, well matched.

Evelyn Stennett is a lovely woman. Everyone agrees that

she is a lovely woman. That seems her lot in life. Unlike Kate, she is gentle, mild of manner and of feature, self-effacing. She is intelligent, well bred, well educated, serious, well informed. People who meet her for the first time at a social gathering tend to treat her politely as extrovert Ted's quiet and dependable wife, and imagine that she must be a great support to him. There is a little truth in this picture, but not much. She also, like Kate, works, and works longer hours; when her youngest child started primary school, she started full-time as a social worker. She is well organised, and runs an orderly home. Kate is well organised, and runs a disorderly home. Evelyn does not make much of her own achievements; she was brought up to believe such things possible, and has made them so, as her mother did before her.

When Ted first met her, out in Gambia, she seemed to represent an unfamiliar world, and a world that he wanted; a world of good connections, security, style. Her father is a surgeon, her mother recently retired from the headship of a large and well-known London school. The Morton girls (there were three of them) were brought up to stand on their own feet, and given a good education to assist them to this end. Evelyn, in those early days, seemed to Ted to know everybody, and to be known to everybody; everybody who was anybody knew the Morton girls, at least in the academic and medical worlds, which were the worlds Ted intended to besiege. In marrying Evelyn, Ted found himself not quite by accident in a charmed circle, and one moreover which included him with the best of grace, for the Mortons were too high-principled to be snobbish, and well placed to appreciate his exceptional gifts. It took him some time to appreciate their limitations, and to become impatient with them. Evelyn could have warned him, but did not wish to. At the beginning, out in Gambia, they didn't think of such things. They were young; they fell in love. Ted rescued Evelyn from a period of terrifying loneliness; she had miscalculated her own strength, in going out alone straight from college to Africa, but was too proud to admit it. Ted arrived like salvation, and brought her honorably home only three months ahead of the end of her sentence.

Their marriage seemed entirely suitable, but of course it too, like Kate's and Stuart's, went wrong, though not so blatantly. The most obvious embodiment of their difficulties is their eldest son, Sebastian, a child who from the first caused trouble, a hyper-active baby who never seemed to sleep. They at first assumed that his oddities sprang from an excess of intelligence, as most such parents might fondly assume, and of course they may have been right, though by now it is too late to say. As soon as he started school, they discovered he had learning as well as social difficulties: fits of intense activity would be followed by periods of intense withdrawal, he alternately bullied and was bullied, he could not sleep at night, he wet the bed. Evelyn kept calm and refused to appear to worry: Ted was far from calm, and would declaim his anxieties to anyone who would listen. At the age of eleven, they sent him to a special progressive school, but that did not turn out too well. He never worked, began to play truant as he grew older, indulged in all the anti-social activities available to a teenager in the seventies—drinking, drugs, late nights, absent nights, theft. He came home one day at the outbreak of the punk vogue with his head more or less shaved, and looked, as Kate's children put it, a mess. Not a very edifying product of so promising a union. All the Stennetts' friends have their own theories about what went wrong, but most agree that it must have something to do with Ted's overbearing personality and ridiculously high expectations, combined with Evelyn's compensatory mildness. Luckily, the second child turned out better; Vicky is a nice girl, tolerably conscientious at school, and a dab hand at such pleasant teenage pursuits as scone-baking and guitar-playing. Again, one could argue, and some do, that Ted did not feel threatened by a daughter, and therefore gave her an easier time. Or that Vicky learned early, from Sebastian's bad example, the virtues of adaptability. Perhaps it comes to the same thing.

Ted had at least one serious affair before he took up with Kate. The woman was an actress whose husband had recently died of an overdose. She too attempted suicide several times, and finally managed it. Her death was unusually horrible: she locked herself in the bathroom of her flat in Notting Hill Gate and drank a bottle of spirits of salt. It is said that she left a vitriolic suicide note for Ted, but this may merely be gossip. Nobody much blamed Ted, because she was clearly unbalanced to begin with, which was lucky for him.

(According to Hugo, Ted spends so much of his time seducing women because he is such an ugly brute that he has to prove he can. When Hugo says this, women tend to look at one another and smile.)

Kate first met Ted at one of his own dinner parties. She and Evelyn were by this time good friends, sharing a woman's world, as we have seen, of small children and excursions to the park. Such intimacies are often fleeting, born of necessity, but Kate and Evelyn liked one another very much, and had become used to sharing their pleasures and their complaints. Kate at this period had fewer anxieties than Evelyn, for her children weren't much trouble either in school or out of it; paradoxically, Kate would suppose, because they didn't have a proper father as Evelyn's did. Stuart, whom Kate had by this stage learned to treat with wary and patronising affection, was a much less disturbing influence than Ted appeared to be—a nice man, gentle, tender, warm-hearted. She and Evelyn would talk of these matters. Kate conjured up in her mind a picture of ogre Ted, the masculine man, the patriarchal bully —not that Evelyn was exceptionally disloyal, but she couldn't help letting her irritations show, and had no inhibitions about analysing them in the calm, objective, intellectual way in which she also spoke of housing problems and immigration, in which she had once with her friends at boarding school discussed South Africa and Stalin and Suez. So when Evelyn invited Kate to dinner to meet Ted, as in the natural course of events (or at least in the natural course of events in a life such as Evelyn's) she did, Kate set off with considerable curiosity to meet this shadowy monster—her imagination also fired, it must be admitted, by accounts of the offstage drama of the suicidal and passionate actress. Men were awful, she and Evelyn agreed, but at the age of twenty-nine Kate had not ceased to find them interesting.

Evelyn invited Kate partly because she was worried about her principal guests, a potentially difficult couple, friends of Ted's, the husband a Swedish birth-control expert who worked for the World Health Organisation, and his English wife, an unknown quantity. Kate, it seemed to Evelyn, would be useful, for she had a lively professional curiosity about almost everything, and a journalist's knack of asking questions when the going got sticky, and then managing to look genuinely interested in the answers.

The other guest was Evelyn's cousin Hugo.

If Evelyn felt slight misgivings as Ted and Kate greeted one another by telling one another how much they had heard about each other, with a challenging look in both pairs of bright-blue eyes, she concealed them. Ted had on occasion expressed irritation at some of Kate's relayed views, but he had also expressed curiosity, and had actually been seen reading some of her current series in the *TV Times* (Kate had some strange outlets); and anyway, Kate was perfectly capable of looking after herself in conversation, as in most other ways. If anything, she enjoyed a skirmish. Kate, for her part, was thoroughly looking forward to her evening; Stuart was baby-sitting, so in theory at least she wouldn't have to hurry back, the spring sun was pouring through the windows onto the pale-gold wooden floor and the stripped pine of the dresser and the blue bowl of orange marigolds and marguerites, it would be a good dinner because Evelyn's oven, unlike her own, was not bought from a junk shop and standing on a slant, the drink that Ted had poured for her was substantial, and she was delighted to find Hugo Mainwaring, one of her favourite recent acquaintances, who treated her with an asexual teasing gallantry that made her feel extremely buoyant. Life, thought Kate, is fun. After all. Or at least, bits of it are. The trees in the square outside were full of new green leaves. What could go wrong?

Her sense of well-being was slightly disturbed by the arrival of the Swede and his wife. The Swede, they silently and unanimously decided, was all right, but his wife, whom neither Ted nor Evelyn had met before, was not at all all right. She arrived looking strained and obscurely agitated, perhaps, they speculated, because she was overdressed; the other women were wearing long skirts and nondescript shirts, but Mrs. Sondersheim was clad in a smart little olive-green jersey silk dress, very low cut, the kind of dress that Kate as a girl in Romley had thought she would like to wear when she was grown up, but which she now recognised was quite beyond her. She was also wearing jewelry, something which Evelyn never did on principle, and Kate because she hadn't any. She was lean and handsome and tanned and very carefully—probably (but who could tell?) unnecessarily—made up. A gin and tonic did little to relax her; Hugo did his best to chat her up about life in Brussels, but got short change. Her replies were short, edgy, evasive. Evelyn hoped that a removal to the dinner table and a portion of mushroom salad might calm her nerves, but no such transformation occurred. She continued to sit erect, taut and silent, toying with her salad in a way that Kate and Evelyn, both healthy eaters just old enough to know that weight was going to be a problem if they didn't watch it, found infuriating. So by a general consensus the party, as it were, metaphorically turned its back on her and talked among themselves. The Swede aired his views on the justification for testing new contraceptive drugs in the Third World, Ted contributed an account of the economics of curing river blindness, Kate as expected asked bright and intelligent questions on both topics, Evelyn worried about the broccoli and hollandaise sauce, and Hugo wished that the emanations from Mrs. Sondersheim would fade, and tried to engage a distracted Evelyn in a diversionary chat about landscape gardening.

They got through the first course tolerably well, but during the second matters became even worse, for Mrs. Sondersheim refused anything but the smallest portion of broccoli, rejecting both chicken and potatoes with unnatural emphasis. Is she, perhaps, a vegetarian? Evelyn wondered, but did not like to ask, fearing the answer would be negative. The Swede, affected by his wife's behaviour, fell silent and began to mope. Even Hugo felt slightly overcome. Disaster, in the form of silence, threatened. And it was at this point that Kate rose, as it were, from the crumbs and did her stuff. Picking up one of Ted's remarks on the economic and social price of containing epidemics, she launched into one of her set pieces, an aria on her father's passion for public health, the embarrassment this had caused her as a girl, her partial conversion due to a scenic trip down the sewers of London, her interest in the difference between the highly skilled, specialised, expensive end of medical care, which affected so few (and most of them already dying), and the crude but effective measures of environmental health care, which affected so many and which received so little applause. This was well before Illyich's attacks on doctors, well before the general public began to ask questions about the real reasons for the decline of certain diseases; she had learned it at her father's knee. Ted was entranced, for this was stuff after his own heart, engaged though he himself was with the rare, the expensive, and the exotic. He responded with like spirit, recommending that Kate should read his book on plagues in history, offering a résumé of his own arguments. The conversation, so nearly dead, fluttered, staggered, took off. Evelyn heaved a sigh of relief and started to worry about the pudding. Ted fierce and expository, Kate pink and excited, the Swede occasionally offering corrections, Hugo contributing a description of cholera in the Congo (which both Ted and the Swede disputed, though they hadn't been there and Hugo had), they continued cheerfully until the cheese. And then Mrs. Sondersheim spoke.

"This winter," she said, and they all fell silent, respectfully. "This winter, Jan and I were in Sierra Leone. On holiday. We were on the beach." She paused. Her husband became very still, made a move as if to intervene, then relapsed, staring down at his plate, as though wishing to dissociate himself. She began again, speaking very slowly, as though trying to explain something very complicated, though what she had to say was simple enough. "Jan had been working for eight months in Senegal. It was decided he should have a holiday. They spend money on their employees, these international organisations." She smiled dishearteningly. "So we went to this hotel, in Sierra Leone. A modern hotel, for package tours. Winter breaks. Second holidays." She paused again, while each listener conjured up an image of the ugly modern hotel, dumped by the shore as confidently and casually as previous generations had set up their trading stations: was she, Evelyn wondered, a woman tormented by guilt, by the rift between the rich and the poor? And if so, why the dress and the diamond brooch?

"We were walking on the beach," she continued. "It was not a very pleasant beach. Too hot, but no sun, no clear sky. Grey heat. The sea and the sky both looked just the same. Grey. And then I saw this dead baby, lying half in and half out of the water. On the water line." She paused, but not for effect. "It was almost a skeleton. Rags of skin and flesh. Like a little drifting cape, going up and down in the water." Another pause. "But it wasn't a baby," she went on, in the same dry monotone. "It was only a cat." She stopped. "It had a little grinning head, with teeth." Nobody tried to say, How horrible, or What a relief. Then she said, not apparently changing the subject, "Jan had no holiday. Most of the children there had syphilis. When they found that Jan was a doctor, they wouldn't leave us alone. In the end, we had to leave."

Her story was finished. She folded her napkin, calmly rose, and left the room. It was assumed, at first, that she had gone to the lavatory. Jan Sondersheim, on her departure, turned to the others, in a mixture of apology and explanation, and said, "Susan was very upset. She was not well." Murmurs of condolence followed; Jan turned to Ted, to Hugo, to Evelyn, seeking support. They knew what Africa was like, they too had seen these things, it was hard to adjust; had they not found the same? Evelyn agreed, warmly, sympathetically. Yes, they had suffered the same shocks, the same sense of helplessness, she for her part had been quite unable to take it. "One has to harden the heart," said Evelyn, who had never herself managed to do so. They talked of such things, in a subdued and serious tone, until it became clear that Susan Sondersheim was not going to come down again. Her absence lengthened absurdly.

Evelyn took the affair in hand. "I'll just go up and see if she's all right," she said, and slipped off, before anyone could comment. They let her go; she was good at this kind of thing, it was her profession. After ten minutes, Evelyn reappeared and appealed to Jan. "She's locked herself in the bathroom," she said, with a calm she clearly did not feel. Then Jan got up and left the room with Evelyn. Some time later, she came back and asked Ted if she should ring the ambulance, the fire brigade. As she spoke, there was a noise of crying and moaning from upstairs, Mrs. Sondersheim had emerged. Evelyn rushed out again hastily, and the by-this-time noisy offstage drama continued until Evelyn, in coat and scarf, came back and said that she was going to drive the Sondersheims back to their hotel, and would they make themselves coffee.

Kate, Hugo, and Ted were left. Kate and Ted were on their feet, animated. Hugo helped himself to another drink. Ted stood by the window, watching the car depart; Kate stood by the dresser. They heard the car round the corner, and then Ted turned back to face the room, saw Kate standing there, and crossed towards her. They were both smiling, and then began to laugh, as they took each other by both hands. "Kate," said Ted, "you are really quite marvellous." And they both laughed again, in unholy and heartless communion, then released one another's hands, and sat down again at the table, helping themselves hungrily to more cheese, to great slices of brown bread, pouring themselves more wine, urging Hugo to more wine. They ate and drank, the survivors, excited, exhilarated, their lease on life renewed by the precarious tenure of others. They discussed the incident, the healthy dissecting the sick, in the best of spirits. They suggested explanations— marital problems, the change of life, real insanity. They were young then. They were still laughing when Evelyn returned to chastise them amiably for not having bothered to make any coffee, to apologise for the disruption of the evening's entertainment. "Never mind, never mind," Kate said, wiping her hot face on her napkin, blowing her nose, "never mind, we enjoyed it, I'm sorry to say."

And that was it, as far as Ted and Kate were concerned.

(Mrs. Sondersheim came to a bad end, though not the kind one might have predicted. Last year she was involved as a hostage in a siege of the WHO building in Geneva, and was one of the victims of a police shoot-out. Kate did not find this so funny. In fact, this was one of the incidents that caused her to sigh to Hugo, "Why isn't life funny any more? Why has it suddenly got so *serious?*" Hugo tried to suggest that the original Mrs. Sondersheim incident hadn't really been very funny either, but she did not appear to be interested in this attempt at re-interpretation.)

It was hard to tell what Evelyn made of Ted and Kate's affair. She was a discreet woman, not much given to talking about her personal problems, if indeed she saw this as one. She can hardly have ignored the way that Ted, after this meeting, would always try to get home early if he knew that Kate was coming to tea, the way he would press drinks on her to persuade her to stay, engaging her in serious conversation amidst a sea of tired and fractious children. He would even, quite uncharacteristically, offer to collect his own children from Kate's whenever an opportunity arose. Such approaches ended, as they must, in bed—or, rather, they did not end there, but continued there, for their affair lasted, to the surprise of some, for a good many years. They had much in common, not least their ambition. Ted had by this time grown accustomed to Evelyn's well-mannered virtues, and was clearly attracted by the flashier aspects of Kate's life: her name in the news (or at least in the newspapers), her photograph here and there, her clever friends in the media. Her image, in a word. She, for her part, found him much stronger stuff than Stuart had been: a man in a man's world, a useful source of information and inside stories. Their relationship, which no doubt began with the usual sexual fervor and emotional declarations, soon settled into a business-like partnership, an exchange process for their mutual benefit, though Kate fancied she was getting more than he took back; and anyway, what he wanted was easy and pleasant to give.

She sharpened her wits on Ted. She knew by then as much as she needed to know about art, the Armstrongs, vegetables arranged in fruit bowls, babies, bailiffs, bric-a-brac. Ted taught her a lot of things. He taught her, for instance, about statistics and government reports. Until she met Ted, she had regarded statistics with an almost personal aversion (a female aversion?), and had taken their findings as an affront to human dignity; she could find so many exceptions to every rule that she found it hard to believe that there were such things as rules and averages. When she read that twins were generally of lower intelligence than non-twins, that infant mortality was higher in Salford than in Sevenoaks, that middle-class mothers talked more to their children than working-class mothers, she would waste her energy thinking of evidence to the contrary, so much did she dislike the idea that human affairs were governed by probabilities of so relentless a nature; Ted suggested to her that this resistance was caused not by being "bad at maths" but by the fact that her own situation was so anomalous, sociologically, that she felt that the law of averages threatened her right to exist. She took this point to heart, overcame her suspicions, and found a new world of enquiry opened; the particular blossomed into the general, and instead of finding her attention caught by the individual hard case—the rare disease, the crime passional, the improbable accident, the unexpected success—she found herself entranced by trends, graphs, percentages, emerging patterns, social shifts. The dullest item in the dullest newspaper gleamed with a new interest. She became a dab hand at questioning official statistics and at quarrelling, usually intelligently, with the findings of surveys.

Her pieces on middle-class manipulation of the health service, on rows about underprivileged gifted children and the preponderance of black children in ESN schools, were classics of their kind, and warmly welcomed, for in those days people were still ready and willing to hear the humane, sensible left-wing view, the so-called progressive view. She and Ted came from backgrounds not dissimilar, and though Ted himself was remarkably indifferent to politics, he was quite ready to provide her with ammunition, to suggest ways in which she could prove her foregone conclusions with a display of reason. They were both in their own ways seeking the egalitarian millennium, which would bring security, opportunity, and prosperity to all, while awarding its faithful and elect (such as themselves) with its own special prestige-bearing blessings: a glittering but carefree life style, amusing classless clothes, a freedom of speech and expression hitherto denied to so-called serious people (in other words, the licence to use bad language at committee meetings and editorial conferences), a certain gaiety that earlier pioneers of welfare and democracy in the Beveridge era had carefully eschewed, and for which

Evelyn, whose inner conviction was that virtue should involve self-denial, had little feeling. The dream of the sixties.

It was easy to be optimistic in those days. The doubts about international organisations which may well have contributed to the unbalancing of Mrs. Sondersheim were not then widespread; there was less talk about people on large safe incomes doing nothing in the UN, in the WHO, in the FAO, in the EEC, there were fewer sour jokes about thick carpets and large desks and free booze in the office. People went to conferences because they were interested in the conferences and discussed the issues rather than the quality of the four-course luncheons. (Though they expected the luncheons.) People had not woken up to the problems of tax-free international incomes, to the lack of answerability. It was assumed that men like Jan Sondersheim were motivated by high principles. Evelyn is very depressed by the shift in attitude. She went to a conference in Denmark recently (one of those free trips we are all told we need so badly, and deserve so much) and returned very downcast by the fact that some of the Danes, people whom she admired, seemed to believe that the high level of social security was turning Denmark into a nation of beggars. Now the social workers in Britain are on strike, and she does not much like that either, though she writes eloquent letters to the *Guardian* and the *Daily Telegraph* defending their case. (*The Times* is also on strike.) Uneasily, though: uneasily.

Kate and Ted, in the early years of their affair, did not have to worry about these things. Kate was happy, busy, successful. Praise and prosperity, beyond her wildest childhood fantasies, flowed in from every side. It seemed that she could do no wrong. Of course, she had her worries: it was hard work bringing up the children more or less single-handed, she was often exhausted, perpetually harassed by domestic problems such as leaking roofs and unpunctual child-minders, she felt guilty about Stuart in his damp basement with his succession of quite inadequate art-student girlfriends (if only, she thought, he would find a nice capable wife and settle down). She worried about her parents, who were growing older and older, whom she found hard to include in her over-active life; she worried about her brother Peter, who was deeply unhappy in his job as chief buyer for Spotwood's Garden Machines, and whose unhappiness had caused him to weigh fourteen stone. Peter was heading for a nervous breakdown, she accurately prophesied, and there was nothing she could do about it, for he had turned against her; and anyway, she was too busy.

But these were small troubles, to an energetic woman, and they did not get her down. The most annoying of them, because geographically the nearest, was Stuart. He seemed to expect her continued attention, and therefore she gave it. She could, perhaps, have moved away, but it did not seem fair to do so, because of the children. Living as he did within half a mile, he was always popping in and offering her utterly useless advice on the leaking roof or the overflowing dustbin, advice ill-directed from one who himself lived in such disorder. He had a knack of arriving just as she and Ted were settling down to a rare evening of illicit peace in front of the television, and although he himself was living with girls of the Amaryllis variety most of the time during these years, he deeply objected to Kate's liaison with Ted—and Kate, for some reason which she couldn't quite explain even to herself, was soft enough to try to conceal it, an endeavour which was pointless from the start, and which involved her in some farcical manoeuvres. Adultery is in itself farcical, and there was a lot of it around in those days, for she and most of her friends were in their early thirties, many of them tied to their spouses by small children, not yet ready to leave and set up house again, and equally unwilling to resign themselves to a life of bad-tempered fidelity; in theory, few of them disapproved of adultery, few of them had embarked on marriage with much hope of survival, most of them professed to believe in sexual freedom, honesty, self-expression—yet, like Kate, they found themselves dodging out of back doors, hiding letters, making phone calls from call-boxes, spying and being spied upon. Of course, these affairs caused a good deal of genuine suffering and jealousy, but they were also comic, if regarded in the right light, or what Kate then took to be the right light: "How strange it is," Kate remarked to Hugo at one point, "that one can feel that loving somebody is the most right and proper thing in one's life, and yet feel simultaneously that it's an offence, a crime, a treachery." Hugo was well placed to know what she meant, for in those days he was, very mistakenly, married himself, to an art historian called Judith, with whom he had two children.

There was no question of Kate's marrying Ted. He never showed the slightest intention of leaving Evelyn, nor did Kate wish him to do so; she wanted to keep them both, to go on as they were forever. She liked being on her own, was never lonely—like many mothers, she prized solitude, and never seemed to get enough of it. Nor did she want to disturb her children by providing a substitute father.

She told some good stories, during this period, about marriage and adultery. About a friend of hers who had an affair with a heavy smoker, and who took up smoking herself, despite a strong initial distaste, in order to excuse the smell of cigarettes on her clothes and in the house; she became addicted and is now on forty a day, though she has long since quarrelled with the man. Not a very nice story. About a man in Broadmoor who cut his wife's head off and baked it in the oven; a psychiatrist friend of hers who had visited him in prison was so impressed with this exploit that he recounted it over countless dinner tables, until on one such occasion his wife, beside herself with rage at his relish, got up, walked out, walked home, and baked the cat. (That, said Kate, silenced him for a couple of years.) About a woman friend who arrived home from work unexpectedly early to find her husband and best friend desperately turning the bed inside out looking for a new contact lens. (This one ended well, with mutual confessions; they all remarried and lived happily ever after. And they found the contact lens.) About a woman who had a child by another man, and never told her husband until all four children were more or less grown up; the occasion she chose to break the news was a Christmas dinner, when her husband was being particularly unpleasant to the odd child out, berating it for its lack of grip on life and its poor examination results. "Don't you listen to him," said Kate's acquaintance, rising from the table in majesty, "he's not your father, your father's a vet and lives in Sevenoaks, so there!" About an elderly man who, thinking himself on his deathbed, confessed to his grown-up children that he had a mistress and two daughters in Canada, and would they please on his death be kind to this extra family, which was due to arrive to take its last farewell; the extra family arrived, was received with heroic courtesy, but the man survived; and lived to regret his moment of honesty, encumbered with a decade of unnecessary apologies, explanations, recriminations, and sibling jealousies. About a university lecturer teaching "The Ancient Mariner," who found her suggestion that perhaps the dead albatross was Coleridge's wife Sarah greeted with silent disbelief by a daytime class of twenty-year-old students (boring old Freud again, she could see them thinking), but with a ripple of spontaneous, assenting, utterly comprehending laughter from the class of adult housewives and retired pensioners whom she taught in the evenings.

People told Kate plenty of stories of this nature. She was an uncritical audience, unshockable, a free woman, set free from the effort to preserve a normal façade of married life. Strangers wrote her letters full of the most intimate details. She became alibi, confessional, money-lender, even provider of rendezvous, a one-woman marriage-guidance council, though she operated on rather different principles. She quite liked this role. The pageant of human love and folly entertained her; it afforded her more amusement than sorrow.

She told one story about herself, about the early days of her affair with Ted. She'd gone to bed early to watch television, taking with her a disgusting little snack consisting of mashed banana, a liberal quantity of cream, and a sprinkling of small aniseed balls nicked from a child, and had just started eating it when she heard, unexpectedly, Ted's key in the door —he'd decided to drop in to say good night on his way home from a meeting. Kate, understandably embarrassed, shoved the plate under the bed, and tried to make Ted welcome, but found herself unable to return his embraces with her usual ardour, smelling strongly, as she did, of aniseed; Ted, offended, released her, and stepped back into the dish. "The awful thing was," said Kate, "that we didn't really know each other well enough to laugh. Love is a funny business, isn't it?"

Not everything, of course, was so innocent, so childish, so painless. Kate had nightmares about Evelyn, and didn't know what to tell her and what not to tell her. Ted wore himself out and bored himself stiff trying to keep two women happy, making love twice over, telling them the same anecdotes. Kate could never remember which stories Ted had told her, which Evelyn, and what she was supposed to know about the other. The penalties of a double life. Evelyn, for her part, worried about how much to let Kate and Ted know she knew: if she admitted knowing (as she of course did) more or less everything, would that destroy the delicate equilibrium that balanced them, and force one or another into regrettable unilateral action? Ted's attentions to Kate served Evelyn's purposes very well, but she did not quite like to admit this, even to herself.

There was a convenient conspiratorial pretence amongst the three of them that Kate, as a woman on her own, needed Ted's advice from time to time, as a man, as a father, as a doctor. "Ask Ted, Ted will know," Evelyn would say, when a child developed an illness, when a wall developed a new crack, when a bicycle was stolen. And Ted was, in fact, quite useful, from time to time. He was a more practical man than Stuart had ever been.

Over the children, an unholy set of alliances grew up.

Kate would listen to the grievances of each Stennett parent in turn, and naturally sympathised with whichever she was listening to at the time, for she could see that it was the conflict between the two, rather than the policy of either, that proved so ill-fated. At times she would attempt, not unsuccessfully, to mediate. She liked both children, was herself a born child-liker, and they liked her. It was, of course, easy for her to behave well towards them. The Stennett marriage confirmed her in her own dislike of marriage, in her own conviction that it was very bad for people, particularly children: yet she had a fantasy that she was herself its true support. A paradoxical role.

Ted behaved towards Kate's children much better than he behaved towards his own, and would listen patiently to her complaints about Stuart's unreliability. He would represent Stuart's hypothetical point of view with an imagination that he completely lacked when dealing with his own affairs. Kate's children, in turn, saw Evelyn's home as a refuge from the frenetic tenor of life in Dacre Road: at Evelyn's, one could actually get a proper meal sitting down at table, a treat which the little Armstrongs were to regard as a luxury for the rest of their lives. (Though when, occasionally, Kate tried to get them all to sit down at once, naturally they refused.)

Shadow husbands, shadow wives, shadow parents.

Kate, it must be admitted, was extremely pleased with herself during these years. She thought she had got it all organised. Her own children prospered, her work also. She felt happy, useful, busy, both in her professional and private life. She would look at herself and think, Yes, you're doing all right. Despite Stuart, she hadn't become a man-hater, as so many of her friends had, she liked men, and in understanding Ted she had an illusion of understanding all mankind. Motherly Kate, safe, affectionate, harmless. She was contained and complacent. She felt she had solved all the problems of being a woman alone; she gave up flirtations on the side, partly because they annoyed Ted, and partly because she no longer needed people to tell her how wonderful she was. Occasionally, with a pitying amazement, she would glance down into the snake pit of sex, where other people were still, apparently, writhing in agony; thank God, she was spared all that. She listened to the horror stories of others with compassionate detachment; Poor things, she would think. Sometimes it would cross her mind that her safe house was built on rotten foundations, but she would banish these thoughts, for they were, after all, nothing but thoughts; they had no substance.

There must have been a point when it began to dawn on Kate that her peaceful middle years could not last forever, that her way of life, which seemed so permanent, could not last. Children grow up and leave home, and journalism is not the most secure of professions, even for the fashionable, the lucky, and the hard-working. She was, naturally, proud and delighted when Mark was offered a place at Waterford, to study architecture in its excellent new department, but felt nevertheless a slight chill at the thought of his departure. What would happen to her busy home when the last teenager left, when the sound of pop music was silenced, when there was nobody in for those inconsequential meals but herself?

A vague anxiety began to invade her complacency, manifesting itself at first in professional restlessness. She left the paper with which she'd been for years and started work for another, a move which she regretted, though she would never admit it. She tried to write about subjects which were really beyond her scope. She began to regret her lack of formal education. She enrolled for evening classes, but never had time to attend them. She envied colleagues who had had the sense to pull out and take degree courses in politics, economics, sociology; she was too old, too ignorant, and too successful to imitate them. The area which she had made her own seemed ever more confining; what had seemed unexplored terrain became well trodden as more and more women began to write about menstruation, battered wives, low career expectations for girls —in short, as the women's movement gathered momentum.

She found herself trapped in stale repetition, and depressed by the fact that as everyone else got more interested in Women she became less and less so. The feeling of deep boredom which overcame her when she opened a woman's novel frightened her. The freedom she had glimpsed as an ambitious girl of twenty had turned into a narrow tunnel, and nobody would let her out. Nobody wanted her to get out. They wanted her to stay in. Am I getting sour, am I getting bitter, and if so, why? she asked herself. She would sit and stare at the piles of letters from women trapped in bad marriages, dull jobs, tragic affairs, abused bodies, and turn faint with dislike. It was all true, all that they said, and it was she that had encouraged them to describe it all to her, but she didn't want to know.

The commercial exploitation of Women began to horrify her in a new way. One could sell anything these days, she began to think, so long as it was angry enough. A best-selling angry feminist novel appeared which seemed to sum up the whole sorry business. She read it because she had to, and found it in many ways impressive, and certainly memorable, but something in it filled her with unease and distaste. The author had chosen to characterise the hardships of the woman's lot with the phrase "shit and string beans." Women, said the author, spend their lives dealing with shit and string beans. Kate stared at this oft-repeated phrase, wondering why it offended her so much, and realised after some time that perhaps it was because her own father had indeed spent his life dealing with shit, real shit, whereas women only have to deal with nice clean yellow milky baby shit, which is perfectly inoffensive, in fact in its own way rather nice. Women do not have to wheel barrow loads of contraceptives, or crawl on their hands and knees through underground sewers, or wade thigh-high in torrents of effluent. No, most women's lives are a piece of cake in comparison, thought Kate. And then felt ill, as though she had betrayed something, renounced something. She tried to remind herself of all the things that were really, genuinely, seriously awful about women's lives, here and in other countries—and God knows she'd spent enough time writing about them—but her faculty of indignation and sympathy seemed to have dried up. I've come to a dead end, thought Kate, I don't care any more, whatever has happened to me?

She found herself envying more and more people with what she called proper jobs—people like Ted and Evelyn, her friend Marina who was a lecturer in Italian at Kent University, her friend Sally who was a doctor, Judith Mainwaring who was an art historian, Hugo Mainwaring whose branch of journalism was so much more serious than her own, who also wrote books. From time to time people, including agents and publishers, suggested that she should herself write a book, but she knew that this was beyond her; she was a short-distance sprinter, a five-thousand-word-at-the-maximum woman (she really preferred the one-to-two-thousand stint, though this preference filled her with a slight shame). She couldn't work alone for long periods; she needed stimulus, events, people, change. And anyway, she wasn't qualified to write a book, was she? Her limitations began to haunt her. She couldn't even accept assignments abroad, because she was frightened of travel in foreign countries.

She mentioned these anxieties occasionally to her friends, but they were not very sympathetic, and why should they be? They too, they said, were going through reappraisals, dissatisfactions, the discontent of realising one would never in this one and only life be anything else but what one was, and some of them said that they envied Kate her free-wheeling existence, her rapid turnover of topics. Evelyn in particular was going through a bad patch of her own. Her work had once seemed worthwhile; indeed, that was why she had chosen it. But it too was becoming repetitive; she spent too much of her time sitting in her office filling in forms. She saw more of failure than of success. The welfare state itself, and all the caring professions, seemed to be plunging into a dark swamp of uncertainty, self-questioning, economic crisis. She recounted to Kate an incident which seemed to sum up her own darkening mood, and the country's. She was walking back from work one day, late, in a hurry, preoccupied by thoughts of the dinner she had to cook and the shopping she had to do before cooking this dinner, when she saw an old woman standing on the pavement outside their local hospital, a large modern teaching hospital. She looked irresolute, confused. Evelyn nearly hurried by on the other side, but paused instead, of course, to help, and the old woman asked her the way to the bus stop. Evelyn, walking that way, offered to accompany her. It became clear, as they walked, that the woman was in a state of shock: indeed, her mouth was covered in traces of dried blood, and she seemed to have lost some of her teeth. "Which bus do you want?" said Evelyn, but the woman did not know. Evelyn questioned her; had she come from the hospital, had she had an accident? Where was she trying to get to? The woman mumbled, in a foreign accent. She did not know. She'd been knocked over, taken to the hospital in an ambulance, didn't know where she was. They reached the bus stop, which happened to be the terminus. Evelyn, although by now even more pushed for time through having slowed her pace to match the old woman's, could not abandon her; she asked her name, which she recalled—Mrs. Fergo, or something like that, she said she was—and her address, but her address she seemed to have forgotten.

"I'd better take you back to the hospital," said Evelyn, but the woman manifested intense alarm at this suggestion and refused to turn back. She wanted to get on a bus. "But you can't go just anywhere," said Evelyn. And they stood there, the tiny woman with her large shabby shopping bag, lost, adrift in meaningless London. Evelyn felt helpless, her mind refused to work, she didn't know what to do. She looked around for help, and found it in the form of a bus inspector, a young inspector in green uniform with a modern moustache, a tall young man. Evelyn explained the problem, and the man gently, tenderly, began to question the woman; she couldn't remember her address, oh dear, but she'd been shopping, hadn't she (looking at

her bag), had she got her pension book? Meekly, the woman
handed over her bag of sprouts and sugar and margarine.
"You've been to the co-op, I see," said the nice young man,
bending down from his great height—was it this co-op, was
it her local co-op, did she have a co-op book—? The woman
shook her head, bewildered. "You can't get on a bus in this
state, dear," said the inspector, "not by yourself." He offered to
take her back to the hospital. Evelyn also offered, shamed by
the young man's attentive concern. After a while, the woman
gave in and allowed Evelyn to lead her off; she took her back
to Casualty, where an extremely disagreeable and abrupt re-
ceptionist in a white coat snapped angrily, "Where's she been
wandering off to, then?" and told her to sit on a chair.

Evelyn, belatedly, snapped back into professionalism,
checked that the hospital had a record of the woman's arrival,
of the location of the accident, made certain that at least some
kind of attention would be paid. She tried to cheer the old
lady with kind words, but failed; Mrs. Fergo simply sat,
shrunk and bedraggled and subdued. "I have to go," said
Evelyn, for she had to get home, had to shop, cook dinner.
The woman hardly looked up. She looked like a prisoner,
caught while attempting escape, awaiting punishment. And
Evelyn left her there, in unkind professional hands, and hurried home. The truth was that Evelyn felt herself to be not
very good with old people; she could hear in her own voice
the horrid inept middle class interfering tones she so disliked
in others, the patronising kindness. No wonder the old woman
had not responded. How Evelyn admired the easy good-
nature with which the young inspector had spoken, the common sense which he had displayed. "Common humanity isn't
dead," said Evelyn, "but maybe we're killing it?"

What Evelyn did not tell Kate was that she was actually
frightened of the old and the frail. Ever since childhood, while
talking to the very old, she had been frightened by visions of
herself attacking them, hitting them, assaulting them, knocking off their glasses. Evelyn, the mildest of women. These vi-

sions would appear, unsummoned, while she sipped cups of strong tea in clients' bed-sitters, even while she entertained her own rambling great-aunt in larger rooms to cups of weaker tea in thinner, more fragile china. Of course Evelyn knew that she would never assault an old person, and that these horrid apparitions must be an image of her own fear of age and death, might even be some kind of safety valve. But they frightened her, nevertheless. Being a sensible woman, she looked on the positive side: she was quite good with delinquent adolescents (her own excepted) partly because she seemed to have some insight into the impulse that makes the young and the violent turn upon the weak and the defenceless, and therefore did not regard this impulse with uncomprehending disgust. She was good, also, with parents who battered their babies, a less unusual talent. But she still, in her heart, grieved over her lack of easy contact with the frail, was ashamed of the relief with which she had abandoned Mrs. Fergo to her fate. How long could she go on doing her job if these feelings grew more powerful? Had she, after all, mistaken her vocation, and was her vocation, after all, a waste of time, a job that could and should be undertaken better by bus inspectors and shop assistants?

Ted, in contrast, seemed unaffected by loss of nerve. The increasingly frequent crises of the National Health Service stimulated him. Revelations about waste of public money and international funds merely excited him to virulence. He displayed little feeling for individual suffering. Lost old ladies with wrinkled upper lips caked in blood bored him. He thought Evelyn wasted her time on hopeless cases. He enjoyed his work.

Kate's dissatisfaction spread. She became restless, unhappy, self-pitying, self-absorbed. She was no longer the amusing companion that Ted had once found her, and Ted had by now exhausted the charms of the world that she offered him; like her, he had seen through it, and, unlike her, he had better worlds to inhabit. He began to find her boring. She sensed this, but could do nothing about it. Their meetings became less frequent. She began to lose interest in sex, which had once seemed such a reliable and renewable joy. She lay dully in bed, worrying. She still, she thought, loved Ted, and was bored by herself rather than by him, but her love seemed to have lost heart and power, to have shut itself in. It no longer animated her, she could no longer even express it, it had sunk into some cold wintry hibernating part of herself. It wasn't dead, she told herself, it couldn't be dead, perhaps it was just waiting for some kind of spring, perhaps it would wake up and blossom again?

But it didn't work out like that. She got worse, not better. She decided she was overworked, took a short holiday by herself, but came back worried about her health, having had nothing else to worry about. She went to the doctor, complaining of tiredness and insomnia. He discovered that she had high blood pressure, referred her to a hospital for tests. The healthy, the indestructible Kate. While waiting for the hospital appointment, she read an article in the paper about the dangers of taking the pill after the age of thirty-five, particularly for those with high blood pressure; the same morning a cutting arrived from an American feminist magazine arguing that the pill was a male weapon, designed by the male sex to sterilise womanhood. It quoted alarming figures. In a saner mood, Kate would have been well placed to see through the figures, or at least to interpret them more soberly, but she panicked, and stopped taking the pill. She told herself that when she got to the hospital she would ask professional advice —perhaps a lower dose pill, perhaps a coil, perhaps even sterilisation? She meant to tell Ted, who was always good at medical reassurance, but their next meeting, a week later, was so dark and so fraught that she never got round to mentioning it.

Ted was in a bad state, ostensibly on account of a friend and colleague who, by indiscreet remarks about private medicine, had managed to bring all the Confederation of Health Service Employees (COHSE) members at his hospital out on strike. Ted was divided between abuse of this friend's folly, and abuse of the interfering press and unions. Kate listened to his imprecations quietly; though not noted for restraint in most situations, she by this stage knew Ted so well that she didn't bother to attack the surface illogic of his position, because she could read the subtext so closely. Ted was worried, and uncertain of the facts of the case, and afraid that his friend, in claiming misrepresentation, was lying. "Oh dear," she said from time to time, like a good wife. But Ted, far from being pacified, got wilder and wilder. He moved on to other, more dangerous topics on which Kate could not keep silent—Evelyn's mother, his daughter Vicky's new stunt of wearing high-heeled shoes with straight denims, Hugo's ludicrous opinions on Iran, Nuffield physics. The evening became grim and drunken, an evening such as they had not had in months, in years; they did not quarrel, for they rarely bothered to quarrel, but plunged together into a dark spiral, speaking of their past crimes, rarely mentioned, of their fears for the future, of age and its inroads. (Ted complained of indigestion so violent he thought he was developing an ulcer, Evelyn feared she was developing varicose veins. For some reason which she never located, Kate did not mention her own high blood pressure, though this would surely have been the moment to do so.)

Kate cried a lot; Ted seemed, in some way that she could not comprehend, desperate. "We ought to get married," said Ted, as he sometimes said at such moments, but this time as though pleading with her to save him from a worse fate. Kate cried the more. Marriage as defeat held no appeal. At midnight, Ted did something he had never done before in all these years; he rang Evelyn and said he was spending the night at Kate's. He was by this time extremely drunk, Kate less so, but too tired to protest. They went to bed, Ted made love to her for hours, seeming unable to reach any conclusion, a rare occurrence; violently, unfeelingly, as though trying to communicate about something quite different, something that had nothing to do with either sex or love.

She woke covered in bruises and scratches, and, though she did not yet know it, pregnant.

And thus she entered into the nastiest patch of her hitherto charmed life, a patch which made all previous setbacks appear in comparison minor irritations.

The discovery of her pregnancy plunged her into confusion of a new order. She was nearly forty; her children were all in their teens, relatively independent. She had, until recently, fancied that she was looking forward to the freedom that was coming her way. It was no time to begin a new family. On the other hand, this was a last chance, and why had she been sleeping with Ted all these years if she did not want a child by him? At the very least, she had to ask herself some not very nice questions about her own past behaviour. Ted, she felt, would stand by her if she resolved to have the baby; maybe he would even marry her. One thing she had not yet thought to question was his loyalty. But she did not want to marry Ted, nor, she was certain, did he want to marry her.

An abortion, or, as the doctor more tactfully suggested, a termination, seemed the obvious solution. Had not Kate herself been advocating for years the woman's right to choose, and who would have more right to exercise choice than herself? But it was not, of course, as simple as that. It rarely is. Part of her felt that the pregnancy was a visitation, an offer that could not be rejected. She was, was she not, a free woman, self-sufficient, as well placed to choose to rear a child single-handed as anyone was ever likely to be? There was no need to marry Ted: she could do it on her own. Many of her friends had chosen to do so, and she had respected their decisions. She was ashamed of the coward in her that shrank from the fuss, the publicity, the embarrassment to her parents (she had caused her parents enough embarrassment already, surely). She was ashamed of the selfishness in her that shrank from the prospect of disturbed nights, curtailed outings, financial worries. She was ashamed, in another way, of her reluctance to contemplate Evelyn's reaction, of her fear of the loss of Evelyn's friendship. Duplicity had caught her out: was not the proper thing to admit it, and see it through?

On another level, she could see that a new baby would give her a new lease of life, would rescue her from the purposeless apathy that had been threatening to subdue her. She liked babies; she was confident that her maternal feelings would revive as powerfully as ever, and that if she had the child, she would in five years be wondering how she could ever have lived without it. Was this an unexpected chance, a gift rather than a threat? Another fifteen years of purpose and selflessness was offered to her. She wondered if perhaps she had stopped taking the pill because, subconsciously, she wanted a baby before it was too late: on the whole she thought not, but how can one ever know?

She did not tell Ted. She was afraid of his response, of the pressure he might put upon her, one way or the other. She feared either his acceptance or his rejection. There was no room for him in her house, or in her life, on anything other than a part-time basis. But she did not like the knowledge that he might feel the same about her. So what had she been playing at? Not love, surely. Maybe she had never loved anybody, except her children. But if she loved her children (which she did not doubt), why not have another one and extend her years of loving?

She let the days drift by, unable to come to any decision. Nightmare days, and worse nights. She slept badly, and when she slept, she dreamed. Of babies, crying for her, calling her. Of babies, forgotten, unfed, neglected. Frightening, rational, irrational dreams, in which she went through every process of reason, in which in sleep she reconciled herself to a new birth, in which she renounced her life, her freedom, in which a baby smiled at her and forgave all. Once she dreamed that she had a new baby, complete with teeth and speech, with a round bald head like Ted's (her own had all been endowed with hair at birth), a baby that lay on the bed and looked up at her and said, malevolently, "You don't know what to do with me, do you? You've forgotten how to do it, haven't you?" Another in which her youngest, Reuben, was a baby again, in his little white Viyella nightdress, but endowed also with speech: sweetly, winningly, he said, "Mum, why have another, you've got me, I am your baby, all you have to do is to remember me." This was a comforting dream; she woke in tears of relief. But continued to dream of babies struggling in her arms, kicking at her angrily, rolling off beds, hitting their heads, falling off window ledges.

She interpreted them thus: I want, and I don't want. This recognition was no help.

After a fortnight of such irresolution, a curious incident took place. It was Saturday morning, and she was setting off, as usual, to do the weekend shopping. A few yards down the road, she met a girl with a dog. The girl was in tears, standing there crying, leaning on a lamp post. The girl had red hair; the dog too was golden, a golden retriever. Kate, being tenderhearted, stopped and asked if she could help in any way. The girl, sobbing noisily, poured forth some garbled story of being on the way to meet her father for lunch in town, but her father hated her and hated the dog, she couldn't take the dog into town, she was going to have to abandon him or her father. But surely, Kate argued, the father could not prevent her from taking the dog. The girl, a strange upper-class girl in hacking jacket and trousers, a rare species in the district Kate inhabited, continued to cry, then looked at Kate and held out the dog's lead and said, "You have him." "Oh, I can't," said Kate, "I don't want a dog, my house is too small, I have cats, I haven't time for a dog." But the girl could tell she had met a friend, and pressed the lead on Kate. "I'll come back," she said. "I'll come back for him this afternoon." Kate's mind raced round all her plans for the afternoon—launderette, cooking, paying bills, an elderly lady to tea, a meeting to discuss the Adventure Playground—the usual round of a working woman's weekend. But she took the dog. The girl promised faithfully to return, but how could one tell if she ever would? There seemed no point in asking for name and address: the transaction was completed as soon as Kate felt the animal move at the end of its leash. The girl disappeared, her tears miraculously dried, down the road to the bus stop.

Kate took the dog home. Her children, predictably, were delighted with him, and he was indeed a delightful dog. Young, hopeful, trusting, obedient, he sat and wagged his tail, eager to please, friendly, at their mercy. "I must be mad," said Kate, but the children laughed, and took it in turns to take the dog for walks, showing him off to their friends in the neighbourhood. They all fell in love with the dog. Golden, gleaming, he took them over. The cats cowered in the kitchen, the dog sprawled on the living-room carpet, panting with life, large, irresistible. By the time the girl arrived to reclaim him, which she duly did, they had all reconciled themselves to keeping him, had started to reorganise their lives on a dog basis. Kate was highly relieved to see the girl reappear, but the problem did not end there, for the girl urged Kate to keep him. "He's a valuable dog, and as good as gold," she kept saying. But here Kate drew the line: overriding her children's protests, she returned him. She did not approve of large dogs in London, had braved ridicule by voicing her views in print on dog licences and dog shit. Reason prevailed, and the dog padded off, disappearing from their lives as mysteriously as he had entered them. Reuben sulked, Mark and Ruth took Kate's side, though reluctantly.

That night, Kate dreamed of the dog. She dreamed that she had forgotten for days to feed him, that he was starving in the sitting room, a skeleton dog. It was a dream of nightmare vividness, and when she woke, she found herself standing in the sitting room, having walked there in her sleep. She had never done such a thing before.

For three subsequent nights she dreamed of the dog, and on the third, found herself standing by Reuben's bed.

She decided to keep the baby. Once she had made the

decision, a wave of relief flowed through her. Cheerfulness returned, she began to sing again about the house. It would all come right, after all. Why try to be a reasonable person when one has such dreams? She would tell Ted, but not yet. She would trust in herself. The bad dreams disappeared.

Then she went back to the doctor to tell him of her decision. He was shocked, though anxious not to show it. He did, however, urge her, in view of her age, to undergo the necessary tests for Down's Syndrome, and Kate, of course, consented, confident that nothing could be wrong. She began to plan, to look ahead; as she put it to herself, she opened her heart to the future. All the little things that had brought such joy in the past came back to her: the stirrings of life, the proudly swelling belly, the drama of birth, the wide eyes, the smiles, the tiny feet and hands, the walks in the park, the lovely noises and gestures, the first steps, the warm embraces, the warm bundle in one's arms, in one's bed, the smell of milk and ammonia. She shut her mind to inconvenience, to difficulties. It would be all right; the older children would help her, they would look after her and the baby, they would be glad. Even Ted might be glad, and if not, well, she would manage without his gladness. It would be so much easier than it had been sixteen years earlier; she had money, she had work, the others would baby-sit, she would still be able to go out. She would be a woman again.

But she went for the tests, to the hospital, and they told her that the baby had not Down's Syndrome, but spina bifida. They strongly advised termination.

Kate went home to think, all over again. She broke down, and, against her better judgement, told Mark of her plight. She had to tell somebody. She cried into her soup at the kitchen table, and Mark patted her shoulder and comforted her. He was too young to know these things, she thought, but then she had presented him with many things in life for which he was too young, and he had survived them. He had grown up with them. She must think no more about it, Mark said, she must get rid of the baby, and forget it. "You have us," said Mark, "you must think of us." "Yes, yes, my darling, I have you," she said, and buried her head against his large shoulder, and cried.

For two nights she wrestled with fantasies of keeping the baby, however damaged it might be. Others coped in such situations, why should not she? She could become a Catholic, to justify her unreason. She would devote what was left of her life to the child. Never again would she have to contemplate the blank waste of freedom. How could she relinquish those reluctant stirrings of hope that she had so wilfully encouraged? She had been chosen for the burden, she could not lay it down.

But in the end, of course, she did. The fantasies were wicked temptations. She had no right to invoke suffering. So she argued, and knew that she was right. But it was not easy to choose the right thing. She suffered. The bad dreams returned, in more grotesque forms. She dreamed not only of babies, she dreamed that Ted and Evelyn were laughing at her. She dreamed that she was in a cage, and that they were outside, pointing at her, laughing at her. She dreamed she was in a cage with great wild beasts. She dreamed of dead babies lying on a butcher's slab, like skinned rabbits.

She went into hospital, and had an abortion. The event itself was trivial enough, and the hospital staff were kind, sympathetic, helpful. The children visited her with sweets and flowers and their homework. She was sterilised at the same time, as the doctor in charge of the ward suggested. Enough of all that, she thought. She told her friends that she was having a D and C, a routine scrape. She told Ted the same. She could not bring herself to tell him the truth. She knew he did not want to hear it. She had never felt so far away from him. And then she emerged, and tried to pick up her life where she had left it.

Two weeks after she came out, Evelyn called round and informed Kate that Ted had for the past year been having an affair with another woman, a research biologist in Cambridge. "I thought you ought to know," said Evelyn.

The information made sense of a good deal that had been obscure to Kate, and she wondered how she could have been so stupid as not to have noticed: too absorbed in her own problems to notice his, no doubt. She felt ashamed, as though she herself were the transgressor, and after one bad scene with Ted, cut herself off from him completely—although their lives remained interwoven and they continued to meet in public and at the Stennett home, discussing children, statistics, schools, much as before, except that Kate's manner took on a certain hard sprightliness which she did not much like, but seemed unable to avoid. She did not fancy the role of victim, but was not sure what other options were open. So she took to talking to Ted in a brisk, challenging, Free Woman way, a no-nonsense, sensible way: you lead your life and I'll lead mine, she seemed to say, as she smiled brightly at him and accepted lifts home, as she'd done in the old days. And yet this was the man that she had, surely, loved, to whom she owed so much? Or was she, as Stuart had so often and angrily alleged, incapable of loving? What Ted made of all this she didn't ask, and would not permit him to explain. She was afraid of explanations.

It was a bad business, and she took it badly. She did not stop working, of course; indeed, she threw herself into work with redoubled energy, accepting ridiculous commissions, rushing around the country in pointless activity, reporting on this and that, afraid to stop, afraid to sleep for fear of dreaming, afraid to lie awake. Work had always been her salvation, and surely it would save her now, she said to herself. After a while, a superficial gaiety returned; she laughed a lot, drank a lot, went out a lot. She started to go out with other men, working methodically through the blacklist of rejects that had accumulated over the past years. Some of her friends thought, Well, good for Kate, she's got rid of that tiresome man and decided to have a little fun while there's still time. Others thought she had succumbed to panic and was looking for a husband. She herself did not know what she was doing, and did not like it much, or herself for doing it. On the rebound, she said to herself, but that didn't help. She couldn't help remembering a friend of hers who, when suddenly widowed, had made a fool of herself by summoning, one after the other, all her past boyfriends to share her highly vocal bereavement. It wasn't, of course, the same—Kate was a free woman, a liberated woman, who had always said there was more to life than marriage and babies, and if she couldn't have a fling, who could?

But she was uneasy. For she had also, had she not, said that there was more to life than men, and here she was seeking their company, as never before. Her conduct may not have shocked others, but it shocked her. And it wasn't much fun, as she could have told herself—though perhaps it might have been if she hadn't been so gripped by anxiety about what she ought or ought not to be doing, if she hadn't been so self-conscious about her role, so aware of the unprogressive/progressive image that looked back at her from the bathroom mirror each morning. She worried hardly at all about the old-fashioned code of sexual guilt, a great deal about the newly forged code of feminist guilt. Or was one merely an updated version of the other? She seemed locked in a bad circle. If all this seems unduly self-aware, remember that Kate had for years earned her living by pronouncing on such topics as sexual freedom for women, the double standard, the right to work, the right to abortion, the maternal impulse, the dependent instincts of women, the exploitative instincts of men. Not in any violently partisan manner; reasonably, seeing the other point of view. (Stuart's, Ted's.) Now reason had abandoned her, in her hour of need. It was inevitable, in her position, that she should feel exposed, that she should feel the eyes of thousands were waiting, some of them eagerly, to watch her trip and fall on her face.

And fall she did, not on her face, but for one impossible

man after another. Looking back over her year of mistakes, Kate told Hugo, "The worst thing was, I couldn't at the time see any of it as funny. I couldn't make any use of my experience, I couldn't tell anyone, I couldn't describe it in any way. I was too shocked, too ashamed, too taken aback by myself. It was bad material, bad copy, if you know what I mean. And yet it would have been such good copy if I'd been younger, if it hadn't been for real. I could have written some marvellous pieces about Matthew, about Adrian, about Emilio, about that extraordinary chap from Dublin, what was his name, Iain, was it? If they hadn't depressed me so much."

Hugo suggested it was merely a question of perspective, of time.

She shivered, and smiled, and said she doubted it. Even at the time, she'd seen it was funny, really. It just didn't feel it, that was all. How can one regain one's feeling for life?

The men, she said, had behaved like caricatures out of a male-chauvinist pin-up book, destroying her naïvely held faith that men were human, after all, and behaved decently if you treated them decently. (Or was it something in her that was *making* them behave like this? How she clung to her own enlightenment: the cries of hate from the sexual battleground horrified her, she could not bear to find herself echoing them, even silently, in her heart.) The fact remained that they did not behave decently. There was Adrian, who let her take him about to expensive hotels and meals, then went into a sulk when he discovered that she'd booked him in under her name: "to let me pay the bills with my own cheque book," she would patiently explain, but he didn't think that much of an excuse for his humiliation (though he never offered to pay a bill, she noted). There was Kevin, who, as soon as he'd spent one night under her roof, and not even in her bed, started to bring round his washing. There was Matthew, who would inspect each plate and glass and piece of cutlery before eating or drinking, as though afraid of contamination, and who finally suggested that her dishwasher needed servicing: she obligingly had it serviced, which did little to check his inspections, and when at long last he invited her round to his bachelor flat for a drink, she found that he lived, not in the hygienic modernity she had supposed from his behaviour, but in a dusty squalor not far removed from Stuart's old potatoes and tins of half-eaten sardines. There was Emilio, a stylish talker, lecturer in Italian history, an aesthete, a would-be dandy, quick with a sneer for decor that failed to pass the grade, adept at placing things and people with quick dismissive phrases—"very Balls Pond Road," "rather Bromley High Street," "a little Lévi-Strauss," and "too much of the Reith Lecturer." Kate politely puzzled over these phrases, trying to distinguish fine shades of meaning, and even felt twinges of apology for her own North-London-bric-a-brac-some-of-it-picked-up-at-Hunt's-in-Highbury-decor, until she visited Emilio's own rooms in college and saw there, to her astonishment, an extremely undistinguished and meaningless conglomeration of furniture and ornaments that betrayed a total lack of visual sense: Chianti-bottle table lamps, alabaster ashtrays, an Italian futurist marble clock flanked by elephants (the only object bizarre enough to suggest some justification), funny little wobbly bamboo tables, a nasty shiny red plastic pouf with a fake African design.

Then there was Conroy, an upper-class beauty whose extreme good looks would have excused almost anything less bizarre than his schemes for marketing seaweed and ozone; Iain, who, quite simply, drank everything in sight and never offered to buy or bring a bottle; Shahid, who wouldn't on religious grounds eat most of the things she could cook, but who never suggested cooking anything himself, though he was always boasting his skills and, unlike Kate, had nothing better to do all day.

Finally, there was Patrick, who was the best and therefore the worst of the lot, in that he raised higher hopes and caused worse disillusion. Patrick had been a friend of Ted's: Ted hadn't liked him much, but then Ted was abrasive even about people he did like, and Kate had put his objections to

Patrick down to a kind of jealousy, for Patrick, like Conroy, was very attractive, in a middle-aged, curly-grey-haired style, and, like Ted himself, something of a womaniser. So Kate had hoped that here might be some real communion, for Patrick was also a serious person, with a serious job; he was an under secretary in the Department of Health and Social Security (DHSS), and his wife had recently died, leaving him with three adolescent children to rear. How quickly Kate's thoughts had flitted to fantasies of herself as the all-loving, all-giving stepmother! And how sadly those fantasies had faded, in the light of reality. For although Patrick was indeed an interesting man, and an attractive man, and although Kate enjoyed listening to DHSS shop talk, there was clearly something very wrong with his attitude to women, and to sex. While talking over a meal, he would treat Kate as though she were a colleague, but in bed he would indulge in baby talk of the most embarrassing nature—treating Kate not as fellow baby, but as mother, of course. Kate tried hard to ignore her own dislike of this, telling herself that everyone has his or her own sexual peculiarities, his or her own language of love, and that maybe she would get used to Patrick's. But she didn't. It continued to astonish and alarm her that an apparently mature and responsible man should be such a Jekyll and Hyde.

Patrick was the last. After Patrick, she decided to give up. Though it wasn't as simple as that, for some of them wouldn't let her go and she was, as I have already pointed out, very bad at getting rid of people. She didn't like to cast them off, or even to upset them, so went on cooking meals, and even, madly, ironing Kevin's shirts from time to time. Nor did she like to cause jealousy, having learned from Ted both by his precept and example that jealousy is the most painful of passions, and not to be visited lightly even on a passing fool. So she had to play them off one against another, trying to keep each one in good spirits. An exhausting waste of time, for the harder she tried, the less she liked any of them, and the more fervently she wished they would all go away.

Why, one might ask, did she not simply get rid of them all at once? She asked herself this constantly. Did she feel responsible for them, was her thwarted maternal impulse misdirecting her, making her treat men as children who wouldn't be able to survive without her care? Did she *wish* so to regard them? Did they treat her so badly because she *wanted* them to? Did she connive at their folly? Well, yes, she did. But *why?* Did she need to be needed, at whatever expense of self-respect?

"Perhaps I really hate men," she told Hugo. "Maybe I had that long affair with Ted in order to avoid having anything to do with men. What do you think, Hugo? I don't hate you, do I? Or do I?"

Hugo had no answers. He did not like to hear her talk this way, and very much disliked the men with whom she had encumbered herself—except for Iain, who was always so drunk that he was a non-contender, and sometimes quite amusing. But then, Hugo thought, perhaps I am jealous. He had no good advice to offer.

In the end, she got rid of all of them. She effected the dismissal of the suitors not by summoning a returning Ulysses to slaughter them, but by collapsing one evening into a fit of hysteria, prompted by a particularly irritating phone call from Patrick about some socks he claimed to have lost. After he'd rung off, she started to cry, then to scream, then to chuck things at the kitchen wall. Mark, who had been having supper with her when the call took place, watched all this calmly and, when she subsided, said to her firmly, "Mum, why don't you just tell them all to *leave you alone?*" The voice of common sense reached her, and she did what Mark said. She abandoned them because Mark said so. Though in a sense, as she explained to him, she had taken them on for him—one of her conscious reasons for wanting to find a new man was her fear that if she didn't have one, she would depend more and more on her children, particularly on Mark, and would invest in them too much emotion, expecting too great a return. As

soon as she and Ted had parted, she had noticed herself turning more and more to Mark for affection, appreciation, advice;
her greatest physical pleasures were to lay a hand on Mark's
head as he sat working, on his springy black curly hair (Stuart's
hair), to embrace her large warm daughter, to entice Reuben
onto her knee for a few minutes in front of television. Was this
right? Was this natural? She didn't know, but certainly attempts
to divert her attention had failed.

A period of deadly peace ensued. She resisted appeals for
renegotiation, most of which were presented in terms that
claimed only to have her own good at heart: you need looking
after, let me come and see how you are, I'm worried about
you, all that kind of argument, nicely calculated to make her
feel extra bad. She resisted the more direct appeals too:
"You'd be amazed," she said, "how many men bring up the
subject of vegetables, when trying to get a free meal. 'Oh, I've
been living on chips,' they say, pathetically. 'Oh, I do miss
fresh vegetables.' It was one of Stuart's earliest complaints
about that Amaryllis girl, that she never cooked vegetables.
Don't men know how to cook vegetables? And if not, why
don't they learn?"

Kate didn't much like thinking these things. They were
diminishing. It's a phase, she said to herself, hoping to see the
end of it. She didn't like being hard. It didn't suit her, it wasn't
herself. She wanted to be affectionate, warm, good-natured,
generous. She was happier being nice. And it was too late to
learn how to be nasty. She knew some nasty women, who'd
been what is called ruthless in their personal and professional
lives, intent on getting to the top. Kate had thought to do it all
the nice way. Oh, there would be a few casualties—Stuart,
Evelyn. But nothing serious. No massacres.

The whole thing had, however, it now seemed, depended
on a natural flow of good spirits, a natural cheerfulness. Now
they had abandoned her, these kindly spirits, and left her in
an empty plain. What on earth should one do next? She had
tried fun, but it hadn't been much fun. What was left? Work?

Living for others? Just carrying on, from day to day, enjoying as much of it as one could? Responding to demands as they came, for come they would?

"In those months," she told Hugo, "I couldn't do anything right. Everything I did went wrong, as though some spell were on me, as though some magic had been taken from me. After one unforced error, I seemed to be condemned to a succession of endless forced ones. I couldn't see where the game would end, obviously in defeat, but how or when I couldn't see. I just had to go on playing. And the oddest thing was that I went on and on feeling bad not about the bad things I'd done, but about the good thing, which was getting rid of that poor baby. I still have bad dreams. But I did the right thing, and I know it. If I know anything. What's the answer to that, that civilised woman can't do the right thing without paying too high a price? Is that the answer? Would I have been full of the spirit of life and love and joy and hope if I'd had a wretched baby with no bowel control and a spine split like a kipper and a head like a pumpkin? Yes, I probably would. Life is rotten, darling, rotten." And she would begin to cry, at this point, and Hugo would give her a Kleenex.

And that is Kate's history, up to date. We will end it with an account of her visit to the Harrogate conference last month. She'd gone up to cover a conference on old age, run by one of the charities that deal with this rather common problem; in the old days she used to enjoy these excursions, combining as they did in pleasant proportions work, company, gossip with colleagues, train journeys, hotels, and a new landscape. This one promised well: the weather was good, a fair break in a wet summer, and the little Diesel train between York and Harrogate revealed pleasant glimpses of small children waving at the familiar driver from small country stations, golden fields, little chestnut-backed kestrels flying low, gardens full of roses, boys fishing by small rivers. Rural England. Harrogate itself, with its vast hotels, was an amusing change from crowded, over-built London; those hotels were like huge great liners, she said, moored on the hillsides, and the vast suburban houses built from vast granite blocks, with big trees in big gardens, all on such a large scale, and the public gardens, with lemon-yellow and salmon-pink snapdragons—yes, it was all very attractive. The flowers were so lovely, they had flourished in the wet summer. Shops with Harrogate toffee in old-fashioned tins, antique shops with displays of expensive china in excellent condition, curiosity shops with strings of Victorian glass beads of every size and colour, such as one rarely sees in London.

Yet the whole experience, instead of cheering her, was oddly depressing. The subject of the conference was not in itself cheerful, the optimism of some of the delegates rang hollow as they outlined schemes for involving old people in the life of the community—"Who wants," said Kate, "the tape-recorded memoirs of ninety-year-old survivors? When most of us can't be bothered to listen to our own grannies, let alone anyone else's? What a pretence we make of our concern." She left the conference at six, to walk back to her hotel, and found the weather had clouded over; rain had fallen during the afternoon, and a purple-grey metallic sky arched over the trees and gardens as she walked back through the town to her hotel. The colours were deep, the smell of vegetation intense. Roses, privet hedges, laurels, jasmine. A sinister smell. She nearly trod on a very dead bird, lying in the middle of the wide pavement. And passed the huge bole of a lopped tree, sprouting with thousands, literally thousands, of tiny transparent toadstools, born of the damp. And pondered on the fact that when she'd had no money, she'd coveted beads and china, and had made do with Hunt's cheaper bits and pieces: now she had money, she didn't want anything, couldn't even be bothered to go into the shops to look.

Back at her hotel, a monstrosity as large as the one that had housed the conference, she went into the downstairs bar to buy herself a drink to cheer herself up. While drinking it, she read the paper, and a large Alsatian which she had noted sprawling in the corner of the bar wandered over to her, cocked its leg, and pissed on her skirt. "Well, can you *imagine?*" said Kate. "Of all things. Never has such a thing happened to me ever, never have I *seen* such a thing. To be pissed on by a dog in a hotel. I was so shocked I couldn't think what to do. And the odd thing was, nobody seemed even to notice. Nobody even looked up. I made a fuss, of course, as soon as I'd registered what had happened, but nobody seemed to care. Isn't that odd?" So she went up to her hotel room and changed, and put her skirt to soak, and found she was shaking like a leaf. And kept saying to herself, Why me? In the old days, no dog would have *dared* to piss on me. How could even a dog tell I was low? Do I radiate abjectness, these days? That dogs are attracted to it?

She was too upset to face going out to dinner; she rang for sandwiches and went to bed. She was shivering, wondering if she was ill. She rang home, but there was nobody there. Tried to remember Hugo's number, but couldn't, though she rings him almost daily. Thought she was going mad. Tried to ring home again, later, but all she got when she lifted the phone was Radio 4 coming through the receiver. Thought about the aged, and how we now live longer than we did or perhaps even should: no wonder guilt walks the land. Thought about forty-year-old women, as strange a social phenomenon in our time as the new aged, and with as few guidelines for behaviour. Unnecessary. Age is unnecessary, but then so is everyone, except during the brief illusion of parenthood. She tried Mark again, longing to receive the comfort she had once been able to offer him when he was scared or lonely, but Radio 4 continued its relentless good will. Wondered what illusion of purpose loving Ted had given her, and why he had so brutally made her redundant. Tried to sleep.

This was last month, the month before the encounter with Hugo with which we opened this history, the encounter during which Kate was somewhat archly searching for ladybirds in her spinach. Since Harrogate, two new elements have entered Kate's life. One is a new job. She has accepted an invitation to make a television film about women, focussing on the choices now made by girls leaving school, five years after the Sex Discrimination Act, and contrasting them with the choices made when she was a girl twenty-five years ago: she plans to revisit her old school at Romley, amongst other places. She thinks it will be a good thing to have a temporary change of colleagues and scenery. The producer, a good-looking chap called Gabriel Denham, has been a friend for years: indeed, they had in the past half-heartedly fancied each other, though the time for any action on such matters is, for both of them, long since past, for by now they know too much about each other. But there will be other people, completely new people. Maybe she will fall in love with a camera man and live happily ever after, she says, laughing unpleasantly at this prospect. She has done a little television interviewing in the past, and is quite good at it; she has an air of deep, interested, friendly, no doubt spurious sympathy which makes the most unlikely people confide in her. She is "good with people," a talent that Evelyn envies. A good listener. She was once very good at forgetting herself whilst talking to others. Maybe, she thinks, she will sail once more into unselfconsciousness, into that happy breeze which has been stilled for so long. "At the very worst," she told Hugo, "it'll make me bloody glad I don't still have to live in Romley. It'll make me count my blessings with a bit more sincerity."

The other new element is the Iraqi. He doesn't connect with Romley, but then not much does.

The Iraqi arrived a fortnight ago, and has been driving Kate distracted in an entirely new way. He arrived not quite but almost out of the blue, a refugee from Bagdad, where he is teaching and pursuing some doctorate at the university, or would be if he had not got into serious trouble by appearing at a demonstration in favour of Kurdish independence. He is the fiancé of a girl whose mother Kate got to know in hospital while producing Mark nearly nineteen years ago: a tenuous connection. The mother, Beatrice Mourre, was half French, half Lebanese; the daughter, several years older than Mark, met Mujid at the University of Beirut, where both were then studying. The mother, Beatrice, kept in touch with Kate after her return to Lebanon, through New Year's cards, in one of which she informed Kate of her daughter's engagement and noted briefly that Simone had become "very political," a convert to the Muslim cause, though the Mourres were Christian Maronites. Kate hadn't paid much attention to this news, though she did register that things in Lebanon were going from bad to worse, and worried vaguely about her old friend, from whom she ceased to hear as the war raged. Beatrice had been a jolly, talkative, worldly woman, full of good advice about babies and breast feeding which as a new mother Kate needed and heeded, and of whom over the years and the next two babies she often thought with affection and gratitude. What had happened to her? Kate wrote once, but received no answer. And now, suddenly, here was Mujid on her doorstep, asking her advice on where to live, how to learn English, which he had determined to do in the next three months. (His French was fluent, but in Bagdad, he said, he needed English.) He had left Bagdad, he hoped temporarily: Simone was still in Beirut, despite her parents' exhortations to leave. They were now in Paris. The baby who had lain by Beatrice's side all those years ago was now dead. He had died in a street battle in Beirut, aged eighteen.

Or that, at least, seemed to be the situation. As Mujid spoke very little English, and Kate less French, she was never quite sure whether or not she had understood him properly. But did grasp that he needed to learn English, knew nobody else in London, had left Bagdad in haste, and had nowhere to go.

So she took him in. "Stay with me," she said, thinking of Beatrice and her stories about breast abscesses and Lebanese midwives and ostentatious Lebanese banquets and the Lebanese jet set: thinking of civil war, of Beirut in flames, of bombs and massacres, of the baby that had grown up only to die, of Mark safely studying architecture at Waterford, far from these dangers. "Come and stay with me," she said. "You can have Mark's room until he gets back from college."

He accepted, of course.

"You must be mad," said her friends, when she reported this new domestic development, "he's probably a terrorist." "Don't be silly," Kate retorted, with her old panache, "of course he's not a terrorist, he's just a boy, and he's got nowhere else to go."

But he isn't just a boy, he is a man of nearly thirty, and although not a terrorist, he is a political fanatic by her standards; and lectures her on politics, in a mixture of French and English, over breakfast. Or so she says, but perhaps she exaggerates. He takes life entirely seriously—as well he might, Kate says—and can hardly believe her ignorance, as he tries to inform her about Lebanon, about the Kurdish question, about the nature of the Ba'ath government, about the Iraq Petroleum Company and the PLO. Before he arrived, Kate did not even know where Iraq was. He comes from a village on the Euphrates, near the Syrian border, where his father is a shopkeeper. His parents are anti-Kurd, but he is pro-Kurd. Neither he nor Simone is religious, he explains to Kate, but they are Muslims nevertheless. And also Marxists. Kate does not understand this at all, nor does she quite understand why, unlike most Iraqis, he speaks better French than English. She listens to him and thinks that she is going mad, but, as his host, listens politely. "It's your own fault," her friends tell her, as she complains, "you shouldn't have taken him in." "How could I not?" says Kate; "he was on the doorstep, *he seemed to expect it.*" "Of course he didn't," they argue. "He *seemed* to," says Kate, "and anyway, I expected it of myself."

He has no other contacts in London, apart from an ex-teacher, a political refugee of a different colour, with whom he does not much wish to spend time. He tries to explain this man's position to Kate, but Kate cannot follow. The politics of

Iraq are very confusing, and Mujid's alignments appear to her to be very odd. Kate has fixed him up with language classes (the cost of which, without his knowledge, she subsidises, though this is hardly generosity: she has to find some way to occupy him). But he finds most of the other students slow and boring, though he attends conscientiously. He wants to be with Kate. He lies in wait for her on her return from work, to harangue her on the triviality and social bias of English television, on the poor coverage of Middle East affairs in the media, on the pro-Israel, anti-Soviet line of the press. He is like an extra conscience and a pedagogue rolled into one. She tries to excuse herself, to explain that her own paper's foreign news has nothing to do with her, but he makes her, nevertheless, feel deeply guilty. For she is, after all, as he rightly suspects, trivial, ill-informed, and biased.

She is trying hard. Having taken him on, she does her best to look after him, but it is difficult, for he is sensitive, touchy, quick to take offence if she fails to include him in any aspect of her social and family life. But the more of an effort she makes, the more he expects, and the worse she feels, the more inadequate she sees she is. He is unhappy about her meals, and particularly offensive, she claims, about British fruit and vegetables. "Vegetables *again*," says Kate, groaning. Apparently they are bigger and better in Lebanon, better even than in France. "Imagine trying to offer a tomato salad to the accompaniment of a passionate description in French of the inferiority of the English tomato to the French, of the French to the Lebanese," she says. "But we've got to eat something, haven't we?" He askes her embarrassing questions about family life in Britain: Is divorce normal? Why are all Kate's friends divorced, is it normal to eat standing up as Kate's children seem to prefer to do, is it normal for women to go out to work as much as Kate does? Although these queries are sociological rather than critical in spirit, Kate is beginning, under their influence, to regard herself as a failure, and her once lovely happy family as a disorganised freak. She is on the defensive.

He brings her pamphlets on the Middle East situation, published by the Council for the Advancement of Arab-British Understanding, and is annoyed (or perhaps it would be fairer to say disappointed) when she hasn't time to read them. He is surprised that she doesn't take him up on his offer to teach her Arabic in return for English conversation, since she readily admits that it would be a great advantage in the modern world. He tries to teach the children French, but they can't understand him, and anyway they haven't time either, they are too busy doing their French homework—though they too, being nice children, try hard to listen politely. "I feel as though a great iron wedge were splitting my *head* open," complains Kate, "and the worst of it is that he's right, I *am* ignorant, I haven't got any answers, I'm nothing but a stupid uneducated woman, and he makes me feel so angry because he makes me feel so inadequate. And he does work hard, his English is improving amazingly, he really sticks at it, and I can't keep a French word, let alone an Arabic, in my head for more than five minutes. Oh, God, I'm an absolute fool," says Kate, "and I've lived all these years without knowing it."

At times her defensiveness lurches into aggression: once he tried to tell her a mildly anti-Jewish joke about poisoned oranges, and she found herself quite unable to smile, unable even to pass it over, and launched instead into a history of the Second World War, of which he in turn seemed surprisingly ignorant. Different languages, different cultures, different history books. "And yet, and yet, what about all the Arab jokes I've heard, over the years?" says Kate. "What about that cheap crack I made about gold teeth once in a piece about that Egyptian film director?"

A ridiculous situation. Mark, over the phone from Waterford, says, "Kick him out," but Kate says, "No, he's a refugee. I must learn to love him," says Kate, seething with rage and irritation. "I must do my bit for international understanding. It won't be forever: when Simone finishes her doctorate, she will come and take him away." In private, alone, she thinks of the boy that died. She can think of nothing more terrible than to lose a child. She cannot help but picture this child as he was when she last saw him, a plump brown baby lying on a blue rug in the garden of the Mourres' rented house near Regent's Park, under the leaves of an apple tree in bloom, and Beatrice drinking lemon tea. A new dream enters her repertoire: Mark lying dead from a sniper's bullet in the placid haven of Waterford, on the South Coast.

The truth is that she knows herself trapped by her own good nature and all its defects, now as never before. "This," she says, "is the Armageddon—or do I mean Waterloo?—of the maternal instinct"; she watches its thrashing and struggling with an amazed and sad detachment. What is it for? In a way, it makes her feel better about all those other men in the past, for at least in this instance there is no question of sex —as a woman, he treats her with entire respect. As an equal. As an intellectual equal. "Which I'm *not*," she says. "Maybe it would be better if he saw me simply as a housewife, as a landlady. Should I put on the veil, in self-defence?"

How extraordinary people are, that they get themselves into such situations where they go on doing what they dislike doing, and have no need or obligation to do, simply because it seems to be expected. (As in marriage, after all?) But expected *by whom, of whom?* Ah, if I had the answer to that, thinks Kate, I should really know myself. As, once, I thought I did. Talking to Mujid, being nice to Mujid, Kate feels herself close to some interesting discovery about human nature; if she makes it, the whole thing will have been worthwhile. She will emerge purified from this trial. It is the ultimately absurd, and, as such, must be instructive. "Mujid is the next stage in my education," she tells Hugo: "first Hunt, then the Armstrongs, then Ted, then all those awful men, and now Mujid. If I fail this opportunity, I have failed indeed." "Absurd," says

Hugo: "you might as well take in meths drinkers from the streets. Or stray dogs." "Yes, I might as well," says Kate, reflectively—then adds with some spirit that Mujid is not a meths drinker nor a stray dog but a perfectly serious and interesting young man, and that, anyway, she does draw the line sometimes, for, after all, only last week she met a woman just outside her house staring with compassion at a dying pigeon—"you know the sort," she says, "one of those dark-grey, streaky, scruffy, glazed-eyes things with missing claws, hobbling on pink stumps, crawling with lice and meningitis, and the woman said, 'Look, poor thing, shouldn't we do something about it?' and I said, 'No,' " said Kate, " '*No*, certainly not,' and the woman said, 'But, poor creature, it's ill,' and I said, 'Yes, it seems to be dying,' and the woman said, 'Is that your house?' and I said, 'Yes,' and the woman said, 'Couldn't you take it in?' and I said, 'No,' and the woman said, 'Perhaps you should ring the police,' and I said, 'What, ring the *police* about a *pigeon?*' and the woman said, 'Why not? If you won't, I shall,' and I said, 'All right, go ahead. I for my part wouldn't have the nerve to ring the police about a pigeon.' " (But even then she had marginally relented, and had run after this interfering but responsibility-shifting woman to suggest that if she really was so worried about the bird, why didn't she ring the RSPCA and see what they had to say?)

Pigeons, dogs, dead babies, washed-up babies rotting on the seashore—is there no limit to these claims? No, clearly not. "They spot me a mile off, like vultures," says Kate. "They hang around, smelling death."

The Friday evening on which Hugo first met Mujid was of a classic social horror such as only Kate, he reflected, would have been capable of organising, though organisation was hardly the word for it. She had decided to kill several birds with one stone, and this was the result. Her ex-brother-in-law

Paul Armstrong had asked her to share one of his social obligations, in the shape of an American visitor and his British-born wife, who had expressed a strong desire to meet Kate: he had invited them to the theatre, to see a preview of a play by a friend who had handed out free tickets. Kate had said she would go if she could take Mujid and Hugo as well, and Paul, equally eager to spread his burden, had accepted this bargain. Hugo murmured dissent, but Kate merely said, "Oh, go on, Hugo, be a saint, help me out, your French is so good, you can even speak Arabic and Mujid can't possibly harangue you too much because you're a war hero, or at least you look like one." Hugo secretly feared that his absent arm might prove a provocation rather than a defence, and the fact that he had spent years in Kurdistan a dubious recommendation, but succumbed to Kate's pleas, for in one way and another he was much in her debt; and, as she pointed out, it might not be too bad, they wouldn't have to talk during the play, and if they had dinner afterwards they could wash everything down with a bottle or two of wine. "And Mujid will be so pleased to be invited to a proper social occasion," she said.

So Hugo found himself turning up at Kate's house for drinks at six, having agreed to move on later to the other entertainments.

When he arrived, there was a not unusual air of emergency. Kate lives in a small terraced house just north of King's Cross which used to be a fish-and-chip shop; at certain seasons, she claims, it still smells of chips, though Hugo has never himself noticed this. It is usually too full of people, and this evening was no exception. The door was opened by Ruth, a large sixteen-year-old who looked, to Hugo, about thirty, and who greeted Hugo with a slap on the back and the news that Mum was on the phone and would he come in and get himself a drink and talk to Mujid. Thereupon she winked, and slapped him on the back again. Hugo stumbled along the narrow hall, over a collection of plastic carriers, broken furniture, piles of books, Adidas bags, and bicycle spare parts, into the sitting

room, which used to be the chip shop; a pleasant room, he
had often thought, but overcrowded, the kind of room where
it is hard to find an empty chair or even a space to put down
one's glass. One of the chairs was occupied by, unmistakably,
Mujid, another by Reuben, two more by cats, and the one that
he preferred (the only one, he had discovered through past
experience, without some serious structural defect) by another large sixteen/thirty-year-old friend of Ruth's called
Tertia. Tertia had very short spiky black hair, and was wearing long spiky black woolly socks, which, on enquiry, she explained to Hugo were called Gorilla Sox. "Gorilla or guerilla?"
asked Hugo, but her attention by this time had returned to
Nationwide, which they were all watching: Tertia and Mujid
had both looked up politely on Hugo's entry, but their eyes
veered quickly back to watch the end of a particularly silly
item about a man who kept hummingbirds in his council
house. Hugo began to see what Kate meant about the embarrassment of seeing Britain through censorious foreign eyes,
though Mujid didn't seem to object to the hummingbirds; in
fact, he was smiling at them.

"Hello," said Hugo firmly, as the item ended, and Mujid
rose to his feet and shook his hand equally firmly, with a
deferential smile. Hugo's heart warmed slightly, for Mujid's
appearance was much less alarming than he had expected; he
was a pleasant, mild-looking chap, small, anxious, serious,
bespectacled, intellectual of aspect. could this be the mad
Stalinist of Kate's complaints? He didn't offer Hugo a drink,
so, over the beginning of a new story about a mugged black
bus conductor, Hugo offered him one and, as soon as he had
his back to the telly, told Reuben to switch off. Mugged black
men seemed more dangerous a theme than hummingbirds,
and Hugo didn't want to start the evening on a wrong note.

Mujid accepted a whisky, and Hugo poured one for himself. He could hear Kate, in the kitchen, getting emotional on
the telephone. Mujid said, in French, but not in very good
French (Hugo noted that he must try to remember to inform

Kate of this), that he was sorry he hadn't got a suit, but that he'd left his only suit in Bagdad, in the haste of departure. Hugo assured him that this wouldn't matter, that he was only wearing a suit himself because he'd just come from a meeting, and that nobody dressed for the theatre these days. Mujid looked disappointed, and they began to discuss, of all things, etiquette, when Kate appeared in the doorway, looking slightly more dressed than usual, but carrying a curious-looking bottle-brush covered in black sludge. "That really was the end," she said, that had been Stuart on the blower complaining about her going out with Paul, complaining that Paul was a rat and owed him fifty quid, and that he, Stuart, was feeling rotten and had got some frightful illness, and that he'd rung just as she, Kate, was in the process of triumphantly clearing out the overflow of the bathroom washbowl with a wonderful new brush that she'd bought in Boot's that morning in a moment of inspiration, and she would just go and finish the job and then she'd come and get herself a drink. But as she spoke, the phone went again. "It'll be for Ruth," said Kate, but it wasn't, it was for her, so off she went. Mujid remarked that it was a very busy house. "Yes," said Hugo with protective emphasis, "Kate is a very busy woman." Perhaps Kate was right, perhaps there was something censorious in Mujid's tone? Kate reappeared in a moment or two to say that it was a friend on the phone in need of a cat basket and could one of the children please look in the junk room to see if theirs was still there, but she had a nasty feeling that the Owens, who borrowed it last, had never brought it back again. The cat basket dealt with, and the bottle-brush disposed of, they were about to settle down once more to their drinks when the door-bell rang (a neighbour collecting jumble), and after that the phone again, so there wasn't much time for political discussion or any other kind of discussion before it was time to depart for the theatre. Kate conducted and orchestrated all these interruptions with a verve that implied she had laid them all on especially for her guests' amusement: here am I, busy Kate, comic Kate, conducting my own little modern domestic symphony, isn't it delightful? Some people find her very annoying, and claim that she disorganises herself on purpose, for effect, but Hugo was sympathetic to such displays, and did not mind playing up to them: "Though why, may I ask," he said, as they hurtled towards the West End in a mini-cab, "why did you choose to clean out your overflow at this precise moment in time?" "I don't know," said Kate, "I suddenly had this vision of how easy it would be with a bottle brush, and once I'd had the idea, I had to get on with it, but look, I've gone and spattered my best dress with muck, isn't that typical?"

Then, abandoning domesticity and its dark charm, she turned her attention to trying to explain to Mujid about the work of the playwright whose latest offering they were on their way to see. In outline, it did not sound very entertaining. Sam Goldman was a South African whose early black comedies were set in his native land: thence he had moved to racism in Britain, though his last piece, a qualified success, had been about technological breakdown and cannibalism in a high-rise block in the year 2000. Kate insisted, or rather insisted that Hugo in his better French should insist, that these works were highly regarded and not as dull as they sounded, though Hugo could tell that she felt herself to be in a tight corner, for she wanted simultaneously to stress their entertainment value (for Hugo's sake and her own) and, for Mujid's encouragement, their political worthiness. There was a contradiction here, and it was being all too clearly revealed by her attempts to conceal it. Mujid's response, however, indicated that he had not grasped it, or was not interested in it; he wanted first of all to know what a Jewish South African was doing in London, and how they could favour the products of such a regime. Once satisfied of Goldman's exiled status, he wanted to know whether or not it was true that the entertainment industry in Britain was run by Jewish Americans. While Hugo was attempting to comment on this, bouncing around in the back of the large red Ford on a broken spring, and trying not to inhale too much of the driver's Gauloise, he remembered that Kate had told him that Mujid had very much enjoyed the one film he had so far seen in London, a particularly prurient glossy American thriller full of blood and violence and expensive office sets and airport explosions and expensive actors and actresses, because it purported to denounce the CIA. Mujid, of course, disliked all things American. When Kate had tried to suggest that the film was not the most sincere or honourable of attacks upon corruption, being in itself highly meretricious, he had thought Kate was defending the CIA. It began to look as though they were in for a sticky evening, whatever happened, and that Sam Goldman's work, impeccably or even excessively radical though it might be by Kate's and Hugo's standards, would fail to please on some more basic level. Kate's tone became increasingly defensive: "Anyway," she kept saying, "Sam's really *a very nice man.*"

It was quite a relief to see Paul Armstrong and his friends waiting in the foyer, though two new sets of problems at once, on sight of them, presented themselves. The first was that Paul, who writes a political gossip column for a weekly, had just been guilty of an extremely vicious and provocative attack on the Foreign Minister's line on Vietnamese refugees, and, incidentally, on a piece by Hugo the week before in muted support of that line. Recollection of this difference of opinion swam simultaneously into both Kate's memory and Hugo's, and a flicker of recognition also passed through Paul's alert and knowing eyes as he shook Hugo's hand: but, like gentlemen of the press, they mutely agreed to ditch their differences for an evening, through loyalty to Kate and their other companions. It would not do to squabble before foreigners. Hugo quite liked Paul, who was a pleasant, smooth, and lively chap, but quite corrupted in style, in Hugo's view, by the New Brutal Journalism, which, in Hugo's view, mistakes policies for personalities, manners for morals, the physical for the intellectual: what on earth is the relevance, Hugo would like to know, and often rhetorically demands, of the fact that such a

Minister has an embarrassing speech defect, or that such another has a delinquent daughter? Hugo's approach is more
austere. He is beginning to feel old-fashioned, and the sight of
men like Paul, in their early thirties, full of wit and malice,
depresses him. Both he and Kate had forgotten that they felt
like this about Paul; but there he was, handsome, pleased with
himself, in-the-know, his curly black hair a reminder of Mark
and of Stuart; but two-faced and, as Stuart had just shouted at
Kate over the phone, a rat.

The other set of problems marshalled itself around the
revelation that Paul's American friend and his wife were, unmistakably, Jewish. Their name was Rubenstein, and he was
a historian. Well, thought Hugo, that figures—Jewish playwright, Jewish friends, Armstrong himself half Jewish, a nice
night out, not at all surprising, but one more topic best
avoided in Mujid's company. A very Jewish audience too,
Hugo noted, as they made their way to the bar: what would
Mujid make of that? Would it confirm his suspicions about
Jewish propaganda and Jewish monopolies? Hugo recalled
that Kate had earlier reported that her own indignant repudi-
ation of these allegations had been weakened by the fact that
in one week's television viewing he had manged to see a
repeat of that excellent comedy *The Barmitzvah Boy*, one
programme about kibbutzim, another about German anti-
Semitism, and, alas, a late-night showing of a ridiculous
schmalzy sentimental tear-jerker about the Entebbe hijack,
complete with Kirk Douglas and Elizabeth Taylor, which
Kate herself had found highly offensive. And not a *single* Iraqi
comedy or Lebanese tragedy or Kurdish documentary, she
had said, wide-eyed in mock astonishment. Nothing but news-
reels of demonstrations, and, in Mujid's view, not enough
of that. "You must stop him watching," Hugo suggested, "pretend the set's broken down." "But then I have to talk," she
said, "and that's so tiring." And they had both laughed, uneasily. Because it wasn't funny, really, was it?

Anyway, there they were, amidst the usual preview

crowd—some, as Hugo had predicted to Mujid, dressed, others undressed. They sipped their drinks and exchanged pleasantries, and watched the blue jeans and denim jackets, the gay young men in ethnic shirts and beads, the ageing greybeards in leather jackets, the billowing long dresses on thin ladies and the little black dresses on larger ladies. Mujid, to Kate's relief, seemed to be enjoying the spectacle, as she had hoped he would; he was looking around him eagerly, noting the variety of faces, the fading gilt, the greasy red damask curtains, the fake marble veneer on the pillars, the electric chandeliers, the occasional elegant woman in full glamour. It was a pretty theatre, a cut above Sam's usual type of venue (the Round House, the Court, the Arts) as the lead was to be played by one of our most famous actors, and a more fashionable audience was expected. Reports from Liverpool, where it had opened, had been guarded. There was an air of expectation. Kate greeted friends, was greeted, waved, smiled, as though in her element. Hugo began to feel better.

Hugo was seated next to Mujid so that he could mutter explanations of the action to him in French between scenes; he began by translating the programme. And at once began to feel worse. There was nothing wrong with Sam's curriculum vitae, nor with those of the distinguished actors and the director, but Hugo did not care much for the information that the setting was an imaginary island, and the date some hundred years B.C., or possibly several thousand years A.D. Clearly, Sam was moving out into the apocalyptic, the unknown. The names of the characters were also lacking in allure. Tiresias, Cassandra, Philoctete. Oh dear, thought Hugo, as the curtain rose on a pale-blue-and-white pseudo-classical set, tastefully referring to the contemporary or perhaps to the timeless by the inclusion of a motorbike, an old-fashioned Victorian camera on a tripod, and some scattered pieces of futuristic furniture. A surreal set, with echoes of de Chirico and Dali, neither of them Hugo's favourite painters: his mother's passion for surrealism had put him off it for life. A large draped object stood at the back, centre stage, as in a Henry Moore drawing. It would no doubt reveal its secrets in due course.

By the interval, an hour and three quarters later, the secrets were still concealed, and Hugo had abandoned his attempts to whisper a précis of the action to Mujid, for he could not understand it himself, and no longer wished to. It was, he decided in the heat of the infinitely prolonged moment, the dullest and most pretentious play he had ever seen, a combination of the worst of Shaw (*Back to Methuselah?*) and those dreary French mythological comedies by Anouilh and Giraudoux from the fifties. Nothing happened at all. The characters talked and talked, about the collapse of civilisation, about androgyny and creative evolution, about the future being the past. Not even the famous actor could animate the text, though one could see why he might have been attracted to the part, as he had to do most of the talking. Boredom and physical discomfort gripped Hugo with unnatural force, and he could feel Kate, along the row, rigid with the same tensions. Sam Goldman must have gone mad, thought Hugo, and he has decided to drive us all mad with him. Though he had spotted him just before the curtain went up, a few rows ahead, looking his usual affable self, and not mad at all.

The interval was not entirely a relief, as friendship with Sam and unfamiliarity with one another prevented them from breaking into the abuse in which they might otherwise have indulged. Some of them would probably have to speak to Sam later, and as they did not wish to be seen to plunge into the depths of hypocrisy within the space of an evening, they contented themselves with muttered remarks like "very interesting," and "a little obscure," and "rather dense"—though in Hugo's view it had not been dense at all, but as thin as weak tea. Kate, sensibly, devoted most of the interval to visiting the Ladies', after expressing a hope that Mujid was not finding it too tedious. Mujid in fact was looking more cheerful than the rest of them, presumably because he didn't know what he wasn't missing.

The second half was as bad, but shorter. The draped object proved to be a Wellsian monster from outer space, a deus ex machina: it had a metallic voice like a Dalek robot, and a lot of shining articulated bits and pieces that clicked and whirred and then fell off, presumably prophesying the death of technology of which Sam seemed so fond these days. It drew a round of relieved applause. Our famous actor made a farewell speech, and the curtain, at last, fell.

Opinions as to whether they should try to speak to Sam were divided. Paul, although the closest to Sam, and the recipient of the free tickets, was in favour of making a quick escape, but Kate thought it would be better to have a short word now rather than a long one later. Kate prevailed. They tracked him down just inside the stage door, where Sam, an extremely equable chap, was trying to organise his aged parents to sit down on a faded dumped crimson velvet prop settee while he went up to speak to his cast. The meeting proved painless, for Sam was already undergoing the full onslaught of attack from his mother, a dumpy little woman who was complaining loudly that she had not understood *one single word*, and that although she hadn't liked or understood any of his plays this was the worst so far. Sam, far from being offended by this approach, was highly amused, kept hugging his tiny mother and calling her a silly old girl, hadn't he warned her she wouldn't like it? Mrs. Goldman clucked and ruffled in her Persian lamb and called him a naughty boy. It was easy, in this situation, for the Armstrong party to stand on the sidelines and laugh, to offer their congratulations without too much insincerity. Indeed, it was made very easy for them, for Mrs. Goldman kept turning to Kate and Paul to say, "Now, you two, you're two of Sam's clever friends, and I bet you couldn't understand a word either, could you? I don't know how he gets away with it." She was glowing with pride, and

Sam with affection. Old Mr. Goldman sat down on the settee and started surreptitiously to read the back page of the *Evening Standard*. Kate's heart was touched: Sam Goldman might have written what her children would no doubt describe as a bummer, but if he had, he didn't care, so that was all right, and whatever his play was like, he was certainly a genius at family relationships, one could tell that at a glance, and what was a good play or a bad play when weighed in the balance with this most difficult of arts? "I don't care, Sam's a nice man," she said, her good spirits restored, as they took their leave, and made their way through a horde of bewildered theatre-goers to dinner.

Paul had selected an expensive but ethnic French restaurant in Soho, one where the prices were somewhat at odds with the routier decor. The table was already set with wine; the menu was chalked up on a board on the wall. Kate insisted on sitting next to Hugo, partly so that she could cut up his dinner (she rightly suspected that when alone he lived on pap) and partly because she felt guilty at having inflicted so long an evening on him, never the keenest of theatre-goers. Mujid seemed the only person anxious to discuss the play, for everyone else was eager to drown boredom as quickly as possible in a carafe or two of wine. A few attempts were made to explain that the play had been an unexpected aberration, quite unlike Sam's earlier efforts. Kate charitably maintained that any writer is entitled to at least one monumental mistake: "If you don't make mistakes, you don't make anything," she said, a motto which Hugo seemed to remember having seen pinned over the desk of the most notoriously incompetent and inaccurate of all his colleagues. Mujid asked some questions about theatre subsidies, and then, unwisely, ventured to criticise not the play, but our famous actor, whom he had found mannered and rhetorical. With one accord Paul, Kate, and Hugo sprang to his defence, a feeble patriotism stirring in the ashes of their embarrassment: they praised his former triumphs, as Coriolanus, Rosmer, Ivanov, Macbeth, though Hugo at least had not

seen any of them. Tom Rubenstein conceded that British acting was still the best in the world, one of the last remaining
fields in which Britain still reigned supreme. This annoyed
them nearly as much as Mujid's complaints.

Over the hors d'oeuvres, they all got down to more serious matters. Hugo, well aware of his social duty, engaged
Mujid in conversation about the Middle East, and particularly
about Kurdistan. He did not reveal the sources of his own
highly specialised and unusual knowledge about this strife-
torn nation, but felt that he was more than making up for
Kate's ignorance. Mujid talked at length and, Hugo thought,
quite sensibly: although undeniably a Marxist, he was no terrorist, and had a much more sophisticated view of the com-
plexities of history than Kate had led Hugo to believe. At the
other end of the table Tom Rubenstein, who was just off with
his wife to visit relatives in Israel, embarked on a recital to Paul
of his own family's escape from pre-war Germany: most of
those that had survived, like Tom and his parents, had ended up
in America. Hugo, listening with half an ear, hoped that Mujid
would be too engrossed in his own narration to catch the subject matter of this conversation and call upon Hugo to translate.
Kate, for her part, had been engaged by Linda Rubenstein in a
discussion on feminism, from which, from time to time, she slid
anxious sidelong glances at Hugo, growing more anxious as
Mujid moved from the relatively safe and isolated topic of
Kurdistan to the Iraq Petroleum Company, the Camp David
settlement, the Palestinians, and the treachery of Sadat. Odd
words from each floated towards Hugo and Kate as the three
monologues unrolled, and Hugo felt a growing sense of un-
reality, as though he were witnessing, in a peculiarly grotesque form, the hopelessness of communication, the bared
roots of intransigence. There they were, the six of them, all
tolerably well-intentioned people, and instead of an interchange all they could produce were these three separate isolated speeches, this mini-Babel. Tom Rubenstein's sense of

perspective appeared to end before Mujid's began, and Linda
Rubenstein seemed to consider her own tangential debate the
only important debate of history. The ideologies of the late
twentieth century mingled but did not mix. Would there be
any point in trying to persuade Mujid and Tom to talk to one
another? Was not this a fine opportunity for creating a small
moment of international sympathy? Not a hope, decided
Hugo as he listened. Sadat, Weizmann (for Tom also had
moved onto the subject of Israel), Dayan, Kate Millett, Begin,
Qaddafi, Doris Lessing, Kazziha (Kazziha?)—the names were
breathed into the smoke-filled air and hung querulously over
their heads, over the checked cloth, question marks, ghostly
presences from distant spheres, unresounding.

Kate decided to abandon the men to their fate, to shut
out their echoes, and tried to concentrate on Linda, though
Linda was making her more and more uneasy: she was one of
those impassioned women who vibrate with a sense of injus-
tice and outrage, and she seemed to assume that in Kate she
had found a sympathetic listener, an assumption which made
Kate even more unhappy, as it could only have been aroused
by Kate's own printed views. She was eaten up by a sense of
opportunities missed, and she said some shocking things about
her husband, even though he was at the same table, and
would have been in earshot if he hadn't been so isolated by
the sound of his own voice. "Of course *he* never thought of
that," she kept saying, "but then he wouldn't, a man wouldn't,
would he?" It emerged that she had given up her own studies
at Sussex to accompany Tom Rubenstein back to Cornell, on
the understanding that she could take them up again when
she got there, but somehow it hadn't worked out—the courses
didn't fit, she couldn't get credits for past work, then there
were the babies, and, anyway, Tom expected her to cook and
keep house, Tom was a materialist, all he was interested in
was domestic comfort and status and cars and electric ovens
and dinner parties for other professors and their unspeakably

boring wives. "You'd think, in a *university*, people would be a little more liberated," Linda kept saying, bitterly, scornfully, her face lined with contempt.

Kate did not like this at all. She feared that Linda Rubenstein, like Susan Sondersheim so many memorable years ago, was on the verge of some spectacular collapse, yet how could she be, when her husband was sitting comfortably a few feet away, enjoying his dinner, apparently oblivious of this torrent of abuse? When she herself was, between sentences, putting away a fair quantity of suprême de volaille? Did she perhaps talk like this *all the time?* Much of what she was saying was true enough, Kate told herself—it is true that women are expected to interrupt their education and their careers to follow their husbands, it is true that babies interrupt studies, it is true that many men have curious expectations of domestic happiness. But how could Linda speak in such a way of the man to whom she was still married, and why, if she was so angry, didn't she do something about it? Had the dark storm of her wrath paralysed her? She didn't seem paralysed: on the contrary, she was burning with energy. Kate listened, trying to make sense of it all, telling herself that perhaps Tom Rubenstein, for all his pleasant round shiny countenance, might be a monster in disguise—but if so, why ever did Linda stick with him? She could hardly be expected to urge a woman to leave her husband while in his presence, could she? Linda moved on, from her own over-personal grievances (of which an odd feature seemed to be Tom's interest in kitchen hardware and its colours—avocado, aubergine, for Chrissake, said Linda, grinding out these insults from between her teeth —was she trying to be *funny*, and if so, why didn't she smile?) to a more generalised invective against the passivity of the British, as distinct from the American, woman: "Things are so backward here, I'd forgotten the whole scene, people here aren't even interested, don't you agree?" asked Linda. (Linda had been born and bred in Kent.)

"Well, no, I don't quite agree," said Kate. "Quite a lot of

people here are interested. And there are plenty of people like me who feel so strongly about marriage that we stopped being married, for one reason or another."

She paused, already penitent.

"It's different for you, you can earn your own living," said Linda.

"So can anyone," said Kate.

Linda stubbed her cigarette out on her side plate.

Kate saw she had gone far enough, if not too far, and backtracked, in the cause of courtesy. Did Linda attend a group, she asked, and if so, what was it like? And did it change people?

"It makes them see differently," said Linda.

"What's the point of seeing, if you can't do anything about it?" asked Kate.

"One ought to know the truth," said Linda.

"I once went to a women's group in Leeds with a friend of mine," said Kate, "and there was a woman there who talked a lot about how much she'd changed as a result, and about how she now saw that it was pointless to spend one's life tidying up the house and making children's beds and cooking meals, and how husbands and children ought to be made to help, and how neurotic she realised she'd always been, folding up newspapers and putting magazines in racks and dusting surfaces. Then she left early because she said she had to get back to warm up her husband's supper, he always burned it if left to do it himself. When she'd gone, the others all laughed and said she still irons tea towels and underpants. Underpants, imagine."

Linda, to Kate's relief, quite liked this story, and countered it with one about a feminist conference on women and the law which had created a scandal because the only two papers accepted from men just happened to have been written by the husbands of two of the organisers. She actually laughed. Perhaps she's all right after all, thought Kate, she just enjoys being angry, gets a kick out of it. Perhaps she and

Tom get on fine. They agreed that change takes time, that perhaps it was better to know one's obsessions than not to know them, they even exchanged a few words about different styles of British and American feminism, Kate conceding that Americans made her defensive, Linda conceding that maybe, as an expatriate, she had become ultra-converted. Slightly cheered, Kate decided that she had had enough of trying to be diplomatic, that it was time to rescue Hugo from Mujid.

Over coffee, Paul, Hugo, and Kate took refuge in gossip about that perennially interesting topic, the editorship of the *New Statesman,* lapsing into the parochial and the malicious in a way that certainly amused them, if not their guests. After all, reflected Hugo, one can't tackle major themes all the time, in fact there is very little point in tackling them at all, from our position on the sidelines. Why not eat, drink, and be merry? They ordered brandies.

It was Kate who broke it up, looking at her watch and saying she had to be up early in the morning. Hugo arranged to meet Mujid for lunch. Kate invited Linda to tea. The bill arrived; the meal had cost more than Kate when first married could have earned in a month. She counted out her notes to add to Paul's, and wondered what Mujid had made of the evening. Were she and Hugo and Tom and Linda as corrupt, in his eyes, as the Lebanese jet set, which, according to Beatrice, had devoured twelve-course dinners washed down with pink sparkling wine, and ordered their clothes from Paris? No, surely not quite as bad, and maybe Mujid had been taken in by the modesty of the red-and-white-checked and not very clean tablecloth, the unofficial-looking waiter in his plastic apron. Maybe Mujid thought you could get artichokes and green beans like that for next to nothing if you knew where to look. Or maybe he didn't think about these things at all. Anyway, he'd enjoyed his steak, he'd said so, and so he ought to have done at £4.95. Oh, help, thought Kate, yawning, how much time I waste worrying about whether other people are enjoying themselves, you can't please everyone all the time, can you?

She and Mujid went home in a taxi, Kate about to collapse with fatigue the moment she stopped talking, but when she got back the evening was not yet over, for her sitting room was occupied by an extremely drunken Hunt, wanting to sell her a large, white, not very attractive jug ("just your kind of thing," as he described it, with an insulting leer), or to borrow some money, or both; and demanding to stay the night, as it was far too late to get back to Highbury. Kate explained that Mujid was sleeping in Mark's room, and that Hunt would have to sleep on the sofa. Hunt at this news became abusive, and poor Mujid, quite unable to understand who Hunt was or what was going on, made some effort to defend Kate: Kate tried to explain that she could handle Hunt, and that he'd go to sleep if left alone with a blanket, but Hunt, enraged by Mujid's intervention, turned on the young man and proceeded to shower abuse on him, abuse which luckily Mujid could not understand, but which ended with an exhortation to go off and float down the Euphrates. Kate, caught between her two ill-assorted and uninvited guests, began to laugh, then suddenly lost her temper too and told Hunt he could shut up or get out, and ordered the dazed Mujid to bed. Hunt was asleep and noisily snoring by the time she had fetched the proffered blanket: she wrapped him up in it, and left him. At least he was too hardened a drinker to throw up. On her way back to bed, she found Mujid hovering nervously outside the bathroom door, waiting to see if she was all right. She patted him on the shoulder, touched by his anxiety, feeling suddenly very fond of him. He smiled, a charming myopic confused smile, and said that he had had a most beautiful evening, a remark which gave her true pleasure. Retreating to her own room, she found a note on her bed, in dried-up red felt-tip, saying:

Sorry about Hunt, Mum, we hid the Teachers in bottom of wardrobe but he got the gin. Nighty Night Darling Mum, Be a

Good Girl, We Love you, Kiss Kiss Kiss, R and R. P.S. DAD RANG
HE HAS GOT SPOTS ! ! !

Kate began to laugh again, as she pulled off her clothes: why
ever bother to try to make sense of so much nonsense, but
however could one stop? She fell asleep in an instant, to wake,
as one does, at four o'clock in the morning, stone cold with
anxiety and remorse.

At a quarter past nine the next morning, Kate and Mujid stood
together on the Underground platform, waiting for a train.
Kate was off to look at Romley, and Mujid to his class. She
had resisted his suggestion that he might accompany her, and
the television company's offer of a car. She had never managed to get used to the idea of keeping a driver waiting, and,
anyway, she didn't want Mujid to get the impression that cars
were there for her asking, even when they were. She wanted
to revisit Romley alone, undistracted. She didn't know what
she would find there, and she didn't want anyone to watch her
finding it.

Mujid didn't look very well. Kate felt herself that she
might have had a hangover, had she allowed herself to give in
to the concept of a hangover, but she didn't. She did not,
however, feel up to the strain of conversation, so gazed instead
at the posters and graffiti, and listened to the thin faint piping
of an early barefoot beggar girl painfully picking her way
through the strains of "Waltzing Matilda" on a hollowly gasping flute. Yet again, she found herself wondering what Mujid
made of London Today, and trying to see it through his eyes.
Waiflike pallid Australian beggars dressed in yellow robes
might not strike him as oddly as they struck her, but what
could he make of that curious couple sitting on the bench,
the large young man on the larger girl's knee, both dressed in
a dirty variety of black leather, smelling even at this early

hour of drink and pot, adorned with buckles and pins and
badges, the girl in Indian sandals, the young man in big brown
monkey boots with yellow laces (no, on closer inspection, not
such a young man, late twenties at least, for his greased flat
hair was smarmed back to reveal a balding patch). The girl's
hair was dyed an intermittent canary orange. What were they,
punk, Ted, ageing hippies, unisex protesters, or simply people
doing their own thing? Unlike the flautist, whatever they were
doing, they were not playing at it. They were for real. A grim
outline of jaw and a defiant slump of the shoulder revealed
working-class origins. What were they up to? Kate hoped that
Mujid would not ask, for she did not know. Her children
might have known, might have come out with a ready cate-
gory, but she herself simply did not know.

And the slogans, what would Mujid make of the slogans?
She had grown used to them, and learned to ignore them, but
in his company they seemed unavoidably prominent. NIGGERS
GO HOME. KILL THE BLACK CUNTS WHO ARE RUINING OUR COUN-
TRY. BRITS OUT OF NORTHERN IRELAND. MUSLIM DOGS. STOP IRAQI
SLAUGHTER OF KURDS. These messages were plain enough even
to one with little English, and Mujid could no doubt also
understand the multitude of Arabic protests that had in the
last few years been added to the indigenous array. Some of the
graffiti had, mercifully, no political message; to an insurance
poster portraying a delightful retreat in Georgian Bath, inhabited by delightful people in Georgian costume, somebody had
added a balloon issuing from the mouth of a wench selling
oranges which proclaimed, baldly, FUR OFF. Kate peered more
closely. Was fur a new way of pronouncing fuck? Was it a
new word altogether? Was it evidence of the rotten teaching
of basic skills such as spelling in primary schools today? Kate
sighed heavily, and shifted from one foot to another, wishing
she had not put on her boots. It promised to be a hot day, and
a piece of lining was uncomfortably crunched up under the
ball of her foot.

She stared straight ahead of her, where, at the opposite

side of the track, out of reach of the felt-tip pen and the spray can, an enormous curved advertisement for stockings loomed. It was her least favourite advertisement, if one could have such a thing. It portrayed two very long pairs of stockinged legs in very high heels: above the legs were two bottoms, clad in the scantiest and wispiest of blue-green garments, far too short to be an evening dress or even a day dress, far too flimsy to be beach wear or sportswear. The models had their arms intertwined, and looked like some horrible four-legged monster, or an unfortunate pair of Siamese twins joined at the hip. The slogan read: FOR WOMEN WHO DON'T WANT TO WEAR THE TROUSERS. Kate wondered whether she should point it out to Mujid; in the past she had drawn his attention to the various feminist remarks and stickers that now adorn advertisements for boots, brassières, bridal outfits (Y B A BRIDE, THIS DEGRADES WOMAN, and so on), but he had been neither pleased nor offended by them, merely perplexed. It would be too difficult to explain why and how much she disliked the poster, and, anyway, why did she dislike it so much? She had nothing against legs or stockings. Was she disturbed by the fact that through the diaphanous drapery one could actually see the gaps between the girls' thighs? Two blunt, straight, short, horizontal lines, representing, not to be over-delicate about it, their cunts? They must have been wearing elastic knickers to have presented so blunt an outline when blown up way beyond life size. How unpleasantly *numb* they looked. As though they'd been amputated, though of course we all know a woman has nothing to lose and therefore shouldn't react this way. Or at least not a woman like me, in this day and age, standing here on this platform, staring glumly at two pairs of giraffe legs and two outsize bums. Perhaps not amputated, perhaps *stitched up* and *sealed over* would be a better way of looking at it?

When she had parted with Mujid at Tottenham Court Road and sailed on to Fenchurch Street to catch her train to Romley, she found herself assaulted by a different variety of slogans. The tatty compartment of the tatty suburban train, which in itself evoked a complex array of memories, was madly plastered with red National Front stickers and scribbles. These were new since her day. She had not been back to Romley since her parents left the district, retiring to Clacton eight years earlier. The trains into town had been shabby enough in her girlhood, but they had not been so exclamatory. The particular gang that had worked the compartment over were clearly susceptible to the possible hostility of public opinion: amongst the usual stuff were two almost apologetic remarks. REPATRIATION NOT EXTERMINATION, said one; the other said (in illustrated form) that the NF equalled the Union Jack, not the Swastika. A very decent attitude, all things considered.

Kate peered into her carpet-bag. There lay, waiting for her attention, her morning's hate mail. She had only had time to glance at it before leaving the house, and had a nasty suspicion that when she looked closer it would prove to be even more unpleasant than at first glance. It was anonymous, but she thought she knew who had written it. It was about homosexuality, that much she had ascertained, and it was knocking her for supporting in print some aspect of the gay cause: her article about a dismissed teacher, probably. She shook her head, partly in despondency, partly to try to remove a faint buzzing in her left ear. But the buzzing persisted. Perhaps it was the faint red buzzing of hatred from the writing on every wall, from the opinions that poured to her through every red letter-box, that poured through her own pen? She was sick of opinions, slogans, ideologies, factions, causes. One could not speak, these days, without offending some pressure group, worthy or unworthy. Sensibilities were inflamed, catching insults where none were intended; an ideological epidemic had swept through Britain, perhaps through the world. The raw membrane caught every passing disease. Swollen organs of indignation impeded natural functioning on every side. And what was the answer to that? This is the disease of capitalism,

Mujid would no doubt say, were he here to say it. The final sickness. And would he be right? God knows, for I certainly don't. Oh, Lord, thought Kate, first I had a Freudian nervous breakdown through Ted and that baby business, and now I'm having a Marxist nervous breakdown through Mujid. To hell with them both, she said to herself crossly, as the train moved out of the station and began to wind its way east. Put them out of your mind. It is to something earlier than either that you must now attend.

BRITAIN OUT OF THE EEC, the red paint declared. Maybe she should simply give up having any views on anything for a year. Shut up for a year. What a relief it would be. But, of course, she couldn't afford to shut up. She had to go on earning her living, and her living depended on peddling opinions. She had brought three children up on views. It was quite an achievement, in its way. At the back of her mind, behind the worries about age and solitude and sex, lay a very real economic fear. What if she found herself with nothing more to say? She had no skills, no training, nothing behind her, and life was more expensive every day. Trapped. She simply couldn't afford to stop, and moreover she couldn't afford to let herself get crosser and crosser and sourer and sourer. The editor didn't like it, the readers didn't like it. They wanted the old sprightly Kate. The old jokes, the old uplift. Her life, or at least her living, depended on keeping it going. She was not indispensable. If she got dull, she would go. A sobering thought, and one not calculated to make her feel any more lively.

She gazed out of the window at high brick walls, at buildings and building sites, at the backs of factories, at tufts of greenery and ragged yellow flowers clinging boldly to stony niches. It was a beautiful morning, and it had altogether been the most beautiful autumn in memory. The sun irradiated the pocked and shabby surfaces. It was now November, but seemed like high summer; the trees had hardly begun to lose their leaves. Kate had not in the past been an admirer of autumn, for it had seemed to her a sad season even at its best; the smell of falling leaves and bonfires had during her good years filled her with premonitions of death. But this year, even she had enjoyed it. A few nights earlier, at dinner with friends, the conversation had turned to the weather, and each had expressed emotion at this spectacularly gracious dying fall, enthusing over walks on the Heath, mild mornings and evenings, country excursions, lunch outside pubs in Covent Garden or Chiswick, picnics in St. James's Park and Queen's Square. Her host had recounted the story of a man who, every October, was seized with rheumatism, until one year a friend pointed out that the rheumatism was merely an annual expression of his fear of death; after this discovery, he never suffered from rheumatism again. And his fear of death, Kate wanted to know, what had happened to that? Nobody answered, they all fell silent, gripped by a companionable terror, a companionable reprieve from terror, slumped in their comfortable leather chairs, nursing their glasses of wine. Maybe they would be spared the slow chill, maybe an Indian summer was in store for each, a contented old age? Though perhaps we do not lead the lives proper for such a conclusion, thought Kate. We gamble on the present, what else can we do?

Perhaps the sun shone so brightly to remind her that, whatever she thought of it, it was still there. She couldn't ruin it or blot it out with the dull disk of herself. If she fell silent forever, it would continue to shine. She couldn't turn the sun into an article, she had no views on it at all. She had spent too much of her life turning things into articles, annexing them, distorting them, colouring them in with her own limited range of colours. Should she attempt stillness? But no, how could one be still, she was an active person, she could only do things her own way. Restless, enquiring, demanding an answer. Stillness was useless, one had to keep walking.

And therefore she went to Romley, looking, as usual, for copy. She could see herself, far away, on the box, smiling insinuatingly, coaxing, assuming a lively interest in the lives of others, wheedling out of them their aspirations and their failures. The picture both cheered and disgusted her.

Romley, she had hoped, would restore a sense of perspective. She thought again, briefly, of Mujid. His stories of Iraq and Lebanon should surely have restored perspective too, but in some curious way he had merely become a part of her own, for, despite his situation and opinions, he was really as interested as anybody in the trivia of existence, in whether or not he could go to the theatre without a suit, in the size of tomatoes and the length of leeks, in whether or not Kate would include him in a dinner invitation, in whether he had managed to impress one-handed Hugo with his political analysis. He had sunk to their own level. People are awful, thought Kate. Petty, selfish, childish. And I the worst of all, all my good things gone sour. Gone bad, like that horrible scar full of grit on Ruth's elbow that went green because the silly woman at school hadn't washed out the dirt before putting on the plaster. The grit was still there, she could feel it throbbing away under each new layer of skin. But did not know how to get at it. Would it fester fatally, a gangrene of the spirit? And I had always vainly prided myself on my good health. A healthy person, conceiving a sick child. Impossible, impossible, she could not accept such knowledge. She had cut out the child, but not the malady. These thoughts will drive me mad, thought Kate, and shut her mind to them.

She had her day planned, after her own fashion. The morning she would spend wandering; in the afternoon she had an appointment at her old school.

The district would have changed. A massive new rebuilding programme had been nearly completed on the heavily bombed district south of her old home; a vast new estate, almost a new town, called Romley Riverside, extending onto reclaimed flat marshland that in her day had been wild. She had never seen it, though she had of course seen photographs, read articles. Some of her old school companions must have ended up there. Her director liked the idea of filming on the

Riverside estate. The architecture was dramatic, the whole project controversial: some considered it the pride of the GLC (Greater London Council), others muttered of vandalism and problem families. Interesting, either way: and one could probably make it look either way.

The little station, however, had not changed at all. Its shabby deserted little platform stood open to the sun; a black porter was cleaning the brown woodwork of the waiting room with a mop on a long handle. It was very quiet. She handed in her ticket, made her way out up the ramp to the street. The street was altered out of recognition. A new main road led to the new estate in one direction, back into old Romley in the other; it was designed for motorists and heavy lorries rather than pedestrians, but not impassable. The sewage bank, half a mile away, linked the two, running parallel to the invisible but not distant Thames. She set off towards it, towards the new estate, which began to loom up before her like grey concrete elephants, huge, split-level, massive, a demotic version of the new National Theatre and the Festival Hall. A modern pub, the Fisherman's Rest, fronted the road, and the housing blocks banked up behind it. On the other side of the road was a new middle-class estate, built in the sixties: neat little houses with smart paintwork and well-kept hedges and gardens and lace curtains, individuality flourishing in odd designs for doors and windows, in carriage lamps and front gates. Riverside was a grey monolith of expensive planning for cheap people, uniform, grand.

And there was the sewage bank, the green ridge. The road rose high over it on concrete stilts. Maybe she wouldn't be able to get down to get up on it any more. But yes, there was a ramp leading down, and then a well-worn path leading up the grassy side, where generations of children, including herself, had scrambled.

She descended, then made her way up again. The mud was dry, the ground parched from the long dry autumn. And there, from the top, was the old familiar view, changed forever. A wilderness of fly-overs and underpasses and unfinished supports spread meaninglessly around her and above her: rusty stakes dug into the earth, protruded in ranks and spears like broken railings, marched away like the aftermath of war, the stubble of no man's land. Though in the midst of construction, the area looked derelict, abandoned: raw, ugly, gigantic in scale. She stood on top of the grassy bank and looked down at the neat suburban houses, up at the soaring blocks, ahead to the unseen Thames: from the top flats in the estate one could no doubt see huge ships sailing. Only the bank was unchanged: it led, to the right, towards Blackridge, its destination.

The path on the top was still well trodden, and she could see two children in the distance, playing some game, as she herself had played. An immense calm lay on the tormented landscape, a mid-morning silence. She could hear birds singing. She began to walk along the ridge.

Her feet remembered the surface, through her high, hot, uncomfortable boots. The worn grass, the trodden earth, the intermittent litter of twisted barbed wire, the round iron manhole covers. Her heart beat uncomfortably fast as she walked over the first of these covers; recollections just beyond the reach of memory gathered in the distance, took shape as she approached. She could now see a side view of the huge estate, and there, to her astonishment, was a large artificial lake, with, of all things, little sailing dinghies afloat: sailing dinghies in the middle of nowhere, on a mid-week morning. The high blocks rose behind it. Workmen were building an edifice clearly designed as some kind of leisure centre, with a terrace overlooking the lake, and a boathouse. How extraordinary! The workmen waved, and she waved back, conspicuous on her high ridge. How odd it all was, how unexpected! Twentieth-century paradise, pleasure gardens of concrete, lakes where land had once been, civic landscape-gardening. She walked on, passing on her left another small recreation park, with a funny serpentine river, and a little Chinese bridge, and ducks, and reeds, and ornamental grasses: thin young planted trees stood and quaked in lonely gatherings, their leaves trembling in the bright still air. Before her, in the far distance, her father's works. When he left, they had presented him with a carriage clock, engraved.

She was uncomfortably hot, and would have taken off her coat, but for the bother of carrying it. Her boots were not only hot—one of them was also, she could tell, on the verge of breaking. The heel felt wobbly, precarious, unsafe, like a loose tooth. If she trod on it squarely, it bit safely, but a slight angle or stumble made the nails pull at the roots, the bridge strain. She concentrated on keeping upright, walking squarely, avoiding the dog shit and the horse shit. Horse shit? She looked around, and there, in this redesigned world, were the gipsies still, who had lived here when she was a child, camping by the side of the bank, their ponies and greyhounds tethered, their chickens scratching in improvised runs. The two children, she could now see, were gipsy children, playing at washing up a plastic doll's tea set in a bowl of soapy water, watched over by a skeletal whippet. They did not look up as Kate passed, intent on their game. She wondered how permanent the encampment was; there had always been gipsies in this region, though the great flood of 1953 had dislodged many of them.

The landscaped pleasure gardens dropped behind, replaced by a tangle of brambles and bushes and long grass. A few shabby horses grazed in an untidy field. Rabbit country, the working man's uncultivable terrain. Half a mile away, square open patches of yellow sand flatly glittered, and far on the horizon cranes and vast silver cylinders stood about, ghostly shining inhabitants of the marsh. Nearby, the bushes were laden with berries. The dark red of the haws scattered the deep green in a fine haze like drops of blood. A crabapple dazzling with pale-orange glowing fruits like a tree decorated for a festival illuminated the undergrowth. Trails of old man's beard and traveller's joy silvered the scrub. This is my country, thought Kate. Tatty, low, obdurate. Was it wrong, perhaps, to move?

Though she had not, in fact, moved so far. She had recreated NW6 in a familiar image, despite her intention of flight and escape. Her chip-shop house, her scrappy district with its funny ramshackle community schemes (there was even a community farm in Kentish Town, a farm by the railway), her corner-shop life, her narrow junkyard of a back garden—it was not so different, after all. She'd thought she had moved and changed, but she hadn't. She'd been offered flight, escape, transformation, but for some reason she'd managed to impose herself, her old self, even on the Armstrongs. Why? How? Whatever for?

She could have chosen to live in a different style altogether. She could afford it now. She could live in a square white house like Evelyn's, with comfortable furniture, instead of in her cramped and seething abode. She had always liked Evelyn's house, Luisa's house. Polished floors, large rooms, bowls of fruit. In Kate's house, the fruit stayed in paper bags, as Mujid had no doubt spotted. Why ever did she go on so resolutely being what she was? What failure of imagination kept her within her narrow limits?

Kate stood still, and thought.

She thought of Evelyn. Evelyn worked amongst the very poor, as Kate did not, and never had. Evelyn cared, Evelyn gave herself, Evelyn tried to understand and to help the dull, the hopeless, the inadequate, the vicious. Evelyn was a good woman, a woman with a conscience. She went out of her own way, and worked long hours. Whereas I, thought Kate, I merely at random scatter my notions abroad like birdseed, and accept the visitations of people like Mujid and Hunt and all those silly men I get mixed up with, and the children's awful friends, because I haven't the strength to say no, haven't the strength to kick people out, haven't the guts to defend myself. Evelyn goes home to her white house and shuts the door.

Then she gives proper dinner parties with proper food. And she has Ted, after a fashion. She draws lines, she makes demarcations. She is a proper woman. And I, I mess about and straggle and excuse myself and giggle and turn everything into a bad joke, because I can't do anything properly. The funny woman. I've even turned Stuart into a joke, and our relationship. God, what a myth I've created about that. "Dear Stuart," I tell people, "yes, I *love* Stuart," I say, "who wouldn't, we get on so well, the children adore him, but he's so clueless and *incompetent*," I say, and laugh, and tell them about his latest mould or rust paintings, and we all laugh, and I tell them about his dirty kitchen and his money problems and how do I emerge from all these stories, the brave woman, the practical nice-natured understanding woman, the woman without malice who gets on so well with her ex and takes him soup when he's ill. And it's all an invention. Because the truth is that I hated Stuart, he treated me like a shit and I treated him worse, though he began first, in fairness I have to say. It was hell with Stuart. I hated him, and I behaved like a child in my rage. And now we have this cosy pretence and I go out to the theatre with his brother and we laugh over old times. As though they hadn't been murderous. Murderous. Once I tried to kill Stuart, with the bread knife. Not very seriously, and I'd never have done it, but I *wanted* to.

Maybe if I hadn't make jokes about Stuart's paintings, he'd be a successful painter by now. I think he's a bloody good one, not that I know anything about it, but I think he's every way as good as, oh, Mark Boyle and Richard Hamilton and all that lot, in fact better, but then when I say that to people, this damn silly stupid woman's tone comes into my ridiculous voice and I start to sound as though I was only saying it because I want to be a nice woman. *A Nice Woman*, for Christ's sake. What an epitaph.

The thing is, Evelyn looks after people because she ought to, and because, despite Ted and everything, she's in some mysterious way OK. And I look after people because I have to, and because in some awful way I only like hopeless cases. I don't like real, serious, respectable people. Well, no, that's not true, I like them, but I never get close to them. What's the matter with me?

The sun beat down on Kate Armstrong's head, as she stood lost in thought on the sewage bank. A small kestrel hovered over the scrub. A dog barked. As she stood, trying to think and not to think, a strange distracting smell began to make its way towards her. She sniffed. Sewage, of course. From the manhole just before her. She walked towards it and peered down. Most of the holes were blocked up, but the fancy grid of this one was open, and way down she could see the dark water racing through its pipe. The smell, powerful and secret, of drains and rainwater rose towards her. A vegetable, organic smell. Well, she had to admit it, a pleasant smell. She actually liked it. As a child, she had liked it very much, had much preferred it to the treated smell of antiseptics and disinfectants that hangs around most potentially unsavoury places. In fact—and a faint prickle of embarrassment raised the hair on the back of her neck—in fact, one of the secret pleasures of her childhood had been sniffing this very smell. What a shocking recollection. When small, she used to climb up this very bank, further back in its Romley stretch, and when no one was looking she would lie on her belly and press her face against the grating and inhale. She knew it was both wicked and silly, this activity, and possibly dangerous, but it was also irresistible. There had been something magical about the dark race of water and the powerful odour of London. She had lain there and thought of the mysterious network of drains and pipes and tubes and gulleys and sewers linking the underground city, her small flat child's belly pressed to the warm summer grass, her bare knees and her feet in their sandals and ankle socks warm on the grass. She shivered as the sensation of childhood overpoweringly returned, the sense of her small guilty child's body covertly sniffing its own strange drug. She looked around, back at the distant workmen, the distant gipsies' camp. Dare she kneel, in her precarious leather boots, and sniff? No, she dare not. Supposing someone saw, supposing she caught bubonic plague? (Peter, at school, had been known as Stinky Fletcher. A trial.)

She moved away, along the ridge, out of sight, out of smell of the grating, and sat down on the grass. Her knees felt slightly weak with shame and excitement. Was this what she had come for, was this the window, the grille through which she should escape the prison of the present into the past, where the dark spirits swam in the fast-moving flood? Well, no, nothing as simple as that, really. No revelations evoked by the smell, just memories. Of the piece she had written, five years ago, about the sewers, at the time of the last industrial dispute. She had persuaded the Thames Water Authority to organise a visit for her, and down she had gone, down in her protective overalls and helmet and waders, down through a manhole in the middle of Piccadilly, climbing down a greasy ladder to the underworld, wading through tissues and Tampax and orange peel, walking through the ancient red-brick Victorian arches, crawling on her hands and knees to see where the flashers, bent double, worked, smelling the odours issuing from grand hotel kitchens and laundries. The dark tunnels, the mysterious network. The men had been so kind to her, teasing and joking, egging her on to crawl further into the darkness, and she had crawled, although frightened, because if they spent their working lives down there, why should she not be brave enough to look? How easy to be a woman, to be able to manifest fear at the end of a rope without loss of face. And how pleasant they had been, in their tee shirts, with their stories of storms and rats, brewing up cups of tea in their mobile van. Why had her father been incapable of such easygoing bonhomie? Why had he made it all so difficult?

What an odd couple her parents were. She had turned them into an acceptable version, in her own mind, as she had turned Stuart. The little clever man and the large idle woman, one suffering from paranoia, the other from agoraphobia. One could laugh about it now, but it hadn't been like that at all. She had learned to laugh, to admire, to forgive. Yet what had laughter, admiration, or sympathy to do with the tangled roots in her heart? For she had loved these two terrible people, in the dawn of time, in the dark before dawn, in the underground she had loved them. And nothing in her conscious self, in her daylight self, had been able to love. Was this the problem, was this the fault, was it for this that she sat here, was it for this that Ted had left her for a woman in Cambridge, that she had conceived a deformed baby, and murdered it and then herself? Those two selves, that prattling chattering journalist in Kentish Town, with her smart views and expensive boots and trendy house (these boots with rotten heels had cost her £80 at Liberty's, she must be mad), and the child in its skimpy cotton dress, lonely, cast out, cut off—what had they in common? No blood flowed from one to the other, the cord was cut, she withered and grew dry.

She could remember, with horrible clarity, one of those dresses. A dull brown with a little geometric pattern of yellow, black, and white shapes scattered pointlessly about on it. Little square short sleeves with a turn-up, like an overall, and a belt like an overall belt, always twisted. Thin cheap limp cotton. A plain child's plain dress.

Oh, God, Kate sighed. She'd never read Proust, but she'd heard of Proust's *madeleine*. How typical of her to have chosen a sewage bank for such stirrings, instead of a nice little cake and a nice cup of tea.

She thought of Peter. Felt in her bag for Peter's letter. Or, rather, for the anonymous letter that she thought came from Peter. Yes, there it was. Carefully cut-out letters pasted onto a large sheet of lined paper. It read:

Sensation-seeking people like you talking rubbish about homosexuality are ruining this country for decent people. Perversion in our schools and colleges, what next?

Not, by the standards of most anonymous letters, a particularly offensive message. No swear words, no personal allegations. It was Peter's style, down to the carefully cut-out question mark, which one could take either as a joke or as a sign of extreme madness. She had had such missives from him before, on such topics as abortion, race, and education, and would never have suspected that they were from him, had he not deliberately betrayed himself at Christmas three years earlier (they rarely met except at Christmas) by interrogating her about whether or not she received many such letters, and if so, what did they say, and did she ever try and track down her correspondents. His apparently open-hearted but excessively lively curiosity had alerted her suspicions, and when the next letter arrived postmarked Hornchurch, she knew she had guessed right.

What was he up to? It was easy enough to think of reasons, on one level. He was jealous of her success. He resented her lack of interest in him. He genuinely disapproved of her fashionable views. He blamed her for his own difficulties. He hated her, and always had. He was mad. Any or all of these were possibilities.

Mad, clearly, anyway, as sane people do not write anonymous letters to their own sisters or to anyone else. But mad in what way, and why? And what could or should she do about it?

Poor Peter, he had had a bad time, though it was hard to see exactly why, or when things had started to go wrong. Maybe he had reacted against their father's hopes, against their father's insane capacity for remembering facts and figures and dates. Kate had reacted against it herself, though at once more blatantly and more deviously—blatantly, by refusing to do any serious work at school at all, though she now perforce recognised that she could have done had she chosen, and deviously, by concealing her capacity very thoroughly from both teachers and parents. Peter had been the real victim, right in the firing line. Being the only boy. Those miserable suppers when Dad would take it into his head to fire questions at Pete—mental arithmetic, what's the capital of Madagascar, when was the Treaty of Lausanne, rubbish like that. Poor Dad, poor Peter. Kate had learned early to giggle her way out of that kind of interrogation, and, being a girl, was let off. And Mum, enormous and querulous, saying, "Don't nag the poor boy," to no avail.

What a paradox he had been, her father, with his fine views on the dignity of labour. During the big strike of 1970, although retired, he had addressed meetings: "No miner would work in the conditions our men endure," he would declare. "For a pittance these men have struggled throughout their working lives for the community, and what is their reward? Their labours are brushed under the carpet, because people don't like to think about these things. And yet which is more essential to the community: the miner or the sewage maintenance worker? Every time a housewife turns on a tap, she should give thanks to the men that make this daily miracle possible. Every time you flush a lavatory, you should remember the past, when cholera was king in London. The nation's health depends on our labours. And what thanks do we get? We are called traitors to our country when we ask for a pay rise of a few pounds a week. No, you cannot flush away our demands." Fine stuff, and Kate recognised herself to be her father's daughter. (Even to the mixed metaphors, alas: the first time an editor tried to explain about mixed metaphors to Kate, she thought he was joking.) Yet this same fighting spirit had nagged at Peter to better himself, had bullied both children into trying to speak properly, had poured scorn on working men in other lines of business, had joined his wife in a rejection of neighbourliness, had opted for lace curtains and bow windows. They had struggled their way up into a semi-detached and respectability, and much joy it had given any of them. A perilous thin veneer had been laid over the past, over Arblay Street. A thin scum of decency. Uncle Bob, with half his brains, had been twice as happy.

And Peter had been terrorised. She could remember now his broad pale frightened face, harangued over sausage, swede, and mash. A sacrifice to progress.

Perhaps luckily, Dad hadn't been in often; the bouts of mental arithmetic had been spasmodic. Dad was always out at meetings. He loved meetings. Dad was never in, Mum never went out. No doubt there'd been some connection between these two things, but as a child she'd never suspected it. She'd assumed that Dad went out so much because it was boring in with Mum, but perhaps it had been so boring in with Mum because Dad was always out and never took Mum with him.

Dad wasn't well enough to get out to meetings any more, and, anyway, he'd cut himself off from his old circle of activity by moving house in the obstinate, short-sighted, suicidal way that old people do. He had become disillusioned, angry, wanted no more to do with the union. The sourness of the seventies overcame him, as so many others. He had taken to reviling strikers, whatever their claims, whatever their griev-ances. Greedy, dishonest, and selfish, he called the hospital workers, the men at Leyland, even his own NUPE (National Union of Public Employees) colleagues. The bitterness of old age and ill-health mingled with a more reasonable resentment. "This isn't the country we were fighting for," he would say. He loathed the idea of comprehensive education. "It's pulled the ladder from under the feet of the working man," he would say, regardless of the fact that he and Kate had ascended without that ladder, and that Peter had fallen because of it. Poor Dad. But what could she do?

Would her own children come to regard her with such a strange mixture of emotions? Would they too reject her as she grew old and sour and crabbed? Were they rejecting her al-ready, in their secret hearts, despite their deceitful smiles and embraces? She had talked of this with Hugo, many times, and he had taken the line that it was not only natural but necessary for children to reject their parents; that it was dangerous, destructive, to try to preserve communion, to try to keep the blood flowing through the severed cord. She did not think that Hugo truly believed this, though he had reasons of his own for wishing to do so.

She thought of Hugo's mother, who had caused Hugo such very different problems. Smart, fickle, eccentric, too interesting by half. Hugo also on the run, for a lifetime, from her curious mixture of obsession and neglect. Kate liked Hugo's mother. (But then, as Hugo said, she would.) No culture gap there, between parent and child: rather a frightening amorous communion, a rapport so quick, so sharp, so intense, that an observer felt himself to be watching a pattern of courtship, a display, at once public and intimate, of mutual possession. Hugo pouring his mother a drink, laughing at her jokes, asking what she was reading, what exhibitions she'd seen, what she thought of them, capping quotations, jumping to conclusions, eliding references. Kate had admired such closeness, had envied Mrs. Mainwaring's charm and wit as well as her handsome clothes and stylish allusions: a woman, an independent woman with a mind of her own and a life of her own (she now ran a gallery that specialised, very profitably, in fashionable surrealism)—what more could one want as a mother? Yet Hugo maintained that as a child she had ignored him, had sent him back to England with relief for schooling, had flirted with him rather than loved him, had kept the wrong kind of distance: he liked to describe the occasion on which she had been to visit him in Cambridge when he was an undergraduate, and as he entertained her to tea, she had glanced around his untidy room and said, quite unselfconsciously, "If I were your mother, I'd tell you to tidy this place up a bit." "But, Mother," Hugo had said, "You *are* my mother," and Mrs. Mainwaring had laughed, happily, throwing back her head, showing off her long throat, amused by herself and her amusing revealing mistake: confident, detached, admired, entire. Poor Hugo.

Mrs. Mainwaring lived by herself in a pretty little house at the end of a cul-de-sac off Knightsbridge. Her husband was dead, and she did not seem much to miss him. Her house was full of paintings and objects on tables and valuable carpets, the bric-a-brac of a life of diplomatic travel: all expensive stuff, unlike the strange medley at Luisa Armstrong's. She had flowers in vases, and understood money. Kate thought she was good fun: maybe Hugo was right, maybe she did expect a great deal of admiration, but why not give it, after all? It cost nothing.

The Fletcher meals in Clacton took place with rigid punctuality, as they had done in Romley; a punctuality even more irrelevant now there was nothing for either of them to do, no appointments for either to keep. On the dot of twelve thirty the chops descended on the willow-pattern plates, accompanied by the invariable two veg. Kate, eating, trying not to watch her father eating, was struck by so acute a sense of inner panic that she was afraid she might cry aloud or start to tear her hair. The routine, the repetition, the sameness. Her father would always start to clear the table before the meal was properly over, producing an extraordinary combined impression of haste and deadly slowness: was this his protest against the sacred routine? If so, it had become part of the routine itself, had become formalised, incorporate. The objects themselves stood on the table as though transfixed in time, congealed in space: the plates, the stainless-steel salt and pepper pots, the bone-handled knives and forks, the spoons, even the very spoon that she and Peter had always sneakily fought to avoid—one with a queasy uncomfortable ripple in its bent handle. The water jugs, the canteen glasses, the wooden napkin rings, the white bowl containing stewed fruit. How could so short a meal take so long? Partly, of course, because they did not make conversation of the sort to which Kate had become accustomed in later years. Not much conversation of a conventional mealtime nature took place in Dacre Road, either, but then meals there were as often as not eaten standing, or with a book or newspaper propped up on the table, in genuine haste or distraction. Hugo had suggested that Kate should try to divert her mind during such ordeals by trying to work out the anthropological or sociological significance of the meal structure, and Kate had tried, but the event continued to defeat her: its imprint lay too heavy in her spirit, too deeply indented, too solid for interpretation. She could interpret easily enough her own disarray, Evelyn's much-disguised formality, the Armstrongs' clan gatherings, Mrs. Mainwaring's unpunctual delays, the various disparate structures of her friends' life styles, but the Fletcher dinner was too much for her. *Why* did she sit there so meekly, so subdued, so silent, with a scream of protest wailing high and inaudible like a bat in her head?

Guilt? Shame? Love? Respect? Fear? No words seemed in any way to approach the reality of the experience, its implacable obviousness. All she knew was that her loathing for stewed fruit verged on the pathological. Hugo said she should reflect on the Cooked and the Raw, but that did not much help her as her teeth met in a sodden apricot. As a child she had found stewed fruit at the worst boring: what sickness had brewed up this increasing disgust? *Why didn't she refuse to accept a helping?* (When she described the apricots to Hugo, he said that she had let the poor dried things swell up with unexpressed resentment, that they were stewed in the juice of subversion, an explanation so fanciful and yet possibly so accurate that even while laughing at it she had been stricken with admiration: "Ah, Hugo," she had said, "if only I had a brain like yours." "You should have tasted," said Hugo, "the dried and martial scraggy chickens of Kurdistan. Not a scrap of spare emotion on those old bones.")

Watching Dad eat was a trial these days. His teeth didn't fit, and he refused to get a new pair, because of some characteristically perverse argument about sticking by the National Health, when anyone knows you can make the National Health provide decent teeth if you try. "You don't have to be the Queen to get good teeth," Kate had argued. But he continued to cluck and chew and sputter and shift them uneasily around his mouth, making the worst of a bad job. (Like me and my bloody boots? thought Kate.) He did it deliberately. (And did her mother cook tough lamb chops instead of shepherd's pie deliberately, come to that?) Dad claimed that it was all the fault of his rotten diet as a boy that his teeth were so bad, and said that Kate and Peter, wartime babies full of orange juice and cod-liver oil, were lucky to have such good choppers. As if that excused anything. Why was he so stubborn? She thought with envy of Sam Goldman and his mother, divided by a culture gap so huge that it ought to be impassable, and yet smiling and embracing over it, laughing and teasing, as though such intimacy were the most natural thing in the world. A deeply ignorant woman, Mrs. Goldman, much more ignorant than Kate's own mother, who had picked up a fine store of information from watching television year in, year out. But in touch, in touch.

And now Peter, despite all, was more in touch with them than she was. Since his breakdown, which he preferred to describe as his "personal revolution," he'd become much bolder at dealing with them. He no longer cared what they thought, would contradict them and ignore them and smoke small cigars all over them, though they both disapproved of smoking and never had any ash trays. He visited them more often than she did, and was much less polite when he got there. No doubt they enjoyed his visits more than they enjoyed hers. What a failure she'd been, after all.

Her feet were swelling, and she unzipped her boots, knowing she'd regret it later, and thought of Peter. There was no denying it, the idea of Peter was inextricably linked in her mind with whatever it was that had gone wrong with her own life. He'd occupied much less of her conscious life than Stuart, Hunt, Evelyn, Ted, Hugo, yet there he was, standing in her mind like a dam in a river. Peter, aged eleven, in his striped pyjamas with their twisted string, pedantically explaining the difference between a Spitfire and a Hurricane. Peter a fat teenager, worrying himself sick, envying Kate her merry life at Romley Fourways, his hair short and neat and carefully parted. Peter at his wedding to June, temporarily thinner, swallowing nervously while June talked and talked and talked. Peter during his worst years as chief buyer at Spotwood's, sixteen stone and depressed, caught between men and management, not up to his job, harassed, learning to talk back in order to drown June's endless chatter. Peter ill, sweating, white as pastry, self-justifying, chucking up his job. (Kate suspected he'd been sacked, but this was never confirmed.) Peter unemployed, "taking himself in hand," as he put it, visiting the doctor, conscientiously losing weight, taking pills for this and that, taking exercise, replanning his life. Taking a job at Dagenham as an engine tester. Starting again. Taking up gardening, jogging, swimming, weight-lifting, evening classes in Spanish and upholstery and home brewing.

The change was startling. Peter in his forties was for the first time a good-looking man, healthy and expansive. He entirely changed his style of dress, abandoning ill-fitting suits for Army jackets with innumerable pockets, trendy two-tone blue shoes with orange stitching, light-hearted caps, check lumberjack shirts. He was tanned all the year round from his outdoor pursuits. He glowed with new vigour and new ideas. Released from office life, responsibility, and middle-class aspirations, his mind wandered happily through articles on microchips, programmes on parapsychology, pub discussions on seed potatoes and East German washing machines. He became a do-it-yourself man, a rebel against technology. "A man who doesn't make mistakes doesn't make anything," he would announce to anyone who wished to hear. He became very keen on the idea of freedom, and believed that the workers were freer than the bosses and middlemen. "If you're a worker, like me," he would say, "your mind's your own, your life's your own." He became fond of comparing his appearance with that of his contemporaries: "Look at them," he would say, "bald, overweight, clapped out at forty, bored stiff, worried to death by their mortgages or their wives, afraid of losing their jobs if they say a wrong word. And look at me! Not a care in the world!"

He was, certainly, a good advertisement for his own philosophy. Fit, cheerful, enterprising, carefree, full of curiosity, more boyish than he had ever been as a boy. Like Kate, he had got his own back at last: like Kate, he had learned to laugh at those who had once teased and tormented him. A successful metamorphosis. Yet it had its drawbacks. His wife June had not much cared for his technical loss of status, and tried to bolster her own sense of importance by clinging to friends who were unmistakably middle-class; she talked in an increasingly refined accent as Peter grew more casual, and made a great play of correct place settings at table, polite little tea parties, visits to concerts. Peter laughed at this, and asked her who she thought she was. But he himself was not the easiest of people, even now. For one thing, he had become as great a talker as June had once been; he would occasionally listen to other people, but much preferred to expound his own views, at great length, to any audience he could capture—in pubs, railway compartments, over the back garden fence. People began to avoid him, as they had once avoided his father. One of Kate's less happy memories of him in recent times was of an evening when he had dropped in on her unexpectedly, an unprecedented occurrence, to find her dishing up supper to an assortment of people including her then lover Patrick of the DHSS, a writer on industrial affairs, and an ex-priest turned teacher: Kate had naturally invited Peter to join them for the meal, and Peter had settled in comfortably and dominated the conversation; he was on his way back from a holiday in Spain, whither he had gone with a group of work mates, and he proceeded to tell them all in great detail about his adventures, about the noise in the discos (even worse than engine testing, and no earmuffs provided), about the local food and wine, about the feebleness of most of his companions who hadn't even tried to speak a word of Spanish, about the swimming, about the man who gave him a lift when he got lost on a walk, about his successful trip through the customs with a bottle of Spanish brandy concealed in a vacuum flask, and another of some oily white liqueur in a Johnson's Baby Oil container. Then, dispensing these liquids generously to the company, he embarked on his Philosophy of Life. Kate abandoned all thought of controlling the conversation, and sat back in despair. The leader writer was in fact quite interested in his views on middle management and the shop floor, and the ex-priest in Peter's change of career in mid-life, so it could have been worse, though the leader writer's wife, a fastidious and intellectual woman of whom Kate had always been rather frightened, did not appear to be much gripped by his narrative. Still, what could Kate do but sit it out and reproach herself for being embarrassed by her own brother? Other people had much worse brothers on the face of it. Ted had a brother who was the dullest man in Britain, an unemployed chemist who lived with his parents and never ever went out or did anything or said anything. Compared with Ted's brother, Peter was quite normal.

Except for the fact that he wrote anonymous letters.

Once, of course, in the far-off mythical past, she had looked up to Peter, and he had looked after her, During the war, according to family history, Peter had refused to be evacuated without Kate (so must have loved her then, so long ago?). Mrs. Fletcher had refused to leave London, less afraid of the bombs than of new places: "I had to stay with Walter, his was priority work," was how she explained this decision. Peter had been evacuated with his school for a brief period, in the initial scare, and then returned when it appeared the bombs weren't going to fall after all; when they began to fall in earnest, he insisted on going with Kate. They went off to Devon, to Great-aunt Martha. Kate remembered the journey; they'd managed to get themselves on the wrong coach at Exeter, despite the labels round their necks, and were rescued by a soldier who spotted them both crying as the names of the towns got more and more unfamiliar. He took them back to Exeter on another bus, and gave them fizzy cherryade and mint imperials before loading them up again. Kate could remember his broad kind face, and the rough texture of his khaki uniform. He had seemed immense, like a giant. He had a kit bag with writing on it, and numbers. A huge figure, he strode through her dreams, the British Army in person, protective, all-powerful, superhuman. The biggest man who had ever lifted her in his arms, with a slow booming voice. A boy, she now supposed he must have been, a country boy of eighteen. Mark's age. The age of Beatrice's dead son.

Aunt Martha lived in a damp little cottage that smelled of plaster and dead leaves and rotten apples. On the first night Kate (who was later to hear dreadful stories in the village of London refugees covered in lice, not knowing about knives and forks, and wetting their beds) wet the bed. She remembered her terror and her shame, and how Peter had stood up for her and said she never did it at home. "What can I do, will it happen again?" Kate whispered to Peter, alarmed most of all by the sneaky mysterious way it had happened while she was utterly unaware and fast asleep—it would have been another matter if she'd just got to the lav late and wet her pants, that happened to everybody and it was always your own fault for hanging on too long. This wasn't your fault, but you were still guilty. Peter, as upset as she was, suggested that she should try not to drink, so for days Kate avoided all fluids, rejecting cups of tea and glasses of water, even avoiding wet looking custard in case it went straight through her as soon as she fell asleep.

Had she missed her Mum? She honestly couldn't remember. She remembered being frightened of Aunt Martha, who was a bad-tempered old lady with an utterly unpredictable set of prohibitions; she was a Plymouth Brother, like Walter's grandfather, and disapproved of the village children, whom she considered ungodly. Kate had no idea what a Plymouth Brother was, but the phrase disturbed her. How could Aunt Martha be a Brother when she was clearly a woman? And what did Plymouth mean? Was it something to do with plumbing, the only word Kate knew that had any remotely similar ring? Or pumping, perhaps? Before meeting Great-aunt Martha, Kate had formed a frightening picture of her, drawn from composite sources, of a semi-human, semi-mechanical figure, half man, half woman, with stiff, straight, tubular arms like pump handles that could be moved up and down: a sinister form, angular, severe, rigid. (Her father's dislike of the faith of his forefathers must have made itself real to her even at this early age.) The reality of Aunt Martha proved different, but she was nevertheless not a homey woman, though she tried hard.

There was, in fact, a real pump at Aunt Martha's, which provided the cottage's drinking water. It stood round the back, against the kitchen wall, facing the vegetable garden. Kate loved this pump, and loved filling the white enamel blue-rimmed jugs for her Aunt. It was magical; you swung on the handle, and out spurted thin gushes of clear water, water that tasted of lead and stone and sun. She also liked the gooseberry bushes and black-currant bushes and carrots. Less attractive was the outside lav at the bottom of the garden path, for it was full of creepy-crawlies and spiders, things that seemed all right in the open air, but which took on a nasty menace in a small confined space. Peter didn't mind them, and would try to clear them out before Kate went, but they always outwitted him. Kate could remember sitting there, not exactly terrified but profoundly unhappy, watching small squat-bodied creatures and long-legged pinheaded creatures trampling round her. She dreamed of them walking on her face. Once Peter, in less protective mood, had cruelly told her a story about a girl who fell into a bog and had her eyes stitched up by spiders.

(When Kate was discussing with Hugo the question of why insects were all right out of doors but not so good indoors, he told her she ought to read Mary Douglas's *Purity and Danger*, but she never got round to it. He confessed himself baffled, however, by her childhood partiality for snails, which she and Peter used to keep in a shoe box and feed with leaves. "If one could work out why you were frightened of spiders but not of snails, why I was frightened of bats, why I like piccalilli and you like tomato ketchup and sandwich spread, we'd have the key to the universe or at least to a bloody good book," said Hugo.)

Kate didn't fall into a bog, but she did manage to fall off an iron railing, and thus to get herself and Peter sent home. The railing was just outside the entrance to the school playground: one of those obstacles intended to prevent children from rushing straight across the street. The village children used to do forward and backward somersaults over this bar, and Kate, competitive in spirit, thought she would do the same, though she had no idea of the technique involved, and was much younger and smaller than the local gymnasts. She climbed up, swung forward, and, to her astonishment, instead of turning neatly through the gap and ending up on her feet again, like the others did, she simply crashed down onto her head. She must have let go. She was very surprised and very cross. What on earth could have gone wrong? This interested her much more than the fact that she was dripping with blood from a large graze on her head.

Aunt Martha was not so philosophical. She sent the children home, declaring she could not cope with the strain.

I suppose, thought forty-year-old Kate sitting on the hot scrubby grass of London, I suppose it's just possible I did it because I really wanted to go home. Is that what a psychiatrist would say? And if it's true, why can't I *remember* wanting to go home?

The truth is, she thought, I no longer trust any of my memories. I've lost faith in them. I thought they all made sense, that there was a nice bright straight pattern, a nice conscious clear pattern. I thought I fell off that rail because I wanted to prove myself. But maybe I've got it all wrong. Maybe there's some other darker pattern, something utterly different. And if so, why can't I *see it?*

How hot it was. She rolled back the sleeves of her jersey, looked at her watch. It was time to move on.

Had their parents welcomed them back? She had no idea. But did recall that Peter's misery dated from this homecoming. He'd lost his friends at school, had been squeezed out, and somehow never got in again. That was when the teasing began, when he began to withdraw, grow fat.

Had she begun to despise him? No, surely not. Her heart had bled for him. She had longed to protect him, to fight for him, as he had protected her, but she was too young, and a girl. He had abandoned her to the wild ones, exposed her to ridicule, but he suffered more than she. She nourished revenge. She could remember trotting along Arblay Street, running the gauntlet of whistles and mocking cries, and saying inside herself, with complete confidence, You *wait*, I'll *show* you, you'll *see* who *wins* in the *end*.

How did she know she had anything to show them *with?*

The more Peter buried himself in books and aeroplane kits, the less Kate read, the less constructive became her pursuits. Why?

Was it because I didn't want to compete? Did I stand down, leave him the field? If that's what I did do, what a bloody awful mistake it was, look what I've done to him now. I should have come clean then. Instead of playing this backhanded game. This sinister female game.

The dirty, tangled roots of childhood twisted back forever and ever, beyond all knowing. Impacted, interwoven, scrubby, interlocked, fibrous, cankerous, tuberous, ancient, matted. Back in the artificial pleasure ground, the dear, solitary, carefully nurtured groups of saplings stood and shivered in loneliness, straight and slim, sad and forlorn. Their roots in artificial loam, reared in artificial fibre pots, carefully separate. Tastefully arranged, fruitlessly deployed.

Kate heaved herself to her feet, resolving to walk back and call at the estate information office before making her way back into Romley. Beneath her feet the water flowed. Well, perhaps so close an infantile connection with sewage would be bound to have some effect on the psyche?

Her heel would last the day. She should never have worn such boots for a day on foot, for, apart from the wobbling heel, the height pitched her forwards onto her toes, and her toes were aching, as though creased at the wrong angle. (Which they were.)

Madness, yes, well, Peter was certainly not one of its more extreme manifestations. People got much worse than Peter, and did much worse things. Take Sally Jackson, for example. Sally had been a classic case, one of those women who revert to eating their own shit in middle age in complete collapse. A trendy psychiatrist, an acquaintance of Kate's, had cured her by trendy loving means. Sally had taken the long journey back over the dark rivers of Lethe, Styx, and Acheron, and had crossed back to the other side of daylight and life. But for what, frankly? For what? Nobody wanted to know the resurrected adult Sally. Certainly the trendy psychiatrist who had cured her didn't want to know her. No Orpheus awaited her. She couldn't do anything clever, like Mary Barnes, who became a painter. She was just a dull woman who had missed out on life. There are plenty of those around without rescuing more from the madhouse. The trendy psychiatrist had tried to palm dull Sally off on motherly Kate, and Kate had done her best, but failed. She couldn't get on with Sally, Sally was a moaner and a time-waster. The trendy psychiatrist continued to feel pleased with himself, Kate felt ashamed and a failure, Sally felt ashamed for having upset Kate, and went off to live in St. Albans with her aunt. A sorry tale.

Eating shit. No doubt it all had something to do with the anal phase, whatever that was. And pot training. Wasn't homosexuality supposed to have something to do with all that too? Was Peter a latent homosexual? Certainly his wife June was a very odd woman. And they had no children. Oh dear, oh dear, thought Kate, waving again at the workmen, the trouble is, anything *could* mean anything. Or its opposite. She trod firmly on her loosening heel, driving the nails back to their homes. Sanity and madness. Well, certainly, sanity is a precarious state, a thin ridge, a tightrope. However do most of us keep upright? Like tightrope walkers, by not looking to either side, I suppose, like horses in blinkers. I should never have looked. I should never have looked, I should never have looked.

As Kate sat on the bank, Evelyn sat in her car in a traffic jam near Finsbury Park, gazing meditatively at the cheap shop fronts advertising perpetual Closing Down Sales and Special Offers, at the banked garbage in black bags, at the dirty pavements, at a stall offering Selected Fruit. (Selected, in this district, meant selected for cheapness, not quality.) Was it getting worse, or was it that she was getting older? she asked herself, as thousands of Londoners ask themselves each day. Though this had never been a good area, or not in her lifetime. The conglomeration of textures and surfaces, all glinting dully in the sun, had a certain beauty, and a varied richness: if hung on the wall of the Tate or the Serpentine, one would perceive them as beautiful, so why not make an effort and try now? Pockmarked sooty bricks, mica-chipped cement, corrugated-iron hoardings plastered with posters, peeling wooden doors, drainpipes dripping with green moss. Craters in the road, abandoned by workmen, revealed greening copper taps and subterranean pipes covered with strange khaki grease-covered rags. Soft bulging plastic garbage bags stood side by side with rigid ribbed grey dustbins. The pavement was ornamented with grey-green cellar skylights of thick glass, with iron manhole covers, with a crazy mixture of paving stones and kerb stones, and the road itself, painted with hieroglyphs of road signs in white and yellow, was an interesting assortment of colours—black sweating tarmac, grey chips, against a background predominantly pink, a dark granitic dusty pink. A delicate mélange, well weathered.

She looked up at the shops as her car edged forwards. A Greek Cypriot grocer spoke to passers-by in Greek, a large old-fashioned butcher announced Lean English Shoulders, Ox-cheek, and a Bargain Tray, an Indian supermarket offered Oriental spices. A mysterious boarded façade announced Foam Bargains, whatever they might be. A barrel of salted pigs' tails stood outside the West Indian shop. A Herbal Remedy shop selling contraceptives and rubber appliances was squeezed into an improbable small sloping space between the West Indians and a shabby Community Health Centre, an unhygienic-looking dump with a flyblown window stuck with DHSS pamphlets and an amateur drawing of a coughing man in a cloth cap wheezing out a great balloon with the unsubtle message CIGARETTES CAN KILL inscribed within it. Beyond that, a temporary fence shielding a permanent building site was adorned with posters for pop groups, featuring a lurid display of images—a huge eye floating in a saucer, a giant target-striped tit, a doll in a coffin, a three-toned snake, a witch on a broomstick, a London bus, the Venus de Milo, a tombstone. What charming names the groups had these days—The Necrophiliacs, The Jam, The Scum, Medea and her Babes, Sore Throat. Evelyn's eye lighted on what looked like a particularly nasty new invention called Baby Seal Slaughter, but closer inspection proved it to be an advertisement for a protest demo at Hyde Park Corner. Evelyn had noticed herself, of late, to be prone to such misreadings: the day before in the hospital she'd had two within two minutes—first she'd read a sign in the lift that seemed to say INFIRM OPERATOR, a slightly chilling notion, and on leaving the lift she'd been confronted by a sign on a hospital notice board that through some peculiarity of the typography appeared to read RENT-A-RAT, instead of RENT-A-FLAT. Evelyn had actually started seriously to wonder, as she walked down the corridor, what anyone could want to rent a rat for, and had recalled a recent case in the paper of a man who'd bought some rats from a sewer worker to shove through the letter-box of his ex-mistress's house. They had eaten up her settee and chewed the wires connecting her washing machine. She smiled to herself, remembering this: she must remember to tell Kate. Kate liked such stories.

The jam moved; she lurched forwards another few yards. One might go quite mad, one's eyes thus assaulted all day long. Evelyn's sister Josephine had just bought, with her husband, a farm in Pembrokeshire, whither she intended to move shortly. What would it be like to find one's daily imagery translated into trees and fields and sheep and hedges? Would it be good for the soul? Evelyn herself, particularly when weary, had fantasies of moving to the country, of getting away from all this, of resigning altogether and digging her own garden. What could one expect but delinquency, of children reared amidst such prospects? What images could one expect them to create for themselves? No wonder they dressed in battledress, adorned with plate armour of badges on their bosoms and clinking chain mail of staples and safety pins and paper clips. Each day they went into battle, along their own streets. Her own daughter Vicky was not exempt. Vicky had acquired a strange new habit of walking around the house with a pair of open scissors. She hadn't yet got round to mutilating the furniture, but she had started on herself, chopping her fingernails until they bled, and then binding them up with decorative green sticking plaster. Crazy. What would Vicky have been, had she attended Evelyn's nice boarding school in the nice countryside, with its nice playing fields and shrubberies and blackberry excursions? It was too late now.

An old man, bent almost double, coughed and spat as he passed. The glob of spittle gleamed, iridescent, blue and purple and green, on the pavement, next to a strange discarded lump of bright orange chemical wadding, the sort of stuff that is used to pad cheap upholstery. Evelyn stared. She had once read, years ago, of a woman—a saint, a madwoman,

Simone Weil, St. Catherine of Siena?—who had forced herself to swallow a gob of spit, as a humiliation of the flesh. A useless but glorious act, like the saints who had sucked the abscesses of the sick, and embraced the lepers, imagining that in so doing they sucked the bleeding wounds of Christ. Evelyn had always been tempted by such masochistic displays. And, indeed, what was she up to herself, but rubbing her nose in the dirt, when, like Josephine, she could have been living peacefully on her husband's income, far from the dirt and noise, amidst the green pastures, by clear waters?

> Not forever by green pastures
> Would I idly rest and stray,

Evelyn hummed to herself. Hard to know what kept her at it in this way.

Her mind wandered back to the evening before, an evening which had promised well, and which had indeed proved interesting. For once, she had managed to assemble both children for a meal, as well as one of Vicky's friends, and an old school friend of her own whom she had not seen in years. Ted was away, in India, at a conference. All seemed to be going well when, while Evelyn was in the middle of carving a shoulder of lamb, a notoriously tricky operation, she had been summoned to the telephone by none other than Ted's woman in Cambridge, to whom Evelyn had never spoken, and to whom she had little wish to speak. She wanted to know where Ted was. Evelyn said that Ted was in India, and the woman in Cambridge accused her of lying. From this, Evelyn concluded that Ted had got tired of the woman in Cambridge, and she tried to sound sympathetic, but guessed she had failed, for the woman rang off.

The interruption was unfortunate, for it dissipated her concentration not only on the lamb, but also on the conversation, and by the time she had finished hacking the meat to pieces and distributed the roast potatoes and courgettes, things had begun to get out of hand. Her friend Stella had been politely questioning Sebastian about his school, and had been met with a muttered tirade of obscure direction, mostly inaudible; Vicky and her friend Puss had tried to help out by a recital of their own activities, which, despite their good intentions, had taken on a lurid tinge. "You don't mean to say that the staff allow you to do that *on the premises?*" Stella was saying, as Evelyn came back from the kitchen with the forgotten onion sauce, a query which threw both girls into giggles. "Oh, they don't mind what we do," Vicky said, and proceeded to give illustrations, until checked by Evelyn.

"It's not really as bad as that," said Evelyn. "They exaggerate, you know."

"Mum, you don't know half," said Sebastian.

"No, and I don't want to," said Evelyn.

And so it had gone on. Puss, as a guest, had taken Evelyn's part, and Evelyn began to see why Kate always maintained that Puss, despite her name and her curious appearance, was a really nice girl—she was a large, broad-faced girl, with long black ropes of hair, and a curiously innocent, kind, bland expression which belied her billowing white paint-stained grandad shirt, her punk badges, her big boots. (Puss, Kate maintained, was very mature for her age, astonishingly mature in view of, or perhaps because of, her violent home life: Kate had once been deeply moved to see Puss walking down Camden High Street all alone swinging her canvas bag, with a purposeful, even padding pace, all alone like a grown woman, a vision of independence, for one hardly ever saw these girls alone, they were always in a gang, moving in droves. But there had been Puss, all by herself, walking unarmed and innocent through the dangers of the world, her child's face serene, unmarked by the deadly struggles for custody of her parents, by the ravages of London, by waits at dark bus stops and panics in telephone boxes, by lost keys and locked doors and stolen bicycles.) And here was Puss at Evelyn's dinner table, smiling in a calming manner, eating her lamb at lightning speed but with evident pleasure, her large bosom swelling strongly and powerfully beneath her shirt, placid, healthy, unperturbed, shaking her head deprecatingly like a fond adult as Vicky proceeded to describe the people she met at the pub and the troubles they got into, which made school life in comparison seem orderly; or that seemed to be the point of Vicky's narration.

Vicky had been going out lately with a young man who worked as a guard on the Underground. He looked alarmingly youthful, with pale spiky hair and an earring in one ear, and he seemed to have taken on himself the task of jazzing up London Transport single-handed, a task for which he seemed to Evelyn to lack the necessary strength of character and stamina: he was always in trouble about his clothes and appearance, and had so far achieved the distinction of a photograph in the *Evening Standard,* standing up to a threat of dismissal for his rights to dress as he pleased. (Vicky had met him in his tube train: he'd been eating an apple, and Vicky had asked for a bite.) When Evelyn had voiced some mild queries about him, Vicky had retorted that Vic was a hopeless case, right, but then Evelyn spent her life looking after hopeless cases, right, and why couldn't she, Vicky, do the same, right? in a more practical manner, right? And Evelyn had ceased to enquire, for frankly she was so relieved that Vicky had friends at all that she was willing to condone or encourage any or all of them. Sebastian had few friends: he was a solitary, locked in adolescent misery. Bad company is better than none, Evelyn had concluded: she had been lonely herself and knew what it felt like. Her concern for Sebastian was by far the most painful emotion she had ever known, and she had coped with it so badly, so foolishly—trying to buy him friends by handing out large quantities of pocket money, trying to buy him off petty thieving by offering him a hi-fi, motorbikes, whatever he wanted. A disastrous course, as she had known it would be, but those who are good at helping others are not necessarily very good at helping themselves.

The revelation of her family's peculiarities before Stella

was not what she had planned, and Stella, who now lived near Worcester, proved easy to alarm, a good audience. When the children finally slouched off to listen to records or hack at their fingers, she and Stella settled down to coffee and compared notes.

Stella, it emerged, had been alarmed: she had heard nasty stories about London schools and London life, and Vicky's stories had tended to confirm them. On the other hand, she told Evelyn, country life was not necessarily an answer, and it would be a mistake for Evelyn to imagine that one could evade the twentieth century by living in Worcester or by sending one's children to school in Dorset. The Orkney Islands, maybe, or maybe even Pembrokeshire, said Stella, but Worcester and Dorset, definitely not. She herself had three children, all away at school, the eldest a girl and, like Sebastian, extremely difficult, the middle one unnaturally docile and hard-working, the youngest a little monkey who managed to charm everyone but Stella (said Stella with a worried smile, clearly not immune to charm). Stella was married to a solicitor, and lived in a large and comfortable house in stockbroker land, with an orchard and two garages and a tennis court: Stella herself worked part-time as a physiotherapist. It sounded like an orderly life; but, Stella said, it was not. The orchards and tennis courts and swimming pools of the West Midlands were no longer the Garden of Eden, had they ever been so. The youth of the district might not look as bizarre as Vic, Vicky, Puss, and Sebastian, but their activities were no more innocent, and they were, if anything, more mercenary, for there was no counter-affectation of working-class culture to keep their aspirations in check. Their pursuits were expensive, the competition intense. Amongst the friends of Stella's children was one whose father had a private aeroplane, on which he would offer trips to Deauville on weekends: one whose father owned a chain of pizza houses and a racehorse: another whose family thought nothing of nipping over to New York by Concorde for a party. With parents like that to set the pace, how could one expect one's children to moderate their demands for electric guitars, ponies, evening dresses ("They still wear them in the country," said Stella, smiling faintly), ski suits, sports cars? "Of course, we try to be firm, indeed we have to be firm because we can't afford not to be, but it's heavy going," said Stella.

Stella, like Evelyn, came from a good solid hard-working middle-class family, and had been reared on notions of thrift, prudence, propriety. The school which they had both attended had been chosen to encourage these virtues, though Stella had married against the grain: her husband Bob was an easy spender, a golf and gin-and-tonic man. Stella at school had been a gawky lively unfeminine girl, interested in hockey and youth-hostelling; a girl with a broad face, poor skin, a determined chin, and powerful calves. Her appearance had improved with the years; she was now handsome, well turned out. But also restless, dissatisfied. It was partly the work, she told Evelyn—she was tired of being a second-class employee, the hospital didn't think much of physiotherapy, though of course it had to pretend to, and her husband didn't like her to work, although now the children were older and away at school and he couldn't find any sensible objections. "I didn't really want to be a physiotherapist," said Stella, "I wanted to be a doctor, like my father, but I couldn't cope with the maths and the chemistry. But, looking back, I don't see why not— was it the school, do you think? I meet these doctors now, and, frankly, I know I'm at least as intelligent as half of them —I mean, I'm not an intellectual like you, Evelyn, I never wanted to be, but I'm not thick; if they can get through, so could I have done."

Had it indeed been the school? They discussed the fate of old school friends, most of them housewives now, though some had pursued careers in medicine, nursing, teaching. The caring professions, the women's professions. The school had laid great emphasis on service, on religion, on the community, but it had not taught its pupils to aim high. Both of them, they agreed, still believed in service, in living, a little, for others. "What else can one believe in?" asked Evelyn, rhetorically. Evelyn called herself a Christian, though Stella said she no longer believed; her greatest pleasure in life was singing in a choir connected with the cathedral—the *Messiah*, Verdi's *Requiem*—but she sang without faith. Art for art's sake. Neither had brought their children up to be religious; Evelyn felt she could not impose her views on others, particularly as Ted, an ardent Darwinian, found Christianity ridiculous. "Ridiculous it may be," said Evelyn, "but people did behave better when they believed, didn't they? Or didn't they?" They talked of the social workers' strike, of striking teachers, nurses, ambulance workers. Stella herself, though she voted Tory, had come out on strike when called upon by her union the year before: "What else could I do?" she asked. "I felt I had to." Evelyn's own council had not yet been affected. She had been spared decision. "Do you think nuns and clergymen will start striking soon?" asked Stella, and they both laughed, relieved to be able to voice their disquiet without a hostile audience, far from the *Daily Telegraph* and the picket line. If one believed in the efficacy of prayer, should one withdraw one's prayers for the sick, in the hope of a pay rise?

"I simply can't get over the idea that self-denial is good for one," said Evelyn. "Do you remember that fund at school, the Self-Denial Fund? We had to pay in sixpence of our pocket money a week. It was obligatory, not a choice. Ridiculous, of course, but maybe not a bad thing. Raising money for wells in India, knitting blankets for victims of Turkish earthquakes. Nowadays charity is so professional, the kids get these silly stickers and badges from rival organisations, all at one another's throats all the time—Help the Aged, Age Concern, Anti-Nazis, Oxfam, War on Want, Task Force, National Council of Civil Liberties (NCCL), Child Poverty Action Group (CPAG), all bickering away in public. No wonder they think they're being ripped off. They are. And so were we, I suppose."

"And the *junk* and the *mess* and the *gear*," said Stella, who had the week before sorted out the boxes in the old playroom for a jumble sale. "Broken toys, toys hardly touched or played with, but broken nevertheless. When they were little, they never put the tops on their felt-tip pens, they wasted beautiful pads of drawing paper, they let expensive modelling clay dry out—and yet they always wanted more, more boxes of paints, more beautiful pads, more clay. And I throw things away myself too, these days. Toasters, hair-dryers. When I was little, I remember how I longed and longed for a box of Derwent Lakeland coloured pencils—you remember them? Those big boxes of beautiful colours with a picture of the Lake District on. And I asked for a box for my birthday, and my mother said they were too expensive."

"Do you remember Glitterwax?" asked Evelyn. Yes, they both remembered Glitterwax.

"Oh, I don't know, we're being ridiculous," said Stella, "it's just that we forget what untidy messy creatures we used to be, and we've got a different time perspective, we expect things to last for years, but to a child, a month seems a long time. Last holidays, my seventeen-year-old said to me, did I remember that when she was little I used to draw little houses and apple trees for her, and she used to colour them in. I'd forgotten, but she'd remembered. She said she used to be very happy colouring in. And I couldn't remember that she'd ever done anything as nice and quiet and constructive as colouring in, or that I'd ever been an attentive enough mother with enough time to draw little houses and apple trees. . . . Now I haven't even time to nag them to pick their clothes up off the floor."

Ah well, such poignant memories, Derwent pencils, Glitterwax, thought Evelyn, as the traffic moved slowly forwards again, bringing her alongside a large spray-can message on a wall which read in letters three feet high: HAPPY BIRTHDAY WENDY several times over. She and Stella had laughed a lot at their own reactionary complaints. The diseases of affluence.

Spray-can art. One was supposed to admire it, these days. One had better admire it, there was little else to admire. Affluence was certainly not the major problem of the mothers at the day-care centre which was her morning's destination, but affluence, nevertheless, had affected their lives; it had set up for them impossible dreams in television advertisements, in hoardings like the ones that loomed over her, beyond the reach of spray cans, portraying happy families eating Danish bacon, glamorous women on tiger skins eating Colman's mustard, dizzy half-clad girls consuming tots of rum and an ominous new variety of pink martini, handsome men standing in the middle of trout streams smoking menthol cigarettes. It had filled them with feelings of failure and rancour and despair, and it was affecting the staff that ran the centre, too. The social workers' strike had not yet hit the district, but the younger staff at the centre were threatening to come out in support of a colleague who had been made redundant. Despite the fact that for months they had been complaining that if this particular colleague didn't leave, they would, so impossible did they find her to work with. "It's the principle of the thing," they told Evelyn. What a muddle, what a mess.

The day-care centre was a large shabby Victorian house in one of London's most forlorn streets; it faced the high brick wall of a railway siding, on one side was an ink factory, and on the other a mean stretch of decaying, almost derelict, turn-of-the-century terrace houses. Evelyn found the door double-locked, despite the new open-door-for-mothers policy which its new matron Joan Kingsley was trying to encourage. She rang the bell. It was opened by Mrs. Oakley, one of the old guard, who had been hand-in-glove with the redundant Janice Ash. Mrs. Oakley was not too pleased to see Evelyn, who had arrived, deliberately, unannounced. Mrs. Oakley was one of those who liked everything to be tidy for visits, quiet, regimented, with children sitting quietly doing nothing much; to her, a silent child was a good child, and she could not adapt to Evelyn's and Joan's view that a certain amount of noise was healthy and desirable. Nor could she take the mess. She could not prevent herself from wiping up paint, from whisking dough and plasticine away as soon as she could, from forcibly and somewhat brutally wiping snotty noses every few minutes. She complained about the smell of the hamster and rabbits, and thought the wormery disgusting. She did not like children, and liked the mothers even less: Joan Kingsley's attempts to encourage those that could to spend time at the centre with their children filled her with disapproval, and she rejoiced, not too secretly, when thefts and vandalism made it necessary to keep cupboards and doors locked. "These mothers, they're not fit to go near their own children," Mrs. Oakley had roundly declared at a staff meeting. "They wander in here, smoking, dropping litter, tramping in mud, they upset the children, teach them bad habits, bad language, they don't seem to have any control. . . ."

It was true that many of the parents were not models of parental behaviour, but that was why the children were in the center in the first place, wasn't it?

Evelyn had once, unobserved, seen Mrs. Oakley forcing a child to finish its lunch. The child, a three-year-old West Indian, had been too frightened to cry, but also too frightened to swallow. Mrs. Oakley held the back of the child's neck with one hand, and forced the spoon into her mouth with the other. The child's mouth had puckered, the food had gone in, the child had gagged, and all the time she had stared up at Mrs. Oakley with a wide wild look of horror in her white eyes. The food had dribbled down again onto the plate, and Mrs. Oakley, refraining from administering an actual slap, had shaken her by the shoulder, and scooped up the expelled mouthful, and started again. Evelyn heard the spoon clank against her teeth, and had heard Mrs. Oakley say, "Now get on with it, Ruby, I haven't got all day, if you don't eat up this nice dinner you'll get shut up in a cupboard tomorrow with no nice dinner, and no toys, and no one to hear you. . . ."

Evelyn, at this point, had stepped forward, and the little scene had come to an end.

Ironically, many of the mothers shared Mrs. Oakley's views on force-feeding. Which was why the children had feeding problems in the first place. A circular problem, caring for the deprived.

What was the point in confronting people like Mrs. Oakley or the vanished Janice Ash? No wonder Joan Kingsley preferred working with pleasant people like Carol and the young man called Dolf, who greeted Evelyn as she made her way through the pram-littered vestibule. Carol and Dolf were drinking coffee, and they raised their mugs in half-hearted salute. "Hi," said Carol. "Have a coffee," said Dolf. Dolf was a dreamy young man who had once been an actor, who claimed to love kids, though according to Ash and Oakley he spent half his time drinking coffee, a quarter of it drinking beer or wine, and the other quarter working the kids into a state of frenzy by playing games that sounded to Evelyn like psychodrama, though psychodrama was not a concept with which Ash and Oakley were familiar. Now he was contemplating strike action on behalf of Miss Ash. Joan Kingsley thought Dolf was a good thing, and so, no doubt, he was: but muddled, muddled. Why can't people be both flexible *and* efficient? thought Evelyn, not for the first time, as she avoided a truck on wheels pushed by a manic toddler, and made her way into one of the large playrooms. It really wasn't impossible to combine the two.

Mrs. Oakley would have approved of swaddling, had she been born only a century earlier. Babies tightly wrapped and bundled and hung from hooks in rows, as they had been in Russia. It upset Evelyn to think of past generations of child abuse. However had the human race survived?

The children were variously engaged, some painting, some making Playdo sausages, some brawling in the Wendy House. Those who knew Evelyn stopped what they were doing and rushed at her, clutching at her knees, wiping their noses on her skirt. She picked up one, then another, and hugged them and squeezed them. They could never get enough of hugging. Damien, a large four-year-old, asked her to play Fly Away Peter, Fly Away Paul, which was Evelyn's most successful party piece, so she sat down and played: sticking bits of paper on the backs of her fingers, reciting the little rhyme, watching the children's astonishment as Peter and Paul flew away and came back again. They could never work out how it was done, it was a recurrent miracle, and Evelyn smiled proudly, touched as ever by their enthusiastic and amazed response. It was, in fact, quite a good game for sorting out children—some were hardly interested, so astonishing and unpredictable and bewildering did they find the whole of life, others were fascinated but content to wonder, and one or two, like Damien, were desperate to know *how*. "*How* d'you do it, Evelyn?" he asked again and again, leaning heavily on her knee as she sat at the tiny table on a tiny chair, pressing into her, breathing into her, breathing her up, warm hands kneading her, beseeching, as she laughed and did it again. She wouldn't tell him: she thought he preferred not to know. Should she tell him, one day? Should she take him aside into the story corner and impart the secret? Or would he then be disappointed, would her magic have gone? Perhaps on graduation day, when he was ready to move on to primary school? She did it once more, then detached his clinging fingers and squashed him and squeezed him once more, and said she had to go and talk to Joan. She loved them, she loved the feel of them, it was like having her own small again, but, like her own at the same age, they filled her with a terrible boredom after half an hour, whereas the staff had to look after them all day, every day, no wonder they got restless. . . .

   She finally tracked Joan Kingsley down in the music room, mending a tambourine, surrounded by yet more infants. "We'd better go into the office," said Joan, so off they went, and Evelyn listened to her expert account of staff warfare, new alliances, new insults, old grievances. Mrs. Oakley, abused by Sharon's Mum, had threatened to resign. (If only she *would*, both women murmured simultaneously.) Baby Kent's Mum, Diane, had arrived with a black eye and stitches in her nose ("Yes, in her *nose*, it looks awful"), clutching Baby (this child had never been named, seemed set to remain Baby all its life, despite many helpful suggestions), saying she'd never go back to her flat while that madman was in it, and was at that moment sitting on a giant beanbag in a corner of the upstairs nursery rocking Baby backwards and forwards to a litany of obscenities. She would, of course, go home: Baby's putative Dad was one of the few Dads who ever took any notice of his so-called wife and offspring, and between bouts of violence and prison behaved well enough to earn Diane's loyalty. Most seriously, little Harry had arrived with a nasty-looking bruise on his face. Harry was on the non-accidental-injuries register, a borderline case, and Evelyn and Joan spent much time worrying about whether or not he should be taken into care. His mother, an obese young woman, had gone into a tirade yesterday, said Joan, about the fact that Harry had forgotten her birthday, and hadn't got her a card. As Harry was only three, this did not seem a surprising omission, but his Mum had taken it badly. She was a very simple creature, a child herself in mentality. She was forever betraying her own dependence, unwittingly. She needed Harry: he was all she had. "I think you should visit," Joan told Evelyn. The whooping-cough scare had proved only a scare: so that was one good thing.

Joan, thought Evelyn, shutting herself back into the safety of her car, is something of a saint. All that, every day, and at the end of every day both mothers and children would do their best to prevent her from leaving the building. She did hours of overtime. What would happen when even Joan had had enough?

Joan had once said that the mothers resented the fact that she, Joan, had a proper home and a proper husband to return to. And must Joan herself not also resent my bigger home, my comparative freedom of movement, my more varied round, my higher salary? Joan's husband was a nice man who worked for the Child Poverty Action Group. He did not earn very much, and neither did Joan. Ted was not a nice man, but he earned a lot.

Oh, marriage is a funny business, thought Evelyn, as she decided to fit in a quick bacon sandwich for lunch before her next visit. Stirring a cup of strong tea, she thought of Stella and Bob and their tennis court, of the woman crying in Cambridge, of Kate, who believed that marriage was the root of all evil. "Marriage is warfare," Kate declared, "how could it be anything else?"

Or had Kate said that so often over the years as a promise to Evelyn that she didn't really want Ted, and wouldn't steal him even if she could?

Evelyn bit into her sandwich, encountering a white shiny knob of gristle. The bread and marge was limp and heavy with cooling brown grease.

Marriage, for-better-or-worse; in Evelyn's mind, it had a kind of admirable cracked solidity, a worn peacefulness, like an old white plate. Why throw it away when it still served? Why change for change's sake? She was used to Ted, and he to her. There was even something comforting about the cracks: something sweet, familiar, sanctified by use.

And Ted would never have married Kate, in any circumstances. He had loved her in his own way, no doubt (Evelyn shut her mind to what this love might have entailed), but he didn't want to live with her. He wanted a big house with polished floors, and a wife who could and would cook dinner for his colleagues. He wanted Banham locks on his doors and double glazing and even, God help him, a garage for his car. He wanted, on one level at least, Evelyn. A life with Kate would not have suited him at all. She was too disorganised for him; he could never have taken the constant flux of her home, the lack of regular meals, the wild opinions, the eccentric outbursts, the haphazard hospitality, the Hunts and Mujids and

Stuarts with which Kate surrounded herself. The drinking companions, the riff-raff, the spongers, the lunatics. The horrible noise of pop music which she permitted her children to play. Kate even affected to like this music, a taste which Evelyn found incomprehensible, and had of late struck up a kind of friendship with two members of a gay group called Black Ice, who loafed about from time to time eating large cheese sandwiches and showing off to the children. Evelyn herself disliked this aspect of Kate. Trendy in the worst sense; time-serving.

Kate had once said to her, "The thing is, Evelyn, I actually *prefer* hopeless people, whereas you want to help them and stop them being hopeless." And, being Kate, she had gone on to say,. "Of course, I realise I probably like them because they make me feel I've got the upper hand, they make me feel big, they make me feel I run the show. You don't need to feel big, Evelyn, you're so much stronger than me."

Well, yes.

Smeared cups, chipped saucers, dirty cats sitting under tables. Kate didn't mind these things. The companionable gutter, herself playing at slumming? Ted hated the way Kate let her cat walk about the kitchen table, lick plates, sleep in beds. Or so he told Evelyn.

Mrs. Oakley, savagely wiping children's faces with fierce wet cloths. Suddenly Evelyn remembered her own mother, thirty years ago, washing her hair as she had done every Friday night, screwing the damp hair up into a towel turban, but tightly, tightly, till the small hairs at the nape of her neck tweaked and her eyes filled with tears. Punitive, satisfied. Leaden nipples, swaddling clothes, liberty bodices, straitjackets.

The café was far from clean. A mistake. A ginger cat with only three legs waited for bacon rind. The woman through the hatch frying sausages was gross, greasy, her hair straying into the food. Evelyn found a hair in her sandwich, and could not finish it. Which was perhaps just as well, for on her next visit she was offered a slice of excellent homemade sponge by Mrs. Meer, and was able to accept with unfeigned pleasure. None of the day-care-centre mothers could make cakes: neither could most of Evelyn's friends, come to that, and she herself had abandoned that habit as soon as the children no longer wanted to play at baking. Mrs. Meer's cake was light and filled with homemade jam, how different from the friendly offerings she had to accept from some of her clients, some of them almost as unpalatable as the sheep's heads, dried grubs, and fried locusts of which Hugo, when in the mood, could tell such amusing stories. Tea so strong you could stand your spoon up in it, ancient biscuits tasting of death extracted with gnarled and quivering fingers from old lacquered tea caddies, slices of shop-made pink-iced pink-tasting cake cut straight from the cardboard, once a bun from the corner bakery (homemade, its presenter had smugly claimed, with a fine disregard of the rather obvious meaning of the words) which had contained a sticky sweet filling full of globs of what seemed to be blue-grey unblended Vaseline. Not that one was ever anything other than grateful for these offerings, when the alternative was a slammed door, or worse. One of Evelyn's colleagues had had a pot of tea thrown at her face, only the other day.

No, Mrs. Meer was an ideal client, in fact more an old friend than a client. Her life story was one of awesome tragedy and immense fortitude; half coloured, she had come to London from South Africa just after the war with her Afrikaans husband to start a new life. Within six months he had died, leaving her with three children and a fourth on the way. Not an easy start, but she had made the best of it, and now the three oldest children were launched, well established, with jobs, husbands, wives, children. Only the fourth was a nuisance, lounging around at home, one of the great army of unemployed. Evelyn, who had ostensibly called to sort out some complication with Mrs. Meer's Widow's Pension and her National Insurance Card (she worked as an office cleaner, unearthly hours but a short day), listened to Colin's latest misdemeanours with deep sympathy.

"You should kick him out," she said, finally. "You make it too nice for him here, Mrs. Meer."

"I keep telling him he'll have to go, but he doesn't listen, he just laughs. And I wouldn't mind so much, Mrs. Stennett, if it weren't for the language. Such language, from my own child."

"He doesn't mean it," said Evelyn. "It's the way they all talk nowadays. It means nothing to them. You should hear mine."

"Peter says I should kick him out and go and live in Harlow, but what would Colin do then?"

"He's a big boy, isn't he? Twenty-six, isn't he?"

"Anyway, I don't want to live in Harlow. It's very nice there, I'm not saying it isn't very nice, but I've lived in this neighbourhood for over thirty years, all my friends are here. And I like being near my Patience. It's Mandy's birthday tomorrow. Seven, she'll be. See that little china dog on the mantelpiece? That's for her birthday. She'll be over the moon when she sees it. She's been on for months, every time we passed the shop. 'Oh, Nan,' she'd say, 'just look at that little dog, isn't he lovely?' She'll be over the moon."

Evelyn gazed at the little china dog, and felt fond tears rise in her eyes at this evidence of grandmotherly love, glad that there were still innocent children left in the world who could set their hearts on china dogs instead of on toy submachine guns and walking, talking, peeing dollies and toy hairdressing saloons and television Ping-Pong. What snobs we are at heart, I only like Mrs. Meer because she's got good taste, thought Evelyn: a curious thought, in view of the fact that the little china dog was really rather ghastly and nobody reared in the Morton family could ever have been seen dead with such a thing on her mantelpiece.

Sensible and capable, perhaps that was a better way of looking at Mrs. Meer. Even Mrs. Meer's lapses from sense were endearing, comprehensible. Just after she'd moved into her new council flat, she'd been conned into buying a roll of carpet by a traveling salesman, and had been so flustered, what with the move, and the cat running away, and the new neighbours staring, and Colin complaining, that she hadn't inspected it properly, hadn't even, she said—"Would you have believed I'd be such a fool, Mrs. Stennett?"—hadn't even unrolled it, and when she did, it was poor quality, not even new, a great mark in the middle, and cheap plastic backing, useless stuff, not worth half the £58 she'd paid for it—"Would you believe it, it's not like me to be such a fool, is it?" And the instant clarity of her own self-judgement, the lack of whining, the solid rock-like sanity of Mrs. Meer had shone out more in this one lapse than in all her proud and stoic years of common sense. "No," Evelyn had said, "it's not like you *at all*," and had confessed to Mrs. Meer, as she had never done to anyone, about the time she herself had been mending a standard electric lamp with a loose fitting, had put a bulb in to test it, taken it out when it didn't work, then gripped the whole thing still connected with her bare hand, her hand closed right down with all its force over the live terminal, and had received such a shock as she'd never had in her life, her hand burned black and blistered, for a horrible moment she'd thought herself stuck to it—and all because she'd forgotten to switch off— "me, Mrs. Meer," said Evelyn, "me, who's changed a hundred plugs and mended a hundred lamps in my life, would you believe I'd be so silly?" And they had shaken their heads and clucked at their own stupidity, their own failures of vigilance, two women used to shaking their heads at the foibles and follies of others, alarmed, ashamed, but in some small way reassured to find themselves as foolish as the next person, victims to common human silliness.

Driving through gentrified Barnsbury on her way to the office, deciding to skip until tomorrow her visit to the alarming Blackwood family with their insoluble problems, she thought again of Stella and Glitterwax, and another image from the past returned to her: not of a china dog, but of a luminous lamb, which had glowed with its pale yellow-white soft woolly light on her mantelpiece night after night with such enchantment that she had tried to stay awake at night to stare at it. The lamb had been a little household god, symbol of a nice safe middle-class childhood. Though, of course, it had subsequently been discovered that these benign little darlings were full of lethal radioactivity, and they had been made extinct. Evelyn couldn't remember what had happened to hers. Had her nice safe middle-class mother removed it, once its dangers had been made known, or had it been allowed to burn its tiny natural life away? It would have been just like her mother to remove it, with a cautionary lecture. But as she couldn't recall such a lecture, it could surely never have taken place? And how mean of her to have assumed the worst of her mother. On one thing professionals and amateurs agree: mothers can't win.

Stalling at the traffic lights, Evelyn remembered those blackish-blue rings round the oldest Blackwood child's eyes, and the mother's curious fast breathing and shaking and twitching of her cardigan, and decided to drive back, after all, to see the Blackwood family.

"Some of the mothers must have been at school with you," said Joyce Scully, headmistress of Romley Fourways, leafing enthusiastically through reports and records in a large, over-flowing filing cabinet in a dark basement stockroom. "Here, just hold this lot, will you?" and she thrust yet another sheaf at Kate, whose arms were already loaded.

Kate's day, like Evelyn's, had taken a turn for the better. She had had lunch in a pub before making her way to the school—a round of cheese and pickle and a double tomato juice, what could be nicer, and everyone in a good mood because of the hot sun streaming through the 1930s stained-glass windows and open door—and had then discovered in Joyce Scully a willing accomplice: somewhat to her surprise, as Miss Scully's letter had been cautious and Kate, from her previous experiences of interviewing heads of schools for articles on education, had assumed the worst. Kate had at once assumed that the caution was justified, and had leaped to the conclusion that Romley Fourways was even more of a dump than it had been in her day. She had, she acknowledged, jumped too far. Miss Scully turned out to be a talkative woman; tiny, with a large bosom and small hips and tiny thin little ankles, a little pigeon of a woman, and she made Kate very welcome.

"I'm so sorry you couldn't come to lunch," she kept repeating, "the girls would have *loved* to have done lunch for you, we have a special catering department now, and though I say it myself, they can produce an excellent meal. But another day, another day."

Kate promised to come another day.

"Well, this is a pleasure," said Miss Scully. "We haven't so many distinguished old girls to our credit, and the girls will be thrilled to meet you."

This was so much better than anything Kate had anticipated that she felt herself smiling foolishly as she looked around Miss Scully's office, with its bright prints and luridly glowing sappy Bizzy Lizzie plants and pinned-up picture postcards.

"I've been checking up on you," said Miss Scully, going straight for the attack. "When we first heard from you, frankly, I thought, 'Oh, Lord, one of those snoopy television reporters wanting to show the girls smoking in the lav and punching teachers in the playground,' but when I read your piece on Risinghill I realised you'd have a much more *balanced* attitude." (Flattery, flattery, thought Kate, flattered: Miss Scully had indeed done her homework, had a whole file of what looked like Armstrong cuttings in front of her. Miss Simmons in Kate's day wouldn't have known what a cutting was, let alone how to get hold of one.) "I've found a few of your old reports too—not that they were much to write home about. A bit of a late-developer, weren't you?" And Miss Scully laughed.

"That's one way of putting it," said Kate—and they had chatted, for a while, about Kate's schooldays, and about education for girls and comprehensives and single-sex schools. I mustn't get too friendly, Kate kept warning herself, maybe she's an ogre in disguise, and if she isn't, maybe she'll expect to have every moment of her school day recorded in television film, so proud is she of its successful struggles against heavy odds.

But she was hard to resist, and had bustled Kate down to the stockroom to look for useful information about vanished students. The smell down there, like the smell of the sewage bank, was overpoweringly suggestive. Ink, damp, dust, dark splintered soft wood, old books. And there were the very same old books, ranged on shelves layers deep—old maths textbooks, geography textbooks, poetry anthologies, English grammars. "I keep thinking we ought to get rid of some of these," said Miss Scully, peering into the depths, "but you never know when things will come in handy, and there's such a squeeze with money for new books lately. . . . I don't really know what we've got down here. Did you read about that librarian up in the Shetlands who burned a lot of old books because he said old books were like old groceries, safer destroyed? Look, here we are, the confidential reports for 1951, these might interest you. Festival of Britain year. I was up in Wakefield then, teaching French at the grammar school. I came to London for the first time, brought a party of girls down to the Festival. Never thought I'd end up here. I know a lot of people would disagree, but I think girls have a better chance in an all-girls school, don't you? Gives them a chance to sort themselves out. What do you think?"

Kate, who had been staring at the spine of a book of fairy stories called *Old Peter's Russian Tales*, started: Miss Scully's mind moved fast, like her small agile body.

"I don't know," said Kate, "I really don't know. . . . I don't think anyone knows. Do you mind if I borrow a copy of this?"

"Of course not, help yourself. Let's take this lot up and sort it out. You can always have another look later. I'll get Mrs. Carey in for a cup of tea, she must have been here in your day." And Joyce Scully set off up the steps at a cracking pace, commandeering on the way a child called Heather to look for Mrs. Carey, who turned out to be a very large woman in a flowing Indian dress, once Fiona Macfarlane, though she'd been through two husbands since then, ending up with (or temporarily attached to) Mr. Carey, head of English and Drama at the new purpose built comprehensive school at Claydon. Like Joyce Scully, she was cheerful, confident, enthusiastic. She did not remember Kate; Kate, staring at her, tried to recall the old Fiona—had she been that very young tall freckled woman with sandy hair in a big plait down her back, or was that someone quite different, or possibly nobody at all, a figment of the imagination? Kate, listening to the reminiscences and gossip of Scully and Carey, had a strange feeling that she had imagined both of them, that they were some kind of mirage, so different were they from what she had expected, and so much nicer in every way. There they sat, pleasantly absorbed, in the little island they had created for themselves, laughing their womanly laughter and discussing the fate of ex-pupils (Mabel Eddison was working in the new drugstore, Miss Scully had bumped into Tracy Baker in Majorca, Sharon Polsen had married a bookie, poor Janice Lumm had cancer, Jayne Tuthill worked as a cleaner in the hospital where Kate had been born, Marylin O'Brien had six children) while outside the tides of traffic poured round the vast roundabout that had given the school its name, and the angry disaffected daubed their slogans on every wall and poster.

Did they think things had changed much? Kate asked, remembering her mission. Had the Equal Opportunities Commission had any effect yet? Or did the girls still want to be vets and nurses and hairdressers and secretaries?

"Well, what do you expect?" said Miss Scully. "These things take time. Though we do have one girl who wants to be a taxi driver, she's doing mechanics. And Marilyn James, who left two years ago, is a plumber now, working for the Council. She trained at a Government Skill Centre. That's new, I suppose. Anyway, what is progress, Mrs. Armstrong? Do we really want to see women making themselves miserable doing men's jobs, jobs that no human being could enjoy doing anyway? Of course it's different in middle-class schools, it's a different matter if you can set your sights on being a doctor or a barrister or a business executive, but why should a girl want to go and work in the gas works? Or at Beckton Sewage Works? There's room at the top, maybe, but only for the clever ones. Life's not fair and never will be. We do the best we can."

"I wonder what happened to Pauline Scott," said Kate. "I always thought she was a clever girl. But I lost touch completely. . . ."

"Ah, Pauline," said Mrs. Carey. "Yes, I remember her. But I knew her little sister better. Shirley—did you ever know Shirley? Well, that was a story and a half." She hesitated: a story of mixed import, clearly. "I suppose we could consider Shirley a success story, Joyce?"

Joyce Scully nodded.

"Yes, you ought to talk to Shirley, if you can ever get hold of her. Well, you remember, they were both beautiful girls, real stunners. Shirley wanted to be an actress. And very good she was, too. I wanted her to go to drama school, but her parents wouldn't have it. They wanted her to help out in the pub. And she did, for a year or two, but then she took up with some man who said he was in films, and our Shirley set off to be a film star." She paused again, then continued in a firmer tone. "And she made it, that's the funny thing. Changed her name to Marylou, goodness knows why. Marylou Scott. You may have seen her, she was in quite a few films in the sixties.

Thrillers, that kind of thing. She was quite a name at one time. Made a lot of money. Yes, you ought to talk to Marylou. I don't know where she is now, the last I heard she was living in Hendon. She married her agent, but I don't suppose that lasted."

"We asked her back," Joyce Scully took up the story, "to Open Day, to open the new language laboratory. Eight years ago? Nine years ago? And she arrived in her mink and diamonds. I've never seen anything like it. She looked a real sight."

Both women relaxed, now the worst was out, and began to laugh again as they went in for the kill: awful Marylou, with her hard elocution voice, and her painted fingernails, and her tasteless jokes, and her cold eyes, and her endless talk of money, money, money . . . a tragedy, really, said Joyce Scully, her little plump hands clenched before her in guilty amusement and horror, not *at all* the kind of thing to present to growing girls, and the worst was, the girls had hated her, they'd laughed at her and hated her, but at the same time, of course, poor things, they'd envied her, how could they not, although she looked so frightful and so dated, like a dummy out of a dress shop . . . not their style at all, the girls were into jeans and long-haired boys and pop and Carnaby Street by that time, and there was Marylou, the only old girl who'd ever made good, present company excepted of course, with the few fathers who ever turned up at functions with their eyes popping out in lust and disapproval, and the mothers horrified, and the girls, oh, well, the girls were just *upset*, "and so was I," confessed Miss Scully, "it was a complete *fiasco*. . . . Yes, you really ought to talk to Marylou. She's quite colourful, that we can promise you."

Colourful and good copy she sounded, thought Kate as she made her way back to the little railway station, pausing only to note that not even the haven of Romley Fourways was immune from fashionable decoration: huge letters on the wall declared

FUCK THE PUNK

SOD THE SOUL

WHAT WE WANT

IS ROCK AND ROLL

a message which Kate found quite cheering in its rhythmic simplicity of sentiment and diction. She must remember it for Evelyn—Evelyn liked that kind of thing, even though she sometimes pretended not to.

Marylou, the wicked princess, the ice queen of Hendon. Had she seen her in a movie with Dirk Bogarde, or was she again inventing memories? No wonder such an apparition had upset decent hard-working Miss Scully, cheery good-natured Mrs. Carey. Naked ambition, draped in mink. And here am I, slopping about in broken eighty-quid boots, non-matching pop socks, a Jaeger skirt, and a two-quid acetate jersey. Whose side am I on, anyway? A walking anomaly, a walking hybrid. Yes, I'd better go and talk to Marylou.

The little train moved slowly through the stations. Kate was half asleep, it had been a long day, but did not like to doze off for fear of waking with a headache. On her knee lay her shoulder bag, stuffed with glossy brochures from the Information Department of Romley Riverside, with ageing papers from Romley Fourways, with *Old Peter's Russian Tales.* Idly, she opened the last of these, which she had as idly acquired, dimly recalling that she had once loved these stories, that a teacher at school had read them aloud in English lessons, that the other girls had said they were baby stories, and that Kate herself had had to pretend to think the same, though secretly she had liked them very much. What a two-faced little monster I was in every way, she thought as she looked at the titles: "The Silver Saucer and the Transparent Apple," "Baba Yaga," "Frost," "The Little Daughter of the Snow" . . . Sad, harsh, cruel little stories, told by a grandfather to his two orphaned grandchildren in a hut in the forest. Yes, here was the one she remembered most clearly . . . "Alenoushka and Her Brother."

"Once upon a time there were two orphan children, a little boy and a little girl. Their father and mother were dead, and they had not even an old grandfather to spend his time in telling them stories. They were alone. The little boy was called Vanoushka, and the little girl's name was Alenoushka." (Had she envied these children their orphaned state? Wished herself and Peter alone in the world?) "They set out together to walk through the whole of the great wide world. It was a long journey they set out on, and they did not think of any end to it, but only of moving on and on, and never stopping long enough in one place to be unhappy there.

"They were travelling one day over a broad plain, padding along on their little bare feet. There were no trees on the plain, no bushes; open flat country as far as you could see, and the great sun up in the sky burning the grass and making their throats dry, and the sandy ground so hot they could scarcely bear to set their feet on it. All day from early morning they had been walking, and the heat grew greater and greater towards noon.

" 'Oh,' said Vanoushka, 'my throat is so dry. I want a drink. I must have a drink—just a little drink of cool water.'

" 'We must go on,' said Alenoushka. . . .''

Reading, Kate was astonished to find tears rising to her eyes. The story came back to her, each sentence before she read it. The sister forebade her brother to drink from water in the print of a horse's hoof for fear he would turn into a horse, from water in the print of a calf's hoof for fear he would turn into a calf, but finally, when she was not looking, he drank from the print of a lamb's small foot, and turned into a little white lamb, and when his sister looked for him, all she could see was a little lamb which leaped around her and tried to lick her face. . . . However sad he felt, he had to leap and frisk in the sun, and toss his little white tail. And Alenoushka sat in a haystack and wept bitterly, until a fine horseman rode by, and married her, allowing her to keep the little lamb always by her side. But one day an ugly old witch arrived, and bewitched

Alenoushka, and drowned her in the river, and took her place and shape, and asked the fine gentleman to have the lamb killed . . . and the lamb ran off to the river and sang:

> Alenoushka, little sister,
> They are going to slaughter me;
> They are cutting wooden faggots,
> They are heating iron cauldrons,
> They are sharpening knives of steel.

And the drowned Alenoushka from the bottom of the river heard, and replied:

> O my brother Ivanoushka,
> A heavy stone is round my throat,
> Silken grass grows through my fingers,
> Yellow sand lies on my breast.

And a little servant boy had heard these two laments, and told the fine gentleman, and he dragged the river, and the sister was miraculously restored to life, the brother to his former self, and the old witch returned to her former toothless ugliness and went shrinking off into the deep woods. . . .

Well, well, thought Kate. One did not have to look very far to see why this story had affected her so much. How mysteriously things turn out. She felt in her pocket for Peter's anonymous letter of abuse. Alenoushka, little sister, they are going to slaughter me. Who was the fine gentleman? Stuart? Ted? No, neither fitted the requirements. But the ugly old toothless witch, she is also me, for sure, thought Kate. How extraordinary was the opening of the story, the brother and sister setting out to walk through the whole of the wide world. But where else could one go but through the whole world?

While Kate and Evelyn were indulging in recollections of fairy stories and luminous lambs, and inspecting the surface of the pavements of Finsbury Park and the sewage banks of

Romley, Hugo Mainwaring sat at his table in front of his type-
writer and the pile of books and papers that he was attempting to process into his own Middle East book. He was not
satisfied with its progress. Too much was happening in the
Middle East, and anything one committed to paper might be
rendered meaningless by the next morning's headlines. On the
other hand, very little was happening in Hugo's own life,
which left him plenty of time to sit and stare. So he stared, at
the debris of his work, and at two empty coffee mugs, a tube
of Redoxon, a plate with congealed egg, a plastic Saxa salt
container, a spanner, a well-chewed toothpick, a packet of
cigarettes, an ashtray, a copy of *Death in Venice*, and a
chrysanthemum in a milk bottle.

He thinks of writing a different book altogether. A book
about himself, in novel form, perhaps. He has friends who
write novels about themselves, so why should not he? His life,
after all, has not been without drama. He rolls a new sheet of
paper into the machine and types.

Here I sit at my kitchen table, typing with one finger instead
of two, a fine figure of impotence. Diminishing powers, leading to
silence.

He quite likes these two sentences, but does not know
what to do with them, so thinks, instead, that he will start at
the beginning, and writes:

I was born in Berlin, the only child of a diplomat, and have
spent most of my life until recently wandering round the world on
one pretext or another, mostly as a foreign correspondent, looking
at disasters. Famine, flood, war, genocide.

Those two sentences aren't bad either, but it depresses
him to find that two out of four of his sentences seem to lack a
verb. What can this signify?

He decides to make one more attempt. Third time lucky.

Peace of mind, that is what I seek. The phrase fills me with
a great and hopeless tenderness.

Now that, he says to himself, is really bad writing, despite the fact that I mean every word of it. There are, it is true, enough verbs, but what about that pretentious inversion, and what about the general vagueness of the whole sentiment? The more I try to tell the truth, the worse I write. But surely, at my age, I ought to have the courage to write badly. What do I fear to lose?

Perhaps he would get on better if he wrote about somebody else, he thinks. His friend Kate Armstrong, for example. He knows a lot about Kate, he has been studying her with interest for years, and she would make a good subject for one of these women's novels that seem to be so popular these days. But it would probably take a woman to write such a book. Nevertheless, he resolves to write something, at least, about Kate. He rolls in a clean sheet of paper, and begins:

I recall one of my first meetings with Kate Armstrong. It was a Sunday, ten years or so ago. Judith and I had been to lunch with Evelyn with our children, who were then still small. Ted, as so often, was away. Kate called round in the afternoon with her children, and for a while we sat around drinking coffee and gossiping, while the children played with Lego and squabbled over the pieces. It must have been '68, because I remember talking about the troubles in Paris, and being surprised to learn that Kate had never been abroad. They listened tolerantly to my analysis of events, which was over-subtle and subsequently discredited. Judith, who had a bad cold, and who had heard it all before, fell asleep.

It was Kate who suggested we should go out for a walk. It was a dreary December day, and the prospect would not have been attractive, had it not been for the fact that the children were becoming increasingly tiresome and boisterous. It would do us all good to get out, said Kate, so off we went to Hampstead Heath, to Kenwood, pushchairs and wellingtons piled into the back of my car and of Evelyn's, leaving Judith sleeping. We started off with a cursory tour of the house, small boots skidding on the parquet, unsuitable little fingers wiping themselves at knee level on pale paint. Kate was wearing a striped woolly hat with a bobble, and her cheeks were pink with cold and health. "What a life," she said, gazing at the Adam library with its bright colours and restored elegance. "Do you think that if one were a rich person and lived in a house like this, one would become a proper person and live at a proper pace? Slowly, I mean?" We paused in front of my favourite painting, Van Dyck's handsome Duke of Richmond sitting back with a knowing smile on his fine lips, his red-gold curls tumbling, his white shirt billowing, his faithful dog gazing up at him with an expression of alert fidelity, a spear leaning against his chair with casual potency. Ease, grace, wealth, power; an embroidered curtain, a distant landscape, a red robe. "Now *there's* a man," said Evelyn, and Kate agreed. Kate dismissed the famous Vermeer, which was to cause such a sensation when stolen a few years later: plump, dull, pretentiously simple, trying to be the real thing, she said, but not the real thing at all. "What do you mean by the real thing?" I asked her, and she said, "Oh, Pieter de Hooch, of course, you know that one in the National Gallery, of the woman and her maid in a back yard with a fish in a bucket and a man coming down the alleyway? That is the most beautiful picture *ever painted*," she said, with mocking emphasis. "And even Stuart says I'm allowed to think so. He says I'm wrong, but he says I'm allowed to think so. He says I'm mad not to like Vermeer, but he lets me like de Hooch just the same. And what about that one with the woman peeling apples and the little girl in the Wallace Collection? That is the other most beautiful painting ever painted."

I had forgotten her husband was a painter. I had not, at that stage, met Stuart. Nor am I sure, come to think of it, if Kate at that stage had met Ted.

When we emerged from the house, the swollen dark-slate

sky had filled with thick white mist. We couldn't even see the lake with its little two-dimensional bridge at the bottom of the landscaped grassy slope. Bare trees loomed suddenly, alarmingly. Some of the children wanted to go back, but others wanted to go on, so on we went, past Dr. Johnson's summerhouse and the high rhododendrons, past a bench with an empty fish tin on it ("That was there last week," said Evelyn, "do you think it's the same one?"), through a deep alley of evergreen, and out into a strange white plain, all distances vanished, only damp white slopes with rooks pecking at pale tufts of straw-coloured grass, and one ominous magpie. It was silent, eerie, all sound muffled. All other walkers had disappeared. We were alone in a sea of mist. Forty rooks, stifflegged, looked up at us, but did not move away. They were in possession, sinister in their assurance, their indifference to our passing. We walked on, careful to keep all seven children in view. On the brow of a small eminence to our left stood a solitary tree. "Look, look," said Kate, and we stopped and looked, and in the tree's branches, unnaturally large, frisked three grey squirrels. They were too large for the thin tree; they looked unreal, out of perspective, like creatures in a medieval painter's allegory. "Aren't they horrid," said Kate, "they're witches' squirrels, don't you think?" The children hung around, open-mouthed, noses running, while Kate elaborated on her theme, breaking off when they began to show signs of real alarm. "No, no, don't be so *silly,*" she said, and bent down and picked up a stick and threw it at the tree, and the squirrels scampered off like ordinary squirrels, the spell broken, and we turned on our tracks and made our way back to the car. Mysteriously, the mist vanished as quickly as it had arrived, and by the time we got back to Evelyn's the sky was clear again, though dark. As we stood on the doorstep a great drifting eddying flock of tiny birds flew over our heads, a wide irregular column like a trail of smoke; a few larger birds flew with them. "Where are they off to?" asked one of the children. "Surely it's too late to migrate?" said Evelyn, her key in the lock, gazing upwards. The birds passed over, into the darkness.

We went in, and had tea and toast and biscuits round the kitchen table, and Judith and Kate talked about Dutch paintings and the cult of the everyday, and whether or not one needs to know the allegorical significance of a peeled apple or a patterned tile or a tablecloth or a game of cards, and Kate's little one sat on her knee, my little one on mine, daubing us with butter, and lurching dangerously every now and then in sudden bursts amongst the tea cups. "I *hate* scholarship," said Kate, vehemently, wiping her fingers on her son's home-knit jersey, "I *hate* the way it tells you that everything you think means something else really, but I know I hate it so much because I know it's true. Sickening to be always wrong, isn't it?"

Evelyn got up and drew the blinds. It was very pleasant in her warm bright kitchen all those years ago, the darkness shut out, the children safely assembled. If we could have known . . . Well, would we have savoured it more? And were we really happy? Were we not, rather, half bored, and surreptitiously tormented by infidelities, unfulfilled ambitions, fatigue, financial anxieties of every sort? Our minds more than half elsewhere as we engaged in desultory chat? Judith, sitting there in my memory so comfortable, was, although I did not then know it, eaten up with passion for a liberal-studies lecturer at the Central School, and with worry about dry rot in the staircase and a lump in our son David's neck: Kate was worried about Stuart, as always, and about money, as always, and about the reliability of baby-minders, as always in those days: Evelyn, historically, must have been worried about either Ted and that girl who bumped herself off so nastily, or about Ted and Kate, or about Ted in general. No doubt all of us were suffering from sleepless nights and coughing children with earaches. If questioned, would we not then have looked back with nostalgia to the carefree days of youth, to unbroken nights, to parties at Hunt's or at Cambridge, to love-making undisturbed by children, to love itself? Yet, nevertheless, one can look back to such afternoons as though they possessed a true tranquillity. In ten years will I look back upon myself sitting at this table and think, Ah, I was happy then?

A peace of mind free from all vicissitude, which cannot be undone by death or time, by falling bricks, by random snipers, by lumps in the neck, by crashing cars. Love, they say, redeems, but it is love itself that exposes us. When they operated on my son David, a year or two after the afternoon I have described, he was given the wrong dose of anaesthetic, and suffered permanent brain damage. Judith went more or less out of her mind, and has spent the last few years pursuing the hospital administration, the ombudsman, the anaesthetist personally, unable to accept the concept of the accidental. I do not blame her. This event certainly simplified Judith, reducing her once-varied colours to a monotone of revenge. She would not call it revenge, of course: she says she is demanding adequate compensation, not only for David's sake, but for the sake of others, for the principle of the thing. Exemplary damages. I do not need to point out that there is no compensation possible for such a tragedy. It is not a question of money. We have plenty of money. It is blood that she is after.

It has been very hard for Judith. She is an intellectual woman, and had had high hopes of the children. She was not good with little ones, would look forward to the days when they could talk and think and read books; would over-stimulate them, even when they were small, with reading schemes and jigsaws and playfully disguised conceptual puzzles. Her attention seemed in some ways to be paying off, for David was, as the insurance reports in the newspapers put it, "a lively and intelligent child." Now he sits about and stares and has to be fed and cleaned. Perpetual peace has possessed him; his mind is at rest. But Judith is on a treadmill. There is nothing I can do to help. There is nothing that anyone can do. She tracked down the anaesthetist, and took to standing on the corner of the street where he lives in Muswell Hill, to watch him come home from work. She became troublesome, and in the end he had to take out an injunction. Our other child, Susanna, is still lively and intelligent, but spends little time at home with Judith. She will go to university; with luck she will escape.

In the early days of this affair, Judith enlisted any help she could in her battle against what she no doubt correctly saw as a professional conspiracy to refuse to admit liability. She tried Ted, but Ted had too much sense to involve himself. She also tried Kate, who was less sensible, and more responsive. Kate wrote the case up in one of her articles, and mounted a campaign, through her paper, for the publication of the results of the enquiry into David's accident. Her intervention proved, for their relationship, disastrous. Kate and Judith had never been close; each claimed to be "frightened" of the other, though I could never determine whether this meant that they felt they ought to like each other and didn't, or whether it meant that they did like each other but felt themselves too different to consort easily, too suspicious of one another's fields of expertise to share confidences. Had they been closer, it might not have worked out so badly, who can say?

What happened was this: Judith took offence at something in one of Kate's pieces—a turn of phrase, a concession to the enemy, a bit of fair-minded journalistic balance—and accused Kate of betraying her cause. Unjustly, of course. I was not surprised by Judith's complete rejection of Kate, which was effected with considerable violence and cruelty: anyone could have seen that Judith was in no state to be objective, and it does not take much subtlety to note that people tend to turn most angrily against those who try to help them, whether they fail or succeed. But I was surprised by Kate's intense distress at this rejection. I had thought she would be more understanding, that she would not take Judith's anger personally. But Kate took it very badly. I spent one terrible evening at Kate's in the midst of this crisis, watching her weep and scream and bang her head about the cushions; she yelled that she would murder Judith, that she would stick a knife in her if ever she set eyes on her again, that Judith had brought it upon herself by expecting too much of the children, that she hated Judith for not being able to go on loving a damaged child, that Judith was a monster with no true love in her, and no true mother. I held her in my arms while she ranted. That is how we became so close. And Kate, of course, recovered: her tears abated, her sobs diminished, she began to apologise, to recant, to beg my forgiveness. I sat and stroked her arm and her tousled hair, and wiped her puffy face, and brought her a cup of tea, and promised to stay by her side until she slept. I sat by her bed and watched her sleeping, jerking like a dog, restlessly turning. Judith would not let me near her. Judith never wept; she talked and talked and talked. Kate let me hold her hand, let me comfort her, which was a great comfort to me, though I do not wish to imply that she staged the whole scene for my consolation: devious she may be, but not to such a degree.

Maybe Judith will recover. I don't know.

While I was walking alone on the Heath last week, as I do often, I saw a strange sight. Two young men, with a large Alsatian, and hooded hawks on their wrists. Hunting small birds, I supposed, which for all I know may be illegal in this country. Falconry is still a sport of princes in the Middle East. The two young men on the Heath did not look very princely. I asked Mujid about hawks when I gave him lunch the other day, but he didn't seem to know much about them. I took him to Simpson's on the Strand: when I told Kate this, she said that I'd overdone it, the Italian self-service on the corner would have been quite all right for Mujid, and no one had ever taken her to Simpson's in her life. Poor Kate, I said, and reported that Mujid did not think much of Yorkshire pudding. Mujid is an interesting chap, and the progress he has made in English is remarkable, despite his lack of enthusiasm for his classes. A serious young man, but, as he says, someone in his position is obliged to be serious. In an old country we can afford our frivolity, and little else. He is also much less rigidly aligned in his views than Kate first gave him out to be, though that may be due either to the fact that Kate, by her own account, doesn't understand politics and is anyway much given to exaggeration, or to the fact that an increasing familiarity with England enables him to express himself less rigidly, or to a little of both. Maybe he is even changing his views, who knows? Certainly he seems more interested in the rights of women than Kate has ever suggested to me, and even quoted her once or twice—he seems particularly taken with her censoriousness about advertising, and noted on his own account and with amused approval a scrawl on a shop selling bridal gear in Oxford Street which read, IS THERE LIFE AFTER MARRIAGE? The position of Muslim women interests him: what will happen to the brave militants of Iran, or are they not brave at all, but Pahlavi whores, as most of their own countrymen declare? An emerging nation needs a sense of identity, but what a pity, says Mujid, that it should find it in the veil. His own fiancée, Simone, he says, would not be seen dead in a veil. (*"Elle préférerait crever que de porter cela"* was how he put it.)

No wonder, however, that Kate finds his allegiances confusing. So does he. How can one reconcile Marxism, an admiration for the Soviet Union, and a faith in the new Islam? No wonder the left in the Middle East has splintered into so many fragments. He is anti-American and anti-Israel in his bones, in a way that would be historically impossible for an Englishman of my age, yet can hardly commit himself to the rule of religion. Yet, he says, religion is necessary. An uneasy position. Religion and nationalism, an old and dangerous alliance. I reported to him the interesting interchange of one Mr. West, Vice-Chancellor of Bombay University in the 1880s, who told Wilfred Scawen Blunt that Muslim religious fanaticism was a fatal impediment to progress, declaring that "You might as well run a race with a knapsack on your back." To this Blunt, that early supporter of Islam, replied, "Perhaps if the race was a long one, and the knapsack full of bread, you might not find it an encumbrance." He liked this.

Blunt, of course, was a Catholic. And, after Islam, took up Home Rule for Ireland.

Mujid is puzzled, as well he might be, by the manifestations of anti-Arab feeling in this country, by the inability of most people to distinguish between "les émirs" from Saudi Arabia reclining in vast suites in the Wellington Hospital, and the poor Egyptian and Jordanian students struggling to learn engineering on grants from the Overseas Development Administration (OAD); between the ethnic archaic figures of the Iraqi National Dance Company currently disporting itself at Sadler's Wells and the Iraqi terrorists who shot an ex-Minister outside the Intercontinental Hotel. We talked about oil and OPEC and the IPC (what a lot of initials there are splattering the air these days), and about money and morality, money and aesthetics. (We both quite like the mosque in Regent's Park, and he listened with interest to my story of a visit I made to the East End with a Jewish friend, who showed me the synagogue of his youth: once a Huguenot chapel, then a synagogue, it is now a mosque. Perhaps there is some point in talking, after all.)

I wish, in fact, that we could have talked less about these matters, and more about his own past. The village on the Euphrates, with its date palms and pomegranates and steamers: his father, the village shopkeeper: his uncle, the village schoolmaster, educated downstream at ancient Ana with its mosques and minaret. His brothers, working at the new chemical plant, in another world. An eclipse of centuries. It is a long journey he has made, and his gentle face bore signs of stress as he sat there in his best tie eating roast beef and glancing around at the prosperous businessmen eating expense-account lunches. The Englishness of Simpson's pleased him. He was, he noted, the only foreigner visible: a comment similar to that of the editor of a new feminist magazine for businesswomen who invited Kate to lunch in the Connaught and then pointed out, with a mixture of pride and anger, that they were the only two women eating in the room. ("Should I," said Kate, "have declared that I'd never set foot in the place before (which I had), or should I have pretended I ate there all the time?")

Mujid says he dislikes violence, is not a fighter, and is too short-sighted to be any use in any kind of army. I find this reassuring. I like his thick glasses.

He also says he wants to be a writer (as do we all?), a topic which led us onto the unfair historical advantage of being born to the English language, and the extreme insularity of English publishers, who do not seem over-eager to translate Egyptian novels, Iraqi poets, Lebanese plays. I said that this situation must surely be changing with the growth of Western interest in and dependence on the Middle East. I was able to inform him that sales of the Koran were rising steadily (Penguin sales doubled in the last four years) and that a friend of mine who is a literary editor had remarked to me only the other day that a remarkably high percentage of books, not to mention films, now make some effort to encompass a wider geographical range, and presumably not only through a direct interest in Arab money. Africa had once been the country to which writers turned; now they look to the Middle East. Mujid was not sure what he thought this meant, or whether he approved of it; he did not entirely believe me, I suspect. The 1970s, the global decade, as Updike said in an interview the other day. Will anyone ever again be able to write, with confidence, a book that assumes the significance of one culture only, will anyone ever again be able to stand upright in one nationality? Relativity, comparisons. Well, I have spent a good deal of my life worrying about these things. Culture dies at the interface, one might reasonably fear.

Mujid had a cutting in his pocket from the *Guardian*, which Kate had pointed out to him, describing the rescue of four children and a dog who had been adrift off the coast of

Lebanon for four days in a refrigerator packing case they had found on the beach. Two Lebanese boys, two Armenians. He seemed taken with the idea of turning it into a drama, inspired perhaps by Goldman's surreal effort. The refrigerator case symbolised American consumer imperialism. Or something like that. I countered his cutting with one of my own also from the *Guardian*, about an Italian homosexual activist arrested in Iran; he had gone to protest against the executions. We agreed that life was too bizarre for fiction, these days.

Hugo's little story took him several hours to compose, and at the end he was quite pleased with it; partly, perhaps, because it shows him in a responsible domestic light; partly because he seems at last to have cast off the dusty mantle of T. E. Lawrence, whose prose style he so admired as a boy. But nevertheless, he has failed to convey much useful information about his own past history, and has failed also to provide much of an interlude. Maybe it is modesty that prevents him, at this stage, from describing his Kurdish adventures in more detail? Or is it something more sinister? Whatever the explanation, there is no need to respect his discretion too much: here are some of the points that he chose to omit.

Hugo, as he said, was born in Berlin, but did not spend long there, as his father was shortly transferred to Cairo, and thence to Ankara. So it was in Egypt and Turkey that he spent his formative years, with the inevitable journeys to England for prep, then public, school. His mother was an intrepid and eccentric lady who loved the Middle East, and who communicated to Hugo an enthusiasm for the more romantic aspects of the countries in which they found themselves. While Kate was reading advertisements in *Woman's Own*, and Evelyn Arthur Ransome, Hugo was making his way through *Greenmantle* and *Beau Geste*, through Doughty's *Arabia Deserta*, through Sir Richard Burton, the *Arabian Nights*, *The Seven Pillars of*

Wisdom, through Fraser's *Journeys in Kurdistan*. He read also a great deal of poetry; his favourite poet was A. E. Housman, whose landscapes of distant blue remembered hills somehow merged inextricably in his imagination with the mauve horizons and pale pink brittle icy dawns of the Anatolian plains. A solitary child both by temperament and circumstance, he cultivated a heroic notion of himself, and dreamed of the desert. When he was a man, he told himself, he would be a soldier, an explorer, a leader of men. Meanwhile, as a boy, he prepared for these exploits. While Kate was testing herself by doing reckless somersaults over double bars in an attempt to prove herself the equal of the village children of North Fawsey, Hugo was training himself to endure extremes of temperature: he would force himself to lie naked by an open window in the bitter nights, staring at the outsize stars of Asia, or to sit in the summer sun in the white courtyard until he fainted. Like Kate, but for different reasons, he experimented with depriving himself of liquids, of food, to see how long he could last. He was a deeply superstitious boy, much given to counting games, magic numbers, salvation rituals—touching a certain stone in the wall, a certain tile on the bathroom floor—and, having no friends, was not aware that these superstitions were normal for children, indeed an integral part of childhood. He thought he was odd, and, thinking so, became so. He liked to frighten himself.

Nobody much noticed his oddity. The succession of nurses who looked after him expected English children to be strange, and Hugo was a polite lad and caused little trouble. He was also pretty, which pleased his mother, herself a beauty, a fair-haired beauty with a fine complexion and pale blue eyes, one of those English women who look good in pink and mauve and blue; she was a restless creature, impatient, quick, dissatisfied, vain, always looking for a flattering reflection, and finding one, in a sense, in Hugo. (Kate and Hugo's mother get on well: they have much in common.)

As Hugo grew older, his conception of his destiny altered,

and his heroes changed. He no longer saw himself as Lawrence of Arabia, and began to read archaeologists and anthropologists, inspired by a classics master at school (in England, of course) and a visiting professor who came to stay with his parents one winter vacation, on his way to an excavation. Here, Hugo recognised, was a more respectable field of endeavour. He started to read Layard, Childe and Montelius, Malinowski and Durkheim. *Rites de passage*, taboos and rituals, magic and myth, the pure and the impure. After his national service he went up to Cambridge to read Archaeology and Anthropology, did well, and decided to continue. Planning his first research project, he turned naturally towards the Middle East rather than towards the then more fashionable terrain of Africa, and managed to get himself financed to visit the Bizhari in the mountains of Kurdistan, in Iraq: this was just before the Suez crisis and the Bagdad revolution would have rendered such an expedition impossible. This field study had bizarre consequences. Hugo had recognised from the outset that the Kurds were not renowned for their peace-loving dispositions—indeed, this was one of the reasons why he found them attractive—but he had not foreseen that he would actually be taken prisoner and held as hostage in a militant local upsurge of the prolonged Kurdish battle for independence.

Being a prisoner, in fact, did not make much difference to his life style, he says—if anything, life with the Kurdish Democratic Party (KDP) army was more comfortable and better organised than life with the Bizhari, who were a primitive lot, in the eyes of their own countrymen, much given to un-Kurdish superstition, which took the form of a curious variety of devil worship, a heretical version of the Yezidi heresy of the Peacock King. The Kurds treated him well, having no personal objection to him, and were pleased rather than not with his interest in their affairs and rapidly acquired familiarity with their language. They explained that they only wanted to hold him in order to publicise their cause; as the son of a British diplomat, he made an ideal captive. (Even guerilla groups were less violent in those days.)

Hugo changed the theme of his studies, abandoning the principles of social organisation amongst the Bizhari with special reference to "roof-top" and "smoke-filled room" cultures for an intensive if involuntary course in Kurdish nationalism. Night after night, he listened to stories of the ill-fated Mahabad Republic, of the heroic march of Mullah Mustafa to the Soviet Union, to more ancient tales of atrocities and betrayals by Turks, Persians, Iraqis, Syrians, Armenians. He also learned to capture quail and to shoot partridge, and to catch unidentifiable large but bony fish, which were almost as plentiful as in the fabulous days of Fraser, when the rivers had seethed and the skies darkened with life. (He was too high up, alas, for the noble bustard, a bird which had always exerted a peculiar power over Hugo's imagination.) Fate seemed to have thwarted his sensible decision to abandon the theatrical military life for a sober intellectual one: glory was to be his, whether he wanted it or not. And he looked very good in Kurdish gear. An image of his own romantic destiny sustained him; his abduction was certain to be creating a stir back home, and life in the mountains was much more free and interesting than life with the British Army had been in Cyprus.

It was also, he could tell, more useful, in a personal sense: he might not have had the best opportunities for fulfilling his obligations to his supervisors at Cambridge, and to the William Pargiter Travelling Scholarship Fund, but he had acquired a good deal of sensational and interesting material of a more topical nature.

So that was the end of Hugo the anthropologist. He was released after three months, with a fair amount of good will all round, and on returning home, sold his story to a Sunday paper, earning more from it than he would have done from years of research. Academic life no longer seemed alluring, and Hugo accepted one of several tempting offers and became a journalist, a decision he has not regretted. The Middle East proved a booming subject, and he flourished. He is now, as we have seen, writing his Middle East book. (His book about his months with the Kurds was quite successful.)

While Hugo was eating stringy chicken and yoghurt and drinking cups of tea in caves that defied any proper division into roof-top and smoke-filled, Judith was studying art history at Glasgow, Ted the life cycle of *aedes aegypti*, and Kate the principles of social organisation in Highbury New Park and West Hampstead.

When Hugo returned from Iraq, he met Judith at a party given by Evelyn's sister Isobel, and married her because everyone else seemed to be getting married. Or that was one way of looking at it. His father at least was relieved, for he had been less than taken with Hugo's posturing, and felt guilty about it, moreover: he was pleased to see the lad settle down into what looked like a more normal life. He had tried, during Hugo's schooldays, to encourage him to spend the summer holidays with his sister's children, the Morton girls, at their cottage in Shropshire. (Hugo, though he liked his cousins, had interpreted this as jealousy on his father's part, and a desire to keep him out of his mother's way.) He would have been satisfied had Hugo chosen to marry one of them, but Judith Street seemed an acceptable substitute—a clever, independent, self-reliant young woman with refined tastes, she seemed a suitable match for Hugo, and did not try to tie him to her apron strings, as Hugo's mother admiringly conceded.

It did not turn out to be a normal marriage—how could it when Hugo was away so much? And that was the smallest of their problems. Judith thinks that Hugo is a louse of a father, and bitterly resents any suggestion that she herself is an inattentive mother. She views the Kate-Hugo alliance with profound distaste, and considers any opinions they may hold about her a grotesque impertinence. She thinks they talk about her, which in fact, since their first union on this subject, they do not. They never mention her. Judith thinks that Hugo

should never have had children. She also does not think much
of Kate's attitude to the young. Facile, trendy, sickeningly
tolerant, ignorant: Kate is the kind of woman who has messed
everything up. She fills Judith with rage. Judith is fastidious.
Kate knows nothing, says Judith. She doesn't even notice she
has fucked up her own children, so vain is she. Kate has
ruined Mark as certainly as Hugo's mother ruined Hugo, in
Judith's view, and she will live to reap the consequences.

Judith, educated at expensive private schools, driving a
car bought for her by her estranged husband, surrounded by a
rapidly changing staff of cleaning ladies, au-pair girls, and
now, alas, resident nurses, is not well placed to appreciate
Kate. Though once they used to get on quite well.

Kate thinks Judith cannot have her cake and eat it. Judith
liked Hugo for his style, because he looked like a Holbein
portrait (the one of Robert Cheseman in a fur cape with a
hawk on his wrist, to be precise, though Kate could not have
been), and she can bloody well suffer for its inconveniences.
"As I suffered for Stuart's," says Kate. Kate does not think
much of the fact that Judith expects and accepts Hugo's
money, but will not have him in the house which it maintains.

On the other hand, though she would not admit this, Kate
herself worries a great deal about the way she has treated
Stuart. The damp walls, the potatoes with their white slug
eyes, their greening bruises, their red wrinkled carbuncled
skins. Gone to seed. Superfluous men. No, the new matriarchy
does not look good. At least one does not have to worry about
hurting Hugo. Whatever happened to Hugo was so remote, so
long ago, and in another country.

Kate thinks Hugo will not stay in England long, whatever
he says. Arm or no arm. He is sure to become restless, he will
be off again to wherever the action is. Sometimes in the old
days, before Ethiopia, he would say, "Why don't you come
with me, Katie, broaden your horizons?" and Kate, shudder-
ing, would turn down his invitations to the world's hot spots.

Danny Blick, Hunt, Stuart, Hugo, Kate, teenage children, Black Ice, the dreadful suitors. Marginal people? And what of the concept of the "real woman" that has haunted Kate, the concept of the "real man" that has haunted Hugo? The soft-hearted fool that cannot turn away a dying pigeon, the lonely disabled warrior writing up the embattled causes of others? Now, Ted and Evelyn, they are not marginal. They are husband and wife, and remain so. For better, for worse. Ted has a man's job, Evelyn a woman's. They keep their ancient places.

The relationship between Ted and Hugo has been interesting to watch. They have always been somewhat competitive, to put it mildly. One of Evelyn's most cherished memories is of the occasion on which, circa 1963, at a Christmas dinner, Hugo informed Ted that it was the Arabs who had discovered the concepts of contagion and infection, and that this discovery sprang directly from their religion, for the Muslims, as Ted surely must know, regard mankind and nature as the living cloak of God, and man as a link in a chain whose other links might well include an infected cloak, infected water, poisonous air. Rubbish, Ted had snorted, exactly the reverse was true; why, in 1348 ibn al Khatib had expressly defied his religion in arguing the case for infection during the Black Death. Oh, that doesn't mean anything, Hugo had replied, Ted ought to go off and read Hunayn ibn Ishaq, al Razi, ibn-Sina, ibn al Nafis before he leaped to any conclusions about the Arab view of medicine. Ted, empurpled with intellectual battle, turkey, fizzy white wine, and the Morton miasma, had nevertheless been humble enough to note these names down on the back of a piece of gold Christmas wrapping paper, trying hard to constrain himself as Hugo held forth on the deep prejudice of the West against the East, a prejudice as ignorant and falsifying as the ignorance of classical culture in the Dark Ages: but his rage had broken forth even more violently when he got home and discovered that at least one of these mysterious characters who had leaped at him so horribly across the white once-a-year damask was not a real enemy, but a disguised friend, for ibn-Sina turned out to be none other than Avicenna, about whom he might have found a thing or two to say had he known who the hell Hugo was talking about. Bloody one-upmanship, stupid Oxbridge twat, Ted had mumbled as he pulled off his socks: the mystic East, the seven pillars of wisdom, if the Arabs are so bloody clever, why are they still subject to malaria and bacillary dysentery to bilharzia and leishmaniasis and anthrax? Why, in Kurdistan bubonic plague is still endemic, I wonder if Hugo knew *that* when he was sitting around so happily making pals with the murderous brutes and listening to their bloodthirsty folk stories, or whatever they spend their evenings doing.

Nevertheless, when he wrote his book on the history of epidemiology, he devoted a certain amount of space to Hugo's suggestions. Without acknowledgement, of course.

One might have assumed that Hugo's friendship with Kate would have annoyed Ted even more than it annoyed Judith, in view of Ted's temperament, and his attitudes to both Kate and Hugo. But, oddly enough, this was not so. In fact, on the contrary, it seemed to please him. Kate always felt that this was a revealing comment on Hugo, but was not sure what it revealed.

Hugo states that he and Kate were brought together by Judith's unintentional intervention, but clearly that cannot be the whole truth: they must have been predisposed to one another to have been in such proximity in the first place. One could perhaps date their alliance from an earlier and more cheerful moment in the acquaintance: after the walk on the Heath which Hugo chose to describe, but before David's operation. It took place in June, a cheerful month, and worth recalling in these darkening days. Kate, sitting in a taxi on the Tottenham Court Road at rush hour, in a traffic jam, on her way home, spotted Hugo walking north with the unmistakable irresolute air of a man uncertain whether to wait for a bus, brave the tube, or continue to look for an empty taxi amidst the hostile fleet of occupied ones: on impulse, she wound down her window, shouted at him, offered him a lift if he were going her way. He joined her, and there sat Kate in the back of the cab, shelling peas. She had a paper bag on her knee, and was dropping the pods into the depths of her carpet-bag, the peas into the paper bag. "Whatever are you doing?" asked Hugo, though it was quite obvious. "Saving time," said Kate, "I got bored sitting here doing nothing. Here, have a few." And they ate raw peas, and chatted, each delighted with the happy accident of meeting one another, Kate charmed to be discovered in what she clearly saw (though she could not have planned the spectacle) as a charming operation, Hugo charmed to have a free lift, the summer sun shining on the traffic and the girls in their summer dresses and the men in their shirt sleeves: "How lucky I saw you," said Kate, but did not describe the gaiety and the affection that had possessed her at the sight of solitary Hugo on the pavement, so agreeable and invigorating a friend, one who always made her feel light of heart, as though she were, after all, exactly the right person in the right place; nor did she describe the joy with which she had seen his face light up with recognition as he saw her calling his name. Spontaneous joy. How could she not warm to one so pleased to see her? And Hugo, for his part, said that it was indeed lucky, but did not tell her that his spirits too had lifted absurdly at the sound of her voice, at the sight of her sitting there smiling in her pink-and-green-check cotton dress. There was no need for them to say these things: they were obvious. When two people are happy to meet by chance, it is obvious. Kate asked him to supper, to finish the peas, but he declined, for he had to go to a party in Hampstead. "But you will come sometime," said Kate, who had never invited him before, for they were not then on such terms. "I will come," said Hugo, "any time that you ask me. There is nothing I would like more than an invitation from you." After this, what could they feel but friendship of a most intimate nature? A friendship devoid of competition or desire. Are such things possible? Will they be so if we imagine them?

So there is Hugo's history, which was intended to provide a change of air, an interlude, a nice dry white perspective, a relief from the grit and traffic: but they have annexed him, they have sucked him in and made him part of themselves, and so he is, and lucky to be so, for one cannot spend one's life, as Hugo once thought, waiting for those moments of pure weightless isolated joy and terror, those moments on a foreign airport, in a strange hotel room, in a wide hot street with the sound of gunfire, on an icy mountainside, on an empty plain with great bustards, fishing in a cold fast river. The moment when the heart stops, the moment before the faceless stranger turns and reveals himself as the friend, the rival, the enemy: it cannot be prolonged. He will turn, he will put on features and make himself known. One cannot disconnect, one cannot hold one's breath and suspend one's being (though Hugo as a boy had practised doing precisely that, and at the age of ten could manage forty-five seconds with his head submerged in a wash-bowl). No, things do not work out as one plans, and maybe that is just as well. But in the end, who knows, maybe the prophecies will be fulfilled and the solitude will return, maybe the false events (an exploding grenade, a botched operation) will turn out to be the true ones after all. How can one know? How can one trace the line? A Saxa salt container, a pile of books, a plate with egg on it. A pretentious sentence, a sentence without verbs, a sprightly précis. The art of selection. The art of omission.

It has not been mentioned, for instance, that a great deal of Hugo's time these days is spent not thinking about the Middle East, or Kate, or his ex-wife, or his children, or his spiritual destiny, or his self-destructive tendencies, or his sexual eccentricities, or his job, but about his mother's state of health. Nancy Mainwaring is, incredibly to him, growing old. Her eyes are not too good, but, more seriously, her hands are becoming crippled by arthritis. She pretends they are not too bad; but they are, they are. It is astonishing, to Hugo, to see her change. He watches in disbelief, and his disbelief is a mirror of her own, for she cannot believe it either. Yet here it is. Not Old Age—that she had already accepted, had resolved to affront with an elegant mixture of resignation and contempt —but Illness. Astonishing. And she had pictured herself flitting to New York at eighty, to Venice at eighty-five. She has trouble with buttons and lids. (So does Hugo, of course.) And, most astonishing of all, it *hurts*. So *this* is what people mean by pain, says Nancy to herself, but not to Hugo, being a proud woman: what a long time it took me to find out, she tells herself. Nearly seventy years to make so simple a discovery.

Hugo is extremely worried about what will happen to her. She has plenty of acquaintances, but no friends, or so it seems to him. She has no one, in fact, but him. She has quarrelled with her sister-in-law Kay Morton, and the wheelers and dealers of the art world that she inhabits are not renowned for their compassion and forbearance. She has no one but Hugo, and Hugo does not know what to do. The lease on her charming little house expires in six years. The thought of his mother in an old people's home, however expensive, however august, however discreetly disguised as a country hotel, fills Hugo with physical anguish. She will refuse to be cared for: she cannot bear the proximity of fools, and who but a fool would choose to do up the buttons of an angry old woman? So that leaves Hugo. Is this the revenge he dreamed of as a boy, or, come to that, the reconciliation? He had imagined a rapprochement, but not of this nature.

Kate, as we have seen, is also worried about her parents. She does not visit them as often as she should, and compensates for this neglect by visiting Hugo's mother, whom she finds entertaining. (Kate, I fear, is a snob.) Evelyn's parents, fortunately for the balance of the narrative, are fine, both still active and in good health, though Mrs. Morton, now retired, is not quite as optimistic about comprehensive schooling as she once was, though she is still as committed to the principle. Ted's parents—but one could go on endlessly, and why not, for there seems little point in allowing space to one set of characters rather than another. Though Ted's parents are rather dull, or so he finds them. Healthy, like his in-laws, but dull, apparently content to garden and watch television and take the dogs for walks. They have retired to Ilkley, and have a fine view of the moors. Ted's brother James, according to Ted the most boring man in Britain, lives with them, but they don't seem to mind even that.

The middle years, caught between children and parents, free of neither: the past stretches back too densely, it is too thickly populated, the future has not yet thinned out. No wonder a pattern is slow to emerge from such a thick clutter of cross-references, from such trivia, from such serious but hidden connections. Everything has too much history, thinks Hugo, sitting at his table, trying to condense his own into a sentence. Even the table has too much history. Everything one does is weighed down with history. The way one mixes salad dressing, or chooses a pair of socks. Pre-history. And as for committing words to paper, it is not surprising that this exercise should present problems. When one was younger, one saw patterns everywhere, for the process of selection was so simple. One simply did not notice most things, having no means of noticing them. So they selected themselves.

How very annoying, thinks Hugo, pulling himself together slightly: I seem in the last week to have been thinking thoughts that I always used to dismiss as extremely uninteresting when other people claimed to think them: namely, that modern life is in some mysterious way too fragmented to be comprehensible (dinner with the Americans and Mujid?) and that modern consciousness is so burdened with its own past that it has worked itself into a state of paralysis, which I myself might all too aptly symbolise; though I might counter-attack by claiming that I got like this through too much action (admittedly while very drunk, and thank God for that; alcohol, in case anyone is interested, is a wonderful anaesthetic which sheds a happier light on some at least of the past) rather than through inaction (though, again, a journalist can hardly claim to be engaged, can he?)—too many data, that's our problem, as I said to Mujid, we all know too much, and haven't got the brains to process the info.

Hugo pours another large drink (it is now two in the morning and he has had a long day) and decides that he is merely going through a phase, like Kate, and that when he emerges, everything will look quite different and much more alluring. This cheers him up no end. "There's life in it yet," he says to himself, aloud, and smiles vaguely at the wall. And if you find Hugo a depressing spectacle, that's your choice. He is at the moment quite happy, even mildly inspired. Let us leave him sitting there, and divert our attention to Ted, who is a busy man and spends very little time worrying about paralysis, but a good deal of time in aeroplanes, where, as you know, one has to think about something.

Ted Stennett, on the BA flight from Bombay to London, found himself sitting in the first-class compartment (expenses paid by a drug company this time) next to a woman called Chloe Harlech, who had once been married to a man with whom he had once worked in the Radcliffe at Oxford. This is the kind of thing that happens to Ted. One could argue that if Evelyn and Kate travelled more often, or in districts more salubrious than Finsbury Park, it might happen to them too.

Chloe Harlech greeted Ted with recognition and distraction. She was preoccupied by the fact that she seemed to have left a gold Parker pen in her hotel room. "What a surprise to see you," she kept saying indifferently, manifestly unsurprised, as she hunted through yet more layers of her multi-zipped leather shoulder bag and delved in the bottom of various smart carrier bags. "Do you mind holding these for a minute for me while I just feel down the bottom here?" she said, thrusting parcels at him: he clutched them on his knee and watched while she struggled, noting with satisfaction the proximity of her long brown gently shining legs, her beige skirt riding up slightly to reveal her knees, her tanned gold-braceleted wrist. Her search was successful. "Thank God for that," she said, displaying her trophy. "I'd have hated to have lost it, I've nearly lost it so often. It's a memento. Such bad luck, losing mementoes."

"Who gave it to you?" said Ted, not one to waste time.

"Never you mind," said Chloe Harlech, not one to be bullied out of her own pace, and sat back in her seat as the plane swooped upward.

The stewardess offered champagne, but Chloe asked for orange juice. Ted echoed her request. They both sipped, warily.

"What have you been up to?" she asked, finally.

"I've been looking at a research project on new resistant strains of mosquito."

"Interesting?"

"To me, yes. And you?"

"Oh, just visiting." She lit a cigarette. "How's Evelyn?"

"Evelyn's fine, thank you. How's Tom?"

"I haven't seen Tom for six years or more. You probably know better how he is than I do."

"Did you marry again?"

"Yes. I did. But now I'm not." A long pause, and then she said, "Fancy your still being married to Evelyn. I call that quite an achievement. On her part, I mean."

"Thank you," said Ted.

"That's all right," said Chloe, politely.

Ted studied her obliquely. A beautiful woman, glossy with expense. He thought of Evelyn's workaday skirts and jerseys, her nondescript neutral safe well-bred evening gear. He thought of Kate's disordered assortments, her odd and usually unsuccessful forays into the exotic, her ethnic yokes and smocks, her girlish gingham dresses. Poor Kate, she'd never been able to decide what she looked like, and it was too late now. He thought of the woman in Cambridge, who looked very good in her overall but not very good in the trousers and sweat shirts she chose to wear off duty. A black cavern of growing dislike, largely for himself, yawned inside him, and he thought that he might as well fall into it as not. He proceeded, treacherously, to recount his experiences with Kate and the woman from Cambridge, to describe the trouble he had had with the women in his life. Chloe listened, reciprocated, responded with a few anecdotes of her own. A nasty excitement mounted in them, a conspiratorial deadly glee.

"One can't expect one woman to unite all the qualities one is looking for," said Chloe, as they looked down over Arabia Deserta. "Nor one man, either."

"No, but one goes on looking," said Ted Stennett.

"Yes," said Chloe Harlech. "I suppose one does. Or, at least, some of us do."

And they both fell silent, contemplating the horrible space beneath them, above them, around them, the yawning, gaping, sucking, hungry air. Love, for both of them, had ceased to be a journey, an adventure, an essay of hope. It had become an infection, a ritual, a drama with a bloody last act, and they could both foresee the final carnage. One could decide not to participate, but there was no way of changing the rules of the game. Was it worth it? Probably not, they decided. Chloe took out a paperback book and began to read, Ted took out his papers.

People who spend much of their time travelling are more likely to meet old friends and potential lovers than those who stay at home, Ted thought as he read the agenda for his next meeting. He always seemed to be meeting people whose paths had crossed his own. A small incestuous elite, with the same protagonists appearing and reappearing, playing out variations on a theme. He had entered this world alone, by his own endeavours, and none of the women he had known had had the guts to accompany him. Evelyn had stuck obstinately to her disadvantaged mothers and deprived babies and derelict old people, Kate had insisted on exploring her own weird, shabby, impossible, sprawling, unstylish noisy underground world, the woman in Cambridge had been no good at anything between work and bed, she couldn't even talk over dinner, and had never read a book in her life. Their horrible daily lives had muddied and bloodied him, they had tried to drag him down. Would it be different with Chloe Harlech? Was there a possibility of a golden world with golden Chloe, with her beautifully cut hair, her gold wrist watch, her gold pen, her gold bracelets, her first-class air tickets, her first-class friends? What was the point of all the hard work he'd put into his life to get up here in this pressurised cabin, if he couldn't have a woman to share his ambitions, to sustain his image of himself? None of them had loved him enough, none of them had loved him as he had loved them. They had not been single-minded, as he had been. They had not given themselves. They had sunk into clutter. Even the woman in Cambridge, who had seemed a better bet, being childless, had sunk into an array of unwashed cups and unmade beds and unironed sheets and angry tears. Ted looked at Chloe, and the smooth sheet of tawny hair that fell forward against her cheek as she read. The survival of the fittest. How Evelyn disliked Darwin, and Ted himself for arguing that she and her tribe were busy saving the useless at the expense of the useful, thus interfering with the natural wastage of society. How Kate had disliked Darwin, with what spirit in the old days she had tried to reject his suggestion that she herself was a fine specimen of nature's ruthless accidental adaptation, how childishly pleased she'd been when she'd come across some half-baked account of Bergsonian creative evolution, how angry when he'd demolished it. At least Kate tried, one could say that for her. She hadn't just shut him out, like Evelyn: she'd answered back. Why had even Kate shut him out, in the end? She had promised to love him for better for worse, in sickness and in health, and he had trusted her. But she had betrayed him to his own lonely dangerous malevolence, his profitless pursuit of an impossible ideal. Treacherous Kate, wicked Kate. She had made him a bad person.

Women crying, women dying in bathrooms. That was how it all ended. A destructive business, love. Time to retire, perhaps. "Put up again thy sword into its place: for all they that take the sword shall perish with the sword." Anger had kept him alive, anger and passion. He had embraced them willingly. And now felt this immense lassitude.

He looked through the small window at the huge white fleece of clouds, the vast sunny pillows and arches. Kate had never been on an aeroplane, she was afraid of flying. She called herself a journalist, and she was afraid of flying. No wonder she had to stick to damn silly articles about women and babies and menstruation and male-chauvinist pigs and whole-meal foods and London life in all its tawdry monotony. With everything going for her, she'd not had the nerve.

Lion-coloured Chloe closed her book, lay back, shut her eyes. Ted had been taken to see lions once, in Kenya. Large protected beasts, first-class beasts, roaming around dangerously in their large patrolled reserves. Stylish, graceful, expensive creatures. The lords of creation. But on their way out, like most of the large and the lovely. The real survivors were tsetse flies and mosquitoes, insecticide-resistant cockroaches, waterborne meningitis viruses swimming their way through the heavily treated waters of London. What amusing chats he'd had with Kate, in the past, about her Dad. He'd read that week of the destruction of farmland near Rotherham through fertilisation with sludge from neighbouring factories; a casualty of the Clean Air Bill. Instead of discharging their waste products into the air, the factories discharged them into the water supply, and thence into Farmer Thornton's fields, and thence into his prize short-horn cattle. A new pollution cycle. What would old Mr. Fletcher have made of that? How much he missed talking to Kate. She still spoke to him, of course, but with such maddening flippancy, so dismissively. Why could she not speak to him straight, in her old voice? What harm had he done to her that she should so refuse him? Now she spoke to Hugo instead. He had not thought it would end like this. They had all died on him, all those women. Was he the murderer or the victim? What had he done to them, and to himself?

When Chloe Harlech was woken by the pilot's final announcement, Ted amused himself by telling her about the cockroaches that were now thriving so busily in most wide-bodied aircraft. Chloe listened, yawning and stretching in the confines of her seatbelt, arching her shoulder, twisting her wrists and ankles elegantly to restore circulation.

"Oh dear, oh dear," said Chloe. "What with cockroaches and hijackers, air travel isn't what it was, is it? And the passengers"—she lowered her voice theatrically, allowing her large brown eyes to wander expressively over the other multi-racial occupants of the first-class cabin—"even in first class, you can't be sure who you're going to have to sit next to, can you?"

He was not at all sure that she was joking, though with a manner like hers, who could tell?

"The district's not what it was, of course," said Marylou Scott, from the midst of her vast off-white, gold-tasselled, slubbed-silk settee. "Arabs all over the show. Shocking, isn't it?"

She pronounced Arabs, for some reason, as Ay-rabs, and Kate could not tell if she were joking or not.

Kate murmured neutrally, and sipped tea from a fluted rose-painted gold-rimmed thin-stemmed porcelain cup. It was a long time since she had drunk from such a cup—not, in fact, since the last Christmas she'd spent with her parents when they had got out for ritual Christmas tea the never-otherwise-risked best. Her teeth felt very large as they clanked on the fragile china. Her teeth, in fact, *were* very large, and moreover very uneven, when compared with Marylou's dainty well-maintained even little set.

"When did you move here?" asked Kate, playing for time, trying to stick to dull topics while her eyes took in the rather over-exciting decor, which included large picture windows swathed with drooped and fringed white-and-yellow curtains, surmounted by a magnificent pelmet: a thick-pile apricot-pink carpet: a peach-coloured wall of mirror, engraved with floral patterns: a bank of electronic equipment: small scattered tables with spindly legs and leather-and-gilt Italianate John Lewis–style tops: various silver trophies and framed photo-graphs: vases of real flowers: an enormous gold clock in a glass case with many surely superfluous moving parts: many standard lamps of dull-white fake-antique wood with large fluted shades and silky fringes: a glittering gold chrome dimpled hostess trolley covered with drinks: tapestry-covered wastepaper bins: brass-and-glass coffee tables strewn with various down-market women's magazines (surprisingly down-market, Kate noted with interest, the same selections as she'd come across at Riverside, Romley, not a sign of a *Harper's* or a *Vogue*): two paintings of waves and seagulls in heavy gold frames: an enormous blue glass fish on the window sill: and, finally and most obtrusively, a statuette on a plinth of a sexy mermaid sitting on a dolphin. Kate's eyes kept straying back, despite herself, to this last object, for its angle was such that it looked as though it must topple over at any moment and crash into the deep foam of the carpet.

Marylou, after a certain amount of small talk, intercepted one of these glances, and, to Kate's initial embarrassment, began to laugh, a loud hard nasal laugh, her pretty head thrown back very indelicately and all her nice teeth showing, as well as some not so nice ones full of gold at the back.

"You're looking at my mermaid," she accused Kate. Kate nodded. Marylou laughed again. "Hideous, isn't it?" said Marylou. Kate demurred, politely, but Marylou insisted. "No, really, you can say what you like about it, *I* think it's hideous, but what can I do with it? It's too bloody big to shove in a cupboard, isn't it? I was given it by the producer of *Sea Change*, and my ex thought it was ever so nice, so there it stays. Solid bronze, you know. Weighs a ton."

"It looks as though it's going to fall over all the time," ventured Kate.

Marylou looked as though this aspect had not struck her, but nodded eagerly in confirmation. "Yeah, that's right, it's unbalanced, isn't it? Makes you feel seasick, don't it?"

After this surprising artistic accord, Kate and Marylou got on well. Marylou expressed curiosity about Kate's impressions of Romley in the 1970s, and about her project, and about the old Alma Mater, and said she'd be delighted to be interviewed, even though the fee would, as Kate said, no doubt not be in her usual bracket. ("My ex sees to all that, but I do what I want, right? I tell *him*, he doesn't tell *me*, right?") They even had a brief chat about their exes, and the eccentricity of men: Marylou seemed impressively hard-boiled, and Kate hoped she'd say some of the things to camera that she was prepared to say in private. They talked about the old days: Mr. and Mrs. Scott had retired, left the Fortunes of War in strange hands, and gone off to Wanstead, where Marylou's little sister Annie lived with husband and three children. Marylou didn't think much of Annie's choice of life style.

"She's really let herself go, has our Annie. Makes herself a martyr. It's a hard life, with three kiddies. She's ruined her figure. One was enough for me. And there's no need, I keep offering to help out, but she won't have it. Me and her husband don't get on, so I mind my own business." Marylou stroked a Siamese cat which had just leaped onto the settee by her. Her fingernails were long and varnished. "See this cat?" said Marylou. "She cost seventy pounds, and she's the dumbest cat in the whole world. Can't even miaow. She's a little stupid, aren't you, my little stupid? Do you like cats?"

"I've got two," said Kate, thinking how pleasant a life it would be, in a way, to lounge forever on large settees reading cheap magazines and stroking expensive cats: there was even something in the decor that appealed to an atavistic pre-Hunt streak in her. Romley Homes and Gardens. She wondered if she dared ask about her old friend Pauline. For some reason, she was apprehensive about Pauline's fate, and the sight of Marylou had merely intensified her apprehension. Was it the fact that Marylou had volunteered information about Annie, but had said not a word about her other sister? This is silly, said Kate, I'm a journalist, I must ask, and did.

She had guessed right. Marylou seemed to feel the need of a large gin and tonic to recount the Pauline story ("It's all right, it's ten to six, the sun'll be over the yardarm by the time the ice has melted," were the words with which she pressed Kate to accept one too) and exhorted Kate not to tell this story to anyone, not to tape-record it or anything like that ("Sorry, but you can't be too careful, I had a man put detectives on me once, the dirty swine") because it could land people in all sorts of trouble.

Pauline, in short, had gone to the bad, or rather had fallen in with a bad lot, with the big time. Her man had been put away for a bank job—five hundred grand, and they only ever found the half of it—and after a couple of years he'd escaped, had a face job done, and they'd scarpered, to Canada. "Oh, they're all right," said Marylou, "never want for nothing, but who'd want to be on the run like that? And he knocks her about something shocking. Carried on like a bloody tyrant. Fetch this, fetch that. I said to her, 'Pauline,' I said, 'how can you let him wipe his feet all over you like that?' And do you know what she said? She said, 'I love him, Shirl.' (That's my real name, Shirley.) 'I love him, Shirl.'" Marylou mimicked, with the utmost contempt, a tone of sentimental devotion. "Enough to make you throw up, isn't it? What a waste of a life. And she was a real good-looker, Pauline, could have made something of herself. Mind you, they've got everything money can buy. But what a way to get it." Marylou surveyed her own possessions, proudly. "Everything here I've paid for, fair and square. It's all mine, every stick and stone of it. All good clean money. And no one tells me where to get off. No one tells me anything."

A chilly silence fell on the silky fringes. Kate and Marylou looked at one another, askance.

"And it's not that she's stupid, either," said Marylou, a note of forlornness tinging her indignation. "She could have made out all right, couldn't she?"

"I don't know," said Kate. "There aren't all that many ways of making out, are there?"

"No, I guess not." Marylou stroked the cat, then said, "They say some women like being knocked about, but I never did, did you?"

"No," said Kate.

There was a tap on the door: an elderly housekeeping woman in a pink overall, to announce that there was a car waiting for Mrs. Armstrong. Marylou, deep in reminiscence, did not want to let Kate go, tried to give her another drink, wanted her to look round the house and see the swimming pool, her private viewing room, her conservatory, but Kate insisted; the children would be waiting for supper.

"You must bring your children," said Marylou, "they could have a swim, it's a lovely pool, it's heated, and my boy, he gets lonely, he needs company, he's away at school and then in the holidays . . ."

An icy loneliness breathed through the room as Kate rose to her feet. Marylou followed Kate to the door, staggering slightly on her precarious high-heeled fluffy mules: the gins had been strong.

"Yes, that would be lovely," said Kate, resolutely struggling into her coat in the vast, square, horse-brass-and-warming-pan, black-beamed fake rustic hallway, thinking

with longing of her own narrow hallway: and Marylou followed her out onto the crazy paving off the drive, the Siamese
cat rubbing and tripping round Marylou's ankles, to the waiting mini-cab. "Mind out, little stupid," Marylou kept saying to
the cat as she waved Kate goodbye, and Kate, on the journey
home, kept trying to remember where she had read a story
about three sisters, two bad and beautiful, and one called
Little Stupid; a line she abandoned in order to worry about
whether to stop off at the supermarket to buy supper or
whether she could fall back yet once more on take-away
curry: simultaneously she listened to the mini-cab driver's
account of why he was driving mini-cabs for his living.
Drivers always told her such stories: did she look such a
docile listener? This particular man had had a paper-box business in Essex, but his wife hadn't liked it out there in the
country and had persuaded him to move into London, where,
of course, the business had gone bust, leaving him heavily in
debt. "Women," said the driver bitterly, "women." People
were always saying that kind of thing to her too: what was the
matter with her, didn't she qualify as a woman, did she look
like a traitor to her sex? And what was her ideological sisterly
duty in such a situation—to present the wife's hypothetical
point of view, to protest that not all women are selfish and
foolish, or simply, like a good woman, to sit back and listen?
She chose the last course, for it let her worry about the supper
at the same time, but not without a bit of her mind thinking
that she ought to forget the sexist angle altogether and try to
listen to the story through Mujid's ears: what would Mujid
have done, would he have countered with a dissertation on the
collapse of small businesses in a failing capitalist economy, or
would he too have listened politely? And thinking of Mujid,
whatever would he have made of Marylou? And thinking of
Marylou, what had happened to her poor ex, of whom she
spoke so dismissively? Had he ended up driving mini-cabs too,
or had he managed to stake his claim to a share early enough?
And that boy, banished to a public school while Marylou sat

alone with her little cat? How quite extraordinarily odd
people are, Kate found herself thinking, as the man talked on
about loss adjustors and management consultants and what
they had ripped him off for, and how interesting, and how
diverse, and how lucky I am, how astonishingly lucky, to be
able to listen to them all, and how I love my job.

Curry it had to be, owing to a traffic jam caused by road
work, and to the presence in her house, when she reached it,
of a lot of extra people, all of them hungry, though some of
them politely said they weren't. Apart from her usual household of Mujid, Ruth, and Reuben, there was Puss Malone,
Vicky Stennett, Vicky's friend Vic, Danny Denham (youngest
son of Gabriel Denham, and friend of Reuben's), and Joker
James of Black Ice, strumming on Vicky's guitar. Seeing so
impossibly large a throng, Kate at once stopped feeling guilty
about not providing a delicious home-cooked dinner with
fresh veg, and switched to the much less taxing role of Generous Millionaire: distributing ten-pound notes like Lady
Bountiful herself, trying to persuade people not to order ten
totally different meals because it always got the shop confused
(or would have confused her had she been the shop), sitting
back with a gin and tonic as powerful as Marylou's while
various people went off to get the supper, describing Marylou's life style in what she herself thought a very spirited and
amusing manner, listening to Joker's equally spirited and
amusing account of an encounter with the National Front at
an anti-Nazi rally in Brixton, and Mujid's more hesitant but
equally interesting story about what a dentist in Wimpole
Street had tried to charge a fellow language student for a
filling: listening to Vicky and Ruth and Puss comparing notes
about their French master and whether or not he or Puss's big
brother could properly be described as a hunk: eating chicken
marsala o.t.b., washed down with pints of water: watching
Reuben and Danny Denham giggling in a corner, thinking
how stunningly Danny resembled his strange, pretty, washed-
out, fey, stylish mother Phillipa (who had become, of all

things, a devout Catholic convert, and a visitor of the dying, much to her ex-husband Gabriel's horror): watching Vic's earring, which had sprouted a strange dangling little bunch of red feathers: watching the tattoo on Joker James's forearm as he plucked away at the guitar, obligingly singing that immortal song "Gordon Is a Moron" for the children (this was Kate's own favourite, she particularly liked the verse

> I was so upset I cried
> All the way to the chip shop,

surely a high-water mark of late 1970s passion) and then moving on to a new lyric of his own, a surreal little folk tale about a porter in a hospital who learned to resurrect corpses as he wheeled them down to the morgue, and who released them into the streets in their long white winding sheets: a lyric inspired by personal experience as a porter in Cardiff, Joker claimed.

> And I saw the white souls walking
> In the streets of the dying,

sang Joker, a mad ecstatic expression of crazy holiness on his colourless London face: and she thought of Joker in the past, Joker aged fifteen, for she had known him for over ten years now, from before the days of his success, and would probably know him after them too, the way things were going, and with the turnover as it was in the music world. She'd met Joker at Hunt's; Joker was a Romley lad, and he and Kate had struck up a friendship on that basis, and Joker had taken to hanging around Kate's as well as Hunt's, rightly divining that Hunt was not really into successful people, and that Kate was, and Kate had listened to his adolescent fantasies, half bored and half impressed, and had fed him on bread and cheese and lent him pound notes and Penguin poets; Kate the Good Angel, the Proxy Mum; until he had disappeared one day for five years, to resurface in his present incarnation, an honoured guest, a way-out darling, a Romley hero, a holy boy. He had spent the missing years in Wales, in a commune, eating leaves, or so he said. Mark thought Joker was a twit, but Ruth and Reuben liked him. He believed in Peace and Love and Harmony.

(Ruth, watching her Mum listening to Joker's song with a respectful look on her face, nudged Puss and whispered, "Hey, look at her pretending to like it, she's not even listening, isn't she a pseud?" but Puss, her stomach full of Kate-bought chicken, to Ruth's relief whispered back, "No, I think she's *sweet.*")

And Kate *had* been listening, for when Joker's song came to an end, she said, after a moment's polite silence, "Well, that's really you, that one, Joker. Sick but elevating," and Ruth conceded to herself that her Mum wasn't, after all, a fool, and anyway Joker seemed to like her, even if it was only for old times' sake, for he took Kate's comment as a compliment and bowed to her gallantly.

After she had chased the younger ones away and to bed, and exhorted the older ones to talk quietly, Kate went to bed herself, and lay there, turning over in her head her encounter with Marylou, and her previous encounters with other ex-Romley Fourways women. Out-of-date Marylou, clinking and shimmering like the old-fashioned solitaire diamond on her finger. Solitaire. A solitary woman in a large house. Perhaps it was only avarice that glittered so brightly? An unusual vice in a woman. And one which Edie and Dora and Sharon and Marlene and Jayne had not had much opportunity to cultivate, though some of them, in their own ways, tried.

WOMEN AT THE CROSSROADS, REEL 1, TAKE 4

INTERVIEWER "So then you registered as an official child-minder?"

EDIE TUCKER "Yes, well, like, I had to, see they told me I had to, I was taking in more than the limit, so I had to register, they make it all so official these days, don't they—oh, do shut up, Kev, and get off the back of that settee, I've told you a thousand times—sorry, Mrs. Armstrong, he's a little devil, that one, look what he's done to the springs—yes, well, where was I?" (*Shot of Kevin pulling stuffing out of back of settee with the absent-minded bored concentration of a small chimpanzee; happy, repressed, frustrated, who could say?*)

W.C. [*the crew's little joke*] REEL 1, TAKE 15
DORA YOUNG ". . . and I always used to try to have a hot tea for them when they got back from school, but when they got bigger they never seemed to want it, they was always out with their mates, so I kind of stopped bothering, I thought, I might as well work full-time, there's never anyone here when I get home anyway, what's the point of putting yourself out, and we needed the money, I don't know, Stanley never seemed to hold down a job, he was always chopping and changing, couldn't settle, so I thought, why bother, I might as well work full-time, no point in hanging around an empty flat. . . ."
INTERVIEWER "And have the children got jobs yet?"
DORA YOUNG "Our Bob's working at a garage. Training to be a mechanic. One of these job promotion schemes, I think it is, something like that."
INTERVIEWER "And what about Patsy?"
(*Shot of Dora Young's face: capable, good-natured, prematurely aged, her hair actually in curlers, which Gabriel Denham had cajoled her into leaving in, though she'd tried hard to explain that she'd only had them in in order to take them out so her hair would look nice for the telly, but they'd caught her before she was expecting them, she'd no idea it would take so long to rig up all those lights . . . , and over Dora's face, at the mention of Patsy, passes an expression of doubt, alarm, shame, anxiety, pride; again, who could say?*)
DORA YOUNG "Yes, Patsy's got a job, she works at the mental hospital. She says she likes it, I wouldn't fancy it, but she says she likes it. Mind you, she's good with people, is Patsy, she's

ever so patient, but still, it seems a funny thing for a girl her age, a funny way to spend your life. . . ."

W.C. REEL 2, TAKE 16

JESSIE PARKER ". . . so off he went and joined the bloody Army, and I said to him, 'That's a mug's game, son, don't you come back here and complain when you find out what it's like, it's not all playing soldiers like in the adverts,' but he would go, the bloody fool, oh, he'd always been a funny lad, dressing up, playing with guns, reading those comics, I don't know what went wrong, and then they send him off to Northern Ireland, just like I said they would, ah, he was only a lad, eighteen he was, it isn't right. . . ." *(Shot of Jessie Parker in tears: so is the interviewer, thinking of Beatrice Mourre's son dead in Beirut, and her own son at peaceful Waterford: Gabriel Denham cuts, embarrassed, for what has this got to do with anything?)*

W.C. REEL 3, TAKE 8

(Shot of Sharon Sparks, with little Tessie Sparks on her knee: Tessie aged five, white ankle socks, bows in her hair, earrings in her ears, sucking a lolly, and wriggling uncomfortably, a doll stuffed upside down under one arm: shot of Tessie's doll's pram, an expensive imitation of a real pram, ribbons, canopy, and all.)

SHARON *(proudly)* "Oh, she's a proper little cutie, aren't you, Tessie? Isn't she cute?" *(She squeezes her daughter, who grimaces, wriggles even more, and rolls her eyes at the camera.)* "Oh, I always wanted a little girl, I loved dolls when I was little, and so does Tessie, don't you, Tess?"

INTERVIEWER "What's the dolly's name, Tessie?"

(Tessie wriggles, takes out the lollipop, and sticks in her thumb.)

SHARON "Go on, tell the lady what the dolly's name is. Lost your tongue, have you?" *(She shakes the child, not wholly tenderly.)*

INTERVIEWER "Oh, don't worry her. . . . So you always wanted to marry and have children, did you? You never had any other ambitions?" *(Sharon looks blank, and tries to pull the thumb out of her daughter's mouth; her whole attention is focussed on the child and the impression she is making.)* "Do you think Tess is going to take after you, Mrs. Sparks? After all, the world has changed quite a lot since we were girls, there are far more opportunities now for girls to follow a variety of different careers. . . ."

(Mrs. Sparks is not listening: she manages to extract Tess's thumb, wipes her mouth rather fiercely with a paper handkerchief, straightens her bows, and tries to persuade her to hold the doll in a more motherly manner, without much success. A brief struggle ensues, during which Tessie throws the doll on the floor and manages to scramble down after her. Shot of doll face-down on floor. "Cut," says Gabriel happily: the first interview so far that has gone according to plan.) (His plan.)

Various highly selective shots of girls in a concrete playground, making sand pies and swinging and sitting disconsolately on a roundabout: mothers wiping knees and noses: boys in an adventure playground, climbing poles and ladders. Teenage girls, *Grease*-style lipstick and high heels, talking about pop music. Mothers complaining about how the lift doesn't work, cement corridors, garbage cans, vomit. A young woman with a double pushchair staring dully at a duck surrounded by soggy bread in a muddy ornamental pond. A middle-aged working mother, Kate's contemporary, describing her Saturday-morning shopping routine. "Doesn't your husband help?" asks Kate, to which the woman looks surprised, then says cautiously, "Sometimes," but that it's no good sending him, he doesn't know what to look out for. "Why don't you tell him?" says Kate, to which the woman says, "Oh, what's the point, it's quicker to do it yourself, isn't it?" to which traitor Kate can only nod in whole-hearted agreement, for why pursue the subject further, why bother to seek confirmation for the finding that one husband in six never looks after his children on his own, one in four never puts them to bed, and one in three never even reads to them? What are statistics, after all? And it *is* quicker to do the shopping yourself.

Artifacts: flowered carpets, best tea sets, an ingenious variety of draped lace curtains, Spanish-style vinyl tiles, wall clocks rayed like the sun in never-dying Deco, china Siamese cats and pigs and dogs, Toby jugs, glass fish, plastic rabbits, rubbery trolls, outsize turquoise teddies, plastic daffodils, plastic palm trees, fake fur rugs bristling with spidery white acrylic electric light, all the wonderful eclectic bad taste of the English, the brave new world of synthesis.

Pockets of eccentricity and resistance: Sally O'Meara with her hundred cactuses, proud winner of various prizes at the Cactus and Succulent Society. Peter Kettle, who was so unstatistically distressed at his inability to read bedtime stories to his children, being illiterate, that he voluntarily submitted himself to the possible humiliation of being taught to read by a nice helpful middle-class girl. Marilyn James the plumber. The cheerful Domestic Science class of Romley Fourways who cooked for Kate and the crew, as Miss Scully had promised, an excellent lunch of leek soup with cheese savouries, steak-and-kidney pudding, and lemon mousse. Kate wishes, but again with a slight sense of treachery, that she had learned anything half as useful while at school herself, but dares not say so. All she ever cooked at school was one grey apple dumpling.

Encouraged by Gabriel, Kate has another crack at the subject of job-sharing and husbandly co-operation, thinking she might have a good subject in Denise Ball, née Scooter, who had remembered Kate and the old days well, and who had confided to Kate, on Kate's preliminary solitary reconnoitre, that her husband Terry had turned out a right bastard in many ways, but then, what do you expect of men, and at least these days he kept out of the way in the evenings, and what more could you ask of a man but that he should keep out of the way? She had laughed while delivering this view, a seasoned and solid laugh, a matriarchal laugh. Denise had, with much effort, qualified as a nurse, and had worked for a year or two until marrying Terry Ball, an electrical engineer; Terry had seemed to like the idea of nursing until the moment the marriage certificate was signed (indeed, had met Denise in hospital while recovering from a hernia operation), but had changed completely once they were wed, had nagged at her until she gave up her job, had insisted on hot meals and clean shirts, while failing conspicuously to uphold his side of the bargain. Unfaithful, mean with his money, always in the pub. Denise hadn't cared too much while the children were small, but when they started school she'd wanted to start work again, reluctant to waste all those hard years of training, all those laborious O Levels. But he'd put his foot down, turned real nasty. "So what could I do?" said Denise. "Anyway, I felt sorry for him, poor bugger, always had a big chip on his shoulder, you should have heard him go on about me being above myself, and him only an ignorant working man. Enough to make you sick. But I did feel sorry for him."

So what was Denise doing now? Working as a home help, looking after a few elderly folk in the estate. Why didn't he mind her doing that? "Well, he does mind," said Denise, "but he doesn't mind that much, it's no threat to him, you see, not like working in the hospital." "Why don't you ignore him and go back?" "Oh, well, it's not worth the trouble, and anyway I've forgotten all I ever knew, after all these years, fifteen years it's been, and things are all different now."

So was she happy with her old people?

"Well, it's not a question of being happy, is it? It brings in a few bob for myself and the girls, and it's useful work, isn't it? No, there's no point in arguing with a man, it's a waste of breath. But I'll tell you one thing, Kate, I'll make damn sure the girls get a fair deal. Our Sally, she's a bright one, she's doing her teacher's training, he's not going to stop her. We had a few rows about that, I can tell you, but Sally stood up for herself, she's got guts, has Sally, and Miss Scully backed her up, and now she's away at Birmingham, she's got a good grant, she loves it there. Out of harm's way. And Janice isn't doing badly either. That's another thing he's never forgiven me for, the fact we only had girls. He wanted a boy. I'd have gone on trying, just to please him, but after Janice I had all this trouble, and I had to have a hysterectomy. He blames me for that too. Thinks I did it on purpose. I told him, 'Do you think a woman'd suffer like that on purpose?' but he didn't seem to get what I meant. Amazing, men, aren't they?"

And Denise had gone on to confide precise gynaecological details of a fairly alarming nature, had listened with sympathetic interest to Kate's own sterilisation story, had told similar stories of friends and neighbours. Yes, Denise had seemed a good bet for a few forthright statements about equal opportunity. But of course, when it came down to it, when Gabriel Denham in his smart middle-aged denim jacket, and a camera man or two, and a lighting man, and a sound recordist, and an apprentice sound recordist had all crowded into Denise's small fourth-floor-front room, with its view of the unfinished marina, Denise had somehow lost the desire to express her views on the irrationality of men: instead she was sitting there facing the camera, smiling nervously, twisting her rings anxiously round and round her finger, straightening her collar again and again, clearing her throat, her gaze constantly straying from Kate towards the powerful Gabriel himself, the handsome Gabriel, that image of all that men might be, charming, smiling, soothing, debonair Gabriel, bedside-manner television-interview-manner Gabriel, fake Gabriel, Gabriel who must be pleased and placated and offered cups of tea, Gabriel whom even her hostile husband Terry dare not treat with anything other than respect: and towards Sandy Stewart, camera man, with his pale blue roll-neck sweater and Icelandic crucifix: and towards all the other lesser males, with

their strange suitcases of male equipment: and Denise could
and would say nothing against men in general or against her
husband in particular, of course not, all she would do was sit
there uttering platitudes about compromise and doing the
right thing for the whole family.

INTERVIEWER "So your husband persuaded you to give up
work?"
DENISE "Oh, no, it wasn't like that exactly, I mean it was a
joint decision."
INTERVIEWER "But you said he didn't like you working?"
DENISE "Oh, no, I didn't say that exactly. . . ."

(And *Damn, Damn,* thought Kate, watching Denise's
wandering eyes, *that's* why women go on about the need for
women film crews and women's publishing houses, how
bloody obvious: and too late now to explain to Denise that
there's nothing Gabriel would enjoy more than a full-blown
feminist diatribe, being, as he is, a hollow man, a media man,
a commercial man, and anyway that wouldn't even be true, as
Denise no doubt guesses, because Gabriel wouldn't like it (the
two-faced time-server) and neither would Sandy or Stu or
Keith or Ivor, none of them would like it, and neither would
that tarty little secretary that Gabriel seems to have acquired:
nobody would like it: Gabriel was a man still, and so were
Sandy, Stu, Keith, and Ivor, and they didn't like hearing other
men abused even if they were making lively programmes out
of the abuse; oh, yes, they liked seeing women making fools of
themselves, they'd enjoyed ghastly Sharon Sparks and her
poor little girl, and that rat bag Julie Girtin with her piece on
the blacks and the Asians, and Connie O'Brien with her poor
hen-pecked little husband, but they didn't like women talking
straight about men, no men working in a group did, though
they might agree individually, in fact Gabriel on his own,
creep though he was, was a perfectly reasonable chap, but put
him like that, behind a camera with his crew, and what could

one expect? Though anyway, even if you'd had a female director, a female crew, a female television company with female
managing directors and a female board, you'd still never have
got Denise Scooter to say a word in public against her husband, and not because she's frightened of him, but because
she thinks it would be treachery. And she'd be right there
too.)

Women's lives, progress. What kind of programme ought
one to make, anyway?

One can make any point one wants, without even faking
the evidence. Kate, in bed after a long day, tried to stop working, going over work in her head, and reached for *Old Peter's
Russian Tales* for a soothing bedtime story, and found there
the tale of the three sisters. Pauline, Marylou, and Annie
Scott. It was called "The Silver Saucer and the Transparent
Apple," and in it were two wicked, greedy, vain, haughty,
older sisters and a good, little, stupid one. When their father
goes off to market, the older ones demand fine fur-trimmed
dresses, and the little one asks for a saucer and an apple.
When the older ones see the visionary magic of these simple
gifts (the little sister can see the whole world in the transparent apple when she spins it in the silver saucer), they lead her
off into the forest to pick berries, and kill her with an axe. In
the story she comes to life again, like Alenoushka and her little
brother: but in real life no doubt she stayed dead, thought
Kate.

"Spin, spin, little apple," said Kate, shutting her book,
shutting her eyes, and the apple spun, and in it she saw, tiny
and far away like the Eiffel Tower in a crystal snowstorm:

herself and Peter, lonely Londoners, playing with a paper
boat on the fairy-tale village duckpond in Devon, oh, so pretty
a scene, but lonely, but outcasts, with the wrong clothes, the
wrong accents, ugly ducklings in an alien flock, bound in a
communion of exile, longing for the familiar resentments of
home (Had they so longed? Had that been it?)

Hugo's mother in her pretty drawing room, pouring

drinks, short-sighted but too vain to wear glasses, and the antique goblets with their square heavy cut stems smeared and dusty, even the gin and water strangely cloudy (or was that just from the lemon?) and a thin film of dust on the leaves of the lilies in the strong spring sunlight, her neat head turning on its stem, an out-of-date and stubborn woman

Hugo in his mountain cavern, huddled in a blanket, singing:

> I'd like to get you
> On a slow boat to China,

a song which the Kurds had much preferred to any of the cheerful Gilbert and Sullivan or mournful Bach chorales with which he also regaled them

Marylou on her settee with her little cat

Danny Blick's house in Arblay Street, and herself and Danny eating thick slices of bread and syrup, standing up in the kitchen, in the warm stuffy smell of oilcloth and tobacco smoke and Alsatian dog

Phillipa Denham in her cluttered kitchen, Phillipa crazed and thin, cutting even thicker slices of bread and peanut butter for the boys, pouring cups of tea, smiling vaguely, as though not in this world at all

herself and Evelyn and the children, years and years ago, transfixed in one of those endless dark dull afternoons, clouds piled heavy in the sky, throwing bits of bread to ducks and moorhens, watching the thin scummy film on the water's edge

Ted Stennett and the Woman from Cambridge, the faceless, voiceless, nameless woman, a face like a white blank potato, for what could one imagine, a face like a stocking mask or a bandaged napalm victim, and all other images of Ted gone forever, gone and lost

herself and Stuart, laughing all those years ago before Mark's birth, laughing as they lay in bed and he rubbed foul-smelling raw cheap yellow lanolin from a big brown pot (for they had been very poor) into her swelling belly, laughing to conceal who knows what threatening fears and resentments

Mark's birth, nearly nineteen years ago, Mark with his damp black hair, wrapped in a hospital blanket with red stitching, and Beatrice in the next bed in her lacy bed-jacket with her little son clamped to her large purple nipple, talking away, as the (now dead) baby sucked, of the beauties of the Lebanese beaches (now not so beautiful) and of the snowy mountains (they perhaps endured) and the ripe fruits, and both of them so proud, there in the past, in the distance, so happy with their babies

and Mujid as a baby in his village—but here the transparent apple dimmed and clouded like Nan Mainwaring's gin and water, for how could Kate from Romley conjure up that village, with or without the aid of magic? A cluster of flat-roofed huts in a flat wide valley, with herds of Biblical goats? A village perched on a mountainside? On a high plateau? Yellow earth, red earth, dust, sand? Coca-Cola signs, gas stations, corrugated iron roofs, oil pipelines? Or islands of date palms in the wide Euphrates? Camel thorns, tamarisks, mosques, minarets? And yet there lay Mujid, sleeping no doubt, a few feet away, his glasses no doubt safely on Mark's bedside table

She fell asleep thinking of Mujid, and dreamed that she was sitting on the floor of a large room with a lot of women, all of them wrapped in black chadors, and she herself wrapped and enfolded in this large shapeless garment, and inside it was dark and safe and comfortable, secret and profound. A reactionary dream.

While Kate and her family were eating chicken marsala from the Taj Mahal, Evelyn was dishing up chicken in lemon sauce to a slightly jet-lagged Ted, a Pakistani friend who was trying to teach her Urdu, her Danish husband, her sister Isobel, and her sister's husband David. The gathering had been arranged before Ted's Bombay dates had been fixed, and Evelyn had decided not to move it, for Ted's return would be better diluted with outside company, particularly that of David and Isobel, a powerful couple who were usually able to restore to Ted the respect with which he had originally regarded the entire Morton family. He was at his best on such occasions, listening with attention to Ayesha (who worked for International Family Planning) and her entertaining descriptions of a colleague of hers (a man, of course) who believed that abortion was the cheapest, easiest, and safest form of contraception; asking her about a project she'd worked on in rural Pakistan; and entering with proper family spirit into an analysis of the eccentricities of the absent third sister, Josephine, who had bought a farm in Pembrokeshire, although neither she nor her husband could tell a cow from a bullock, and would not possibly, they all predicted, survive six weeks away from the comforts and distractions of the metropolis.

Isobel was a harder, darker, sharper, brighter version of Evelyn. But perhaps, after all, not quite as intelligent, Ted thought, listening to her. Nevertheless, they were an impressive package, the Morton sisters. Well informed, well read, witty, original, and above all so unshakably, so unquestioningly confident. Never a moment's doubt of their own right to their own opinions ever seemed to cross their minds. One could never put them down. One could mock them, besiege them with facts, overwhelm them with theory, and they were always right there, fighting back, answering back, undismayed, unsubdued, and quite often right into the bargain. Breeding, intelligence, and education, all in the same deal. Whatever uncertainties they suffered in private, they brought none of them to the dinner table. A fine public manner, they had, all three of them. He'd done a clever thing in marrying Evelyn. He'd learned a lot from Evelyn.

Evelyn, watching them, serving second helpings, wondering how Isobel managed to eat so much and stay so thin, caught a reflection of this reflection as Ted refilled their glasses, and thought, Yes, well, grateful indeed he should be, grateful he intermittently is, what more should I want? Whatever bad things one can think of Ted, and one can think plenty, at least he is never boring, he never repeats other people's ideas, he never tells an old joke, he makes it all up as he goes along, and that's something. But if he thinks I'm going to start sleeping with him again because he's quarrelled with his woman in Cambridge, he can fucking well think again. So thought Evelyn, smiling pleasantly as she extracted a lemon pip from her rice and laid it neatly on the side of her large yellow hand-made plate.

And they talked on, over cheese, of farms and subsidies, of the simple life, of communes in Wales, of modern technology and solar heating, of Wordsworth and the romantics, of nature and Rousseau. Isobel was a lecturer in English Literature at Sussex, whither she surreptitiously commuted, and Wordsworth was her passion. She quoted from "The Prelude" at length. She was very fond of the sound of her own voice. Ted, who predictably hated any back-to-nature rubbish, listened entranced and enraged, enjoying a favourite combination of emotions. A clever woman, who couldn't bear to leave London for long enough even to fulfill her job's rather limited residence requirements, sounding off in resounding melodious tones about how nature never did betray the heart that loved her, and saying, with mounting excitement, slicing into her Brie, "But listen to this, listen to this bit, do you mean you don't even like this?" and she declaimed:

> A single tree
> There was, no doubt yet standing there, an Ash
> With *sinuous* trunk, boughs *exquisitely* wreathed;
> Up to the ground and almost to the top,
> The trunk and master branches everywhere
> Were green with ivy . . . something something something . . .
> > Oft have I stood
> Foot-bound, uplooking at this lovely tree

> Beneath a frosty moon. The hemisphere
> Of magic fiction, verse of mine perhaps
> May never tread; but scarcely Spenser's self
> Could have more tranquil visions in his youth,
> More bright appearances could scarcely see. . . .

"I mean to say," said Isobel, "there's nobody like him . . ." surveying her audience triumphantly, but correctly suspecting that, alas, none of them knew "The Prelude" well enough to be able to appreciate the relative obscurity of the passage.

"Oh, I've got nothing against Wordsworth," said Ted. "After all, he did what he said he was going to do with his life, and not many people manage that. In fact, some of my favourite poetry is by Wordsworth. When I was young, somebody wrote me a love letter, and quoted a poem that went something like this, do you know it?

> You have so loved me, that no place on earth
> Can ever be a solitude to me.

And I thought that was wonderful, I wasted hours trying to find who said it, I even looked in all the love poets, Donne, Robert Graves, Elizabeth Barrett Browning. But of course it was Wordsworth. To his sister."

" 'On the Naming of Places.' 'There is an eminence,' 1800," quick as a flash said smart competitive Isobel, betraying not a flicker of surprise at Ted's acquaintance with at least the names of poets; and they discussed, over coffee, the Wordsworths and Coleridge, and whether William and Dorothy had suspected that their feelings for one another were incestuous, and if so, what they had done about it, and whether sibling incest was rare or commonplace, increasing or decreasing, more traumatic or less traumatic after Freud, and whether Dorothy had been a good influence on William or a restrictive one.

And Evelyn sat back in her chair and let the conversation wash around her, comfortably, watching vivid Isobel in her scarlet grandad shirt, elegant Ayesha in her pretty peacock sari, lean and bespectacled David (a psychiatrist with strong views on siblings and incest), neat and dapper Henrik, a historian who thought Wordsworth wasn't a patch on Goethe; they talked on, of sex and poetry, and Evelyn sipped coffee from a brown cup and wondered whether to get out her patchwork, her gaze straying to the pale yellow, shaggy, spindly, sea-anemone fronds of the chrysanthemums that Ayesha had brought her, to the ominous crack in the wall over the brass rings of the curtain rail, to the tawny carpet that would soon need attention from Patent Steam Cleaning Ltd., to the grandfather clock that she had inherited from, indeed, her grandfather. The other two sisters had been quite ridiculously jealous, with no justice but some reason, for it was a lovely clock, with charming enamelled pictures of the four seasons, a farmer sowing, reaping, gathering apples, feeding a robin in the snow, memorials of time's passing and time's rebirth, and there it stood, ticking away, its pendulum swinging, recalling childhood afternoons, Grandpapa's death, Sebastian and Vicky playing with their Summer and Winter wooden jigsaw as good children should: continuity, tradition, safety, pleasantness. Balm to hurt minds, thought Evelyn, though she could not remember where the phrase came from; she didn't read much poetry these days, though Isobel tried to keep her in touch by presenting her, each Christmas, with new poets that she really ought to tackle. After a day struggling with the inarticulate and the bureaucratic, a day of being abused on one doorstep in the vilest language, welcomed over another to dirty floor-cloths and the dank smell of too many small chil dren and sour milk; after an encounter with a distraught thirty-year-old seventeen-stone woman with the voice and face and mental capacity of a child, who wanted her seventy-five-year-old father put away before she killed him or he killed her; after an interview with a weeping devoted foster mother whose foster child had shot a fireman on a ladder with an air gun; after such a day, what a relief to hear people talk of sex and poetry, to eat lemon chicken and green salad and Brie, to sit in one's own home. Why ever venture out of it? Why not stay inside in the warm, like Isobel and Josephine? Ayesha knew why. Ayesha was quite pleased with her progress in Urdu.

Evelyn's eyes began to close, her head nodded. Vicky, coming in late, opened the drawing-room door to say good night, and there were five animated adults, including her father back from India high on jet lag, and her mother asleep in an armchair, a sight which filled her with indignation and tenderness: Never, thought Vicky, never will I let myself become a slave to convention, never will I marry and cook dinners and wear myself out trying to do too many things at once, and she waved good night to anyone who wanted to wave back, and kissed her mother on the top of her soft greying hair, and disappeared into the kitchen, where she finished off the lemon chicken, augmented (for they hadn't left much, the greedy swine) with a tin of cold baked beans.

In bed, after a brief chat about the resistant mosquito, Evelyn asked Ted who had written him lines of Wordsworth in a love letter, and Ted said, "Why, it was you, or at least I thought it was you." "Good God," said Evelyn, and began to laugh, "Good God, I didn't know I'd ever known any Wordsworth, I must have got it out of a dictionary of quotations, are you sure it was me?" "Almost sure," said Ted, and they both laughed, for, whatever else one thought, it was amusing to have a past behind them so long that they'd forgotten part of it, and Evelyn, as she fell asleep on her side of the bed (which had developed something of a slope, through years of effort spent keeping well away from Ted in the night), could perhaps dimly recall writing such a thing in a letter, and certainly could remember thinking such a thought, even though Wordsworth, clearly, had expressed it more memorably than she could have done. And maybe, therefore, in one way or another, it was true.

(Neither of them ever found out how significantly they

had misquoted Wordsworth. The grand old man had been a step ahead of them. Even clever Isobel had not spotted it, a lapse that would have annoyed her had she ever discovered it, for she liked nothing more than correcting other people's quotations. An interesting lapse.)

This document began in October, with Kate and Hugo at lunch.

During November, the following events took place.

Stuart Armstrong recovered from measles, only to succumb to a lingering malaise which was tentatively identified as glandular fever, an illness in which his ex-wife Kate says she does not believe.

Hunt's house was burgled and set on fire, not seriously, probably by ex-inmates, who also ground half a pound of Camembert and some taramasalata into an old Afghan rug. Hunt did not complain to the police for various reasons, and did not complain much to anyone else either, to some of his friends' surprise: had the old boy lost his grip, or was he mellowing at last?

Hugo Mainwaring finished another chapter of his Middle East book, and caught himself wondering whether or not he ought to go and have a look at the Shi'ite demonstrations in Bagdad. The thought of catching an aeroplane again produced in him the faintest stirrings of physical excitement, like the stirrings of sexual desire: the first in many months.

Mujid enlarged his active vocabulary to a thousand words, his passive to goodness knows how many more, bought a pair of Clark's shoes with which he professed himself delighted, and received a letter from his fiancée, Simone Mourre, the first for many weeks, telling him that she had finished her doctorate and would, after presenting it and herself at the Sorbonne, join him in London.

Mark Armstrong passed his driving test. He also won a prize in a British Airways national competition for a design for a luggage trolley, and could not decide whether to spend his prize money on a car or a holiday in Morocco next spring with his two girlfriends Lucy and Lily. Or could he wheedle Kate into subsidising both, on the pretext of his approaching birthday?

Vicky Stennett had her hair cut very short and dyed orange, which enraged her father, depressed her mother, and, I am sorry to say, amused Kate.

Ted Stennett had, in most ways, an excellent month. He was offered a highly lucrative appointment in America, but refused this opportunity to join the brain drain, for the truth was that Ted remained deeply satisfied by the fact that he had made himself so acceptable to the British establishment: what was money, to a boy from Huddersfield, compared with the pleasure of government committees? He was also much stimulated by the discovery of an extremely interesting new virus which killed a laboratory technician in Wolverhampton, and which seemed potentially even more lethal and mysterious than the Marburg and Ebola varieties, for the technician in question had finished working on monkey-cell cultures three months before the fever set in, and he died after only three days. A wonderful enigma. Ted, gazing at the innocent wizened little faces of the sprightly green vervets and diminutive talapoins in the laboratory farm at Midhurst, pleased that no murmur of this exciting new development had reached the press (for Ted, once an admirer of open government, was now one of its keenest opponents), reflected with admiration on the unpredictability of nature. Who could tell what secrets lay hidden in these enchanting little creatures? He waited for another case, and was not disappointed: despite all the precautions, a mortuary attendant also developed symptoms. His joie de vivre was only slightly marred by unbidden nightmares featuring the drawn, ghost-like, sullen features of the victims he had seen in the Sudan, and by the discovery that he had himself contracted a resistant strain of non-specific urethritis, presumably caught some time ago from the woman in Cambridge, an unfair legacy in view of the fact that she was herself a biologist and should have known better.

The social workers' strike and the garbagemen's strike ended, and new strikes by schoolteachers, sewage maintenance workers, and civil servants began.

Joan Kingsley at the day-care centre in an inspired move added mothers' birthdays to the large Birthday Chart in the Blue Playroom, and resolved to ensure that all mothers received a homemade (i.e., day-care-centre-made) card from their own offspring on the appropriate day.

Gabriel Denham's second wife Jessica accused him of having an affair with Kate Armstrong, and Gabriel truthfully said that he was having no such thing. He did not add that he was in fact having an affair (if so it could be called) with his research assistant.

Reuben Armstrong fell off his skateboard, and his mother said he had only himself to blame.

Hundreds of students shot one another in universities in Turkey, Iraq, Pakistan, and various other trouble spots.

An article in the *New Statesman* argued that the Western view of the veil as a garment of female repression was fundamentally ill-informed and misguided.

Another corrupt African regime fell, to general rejoicing.

Sam Goldman's play came off after only twenty-six performances, though Hugo had decided on reflection that it was, after all, quite a memorable work.

The *New Statesman* acquired a new editor and several of its staff resigned, and the paper for which Kate and Hugo write teetered on the brink of closure, filling both of them with apprehension and excitement.

Another Iraqi diplomat was shot in Piccadilly.

An Irishman claimed to have planted a bomb in Beckton Sewage Works that would spread disease and destruction for many miles around, a claim which filled Mr. Fletcher with

delight, for it seemed to indicate that people had at last realised that sewage plants were vital organs. The bomb scare
proved to be a hoax, but it provided Kate with an interesting
article on a theme she had not treated in years, and it also
proved a good bargaining point in the sewage maintenance
workers' pay claim, though presumably that had not been the
intention of the unidentified Irishman.

Kate Armstrong interviewed dozens more women for her
television programme, and argued with Gabriel Denham
about the editing of these interviews, which he wanted to use
to paint a picture of women's innate conservatism and resistance to change: "Don't you see," said Gabriel, "that would be
much more provocative, inspire people to greater efforts, and
all that crap?" Kate argued that the interviews fell into no
recognisable pattern, and that it was unfair to try to force
them into a general statement about Women Today: it would
be much better to let them speak for themselves. She also
accused Gabriel of making her look fat and shooting her from
strange angles so that it looked as though she'd got a double
chin. (Her horror at her own facial expressions was so profound that she kept it to herself.)

Hugo Mainwaring saw the rushes of Kate's programme
and pointed out to her and to Gabriel that the reason why
they couldn't make it into a proper shape was because it
wasn't about women and equal opportunity at all, nor even
about sexist conditioning in early childhood, though it contained plenty of instances of that. Hugo said it was about
sibling rivalry and sibling conditioning, and pointed out that
there were interesting co-relations between the behaviour of
children reared in all-male sibling groups and all-female sibling groups (the Scott family being a striking example, and
the interview with martyred Annie in Wanstead a masterpiece
of unwitting self-revelation). Kate, said Hugo, ought to have
been asking different questions altogether. Kate and Gabriel,
astonished by this fresh light, looked at one another open-
mouthed in the comfortable dubbing studio off Wardour

Street, sitting up to attention from their slumped positions on the low black leather chairs, and said, *"What?"* Meanwhile, said Hugo, Kate ought to stop messing around and take a degree in sociology, as that was clearly what she was interested in and it was a subject perfectly adapted to her talents.

Then Kate and Hugo and Gabriel went out and had a late lunch together in Soho and talked about these things over a carafe of wine, and laughed a lot, and Gabriel told them that he had always been passionately jealous of his older brother Marcus and in love with his sister Clelia, and that he'd cocked his own life up trying to do all the things that Marcus couldn't do, although he, Gabriel, couldn't do them either, and Kate told them about Peter and his anonymous letters, the first time she'd ever mentioned them to anyone, and Gabriel said, "How do you know it's him?" which took her aback a bit for after all her evidence was slight: and Hugo told them that having been an only child was no doubt what had lured him into his own strange fantasies, and that his mother had once said to him that she'd thought of having another child to keep him company but her psychiatrist had warned her off when she told him she kept having dreams of chopping off babies' fingers like butter with a large knife on a breadboard, and when Hugo had looked unavoidably alarmed at this story, she had said, "But, darling Hugo, it wasn't *you* I was dreaming about, it was a little tiny new baby," as though that made the whole thing all right. Kate, Gabriel, and Hugo celebrated the wonderful variety of life and the delightful richness of potential disaster by ordering, quite uncharacteristically, a Sambucca, crowned with a flaming coffee bean (it reminded Gabriel of a weekend in Rome with an old flame), and Kate, unaccustomed to what she described as such poncey luxury, drank hers before the glass had cooled and burned her lip. Still filled with good fellowship, they had wandered out into the darkening afternoon and down the Charing Cross Road to the National Portrait Gallery to look at a painting that Hugo said his wife Judith said was the spitting image of his mother. "I won't tell you who it is, it's a surprise," said Hugo, and they went in through the entrance hall beneath a lot of scaffolding (Kate as ever embarrassed to open her bags for inspection, so full were they of untidy-looking garbage, including some rather high-smelling cheese she had impulsively bought for supper in Old Compton Street) and up the wide stone staircase and past an assortment of kings and queens and poets until they finally came to a halt before Vanmour's portrait of Lady Mary Wortley Montagu. They stood and stared, Kate trying hard to remember who Lady M.W.M. was, and Gabriel congratulating himself upon knowing, for earlier that year he had made a documentary about vaccination and immunisation (the falling rate thereof and reasons for), and Lady Mary stared back, elegant, tall, slim, poised, posed, beautifully dressed, from her Oriental background, her neat little head indeed as alert, her neck as well turned as Mrs. Mainwaring's, and a similarly provocative narcissistic look in her faraway eyes.

"Fie, fie upon her," said Gabriel, who had once played Troilus at Oxford,

> There's language in her eye, her cheek, her lip,
> Nay, her foot speaks

—and so it did, peeping from beneath her long shimmering feather-trimmed gown with engaging lightness. She was holding by the hand her little boy Edward, dressed in white gauzy Oriental bloomers. He didn't much look like they imagined the infant Hugo must have done, being pinker and plumper, but that didn't matter, the ensemble was telling. "You see," said Hugo, "the *way* she's holding that poor child"—and they did see, even as he pointed it out: the pretty young mother had her son's arm slightly raised at an uncomfortable angle, almost above his head, an angle that must have hurt had he been asked to hold the pose for long. An unfeeling, forced, unnatural angle. "She kept it up so long the arm withered and died and dropped off," said Hugo, and both Kate and Gabriel turned involuntarily to check to see whether it was indeed the same arm that Hugo had lost, and it was; then all three of them laughed, and Gabriel said that age had at last caught up with his own indomitable mother, she had had a slight stroke, and had to take things very easily.

They wandered on through the gallery, in search of further resemblances, Kate commenting as they went that she and Hugo had often expressed a willingness to swop mothers and a disbelief that the other could ever put up with their own, Gabriel countering with the information that he wouldn't swop his mother with anyone's, so fond was he of her, and came to rest once more in front of the First Duke of Buckingham, tall, effete, deformed by languor, his long white-satin legs displayed with disproportionate pride. "Look at his *shoes*," said Kate, peering at his little high-heeled pumps with their great rosettes of lace, "I wouldn't dare to wear anything so pretty, and I'm supposed to be a woman."

"How very dully we dress these days, Gabriel," said Hugo, and the two men looked at one another appraisingly, Gabriel at Hugo's fading cords and wilting frayed limp pale-blue cotton shirt and shapeless jacket, Hugo at Gabriel's denim jacket and low-slung trousers. "Do you know," said Gabriel as they made their way to the exit, remembering other appointments, "I keep getting letters addressed to Dear Mr. Denim these days? Do you think someone's trying to tell me something? But if I stop wearing this kind of gear, what the hell do I move on to next?"

On Charing Cross Road they parted, Hugo wandering off to meet a man at the Garrick, Gabriel hailing a cab to return to his office, and Kate waving goodbye, irresolute, for she had half an hour to kill before she was due in Whitehall to talk to a man from the Department of the Environment about Adventure Playgrounds. She would, she thought (impressed by how much she had enjoyed the portraits), drop in at the National Gallery and have a quick look at Pieter de Hooch, something she was always meaning to do but never found time for: but somehow when she got there the Dutch masters seemed to be not what she was looking for, they even had, was it possible, a certain dull gleam of complacent claustrophobia, for there was more to life than back yards and fishheads and apple peel, so she strayed on, thinking of Stuart and the old days and how much he had opened her eyes, for when she first met Stuart and Luisa she had been as stupid as a cat or a pigeon when presented with paintings, more stupid perhaps, for a psychologist friend had recently told her that cats and pigeons are highly discriminating when presented with figures, figures in landscapes, landscapes without figures, and she herself was still, she had to admit, slightly self-conscious in an art gallery, aware that she was being cultured and virtuous, like a character in an Iris Murdoch novel: and strayed finally into the room where the Claudes hung, and looked at Isaac and Rebeka's marriage, and at Aeneas at Delos, and at the embarkations of St. Ursula and the Queen of Sheba. Small enigmatic figures, gesturing calmly, while in the foreground or background the sea glittered, the surface of the water ruffled, the ropes of the rigging plucked and rapped and tightened, the canvas began to lift and swell, the heart to rise; the open sea shining with invitation, and radiant, far out, the paths of the sea. The little white waves, the mares' tails, the rising breeze. Embarkation. Her heart stirred, and she walked on, pausing before a painting she had never seen before: *Psyche Locked Out of the Palace of Cupid*, it called itself, or, alternatively, in quotation marks, "The Enchanted Castle." There sat Psyche in the foreground, in an attitude of despondency, heavy, dull, large-limbed, dark, a large woman clearly abandoned, though Kate did not know the story, not having had much of a classical education. In the middle rose the castle, solid, impregnable. And there beyond them, again, the sea, and little white sails free in the wind, in the sunlight. Why did not Psyche look up and see all that glittering expanse? How could her heart not rise if she were to look up? Why did she sit there so dumbly, so inelegantly, so much of a heap, so intent upon the earth? She should look up, and move, and go.

The castle of love was a prison, a fortress, a tomb, how could she not appreciate her luck in being locked out, in being safe here in the open air? Let her rise and go. (Yet in there, locked within, had she not had the illusion of possessing infinite space?) Kate stood and gazed, almost managing to forget to congratulate herself on her interest, so significant did the painting seem, so full of promise and of possible hope: I won't remember it properly, I know, she said to herself, I will buy a postcard to remind me, a memento of this small promise, and off she went back to the Gallery Shop, but there was no post-card, so she tried the woman who sells prints and black-and-white photographs, and the woman had no photograph, and, indeed, when she looked the painting up in the catalogue, there was no record of it, nor in the appendix nor the addenda. "But I saw it," Kate said, "it was there." "That's very funny," the woman kept saying, and in the end Kate said she would go back and check the painting's reference number, wondering as she went if she had invented it, though how could she have done, she wasn't clever enough to invent a painting, even in a dream; or had she embarrassingly got the artist confused, was it perhaps by Poussin or someone like that, or was Claude's name really Lorrain, or had she pronounced Claude so badly in her ignorant Romley way that the woman had misunder-stood her? She got lost on the way back, looked at her watch, saw she was going to be late for Mr. Spofforth unless she set off at once, and had to abandon Psyche to her gloom, the mystery unsolved. (When she got home, she rang Stuart to ask him about this adventure, and he told her that the painting had probably been on loan. Which it had.)

Later that same evening, Hugo's daughter Susanna, on an unfrequented Underground platform, on her way to spend the night with the Stennetts after a party, saw a man drop a ball-point. She picked it up and ran after him to return it, as a good girl should, but as she was about to tap him on his broad donkey-jacketed shoulder she had so vivid a vision of his turn-ing round and hitting her, for no reason, in the face, of his throwing her on the tracks, raping her in the tiled passage, that she hesitated: but tapped him on the shoulder just the same, and suffered no worse a fate than the glare of his equally terrified surprise at her unexpected timid assault.

Sitting on the tube, in the safety of company, breathing fast as a result of her ridiculous past moment of terror, elated by her own ridiculously tiny bravery, she looked forward to recounting this episode to Evelyn, for Evelyn maintained that cities were made safe only by a conspiracy of faith. "We ought all to behave *as though* we trust one another, for the more often ordinary people walk across the Heath, the safer it is, the more we use public transport, the safer it will be," Evelyn had said on the occasion of her own children reprimanding her for walking home one night from a party alone. "You're a hysterical lot," Evelyn had said, "and your hysteria makes things worse." This attitude had pleased Susanna immensely. Sebastian and Vicky had disappeared, bored (for they had heard it all before), but Susanna had stayed to listen to Evelyn on Kant and the categorical imperative. Act so that each act may be a general law. This came well from Evelyn, thought Susanna, for Evelyn knew the dangers, the rough side, the seamy side, and continued to brave them. Susanna, her home life wrecked by Judith's pursuit of revenge and by the tragic spectacle of her brother, was easily moved by appeals to faith and forgiveness. Of course one must trust the anaesthetist, the train guard, the hitchhiker, the lost tourist, the man who drops his ball-point, for how else can society function? Everyone must be extended faith, everyone must play a part in keeping whole the fabric: one must not panic, one must not run away, one must not spread alarm. (No need to go to the other extreme, of course, as Hugo had done: looking for trouble was just as wrong as cravenly running from it or wantonly inventing it. Susanna had her own opinions about her father Hugo's accident; she thought he had incurred it on purpose, seeking to compensate for or to expiate his guilt at her brother David's misfortune.) Evelyn would like to hear, thought Susanna, waiting for the ancient lift, of the non-existent blow from the man with the ball-point.

But when she got to the Stennett household, Evelyn was not there to hear the story, for the blow, when it fell, had fallen on Evelyn.

It was not lethal, nor entirely random, nor entirely unexpected, but it was bad enough, near enough.

Shocked, shaken, oddly convinced that she had herself escaped injury through Evelyn's substitution, Susanna listened to Kate and blotchy Vicky and subdued Sebastian as they relayed to her their version of events: Ted had been away in Liverpool, speaking at a dinner, and was now on his way home. The hospital had summoned Kate, at Evelyn's request; she in turn had tracked down Vicky and Sebastian, broken the news to them, and was now waiting with them, amidst the debris of supper, for Ted's return.

What had happened, it seemed, was this. Evelyn, on her rounds, had called on a client, one Irene, in Jubilee Park Road in Stoke Newington. While talking to Irene in her kitchen, Irene's man Joseph Leroy, a black six-foot Rastafarian, had appeared unexpectedly, and had attacked either Evelyn or Irene with a bread knife; in the ensuing fracas Irene had thrown a chip pan of hot fat at Leroy and followed it up with a few plates and a bottle of cleaning fluid, the last of which hit Evelyn in the face. Leroy, staggering under the onslaught, had tripped over the paraffin heater, and had set himself and the room alight. Police, ambulance, and fire brigade had been summoned by a little Sylheti girl from downstairs, the only person in the house, apart from the victims, to speak intelligible English. The man and Evelyn had been taken to hospital in the same ambulance, and by the time Kate got there Evelyn had been taken from Resuscitation to a ward, where she lay bandaged but conscious and, according to Kate, perfectly OK.

A domestic tragedy, but one that had been smouldering for some time.

In fact, Evelyn had not looked particularly OK; she had

looked, in fact, ghastly, her face red and swollen almost out of recognition from the ammonia, and her eyes propped open by a strange irrigating contraption rigged up by the ophthalmologist, but Kate did not impart this information to the children. Instead, she repeated what both the Sister and the ophthalmologist had said to her, which was that Evelyn would be all right.

"In fact, I *know* she's all right," said Kate, "because when I spoke to her, she was already worrying about what was happening to that wretched man, she wanted me to go round and speak to him and tell him to keep his mouth shut and not start making any statements to anyone. So she can't have been feeling too bad, can she?"

"I don't know," said Sebastian, in his strange, deep, broken, rarely heard voice. "It would be just like Mum to start worrying about other people on her deathbed, wouldn't it?"

A silence hung, at this unexpected formulation. Susanna looked sharply at Sebastian, who blushed.

"Well, I know what you mean," said Kate, "but, honestly, I don't think she's so bad. She'll be all right."

"Did you get to see the man?" said Susanna.

"Not a hope. He was still in Resuscitation, they wouldn't let me near. Evelyn said he kept apologising, in the ambulance. He kept saying he hoped he hadn't hurt her. Aren't people extraordinary?"

Evelyn had also gone on to tell Kate that the smell of the accident had been its worst feature: the mingled smell of burning onions, burning hair, burning flesh, burning clothes, and ammonia had been quite something, she had said, smiling faintly, her swollen tongue stiff in her swollen lips; but this too Kate did not see fit to report.

They talked on and on, about the accident, as people in such crises do, and about more trivial aspects of the drama, such as Kate's difficulty in tracking down Vicky and Sebastian in order to inform them of it. Kate had been contacted just after six in the evening, and with the help of her own children

had finally located Vicky doing homework innocently enough
at a friend's house, but Sebastian had been harder to find: in
the end, it turned out that he was in the local cinema, sitting
through the second continuous showing of a film about an
American businessman pursued in his car by a mad lorry.
Vicky, once she'd worked out where he was, had insisted on
getting him out rather than waiting for the end of the
programme; not, as she insisted, in order to make him feel
bad, but to make him feel less bad. "He'd feel rotten," she had
assured Kate, "if people thought he'd just been sitting in there
goggling for hour after hour while Mum was in hospital." And
in she had marched, into the smart little green neo-Deco arty
cinema, and extracted her brother from his comfortable green
plush seat.

And now they sat there, the four of them, talking of acci-
dents, and of the time Sebastian had broken his teeth falling
off a slide, the time Ruth had crashed her bicycle, the time
Vicky had scalded herself with a panful of boiling soup. They
talked of London, and cities, and whether or not life was getting more unsafe. The kids are so tough, thought Kate, listening to them, they are so used to it all, they are born and bred
to it, and I thought life was tough in Romley when I was a
child. Pub brawls, skin heads, Paki-bashing, school gangs
waiting at the gate, stolen bicycles, bicycle chains. Vicky's
friend Vic had been punched the other night as he stood in a
queue at the chip shop—but then, conceded Vicky, he did go
around looking for it, dressed as he was. Irene's man Joseph,
according to Evelyn, had not been of a violent nature, despite
his ominous dangling dreadlocks: it was Irene, a runaway
from Bradford, who had been the troublemaker. Kate shut her
eyes as she listened. It had been a long day, and a dreadful
one, and now she had to sit there with these children until
Ted came home. But, of course, she couldn't shut her eyes.
She forced them open, poured herself another cup of tea.

"I think we're all capable of violence," Vicky was saying.
"It's in all of us."

"I don't think it's in *me*," said Susanna. "I couldn't even kill a mouse. Or a dying hamster. I tried once, but I couldn't."

Kate shut her eyes again, despite herself, as the children talked on, children who had never known a war, to whom violence was a matter of streets, not armies, and her mind moved back over some of the things those women had said to her in Romley, about blacks, punks, kids, the Irish, the unions; none of it serious, just a scum of opinion, or so she had thought—but what if each act of personal violence were after all an expression, a cumulation of all that vaguely directed ill-will, hatred, and frustration, of the terror we each now feel when walking down a concrete underpass, when we fumble for a key on our own doorstep with the sound of footsteps behind us, when an unknown car pulls up at a kerb? Belfast, Beirut, Bagdad. And was this London, a bed-sitter in flames, a girl from Bradford, an insane Jamaican, a child from East Pakistan? No, surely not, surely not.

Luckily the baby had been downstairs, with the Sylheti girl's mother.

What on earth do Rastafarians believe, anyway? wondered Kate, as she sat there nursing her tea, rocking gently in the old Windsor chair in which Evelyn had nursed Sebastian and Vicky: something to do with Ethiopia, wasn't it? The children had been very put out by the Rastafarian aspect of the drama, no doubt because of their admiration for various reggae singers, and their faith in the peaceful properties of gunge, or whatever they called cannabis. Perhaps Joseph Leroy hadn't been an orthodox Rastafarian. Certainly he had been more given to inflammatory drink than to gunge. What would the press make of the case, if they got onto it? UNEMPLOYED BLACK ASSAULTS SOCIAL WORKER? Well, yes, luckily the press loathed social workers as much as they loathed unemployed blacks. If Evelyn had been murdered, which papers would have adopted her as a martyr, and which would have portrayed her as an interfering busybody who got what she

asked for? UNEMPLOYED RASTAFARIAN ASSAULTS DOCTOR'S WIFE?
SOCIAL WORKER PROVOKES UNEMPLOYED RASTAFARIAN?

Kate rocked, and her mind wandered. Headlines, she had lived too long with headlines. Too much half-baked second-hand sociology, too many questionable statistics, too many soundings of public opinion, if there was such a thing. How gloriously indifferent she had been of these things when she had started out, so many years ago, how innocently certain of her own views. Where had it gone, that innocence? How had she managed to acquire the deadly notion that everything she did or thought had to be *exemplary*, had to *mean something*, not only for herself, but also for that vast quaking seething tenuous mass of otherness, for other people? WOMAN APPOINTED AMBASSADOR. WOMAN FLIES TO MOON. WOMAN KILLED IN BANK RAID. WOMAN OF FORTY-SIX HAS TWINS. Well, no wonder, of course, one couldn't be all those women at once, nor was there any possible way of being all the things that women might be, in one lifetime. No wonder, if writing interpretative or accusing headlines for your every act, you encounter paralysis. You can only be one person, not a sum or cross-section of many, and if other people don't like what you do, or think you ought to do something different, they can GO OFF and DO IT THEMSELVES. (Applause, please.)

A wonderful if temporary relief flowed through Kate, at this release from the grip of the representative. Henceforth she would represent nothing but herself. And if she liked to sit here with three teenagers not even her own, and happy, yes, she could not deny it, happy to have been called in, to be of use, to be able to do something for Evelyn and for them, if only to make cups of tea, well, that meant nothing at all but that *she liked it*. She liked it. No more headlines, no more underlinings, no more stories about Women of Our Time. No wonder those women in Romley hadn't fitted into a pattern. Why the hell should they? Enough of patterns, she'd spent enough time looking for patterns and trends. Hugo was right, she'd get nowhere if she spent the rest of her life forcing things into articles and programmes when they didn't want to be forced. Shapeless diversity, what was wrong with that? WOMAN OF FORTY PREFERS INDIAN TEA. THIRTY-YEAR-OLD RAS- TAFARIAN PREFERS ALCOHOL TO GUNGE. BRADFORD GIRL RUNS AMOK. Kate smiled to herself, and opened her eyes to see three anxious faces staring at her.

"What's the joke?" said Sebastian, but in quite a friendly tone.

"Oh, I don't know," said Kate, improvising, "I was just thinking about names and labels. Do you remember that pic- nic we all went on when you lot were little, and Ruth got in such a rage about the sandwiches? She wanted to know if there was any mayonnaise in the egg ones, because if there was she didn't like them, and we said that if she couldn't tell what they were made of from what they tasted like, then what the hell did it matter. And she said that wasn't the point, it tasted different if you *knew* what was in it. Do you remem- ber?"

"Was that the time Reuben was sick all down the car window?"

"I think it was the time Dad found a penknife stuck in a gate," said Sebastian.

"Dad wasn't there," said Vicky.

"Yes he was," said Sebastian, "I remember him going on and on about how most people can't tell malt whisky from brandy if they drink it with their eyes shut."

"Once I had a bite of a ham sandwich," said Susanna, "and it was all slimy, and I spat it out, I thought it was a piece of nasty slimy jelly fat, you know the kind you get on plastic ham, but it wasn't. It was only cucumber. It tasted fine once I knew it was cucumber. It's all in the mind. Like Sartre's essay on treacle."

And they discussed slime and stickiness, the extraordi- nary fussiness of small children, sandwiches they had eaten, picnics of the past; they even got out the photograph album and looked at old photos of Evelyn brewing up soup on a Buton Gaz camping stove in what looked like pouring rain, and Kate in her bathing suit with a naked Reuben on her knee, and Ted, Mark, and Sebastian trying to light a fire, again in pouring rain, and Vicky staring at a dead frog, and Evelyn's mother in a deck chair on an unidentifiable inhospitable shingled beach, reading *The Times*. They were still looking and remembering when the phone rang; it was Ted, at the hospital, about to leave for home. "I'll get off, then," said Kate, but Ted said no, stay, and so she stayed, because she wanted to hear his professional opinion about Evelyn; her own children would be all right, Mujid was looking after them.

Sandwiches, picnics, packet soup, wellingtons. Knives, boiling oil, flames. Waiting for Ted, watching Sebastian, Kate remembered an incident years earlier when Sebastian for some reason had been left in her charge; about five or six he'd been, and both she and he'd been for some forgotten reason in a terrible mood, and he had kept turning the knobs on the telly, on and off, on and off, and Kate had kept telling him not to but he wouldn't listen, and in the end she'd lost her temper and slapped him, and he had looked at her with such shocked amazement, and she had felt that she had forfeited his trust forever, that he would never speak to her again. And maybe it had been so.

Ted, when he arrived, did not look too good, though he did not look like an imminent widower either, or so Kate hoped. He was very pale and gleaming in an unhealthy way, a pallor accentuated by the fact that he was wearing his dinner jacket, a garment in which Kate had never seen him, and which made him look even more thuggish than usual, crumpled as it was from hours of driving. The three children stared at him, silently, almost in accusation, to which he responded impatiently, telling them all to get off to bed, that Evelyn was fine, she'd be in there for a week or two, but there was no permanent damage, it could all have been much worse. "Go on, clear off," said Ted, and the children, reassured by the aggressive familiarity of his manner, made their farewells and escaped.

Ted shut the door on them, and came back and sat down, heavily. Kate was still sitting.

"Well?" said Kate.

"I've had a bloody awful drive," said Ted. "There's fog on the motorway. And everyone driving like lunatics."

Both fell silent.

"Well?" said Kate again, after a while.

"Well what?" said Ted, unhelpfully, and followed it up quickly with "What's Susanna doing here, anyway?"

"Oh, just spending the night."

"Why can't these kids ever spend the night in their own homes?"

"Yours are both here," said Kate.

"Well, that makes a change."

"Would you like a drink?" said Kate.

"I think I'm past drinking," said Ted.

"Stop frightening me," said Kate, crossly, "and tell me how she is."

"You saw her, didn't you?"

"Yes, I saw her, but I thought she looked pretty frightful, and anyway, thanks largely to you, I never believe a word that hospitals say, but I imagine you could make more sense of them than I could."

"Oh, she'll be all right," said Ted. "You know how long it took to get that ambulance there? They ought to be shot. And all because the voice on the line was Pakistani. Not that it wasn't a miracle to find a telephone working in that district. This country, it makes you sick. And the doctor in casualty's a fucking half-wit."

This sounded so like the real Ted that Kate relaxed: if Evelyn had been seriously ill, surely he'd have found a new voice to express it. In fact, Ted sounded like the Ted of the old days, and she herself seemed to have managed to drop the nasty female sprightliness to which she had been treating him for the last year or so; that was a mercy, if a small one. Ted seemed to be thinking along the same lines, for he looked up at her suddenly, smiled, said, "Good old Kate," stared at her a little longer, and then said, "Christ, Kate, you do look a fright. Where did you get that outfit?"

Flattered by this attention, Kate stared down at her clothes and found she was wearing one of Ruth's sweat shirts, emblazoned with the motto SOLIPSISTS MAKE THE BEST LOVERS, and her everlasting flowery skirt: not a very nice assortment.

"Well, you look a bloody fool yourself," said Kate. "Thank God I never had to go around with you when you were wearing one of those things."

Friendliness re-established, both continued to smile, until Ted stopped smiling and said, "Ammonia's dangerous stuff, you know, it binds with the eye protein. I used to know all about it, but of course I've forgotten."

"Did you speak to the ophthalmologist?"

"He said it could have been much worse. They have to keep irrigating for forty-eight hours, to be on the safe side. Luckily she shoved her head under the tap as soon as it happened. How she managed to do that, with the whole place going up in smoke, God knows. It must have been quite a scene."

"What happened to the bloke?"

"They took him off to Mount Vernon Hospital. He's in a bad way, but don't tell Evelyn. Fifty per cent burns. Serve the bugger right."

"What does that mean?"

"It means it's touch and go. Poor bugger. Don't tell Evelyn, she's in a bad enough state about him as it is. She thinks it's all her fault. She's mad, of course."

"How on earth could it be her fault?"

"For interfering. Has she told you about the terrible Irene?"

"Not much."

"Oh, Irene's a nut case. A real mess. It's an odd story

altogether. Irene's from Bradford, a working-class kid, ran away from home when she was fifteen, ended up in Hackney with a lot of female layabouts, decided she was a Lesbian, got into all sorts of funny business—drugs, Ouija, God knows what. She keeps telling Evelyn stories about faith healing and the spirit world. Then she got together with this chap, and he persuaded her to go straight, if that's what you can call it. He's nutty too, but Evelyn didn't think he was dangerous. In fact, she rather liked him. And he was mad about Irene, who's certainly no beauty. A scruffy-looking creature, our Irene. He kept her shut up for weeks on end. She quite liked it, to begin with, Evelyn says. Then she had this baby, a few months ago. That's how Evelyn got onto them. She went very odd after the baby was born, she kept running away and he kept getting her back. She used to dump the baby on the Pakistani woman downstairs and run back to her Lesbian ladyfriends, who of course took her in and told her she was a martyr. Then he'd go and get her back. Evelyn got onto her through the Pakistanis. The woman downstairs doesn't speak a word of English, but her eldest girl is a bright little thing, and she told her teacher at school about Irene, and the teacher told Evelyn, and Evelyn went along and found this wretched woman with three children of her own, one of them suffering from anaemia but otherwise all reasonably all right. Sewing skirt lengths and minding Irene's baby. For nothing, of course. And terrified, of course, of the big black man upstairs."

"What an upside-down story."

"Amazing, isn't it? So Evelyn tried to help Irene to cope with her own baby instead of dumping it, but the bloke got it into his head that Evelyn was trying to persuade Irene to leave him. Which she wasn't. If anything, Evelyn thought he was saner than she was. Not that either of them was exactly a responsible citizen. He's pathologically jealous, and she says she hates all men."

"Poor baby."

"I suppose it'll get taken into care now."

"Poor baby."

"Poor bloke."

"And poor Irene, I suppose. But for the grace of God, one might say. What it is to suffer from violent passions. You know, when I was younger, I never even used to know what jealousy was. Or so I imagined. But you kept telling me that all men felt it, and I believed you."

"Did I really say that?"

"I think so." Kate paused, and looked at Ted, tried to speak, thought again, and said nothing. What was the point? Unless one drew a knife, fell into the flames, or hurled a pan of boiling oil, what was the point? It was all done and gone, irrelevant.

Nothing can help me now, thought Kate. It had nothing to do with Ted, or with Evelyn, or with love, or jealousy. All these things were not the point, at all. For the first time in months, she thought of the baby she might have had. Ted's baby. She had murdered it. For every good reason, she had murdered it. Maternity had been her passion, her primary passion in life, and she had been forced to deny it. Fate had forced her to undo her own nature. I denied my nature, thought Kate, therefore nature cannot help me. *Doing the right thing has destroyed me.* What shall I seek, what help from the unnatural? Or must I simply admit the violence done, the death of a soul? Her eyes filled with tears. There was no way out of this, it must be borne forever and ever, repeatedly, and she could not tell Ted, there was no point in telling Ted, he could not help her, her dream of some final reconciliation was an empty dream: death lay between them. Just as she could not, in her heart, understand the jealousy that could lock a woman in a room for months or draw a knife on her for love, so he could not understand the deep drag of her nature, its steady pull towards the lost. They would gaze at one another forever, good friends perhaps, old allies, old enemies, across this impossible void, trying new voices, new gestures, making true efforts to hear, to listen, to understand.

But hopelessly, hopelessly. Admit defeat. I have not the strength, thought Kate, I am too old, I have not the strength. Men and women can never be close. They can hardly speak to one another in the same language. But are compelled, forever, to try, and therefore even in defeat there is no peace.

"I wonder," she said, to change the subject, "if anyone's looking after Irene," and as she spoke, the phone went. Ted and Kate looked at one another quickly, and both said, simultaneously, "I bet that's her." And, as in the old days, laughed.

"You answer it," said Ted.

"No, you," said Kate. "It's your house."

"It's probably only some child ringing some other child," said Ted, as he got up to reply: but it was, Kate could tell at once, indeed Irene.

"Where are you?" Ted kept saying, but clearly received no very satisfactory answer. He listened for a while, with tolerable patience, asking the odd question, and then, having described Evelyn's condition, suddenly said, in a total loss of patience, and in the broadest relapse into Yorkshire Kate had ever heard from him, "Well, there's no point in shouting at me, it's hardly my fault Evelyn isn't here to listen to your rubbish, I'm not the fucking social worker, she is, and it's hardly my fault you've put her out of action. I'm not paid to listen to your ravings. Why don't you go to bed, or try the Samaritans? What? No more money? Well, I'm sure you can reverse the charges on the Samaritans, they must be used to that kind of thing. *Good night.*

"What a fucking nerve," said Ted, exhilarated by conflict, returning to his chair. "Complaining to me because I'm a man. I should have put her onto you. She hates me, that creature, she thinks I'm in league with the devil."

"Why?"

"Because I'm so bald," said Ted.

"*What?*"

"You heard me. Because I'm so bald. According to Irene, all bald men are evil. Well, all men are evil, but bald ones particularly so. Have you heard that song Bob Marley sings? About how Jah would never give the power to a bald head? Well, apparently, our Irene takes it rather literally."

"You poor darling," said Kate, "you really are a bit bald, aren't you? But however does she know?"

"Because the silly creature looked us up in the phone book and tracked us down one evening. Called round just when I was trying to pour a neighbourly gin and tonic for that Stacey woman over the road. A nice quiet evening drink, we were going to have, and in comes Irene, like a drowned rat, barefoot and dripping. It was raining. And she looked at me and gave a great scream and denounced me as the devil's henchman. Didn't Evelyn tell you? I thought she told you everything."

"No, she missed out this particular gem. But the woman must be mad."

"Yes, that's what I was telling you. Mad."

"But in quite an interesting kind of way, you must admit," said Kate, her spirits revived by this evidence of energetic rather than downtrodden lunacy. "And I have to say, Ted, that, much as I've always loved your nice round head, I do rather fancy dreadlocks as well. I mean, I can see what Irene means. But tell me, where was she, was she all right?"

"I couldn't care tuppence how she is, the silly girl. She was in a phone box at Finsbury Park."

"God, what a dismal place to be at"—glancing at her watch—"half past one in the morning. And where was the baby?"

"With the long-suffering Mrs. Subhan, I imagine. Perhaps she could be persuaded to foster it. At least then she'd get paid for the job. Though I don't suppose her accommodation would pass council regulations."

"I must go home," said Kate.

"I'll drive you," said Ted. And back they went together, in a silence deferential to Evelyn's open-eyed vigil: when she got into bed, Kate was ashamed to find herself wondering if the reason why Evelyn hadn't reported the Irene–Rosamund Stacey gin-and-tonic incident was because Ted had now got his eye on neighbour Rosamund, whom he had always rather admired. What price jealousy? thought Kate, and diverted her mind to more worthy subjects, such as the delightful rouge-touched bloom which had begun to irradiate Susanna Mainwaring's olive cheeks, and the hesitant earnest friendliness of her manner. A nice girl, thank God.

Evelyn, her wide unseeing eyes awash not with tears but with strangely dry scratchy prickly water, lay in the double darkness listening to the creaking sounds of hospital life, and trying not to watch the playback of the little melodrama in the second-floor back room in Jubilee Park Road: she had never had a strong stomach for scenes of violence even in the cinema, and when she went to see a film, which was rarely, she usually had to shut her eyes through half of it, so perhaps it was just as well that she hadn't been able to see much of Joseph Leroy in flames. His long limbs thrashing wildly, his white eyes rolling, his knotty rats' tails flying, his hard pale bare feet stamping. She had seen this as though in a dream, through the tap water and her burning eyes. But the smell, as she had said to Kate, the smell had been the worst. Not that Irene's room had ever smelled less than awful, even in more normal times. But the smell of burning—well, one must not think about these things. They had taken Joseph Leroy to Mount Vernon. In the ambulance, he had not appeared to be in terrible pain, but Evelyn knew enough about burns to know that this was no good sign. Full-thickness burning, he must have suffered. Ah, he had lain there like a tree, moaning in his strange high-pitched voice, calling upon his God Jah and calling upon Evelyn for forgiveness. The police had not been tender with him. In fact, they had manhandled him. Perhaps a dying man. The ambulance men were gentler, seeing the gravity of the case. One did not have to be a saint, in Evelyn's view, to feel pity for Joseph Leroy.

And all for Irene. White-faced, hallucinated, undersized, butch, pugnacious, foul-mouthed Irene, who had been born a woman by mistake, and who had paid the price of woman-hood in giving birth: no wonder she loathed the baby, con-firming as it did that she was after all a member of her own sex. And yet there had been something remarkable in that ludicrous union. Two people bent on forcing nature to be something quite other than itself. Irene, the most unlikely cause of tragic passion.

The baby would have to go into care. And thinking of the baby, Evelyn thought of little eight-year-old Rubia Subhan in her little purple dress and white socks, Rubia from downstairs, who had run to the phone on the corner, who had run back to cling to Evelyn's hand as she staggered down the stairs, who had stroked her skirt with her small hands and murmured comfort: Rubia, who had done all she could to handle adult tragedies, in an alien country, interpreter, messenger, go-between: Rubia, persuading her mother to admit Evelyn, to take the babies to the clinic, to try to learn a little English: Rubia, old before her time, a mother to her mother, a mother even to mad Irene, valiantly making her way through primary school, singing heartily, "Glad that I live am I," and playing a triangle in the school percussion, and running home through the dingy streets to do the shopping, to play with the little ones, to stitch up a seam or two on the rackety old machine: Rubia, who had learned from neighbourhood gossip which phone boxes usually worked, who had learned from television programmes about dialling 999: Rubia, who had found it hard to make the ambulance men believe her story: Rubia, child of Britain, child of Stoke Newington. How wonderful people are, thought Evelyn, how wonderful.

Irene's family, back in Bradford, had been violently anti-coloured. Her brothers belonged to the National Front. Mad though she still was, at least Irene had escaped that kind of madness.

Evelyn lay there and prayed for the recovery of Joseph Leroy, for the consolation of Irene Crowther. She was not particularly anxious on her own behalf, somewhat to her own surprise. She trusted the ophthalmologist's confident predictions. She knew her eyes would recover; it was impossible to imagine that they would not. How odd, she thought, that I should be so unworried.

Evelyn's confidence was not misplaced. Within twenty-four hours she could see again, though she was told she would have to stay in hospital for a fortnight. She was also suffering from a superficial knife wound on the shoulder, an injury which she found much more attractive than her peeling face. "With any luck I shall have a proper scar," she told her visitors, "I've always wanted a scar"; but alas, they had stitched her too professionally. The casualty doctor, for whom Ted had expressed such contempt, turned out not to be an idiot after all, and a dab hand at stitching. (When Evelyn set eyes on this young man, she could see at once why Ted had so disliked him, for he was a ridiculously youthful lad with a marked resemblance to the young Steve McQueen. And a wizard with the needle and thread.)

All in all, the accident turned out quite well. For one thing, it restored Sebastian to a good nature he hadn't displayed in years. He became attentive, co-operative, affectionate. He started to attend his College of Further Education again, abandoning his ambition to be a motorbike despatch rider. (Though it is fair to say that the near-fatal crash of an acquaintance, who ended up in Stoke Mandeville Hospital, also played a part in this decision.) When he wasn't at college or in the cinema (for he didn't seem able to relinquish his compulsive cinema-going) he would go round and visit Evelyn with little offerings. A pomegranate, a book, a handful of flowers, a pot of cream cheese. This made Evelyn very happy. She was also made happy by the attentions of a multitude of people whose sympathy she had not expected. Children drew her pictures and get-well cards, old ladies sent messages; even some of her most hostile and disagreeable clients claimed to miss her. Her misfortune seemed to have unlocked a fund of good will on which she would never have counted. She lay there gazing at her flowers, filled with a renewed assurance that her work was, after all, despite all, worthwhile. Why expect results, progress, success, a better society? All we can do is to join the ranks of the caring rather than the uncaring. All we can do in this world is to care for one another, in the society we have. It seemed enough, it seemed a great blessing. Evelyn lay there and made herself do half an hour's Urdu a day, trying to put to the back of her mind the thought that she ought also to tackle Bengali, Sylheti, Punjabi and Gujerati. One has to start somewhere, and Evelyn had never been very good at languages, though Ayesha, who called in frequently to see how she was getting on, said that she was learning very fast.

Joseph Leroy, in Mount Vernon, was recovering. It had been a near thing: he had been lucky, it appeared, in that the eccentricity of his dress had protected him from a more severe fate. His terrible twisted locks had been more or less flame-proof: the smell of burning hair had been worse, in this instance, than the actual damage. Irene, also, was recovering. The police had decided not to press charges, and Irene had gone off to her women's refuge in Hackney, whence she emerged from time to time to visit Evelyn. Evelyn could have done without these ministrations, but did not like to say so: after all, if one has decided to turn the other cheek, one might as well do it with a good spirit. On one of these visits Irene met Kate, a convergence that Evelyn had seen coming, but had been helpless, in the new modern free-visiting-hours régime of the new modern hospital, to prevent: Irene, in some ways no fool, spotted an easy victim in Kate at once, and, to Evelyn's embarrassment, set off with her, talking darkly and rapidly about some nuns she had once met in a pop festival in Hyde Park. Evelyn hoped that Kate would not end up in the next bed doused with another bottle of ammonia: she did not, for she was back the next day, having shaken off Irene some-how in the meantime, and bearing a clean nightdress which Evelyn had requested.

"Oh, Kate, I am *sorry*," said Evelyn, taking her Viyella nightie out of its plastic bag, "I just didn't know what to do when I saw Irene start on you. How long did it take you to get rid of her?"

"Only an hour or so," said Kate. "She wanted to come home for tea, but I said I had to go into town to meet some-one, so we had a cup of tea downstairs, and then she came with me on the bus, and then I went into the office and hung around for a bit talking to Hugo and Seamus, and by the time I came out she'd gone. For the time being, anyway."

"You didn't let her have your address, did you?"

Kate looked sheepish, and smiled, and then said, "Well, I *tried* not to," and both women laughed. "Oh, Lord," said Eve-lyn, "I don't think she's dangerous, but what a nuisance she can be. What on earth was all that about those nuns? No, don't tell me, I can't bear to hear. I suppose nuns are better than Ouija boards, and possibly even than Jah himself. At least she seemed sober."

"She hadn't touched a drop for a week, she told me," said Kate.

Evelyn sighed, not unhappily, offered Kate a grape, and stuffed the nightdress into her bedside locker. "I've had that nightdress since Vicky was born," she said. "In fact, Vicky was born in it, or rather I was in it when Vicky was born. Wonder-ful stuff, Viyella, isn't it? Were you out in that storm earlier?"

"Spectacular, wasn't it? I was at the Elephant, going to see some people in Alexander Fleming House, but it was raining so hard I couldn't get out of the tube. And when I plucked up courage, the wind was blowing at right angles, and there was a sea of water all over the courtyard, I was practically blown away, and the sky was dark brown, and by the time I got to my bit of the building I was soaked through, and I thought, Well, at least they'll know why I look such a fright, but when I got in there, would you believe, all those tidy men with their well-polished shoes were sitting in an inside room with sound-proof walls and no windows, and they didn't even know it was raining, let alone such rain. They looked at me as though I'd come from another world."

"It looked marvellous from up here," said Evelyn.

"Yes, what a view you have," said Kate, wandering over to the window and gazing out over London: the sky had been washed clear, and a clear pale luminous band of duck-egg blue-green light lay low over the city, heaping up overhead into deeper shades of cloudy blue, a thick canopy of cloud above, from behind which a gold evening radiance fell on the glittering distance. From the twelfth-floor window, London stretched away, St. Paul's in the distance, and the towers of the City, and beneath them, nearby, the little network of streets, back yards, cul-de-sacs, canals, warehouses, curves and chimneys, railways, little factories tucked into odd corners; unplanned, higgledy-piggledy, hardly a corner wasted, intricate, enmeshed, patched and pieced together, the old and the new side by side, overlapping, jumbled, always decaying, yet always renewed; London, how could one ever be tired of it? How could one stumble dully through its streets, or waste time sitting in a heap staring at a wall? When there it lay, its old intensity restored, shining with invitation, all its shabby grime lost in perspective, imperceptible from this dizzy height, its connections clear, its pathways revealed. The city, the kingdom. The aerial view. Kate gazed east towards Romley. The little sister is resurrected, dug up, dragged from the river, the stone that weighted her dissolves, she rises up. Perhaps, perhaps, thought Kate, and turned back to Evelyn, who was sitting up, her arms around her knees, looking like a child in her striped nightdress, a child except for her greying hair. The aerial view of human love, where all connections are made known, where all roads connect?

"It's wonderful," said Kate.

"Yes," said Evelyn. "You wouldn't believe how much the most unlikely people respond to it. People who you'd think would never look at a view in their lives. I can't wait to get out into it, I want to see all the things I've never seen, I want to see the Rubens ceiling in Whitehall, I want to go to Greenwich, I want to go to Kew and see the aconites in February, I want to walk in Regent's Park, I want to walk down Bond Street and look at the amber-shop window, I want to walk over Westminster Bridge, I even want to go to Finsbury Park to look at the garbage."

"When you get out," said Kate, "we'll do all those things."

"Ted says I ought to go and stay with Josephine in Pembrokeshire, but I just want to get back. Anyway, Josephine's so neurotic, and her children are so exhausting. However did one survive having little children? I just want to get home, it's much more restful at home."

"Did Hugo tell you he was going to Bagdad?"

"I knew he would. I'm glad, aren't you? It was so unlike him to stay in one place for so long."

"He asked me to go with him, but I don't think it's quite me, do you?"

"You could try," said Evelyn. "Why not try?"

"I'm frightened of aeroplanes," said Kate, "and I don't like heights." And they both laughed.

"Yes," said Kate. "He seems to have got it all together again, as the children would say. I'm going with him tomorrow to the Artificial Limb and Appliance Centre. What about that for an outing? He says I can use it in an article."

"I was beginning to think he'd never face it, weren't you?"

"Yes, I was. But he says at least he'll go and see what they can do. That's a good thing, do you think?"

"I suppose so. Artificial limbs in this country aren't very nice, you know. Nasty pink elastoplast colour, they are."

"Hugo says he fancies a hook."

"Hugo's so vain."

"He is, isn't he? But that's partly why I like him."

"Do have some more grapes, Kate. I'm getting fat, lying here eating. Did you know grapes were extremely fattening?"

"I'll tell you what," said Kate, helping herself, throwing off the slight gloom that the thought of pink plastic hands had cast over her, "when you come out, we'll have a party. It's ages since I had a party. It can be your coming-out party, and Hugo's going-away party, and Mujid's going-away party, and Mark's birthday party. What about that for an idea?"

"It sounds lovely."

"I'll organise it. That'll give me something to do, now the paper seems to be going on strike for real."

"Are you going to take that other job?"

"I don't know, I can't decide. I thought I might try and do a degree at the Open University. Or even at the non-open university. I wrote off for the forms."

"Did you really?"

"Yes, really. But I don't suppose I ever will. Do you?"

"I don't see why not," said Evelyn.

"I can see lots of reasons why not," said Kate, "but it's a nice idea. Have you got your diary with you? Let's fix a party date."

"Are you sure you really want to? It's an awful lot of work."

"It would be good for me to give a party. It would make me clear all that stuff out of the hall. I've been meaning to shift it for months. And buy some new glasses in time for Christmas. Did I tell you I've asked my parents and Peter and June over for Christmas? I couldn't face Clacton again, so I asked them all to come to me. They seemed quite pleased."

"I should bloody well think so. But you mustn't get carried away, you'll regret it."

"No," said Kate. "I quite like being carried away. And now I must leave you, I've got to go and have a drink with a man."

"Oh, Kate, how daring."

Kate laughed, rather loudly, so loudly that the other three patients in the ward turned to look.

"Yes, it is a bit, isn't it? A *drink* with a *man!* What fun! Do you know what Ruth said to me this morning? She said, 'You know, Mum, you smile too much.' What about that for a direct hit?"

"I was thinking just the same, the other day. Watching Vicky and Susanna. They don't smile *in the same way*, do they?"

"They're lucky girls. Well, off I go to drink and smile and wink and beguile. It's too late for me to learn to keep my face still. Ruth's right—it moves about far too much. I was so shocked when I first saw the rushes of Gabriel's film. All that grinning and ogling and placating. My face felt stiff even with watching it. You don't do it, you have repose."

"Of course I do it. I just don't bother to do it to you."

"No, I've watched you in public, you don't. Neither does your sister. It must be something to do with confidence. I feel I've got to keep switching all the lights on and off. Like Piccadilly Circus. Like a Christmas tree. It looks crazy, Ruth's right."

"I like it."

"You're just loyal. You will look up a date for our party, won't you? He's a very boring man, I don't even want him to like me, I don't like him, and I rather disapprove of him. Shall I try not to smile at all at him?"

"Who is this boring man?"

"He's a Eurocrat. He wrote me a letter about some flippant remark I made in an article about butter mountains, and asked me to lunch to explain to me why I'd got it all wrong. Which I hadn't, actually, I was just making a joke. God, he was awful. I don't think a woman would be capable of being boring in that particular way. He kept telling me what a wonderful public speaker he was and how audiences ate out of his hand, while my eyes were closing with boredom. Can you imagine?"

"All too well," said Evelyn. "But why, if he's so dull, are you going to meet him *again?*"

Kate waved her hands in a parade of helplessness. "I don't know. I really don't know. He kind of hinted he had something important to tell me that he'd forgotten, so I said I hadn't time for lunch, but a quick drink after work I could do."

"That was strong-minded of you."

"Don't mock, Evelyn. I felt sorry for him. I didn't want to let him know how dull he was. Is. I wanted to protect him from himself. Poor chap."

"I think you're crazy."

"Yes, I am."

"Kate?"

"Yes?"

"Don't go and invite him to our party, will you?"

"No, I'll try not to."

"And don't invite Irene, either, come to that."

Kate and Evelyn stared at one another, Kate toyed with the idea of pulling another sheepish helpless face, abandoned it, stared on, and then said, "You're paid, dear girl, paid by the hour. That's the only difference. You're as bad as I am. But I do agree, no Irene."

"Just try, for my sake. Think of me, and keep your mouth shut."

"I promise. I promise."

"Do you think," asked Evelyn, "really, seriously think that life is very different for men?"

Kate stood still and thought, apparently earnestly, and

then said, shaking her head, without any flippancy at all, and no facial expression whatsoever: "I don't know. The truth is, I do not know."

"No," said Evelyn. "After all these years of thinking about it, neither do I."

They looked at one another soberly, and sighed.

"I must go and see my Eurocrat," said Kate. "What a bore."

"Is he one of those men who tell you what you really need in life is a strong man?"

"Not yet. Not yet. But he will be. He will be."

And they smiled again at one another, a smile of complicity. No wonder men find women so irritating these days.

When Kate had gone, tripping off into the dangerous outside world, Evelyn indulged in a little chat with her three neighbours about such interesting female subjects as previous operations, children and grandchildren, and whether they would actually get, this evening, what they had ordered for supper, then abstracted herself and tried to read. It was hard to concentrate, she found, and the glossy laminated novels that people had brought to cheer her didn't seem very relevant to anything, in here, though she had always supposed it would be pleasant to have time to read. (And eyes to read with, thank God.) So she turned to Isobel's offering. Isobel, true to form, and to her desire to improve Evelyn, had brought a new collection of Emily Dickinson. Well, at least the poems were short. Turning the pages, her eyes fell on a couple of stanzas, attracted no doubt by one word in them, and remembering Hugo. She read them, and reread them.

> Those—dying then,
> Knew where they went—

They went to God's Right Hand—
That Hand is amputated now
And God cannot be found—

The abdication of Belief
Makes the Behavior small—
Better an ignis fatuus
Than no illume at all—

Not a very pretty little poem, but interesting. So even by
Emily Dickinson's day, in the mid- and faithful nineteenth
century, people had lost their expectations, had they? Better
an *ignis fatuus*. Was that what Evelyn's own faith consisted
of? She had put her own religion down as Quaker, not much
wanting to see the C. of E. vicar on his rounds, but he had
visited her nevertheless, apologising for the absence, that day,
of a suitable Quaker: should he instead try to find the Metho-
dist minister? Not to bother, Evelyn had said, for such demar-
cation disputes seemed even more irrelevant than the glossy
novels. She had conversed civilly with the vicar about the
threatened demolition of huge, draughty, disused St. Matthew's church on the corner. Sebastian had once attended cub
meetings in one of its damp halls. What would replace it? A
block of flats, a nursery school, a youth club, a community
centre, the new offices of the National Book League? Secular
substitutes, and so much more useful than the original, dear
God, which had not, even in its prime, been a handsome
church, though Betjeman had found a few kind words to say
for it: it had been built in late Victorian days, when people
built grandly and vainly to conceal their waning faith. Why
regret its passing? Religion was very out of date these days,
and would probably not revive, though the vicar had not been
able to admit as much. Most people did not find religion at all
interesting, and those that did were an odd lot. The vicar,
Evelyn suspected, was not one of them. She thought with
some envy of Phillipa Denham, who had become a devout

Catholic. Belief had certainly enlarged Phillipa's behaviour, for instead of indulging in idle gloom, she now devoted much of her time to visiting the terminally ill. Some considered this neurotic, though Evelyn did not. But, nevertheless, could not share Phillipa's conviction. She herself would never manage anything better than a pretence of belief, a working hypothesis. Better than nothing, perhaps. And yet some people appeared to manage quite well without any pretence at all. Kate, for example. But then Kate had not been brought up to it.

"Blessed are the poor in spirit. Poor is he who has nothing. He who is poor in spirit is receptive of all spirit. Now God is the spirit of spirits. The fruit of the spirit is love, joy, and peace. See to it that you are stripped of all creatures, of all consolation from all creatures. For certainly as long as creatures comfort and are able to comfort you, you will never find true comfort. But if nothing can comfort you save God, truly God will comfort you." Meister Eckhart. Evelyn knew the passage by heart. She lay back on her high hospital pillow and shut her eyes. Meister Eckhart had written that a good few centuries before Emily Dickinson, and had no doubt believed it. Had he himself found love, joy, and peace? Perhaps, perhaps. But how could one strip oneself of all creatures when it was only through them that one could express one's love? Love, joy, and peace. Well, one could probably manage without them, after all. For the time being, at least.

A fatuous flame. A small ghostly light, a marshy phosphorescence. Misleading the night traveller, betraying him, leading him to a lonely grave. A pink plastic hand. A burning man. What a lot of very nasty images, thought Evelyn, opening her eyes to the sight of the supper trolley bringing her (oh dear, what a bad choice it suddenly looked) liver and bacon; and infidel Ted in its wake, with a more appetising pot of mushroom salad from the delicatessen and the interesting news that he had found the long-lost radiator bleed key in the bathroom cabinet, information certainly more cheering than

any she was likely to find in Emily Dickinson. As for Meister
Eckhart, he could wait. She didn't need him yet.

Kate was to regret from time to time her impulse to have a
party, particularly when she realised that Mark's birthday inevitably fell uncomfortably close to the birthday of Simone's
dead brother, who would also have been nineteen, had he
survived. But Simone, who turned out to be a tall, grave,
rather silent young woman, did not seem to object to the idea
(perhaps the Lebanese don't go in for birthdays), and by
then, anyway, it was too late to cancel. Mark, ringing from
Waterford, was graciously enthusiastic. If Mum wanted to
have a party, by all means she could have a party, and of
course he would get back in time, and of course he didn't
mind sleeping at his friend Ben Eisenstein's until Simone and
Mujid vacated his narrow bed the next day, and would Mum
mind putting Ruth on the blower so he could give her careful
instructions about whom to invite and whom not to invite
from their own circle?
  Kate, issuing her own invitations, felt herself running a
little wild, tried to check her exuberance, but failed. She invited at random—Stuart, and all her ex-in-laws: the Morton
girls (though Josephine declined, being too absorbed in Pembrokeshire) far too many of her idle strike-struck colleagues,
Joker James and his mates, Sam Goldman, Gabriel Denham
and his second wife Jessica and his first wife Phillipa and half
the crew of *Women at the Crossroads*: Hugo of course, Ted of
course, and even some of the ex-suitors. She invited Marylou
and an American woman she met at a bus stop. She invited
Hugo's mother, and the Irish teacher with whom Mujid had
become so friendly. She did not invite Hugo's wife Judith,
for benevolence cannot conquer everyone, and she feared a
rude refusal. Mujid invited some of his fellow language students, who over the weeks had proved less dull than he had at

first feared, and Evelyn suggested Ayesha and her husband, Joan Kingsley and her husband, and her colleague the sad and widowed Mr. Campbell, who was having such trouble with the rehousing of Boat People. *"Too many people,"* groaned Kate three nights before the event, counting on a list, "we'll probably kill Evelyn, not cheer her up: sixty people, however shall we cram them all into this tiny house?" "Oh, they'll fit," said Ruth, who was of an age to enjoy a squash: she had herself, as she saw it, saved the good name of Rastafarians by inviting an extremely peaceable and musical one whom she had met reciting his poetry in a pub the week before.

"And however much will they eat?" asked Kate. They went once more through the list of drink and food. Simone and Mujid offered to do a couscous, Ruth and Vicky to take care of the salads, and Kate was going to—well, Kate couldn't quite make up her mind, she dithered from crisis to crisis of indecision: lamb and haricot beans, boeuf bourguignon, quiches, or the Italian caterers round the corner, or a compromise between all these things? Do I *enjoy* this? Kate asked herself, and her household, writing down *lemons*, excited by the prospect of so much sheer panic: Kate, whose indecisions inhabited every jar of salad dressing she ever mixed (salad oil or olive oil, garlic or garlic powder, made mustard or powder mustard, cheap vinegar or French vinegar, oh, the possibilities of success and disaster in one jar are endless, and Kate for some reason seemed determined never to decide upon a formula, to improvise each time, to take the risks as they came)—Kate had to admit that she must enjoy uncertainty, for why ever else would one encounter it so often, so willingly? She even quite liked the prospect of being out of work, a sure sign of madness, some might say.

A lot of clearing up had to be done before the party, simply in order to make space to let people into the house. Objects that had lain where they were dumped for months had to be thrown out, taken upstairs, hidden under beds, heaved onto wardrobes, thrown into the cellar. Books, bicycles, bags full of cast-offs intended for jumble sales. The debris of years, ancient homework, long lost, stuffed down chair arms, was rediscovered under cushions, with a fine array of ball-points, buttons, needles, scissors, unanswered letters, unposted letters, all offering diversions, temptations to speculation and reminiscence. In the back yard stood a lidless bin full of pre-strike garbage, which Kate and Reuben tried to carry through to the front for the bin men to collect, but found it appallingly heavy, unnaturally heavy: Reuben worked out that this was because it was full of rainwater as well as garbage, and Kate bored a hole in the bottom of the bin with a corkscrew, and out poured the most astonishing thick black liquid, the rotting sediment of ages: down into the drain it went, smelling of the Black Death, as Ruth said, disgusting, putrid, but somehow not unpleasant, oddly satisfactory, to see the fluid ooze away. "Oh, God, what a slut I am," said Kate, "it's a wonder we haven't all got the plague"—but they were all cheerful as they scrubbed and parcelled and incinerated, sneezing in the disturbed dust, black-fingered, heroically cleansing the Augean stables. The cats ran away into the attic in dismay.

"Don't let's make it *too* smart," said Ruth, the evening before, as Kate, carried away, started to spray furniture polish and rub at the brass knobs of the doors, "or people will think they've come to the wrong house"—and indeed Hugo's first words, as he called in to see how they were getting on, were "What a very unusual *smell*, Katie." Kate, in her apron and rubber gloves, put down her spray can and said primly, "That is the smell of cleanliness, Hugo," and agreed to knock off for the evening, releasing her gang of assistants, all of whom disappeared promptly to bed or the pub, leaving Kate and Hugo to sit back with a drink and a plateful of scrambled eggs, amidst the unfamiliar shining surfaces.

Hugo was off to Bagdad. It was too late, he said, for Kate to change her mind and come with him, as it was impossible to get a visa at such short notice.

"I never meant to come anyway," said Kate, and gazed at Hugo fixedly, as though for the last time, as though trying to work out for the last time what she thought about him. He reached out his hand, across the kitchen table, and laid it on her arm. He did not often touch her, or indeed anyone, and she stared at his hand as though she had never seen it before.

"I'll never go anywhere with anyone," said Kate, thinking of those little white waves lapping on the aquamarine-and-yellow quay, of aeroplanes taking off, of foreign cities and minarets, of nice hygienic little meals on plastic trays with plastic cutlery. "I shall stay here, amidst the fish heads. This is my place."

"I don't see any fish heads," said Hugo.

"You know what I mean," said Kate.

"Yes, I know what you mean," said Hugo.

"What do you think will become of us?" said Kate.

"God knows," said Hugo.

"I shall miss you," said Kate. "You are my good friend."

"I'll come back," said Hugo. "Lightning never strikes twice. I am safe now, wouldn't you think?" And Hugo thought of gunfire, and snipers, and explosions, and wondered whether he could ever tell her the truth about his accident, which had in fact resulted from the one true act of bravery in his life, and which therefore had not been random, pointless, purposeless at all, though there was no one left to tell the tale for him, no witnesses, for they had all died anyway, all but one, and that one too young to speak, and, please God, thought Hugo, to remember. What had it all proved? Nothing much, it is too much to hope that one act will ever resolve us, we have to go on acting till the end. No, he would not tell her, he would tell no one. Secrecy would dignify the ambiguous memory.

"Yes," said Kate, not knowing all this, "you are surely safe now."

And she smiled at him tenderly, thinking of the horrible ordeal of the Artificial Limb and Appliance Centre, whither she had gone to hold his hand (shocking how many black jokes about hands and arms leaped to one's lips in such circumstances), and which had reduced Kate, not Hugo, to tears: "*Not* what I'm meant to be here for," she had whispered into his jacket, furtively wiping her eyes and nose, laughing while she cried, shocked and disturbed by the queue in the waiting room, by the inelegantly phrased notices, by the jumbled heap of bright pink spare parts with which Hugo was finally presented, by the doctor's embarrassed manner, by the patient faces of other victims, by the angry tired tears of a small waiting child (from what deformities might her own have suffered, was Hugo her deformed baby, after all?), and Hugo had said, "There, there, you can cry for me, you can be my official mourner, you do the job so well." Hugo's case proved to be fortunate, according to the doctor: they could fit him without a harness. Lucky Hugo to have an elbow. And Hugo was right, there was a good article to be written about the Artificial Limb and Appliance Centre. A plea for more tact, for more sensitivity to aesthetics, for small technological adjustments? She would have to do some research. Yes, a good subject, a worthwhile subject, and one right up her alley.

"I think," said Hugo, whose mind had been moving over the same scenes, "that it will be all right for us. I don't know why, but I think so. There's life in it yet. What a strange year this has been."

"It doesn't look so bad, now we can look back on it. Nothing seemed to be happening, but perhaps it was, after all. It all seemed to be so *sticky*. So *stuck*."

"Perhaps the world moved by while we stood still."

"Well, it certainly wouldn't stop for us." Kate got up, cleared the plates, poured another glass of wine, sat down.

"You know," she said, "for months I had this strange sensation, as if the world had in fact slipped, and I'd fallen off it. Lost my footing. I can't explain, as though it had all tilted away from where I thought it was, and had slid away. This picture kept coming into my head, of a great dark globe rolling through the darkness at a strange angle. Though how could a globe be at an angle? A giddy feeling, as though I'd fallen off into space. The ground gone from under me."

"A dream, was it?"

"No, not a dream, it was conscious, or rather it was one of those half-conscious thoughts that you can never quite get hold of. A thought just beyond the edge of something. Like a memory of a dream. But I don't think I ever actually dreamed it. Though, of course, how would I know if I hadn't? Or had?"

"I had a very good dream last night. I dreamed I was lying in this very large grand fourposter bed with crimson hangings, and sitting on the end of it, on a carved post, was a huge eagle. It was chained up but screaming. And hanging on the other bedpost was a basket full of pieces of meat. And I knew I had to get up and feed the eagle, but I couldn't move. And as I was lying there, a whole flight of little flat paper angels dressed in red and gold flew past the window."

"Hugo darling, what a wonderful dream. What an extraordinarily classy dream. How like you to have a dream like that! What do you think it means?"

"I think it has something to do with those pink plastic hands, and something to do with Prometheus and his vulture, but I haven't worked out the connection yet. If thine right hand offend thee, cut it off and feed it to the eagle, do you think? Something along those lines?"

"You *are* wonderful, Hugo. I never dream anything poetic or mythological. I just dream about having babies and not having fed the cats, or the goldfish or the dog which I haven't even got. My dreams are so obvious. Just maternal-anxiety dreams. Occasionally I vary it by dreaming a child is falling out of a window. But that's about it. Do you think it means that I never really wanted children at all, and wish they'd all die or starve to death?"

"I don't see how it could mean that, do you?"

"But nowadays, when I dream I'm pregnant, which I do so boringly often, I feel *so* relieved when I wake up and find it's not true. What does *that* mean?"

"It means the time for children is over."

"How clever you are, how well you put it. The time for children is over."

"It is time for the next thing, whatever it may be."

"For you, the next thing is Bagdad. Will Mujid's addresses be any use, do you think?"

"We shall see. One has to be so careful. Not to compromise people."

"How strange it all is. I kept thinking, while I was in Romley, that I was going to find out something really interesting about myself. But I didn't. It wasn't there, after all. Or if it was, I couldn't see it. I shall stop looking. The past is the past."

"If only it were," said Hugo.

Kate smiled, faintly.

"I had another letter from Peter this week," she said. "Here, look at this one." She fished it out of her bag.

Hugo looked; the letter, in Peter's anonymous cut-out style, read: WOMEN LIKE YOU WALK AROUND ASKING FOR TROUBLE. RAPE IS TOO GOOD FOR YOU.

"Not very nice, is it?" said Kate. "But what can I do? There's nothing I can do. And yet I kept on thinking that maybe he would forgive me, maybe we would understand one another, maybe we could cut through all this crap and speak to one another. But it's not possible. The past is the past. It can't be put right."

"What inspired this particular missive?"

"Oh, that piece I wrote about those women who go round Soho claiming to Reclaim the Night, I suppose. Did you read it?"

"I can't say I did."

"You didn't miss much, it was very indecisive. But it's not very nice, is it? From one's own brother?"

"And yet you say that when you meet him he's perfectly friendly?"

"Yes. He is. But he must hate me, to write like that. It's

not very nice to be hated. But I suppose I just have to resign myself to it."

"Perhaps he only hates you with a part of himself. Perhaps he *needs* to hate you."

"Well I suppose it doesn't really hurt me. Or not very much. At least I don't lie awake at nights worrying about him any more. In fact, I don't lie awake much at all, these days. I've been sleeping so much better, this last month or two. I can't tell you what a relief it is."

"Time heals all. As I said."

"Yes. Perhaps."

"You should have agreed to come to Bagdad with me."

"Another day, Hugo, another day."

Hugo, who had been inspecting Peter's note closely, looked up at Kate, whose face, despite her words, betrayed deep hurt, and said: "You know where he cut these letters out from? From our very own paper, I'd say, wouldn't you?"

Kate took the note, looked at it, and nodded agreement. "Yes, of course, I never thought of looking for that. Our own inimitable typography. From our poor dead paper." The discovery cheered her, animated her a little.

"Well, what a swine," she said. "I call that really low. He probably cut them out of my very own piece. I think that's rotten. Like stewing an octopus in its own ink. Or a kid in its mother's milk. If you see what I mean."

"It's not your fault he's mad."

"Isn't it?"

"No more than it's my mother's fault that I am."

"Well, that's not saying much." And they both laughed.

"Well," said Kate, "the next generation will have to do better. I pin my faith on the next generation. I'm looking forward to meeting Mark's girlfriends. He's got two, did you know? Is that the modern thing?"

"Sebastian and Susanna seem to be getting together these days, had you heard that? Apparently they're on the phone to one another day and night. Or so Judith says."

"Oh," said Kate, who had not thought that Judith ever spoke to Hugo, and who slightly resented hearing any gossip she had not invented herself, and who was pleased to find herself suffering from such normal irritations. "And what does Judith think of that?"

"Judith thinks it will interfere with Susanna's A levels."

"Nothing will interfere with Susanna's A levels. She is a girl of strong character, that one. She will be very good for Sebastian." Kate forbore to say that Susanna was working for two, though this is what they were both thinking.

"Do you think you will ever fall in love again, Katie?" asked Hugo.

"I doubt it. Why should I?"

"Why should you indeed?"

"I've done all that. Once or twice too often, in fact."

"You could try loving me," said Hugo.

"But I do love you. I adore you."

"Of course."

"This," said Kate, "is turning into a terrible conversation."

"But we both like terrible conversations."

"No, I think this is just a little bit too terrible, even for me."

"Nothing is too terrible," said Hugo.

And they both fell silent, and looked at one another. A lot of past time filled up the space between them, solid but transparent, as thin and clear as water. Unlived lives, roads not taken, roads blocked, children not born, ghosts and shadows.

"It's a pity," said Hugo, "that we have only one life. In another life, things could have been so different."

"I sometimes think," said Kate, looking at Hugo, so close and so remote, so familiar and yet so incomprehensibly obscure, "that that's not even true, that we are all of us living other lives, kind of just out of sight, just round the corner from our conscious lives, that if you were to roll it all up together, your life and mine, the lived and the unlived, it would be something quite different, a whole life, not a half-life, many whole lives, the shadows of our own as they roll along, and perhaps this one, you and me sitting here, is just the shadow of what we are doing elsewhere, in some other world, in some other part of our being. I can't believe that this is all. Us at this table. How can it be all?"

"Two minutes ago," said Hugo, staring at her intently as she paused, breathless, after this little flight, "you said you were resigned."

"Yes," said Kate. "Yes. It is because I am resigned that I am obliged to invent all this stuff about other worlds."

And she smiled at him with an air of slightly crazed triumph, of logic, of conquest, her head lifted, her bright blue eyes meeting his cold grey eyes with a challenge, for all those things to which they, perforce, had resigned themselves.

"Kate," said Hugo. "You are wonderful. In fact, you are sublime."

"How lucky we are," said Kate, still staring back, "that we should each think each other so wonderful." And she got up, and started to wipe the table, sweeping the crumbs carefully into her open palm, and Hugo, watching her, thought that sublime was indeed the word, for at such moments something in Kate seemed to shimmer just beneath or above the surface, *sub limen*, a breaking light, and she had this knack, this gift, for catching a little of it and bringing it, but just, but just within range, like an astral halo flickering on the sight, calling from him a corresponding gleam: a bright person, an angel in the house, among the crumbs and dustbins and fish heads. Ah, folly, thought Hugo, as he watched, she is just a woman, and a rather gullible, foolish, self-centred, vain woman at that: and Kate, washing her hands under the rubber swizzle tap, looked back at Hugo, his delicate, intellectual, ascetic features, so elegant, so precise, so finely drawn, and thought, After all, Hugo is only a man, and rather a selfish, dangerous, and self-deluding one at that; with something effete, cruel even, in the turn of his lip: a poseur, a monkish poseur, and who knows what he has repressed and mutilated to achieve this nice balance? And she felt the spikes of her rocky expensive boot biting into the heel that she had still not found time to take to the cobbler, as the water splashed onto the cuffs of her shirt, and she turned to smile at Hugo, and said, "Ah, well, at least we stay upright."

"Yes," said Hugo, "indeed we do."

"Though," said Kate, sitting down again across the table from him, "I sometimes think that if so many people weren't leaning on me, from different directions, I might fall over. Why ever did I invite so many people to this party?"

"You ought to come away with me. They'd manage without you."

"Yes. I'm afraid they might."

Hugo laughed.

"In five years," said Kate, "let's go to Timbuctoo."

"I've been to Timbuctoo," said Hugo. "It's not very nice. But I'll take you there, if you like."

"I expect it's just like home, really," said Kate. "I expect I'd manage to find a perfect replica of Dacre Road, even in Timbuctoo."

"Yes," said Hugo. "Maybe you would. And now I must go home, you must go to bed early, and get some sleep."

"I'll ring for a cab," said Kate, reaching for the phone from the dresser.

"I wonder," she said, as she helped him into his coat, "what a psychoanalyst would make of our relationship."

"Goodness knows," said Hugo, though in fact he knew quite well what at least one analyst, namely his own, would have thought of it, and startling the suggestions had been, for his analyst had had a lurid imagination full of the strangest imagery and interpretations, a veritable snake pit of entwined possibilities; most of them, it seemed to Hugo, colourful but irrelevant: poisonous snakes, innocent pretty emerald-green snakes, monsters and mermaids, fish-tailed sirens and bright-eyed toads, coiling and swimming in a dark watery hollow. On the whole, the analyst had preferred to see Kate as an archetypal castrating woman, which perhaps, thought Hugo, sitting in the back of his cab on the way back to his silent flat, was fair enough, for a Freudian: she had certainly managed to castrate poor Stuart, who would undoubtedly have dealt with life much better if he had not had the misfortune to marry a woman so set on proving that she could manage single-handed. Fish heads, fish tails. A dangerous woman, rendered harmless by sterility. He thought of her party with pleasant anticipation. She had given some good parties, in the past.

Kate too thought of past parties, as she lay in bed. The dinner party at which she had first met Ted. The party she and Stuart had given to celebrate Mark's arrival nineteen years ago. The press party at the Dorchester last week to launch a new book on the menopause, at which a fierce woman had cornered Kate and talked at her angrily and intensely for half an hour, advancing inch by inch as she talked, until Kate was in peril of falling backwards over a table covered in bowls of olives, while Kate tried in vain to catch the eyes of various possible rescue forces: she had finally hissed at Kate with unnatural venom, "Well, I mustn't monopolise you," and had marched off, as though offended at Kate's having wasted her time, to leave Kate alone, stranded, far from help. The party three years ago at which her friend Marina had gone into labour prematurely and disconcertingly, and had been carried off in an ambulance, furious at having to miss, as she put it, the fun. The party during which some bloody fool had managed to pull the bathroom washbowl away from the wall, ruining the plumbing and flooding the kitchen below. The summer party during which the famous storm had broken, flooding the whole of North London: they had all gone out and stood in the garden in the torrential hot rain, wet to the skin in seconds, thrilled by the grandeur of the elements, barefoot on the paving stones, rivers of water running through their toes, the dye of their clothes leaking and streaking, their hair plastered to their heads, a drowning party, a Day of Judgement party. Betsy Kay had taken off her shirt and stood there half naked, streaming like a fountain. Oh, yes, as Hugo said, there was life in it yet, and no end to life's surprises.

At three in the morning she was wakened abruptly from an interesting variation of the starving-to-death dream (she dreamed she had left the goldfish on the hotplate, and that the poor dears were gasping and bubbling in their boiling bowl) by a shocking racket under her window. Her room looked over the street, and disturbances in this street were not unusual, but this one persisted and seemed to be taking place amongst her very own dustbins, so after a few minutes she reluctantly got out of bed and went to look out. Cautiously she pulled aside the curtain, and there, below her, stumbling and lurching dangerously around on the front steps, was a figure that she identified, after a few moments, as a very drunken Hunt. He was trying to get up to the door, but not making it very well. He ascended two steps, fell back three, and crashed once more into a bin. Sat there, then picked himself up, and started again. Crashed again, and a lid rolled down into the street. He was swearing and mumbling to himself: snatches of song intermingled with the oaths. He got up and fell over again several times, Kate by now watching with growing amusement, until it seemed that he might do himself some real injury: also she could see curtains twitching across the road, so she got up and ran barefoot downstairs and opened the door.

"Hunt, you silly old fool, what the hell are you up to?" she asked him, as he swayed perilously on the top step.

"I've come to the party," said Hunt.

"Well, you've come on the wrong day," said Kate, pulling him inside away from the eyes of the neighbours, propping him against a wall, and dodging quickly out again to rescue and replace the bin lids, then shutting the door firmly behind her.

Hunt stared at her, leaned back against the wall, then sagged and slowly subsided, folding up at the knees, his long length slowly crumpling and creasing until he sat slumped in an angular heap, his bony shanks doubled up. He sat there for a while, then suddenly opened his eyes and said:

"Why didn't you ask me to the party?"

"Because you're a drunken old fool, that's why," said Kate; then, peering at him more closely, with horror, "And you've been *sick* too, whatever's the matter with you, that's not like you"—for Hunt's clothes were indeed in even worse array than usual, and vomit clung to his trouser legs.

"I've been fucking poisoned," said Hunt. "They took me out and fucking poisoned me."

And to demonstrate the truth of his words, he heaved and spewed up again, though not copiously, on Kate's newly polished floor.

"Oh, Hunt, you are *disgusting*," said Kate, averting her eyes politely, and wondering what to do first: undress Hunt, fetch a bucket of water, chuck him out on the steps till he'd finished? She decided on the bucket of water, but by the time she'd got back from the kitchen with it Hunt had dragged himself into the sitting room, where he was lying propped up on a chair. He opened his eyes, stared at her with dignity, and said in his best voice, "So sorry, dear Mrs. Armstrong! It was the whelks," and passed out.

Whelks it might well have been, for there was a powerful smell of seaweed and vinegar mingled amongst other odours which took a good deal of scrubbing to shift. She managed to get his trousers off, pulling them gingerly over his large feet, and went off to the kitchen to throw them in the washing machine: when she came back, Hunt was snoring, his eyes shut, his long white legs sprawled before him, in mustard-coloured socks. Kate knelt at his feet, and looked up at him curiously. Battered and violently coloured, half-dressed as he was, he had nevertheless a certain lanky elegance. His legs, which clearly never saw the light of day, were blue and white, scarred and bruised, with what looked like a permanent if shifting display of bruises from previous drunken ramblings, oddly youthful compared with his misused beaky broken-veined empurpled face. Grasshopper shanks. Like a dried-up insect, he was. A pickled cockroach. What was that song Stuart used to sing to the children?

> Grasshoppers three a-fiddling went,
> Heigh ho, never be still,
> They earned no money and paid no rent,
> But all day long with their elbows bent
> They fiddled a song called Rillaby Rillaby,
> Fiddled a song called Rillaby Ree.

Should she try to ease off his socks, or would she find inside them a chiropodist's nightmare? How old was he? Impossible to say, and impossible to be cross with him, really, impossible to be anything worse than irritated, for what stamina he had, the old bat, with what impressive perseverance he had abused his system over the years: how could one feel anything but admiration for such dedication? And how clever of him to choose, perversely, so uncharacteristically clean a floor. She got up, quietly, and fetched a blanket, a blanket which had been used so often for the same purpose that the children called it a Hunt blanket. As she was draping it over him, he stirred, muttered, opened his hooded eyes, and said:

"Thank you, my dear."

"Any time," said Kate. "Any time you feel like throwing up, come and do it in my house. How do you feel now?"

"Never felt better," said Hunt.

"And just when I'd cleaned everything up," said Kate.

"You should always clean up *after* a party, not before," said Hunt, not unreasonably.

"Was it really whelks?"

"A bagful of the best. They must have been off, I haven't been so ill in thirty years. I've got a stomach like an old boot. Like the inside of an old boot. What have you done with my trousers?"

"They're going round and round in the washer. Listen, can you hear them?"

And both sat silently for a moment or two, in the dark middle of the night, listening to the comforting distant rattle and swish from the kitchen, as modern life went on its pure mechanical way, trousers turning and buttons and zip rattling against the thick glass eyeball of the machine. An absurd thin purposeless light-headed light-hearted gaiety possessed Kate, as she sat there on the floor in the early hours of the morning with a not very clean old man. The worst is already over, thought Kate; and it wasn't so bad, was it? It won't be so bad, after all.

Her good mood lasted through the next morning, accompanying her as she collected the drink from the Off Licence, as she chopped beef and tomatoes and onions, as she listened to Simone's descriptions of Damascus, as she answered the phone to people who wanted to bring extra friends to her party, as she dusted borrowed glasses. She finished all her own cooking in good time, leaving the kitchen table and surfaces to Mujid and Simone and the girls, and to Hunt, who, recovering with his usual rapidity, insisted on contributing a mushroom salad. Hunt, when in the mood, was an inspired cook. Kate hovered around, watching them. Mujid was off the next day, back to Paris with Simone. He had become so familiar to her, one of the family. Would she miss him? No, of course not, one must not exaggerate. But was glad to have known him, had learned from him. The difference between Sunni and Shi'ite, the location of Kurdistan (which was more than she'd ever learned from Hugo). A few phrases of French. (Gone were the days when she would confuse the Croix Rouge with the Khmer Rouge.) Her progress had been less impressive than his, but then, she had had less time. She had grown used to his ways: particularly she liked the way he made tea. Instead of spooning tea into the pot, he would pick up pinches in his fingers from the caddy, in his pale brown fingers. An Oriental timeless gesture, graceful, intimate, personal. He made a good pot of tea, and had learned to like it English-style, with milk. He had even devised a new labour-saving and hot-water-saving way of warming the pot, by propping it over the spout of the electric kettle; a permanent contribution to Armstrong domestic life. And such nice things he said, from time to time, like on the morning on which she had reprimanded him for taking out of the airing cupboard and putting on, at breakfast, a sweat shirt that was visibly damp, and he had replied in French, "*Ça va sécher sur la bête,*" which he had promptly though not very idiomatically translated for her. "It will dry on the animal." He, in turn, had learned that from Simone, he said. An attitude that augured well for domestic harmony. What a nice man he is, thought Kate fondly, as she watched him and Simone stirring up their couscous, and how unlike what would have been her idea of an Iraqi, had she ever had one. Walking up Tottenham Court Road the other day, she had paused outside the window of the Iraqi Cultural Centre and peered within: the little gallery, usually almost empty, was crowded with men—a party, an opening?—with men in white and beige suits, drinking cans of Coca-Cola, turning to stare at Kate as she stared at them in a way that Mujid would never have stared at a woman: but perhaps each of those men, separated from their group, might prove as amiable? Unlikely, thought Kate: you could tell they were different from the cut of their cloth. All the more credit to Mujid, who had never made a sexist remark, except about vegetables, during the whole of his stay. The world is changing, thought Kate, and all the nice friendly people will inherit it. What a hope, what a hope. But what else can one do but hope? Her own kitchen seemed hopeful enough, charged with an atmosphere of excitement, of end-of-term abandon: even the serious Simone was laughing as she stirred, and Mujid and Hunt were now on the best of terms as they quarrelled over possession of the sharpest kitchen knife.

"How busy you are," said Kate in her apron. "I've left myself nothing to do."

"Go and read a book," said Reuben.

"Read a book? How do you expect me to concentrate on a book at a moment like this? There must be something else I ought to be doing. What else do you need for a party?"

"Go and arrange the flowers," said Ruth. "That's what people are supposed to do before parties." Ruth was doing *Mrs. Dalloway* for A level.

"Do they really? I haven't got any flowers. Shall I go and buy some?"

The notion, once acquired, appealed to Kate immensely. Flowers, that would be the thing. Why not? Ruth was right, other people had flowers, why on earth shouldn't she have some too? She took off her apron, and was just trying to work out where the nearest florist's was to be found when Mark arrived, back from Waterford, and distracted her with greetings, embraces, birthday kisses, and the usual fuss of a returning son. Mark, it appeared, had not only won a prize and passed his driving test, he had also acquired with his prize money a car, bought from a friend cheap, and the whole family was summoned to stare at it as it stood in the road.

"I'll take you for a drive, Mum," said Mark.

"Yes, take her away," said Ruth, "she's getting under our feet."

"You're very eager to get rid of me," said Kate.

"Yes, we are," said Ruth. And they laughed at her, and patted her on the head, as children do when they have grown taller than their mother.

Kate consented to be driven to what she described as the posh florist in Highgate, but was overcome with hesitation when Mark politely held open the car door for her. It was years since she had driven herself, and had humbly acknowledged herself to be the worst driver in London: a near miss of a marmalade cat had put her off for life. And Stuart had never learned at all. Could Mark really have escaped his heritage?

"I say, Mark, can you *really* drive?" she asked, half in, half out.

"I passed my test," said Mark.

"So did I," said Kate, "and I know how little that meant."

"Come on, hop in," said Mark.

And she got in, and sat herself down, and put on her seat belt. And as Mark sat down beside her and switched on the ignition, a most extraordinarily powerful wave of fear, love, and admiration poured through her: what an adventure this was, how astonishing, how impossible to have a son so old, so clever, so capable, so large! With what passion for so many years she had loved him, and he had survived her love, he was a proper whole person, who went away and led his own life, and came back with skills and possessions, to take her to the florist! It seemed extraordinarily unreal, an event in a dream. Her heart lurched forward as the car moved forward, she stiffened with fear, bracing herself for a crunch, but, astonishingly, impossibly, Mark could, after all, drive, as he had said he could, and off they went, with no trouble at all except for one slight grinding of the gears on Highgate West Hill. "My God," said Kate, awe-struck, "you can do it, you can really do it."

"Of course I can," said Mark, smiling affably, amused by her little drama of terror.

"And you're so *big*," said Kate.

"I'm nineteen," said Mark.

"Well, I think that's amazing," said Kate, and sat back, relaxing, a passenger; through all the years she had brought him, and now he was a grown man, able to take charge of her in his turn. She was filled with tenderness, delight, wonder, gratitude. In the back of her mind lay the suspicion that she had been one of those women designed to ruin their sons through excessive devotion, through emotional dependence, and would have done so, had her life turned out a degree less luckily: how fortunate that Mark had been saved from her attentions by her own need to earn her living, by the other two and their needs, by Hugh, by the tatty diversities of tatty distracting modern life. Some power had watched over them all, and let the children free. Or so it seemed, or so it seemed. How could one ever tell? Let the years be kind, let there be no revenge, she prayed, thinking of Beatrice Mourre's son dead in Beirut, of Jessie Parker's son dead in Belfast: and pushed these selfish fears away, to relate to Mark the interesting changes in Sebastian, and to ask Mark if he thought it was true that Sebastian was keen on Susanna.

"None of your business," said Mark, smiling broadly.

"Quite right," said Kate, "none of my business at all. But you can't blame me for being curious."

"You're too curious by half," said Mark. "I wonder anyone tells you anything. You're the worst gossip in London."

"What rubbish," said Kate, crossly. "I'm a very discreet person. As silent as the grave."

"Well, so am I," said Mark, smiling his enigmatic smile. "I must take after you. Shall I park here?"

"Come in with me and choose some flowers," said Kate.

"I don't know one flower from another," said Mark. "I'll stay here and read the paper."

"Do come, darling," wheedled Kate, wishing to prolong this unexpected intimacy, but Mark shook his head, and said, firmly, smiling implacably, "No, thanks."

"My goodness me," said Kate. "You said that just like a man. You sounded just like a man when you said that."

"I am a man," said Mark, benevolently, and leaned over to kiss her cheek. But, beyond that, did not move. And there he sat, reading the paper, while Kate tripped off to the shop on her wobbly heels: how could one ever know what he was thinking? Night and day for years she had watched over him, and now he just said, "No." Or, rather, "No, thanks." A wonderful accomplishment, an accomplished person. Her heart sang with pride as she entered the shop, a green and leafy bower, dank, expensive, warm, a grotto smelling of peat and freesias and carnations, quaking and shivering with maidenhair ferns, flooded with a pale green sunny light. What should she choose? Something exotic, something expensive, for you don't have a party every day of the year, thought Kate; why not be extravagant, for a change? Large orange thick-stemmed bold South African daisies, little pink Israeli carnations, carnations from British Columbia, golden enchantment lilies, freesias, anemones, violets? "What a marvellous selection you have, for the time of year," said Kate, to the woman in her white over-all. "I thought it might just be chrysanthemums. What are those little pink things?"

"They're nerines, from the Channel Islands."

"They're *beautiful*," said Kate, fluttering indecisively from one vase to the next, from one delicate sheaf to another, the perfect blossoms poised, spires and whorls and little neat plates of petals. "And those pale green ones, what are they?"

"They're a new variety, those. *Asphodalos orcinus*. From Jersey."

"Pale green flowers, how charming! But I ought to buy some colours, something with colour. . . ." and Kate tried to remember what colour her rooms were, but they were such a mixture, such a haphazard mixture, her decor was so acci-dental, whereas Evelyn's was so purposeful, one always knew what to take Evelyn, yellow roses, marigolds, blue irises. Yellow and blue. "I'll have some of those," said Kate, "and some of those, and those . . . ," pointing, collecting; but as the bunch gathered, a feeling of slight sorrow came over her, for the poor cut blooms, so fragile, so short of life, so delicately nurtured for this one moment, so bravely out-of-season, so extravagantly imported, and she began to look around for something more lasting, something that would not perish in a day, and her eye lit on a tree, a tree in a pot, a green flourishing tree.

"And I'll have that too," she said. "What is it?"

"It's a bay tree. And it's thirty pounds, I'm afraid," said the woman, in deprecation.

"Never mind," said Kate, "I'll have it, I've always wanted a tree. It'll last, won't it?"

"If you look after it," said the woman, "it will outlive you."

"That's what I want," said Kate, "a tree that will outlive me," and she thought of Mark's face when she staggered out with a tree in her arms. Would it fit in the car? To be able to buy, on impulse, a tree seemed for an instant the height of happiness, and Mark's face, when he saw her, was well worth the thirty pounds.

"Mum, what on earth have you done?" he said, winding down his window and staring as she dumped the tree on the pavement.

"I bought a tree," said Kate. "Will it fit? You put it in while I go back for the flowers."

It did fit, and Mark, as he set off for home, patted Kate on the knee and said, "Mum, you're a very silly girl," but he was pleased with her, she could tell, and he started to whistle as they drove back down the hill, past lighted windows through the gleaming darkness, down towards the grime, the tree nodding and flopping greenly on the back seat, and Kate with her arms full of flowers.

When they got back, the tree created a small sensation; everyone poured out of the house to greet it, to exclaim, to admire. They carried it into the sitting room, and stood it in the window. Even Hunt admired it, though he did mutter some warning about Kate's home looking like a second-rate Greek restaurant in Charlotte Street if she wasn't careful. "That's exactly the effect I was aiming at," said Kate, undeterred. More practically, Reuben said he feared the cats might piss in its pot, and pointed out that guests would certainly stub out their cigarettes there unless strictly forbidden to do so. "Never mind," said Kate, "it has to go in the back garden, really it isn't supposed to live in the house, but a few days won't kill it. It's a hardy tree."

"Is it time for a drink yet?" asked Hunt. "We should welcome the tree with a drink. With a small libation."

It wasn't really time for a drink, it was only half past five, but nevertheless they opened a bottle of party wine, and sat around in amity, chattering of this and that, of which guests would behave badly, of whether or not Joker or the Rastaman would burst into song, and if so, whether each would appreciate the efforts of the other.

"You wait till you see my Rastaman," said Ruth, "he is the most beautiful man in the whole world, you will love him, Mum."

"We drink your health, Mark," said Hunt, raising his glass. "May you flourish, not exactly like the green bay tree as I have done, but in a more godly manner."

"What's wrong with my tree?" asked Kate. "It looks healthy enough to me, has she sold me a dud?"

"You clearly don't know your Book of Common Prayer," said Hunt.

"No, I don't, and I'm surprised that you do. I was brought up as an atheist, remember? Anyway, what have bay trees to do with the Book of Common Prayer?"

Hunt explained that the ungodly therein flourished. "Oh dear," said Kate, staring at her innocent plant, "is it a bad omen?"

"No," said Hunt, "just a small sign that our common culture is perishing. If you had spent as many years of your youth in church as I did, you would turn out virtuous like me, and like me, you would have the inestimable advantage of knowing the English Hymnal and the Prayer Book off by heart. You can imagine what a strength they have been to me in times of trouble. And none of you can recognise a single quotation."

"I'm sure Evelyn would know about bay trees," said Kate, rather offended by these slurs on her learning and her tree, "you must ask Evelyn. Do you do the Prayer Book in Religious Knowledge, Ruth?"

"No," said Ruth, "we do things like abortion and euthanasia and capital punishment."

"Modern learning," said Hunt. "You see where it gets you. Picking up black men in pubs."

"We did racism too," said Ruth. "And the Gospel of St. Mark. And I didn't pick him up, I just got talking to him. There is a difference, you know."

"Mark," said Kate, suddenly starting to her feet, side-tracked. "Oh dear, I completely forgot to give you your birthday present. Do run up to my bedroom, there's a love, it's in my stocking drawer, in a brown paper bag. It's only a very *small* present, I couldn't think what to get you, now you're so grown up"—and Mark went off, Kate defending her tree the while, protesting that it was not merely decorative but edible, and Mark brought down his present, which was a smart dull-black Parker pen, and kissed his mother and told her that over the years she had bought him at least a dozen Parker pens, but that he solemnly promised not to lose this one, and Kate apologised for being so unoriginal, and said she would contribute to the cost of the car, and then Mujid and Simone and the girls went into a huddle, from which they emerged, Mujid declaring that he thought this was the moment to present Kate with the present he and Simone had bought her for all her hospitality.

"My goodness, presents all around," said Kate, "what fun!" hoping that the fact that the girls seemed to be in on whatever secret was about to be revealed indicated that it would be something more exciting than a tome on the integration of modern Iraq, the history of the British mandate in Mesopotamia or another catalogue of Free Palestine posters from the Iraqi Cultural Centre (though of late, to be fair, Mujid had slacked off in his attempts to educate Kate, presumably having found her ineducable)—and the gift, when it was unwrapped from its crinkling white tissue paper, proved indeed to be exciting, and entirely unimproving, for it was a pair of little emerald-green slippers, embroidered with pearls and sequins and golden stitching, a pair of Arabian slippers. "How lovely," cried Kate, "how lovely, they are slippers from the Arabian Nights!" and she unzipped her boots and tried them on, and everybody smiled indulgently as she twisted and turned her little ankles. "Oh, they are darlings," said Kate, "and I so badly needed some slippers, how clever to choose such a present," and Mujid smiled, and said, "You should not be walking always with your feet on the cold floor."

"No, no, you're right, I shouldn't," said Kate, "and now I won't have to any more." She was deeply touched by his solicitude, charmed to think that over the weeks he had noticed her walking barefoot in the kitchen of a morning, and had felt sorry for her cold feet. She had not expected a present, had not thought of such a thing. He was human after all, he had noticed her, had noticed even her feet, had paid attention to her needs, had felt gratitude. How could she ever have found him so irritating? Could you get to like anyone, given the time? Not that she wasn't glad to get rid of him, enough is enough, but nevertheless, how good that it should end so well, and even as she was thinking this, looking around her family circle, feeling as she sat there a sense of immense calm, strength, centrality, as though she were indeed the centre of a circle, in the most old-fashioned of ways, a moving circle—oh, there is no language left to describe such things, we have called it all so much in question, but imagine a circle even so, a circle and a moving sphere, for this is her house and there she sits, she has everything and nothing, I give her everything and nothing—even as she sat, the phone went, and it was Beatrice Mourre from Paris, wanting to thank Kate, wanting to wish Mark a happy birthday, screeching excitedly, a voice not heard in nineteen years, "Ah, my dear, I remember you as though it were *yesterday*"—and Kate shouted back, unnecessarily loud across the many miles of land and sea, that it had been her joy, her pleasure, to have been able to look after Mujid and Simone: and as soon as she put the phone down, it went again, this time for Ruth, then again, and the lull was over, and the circle broke up into its various spheres of activity, and Kate, in the end, having broken a jug and run down to the never-closing Pakistani shop on the corner to buy some paper napkins, found herself alone in her room, about to change, sitting on her bed, wondering what to wear.

And let us leave her there, pondering the choice between various garments, each of which seemed to present some minor disadvantage. The long all-faults-concealing pink cheesecloth had a drooping hem and tripped her up. The too revealing dress from Richard Shops always showed bra straps as well as a daring amount of bosom, and the Indian one smelled rather strongly of Ruth, who had borrowed it recently for a school concert, a smell delightful to Kate but not perhaps to others. The old black one was marginally too tight, and even when it had fitted had been a bit on the vulgar side. Perhaps none of them suited her at all, perhaps none of them had ever suited her. Why ever had she in a fit of folly bought that expensive French silk, had she really ever thought she'd have the nerve to wear it?

Let us leave her there, in an attitude of indecision, confronted by choice. Not, of course, a very serious choice, unless you wish to read it symbolically; but not, you will agree, an uncommon one. A lot of time is spent in such attitudes, by many of us who would not care to admit it. There she sits, Kate Armstrong, in her black Marks-and-Spencer petticoat, her feet dangling in their emerald Arabian slippers, wondering what to wear, and wondering what will happen at her party. Will Hunt stay reasonably sober and refrain from insulting people, will Marylou turn up, and if so, what on earth will people make of her, will Stuart be civil to Ted, will Ted make a pass at Rosamund Stacey, will Evelyn find the whole thing too exhausting, will Hugo's mother find it too much of a squash, will the neighbours object to the noise? Will she herself abandon all hesitation and agree to fly out to Bagdad with Hugo, will she find a voice in which to speak, at last, to Ted, there, amongst so many people? Will she fall in love with

Ruth's Rastaman? (The Rastaman was to prove to be as beautiful as Ruth had promised, though disappointingly lacking in dreadlocks: he and Marylou were to dance together, he striped in red, green and gold, she in her beige pink lace, a sight not to be forgotten.) Anything is possible, it is all undecided. Everything or nothing. It is all in the future. Excitement fills her, excitement, joy, anticipation, apprehension. Something will happen. The water glints in the distance. It is unplanned, unpredicted. Nothing binds her, nothing holds her. It is the unknown, and there is no way of stopping it. It waits, unseen, and she will meet it, it will meet her. There is no way of knowing what it will be. It does not know itself. But it will come into being.

A child calls her from downstairs. The doorbell rings. The telephone also rings. She hears her house living. She rises.

This book was set on the Linotype in Janson, a recutting made direct from type cast from matrices long thought to have been made by the Dutchman Anton Janson, who was a practicing type founder in Leipzig during the years 1668–87. However, it has been conclusively demonstrated that these types are actually the work of Nicholas Kis (1650–1702), a Hungarian, who most probably learned his trade from the master Dutch type founder Dirk Voskens. The type is an excellent example of the influential and sturdy Dutch types that prevailed in England up to the time William Caslon developed his own incomparable designs from them.

Composed by The Maryland Linotype Composition Corporation, Baltimore, Maryland. Printed and bound by American Book–Stratford Press, Saddle Brook, New Jersey.